DANGEROUS PHYSICS

A CIP catalogue record for this book is available from the British Library

ISBN 978-1-7397814-3-9

Published by 186 Publishing Limited 2023

186publishing.co.uk

DANGEROUS

PHYSICS

Rose Mandelson

186 Publishing

I

Plubb

Peckler's hi-tech Bakelite computer terminal only made that sound for one reason. Heart racing, he tapped at the keyboard to access his Confidential folder. In less time than it would have taken him to tie his shoelaces, a line of green text flickered across the bottom of his screen.

And there it was! Codename Wellbeck had done it again. A notification that Peckler had received a copy of the full report, written by the woman herself.

Peckler looked at the file details and his heart sank. It was huge. It was the size of a book.

Think of what it contains, he told himself. This will be dynamite. All the names, all the secrets. It might be heavy going but the information in it will change everything.

He sent the file to print. The following half an hour seemed to last an eternity but finally the magic phrase 'Print complete' appeared on his screen. He fetched the hard copy from the print room himself, his excitement building again. However dry this was going to be, Peckler would be equal to it. He was no stranger to hard graft. In fact he was famous for it.

He sat at his desk and turned to the first page.

What the fuck...

Adventures in Sputteridge by Bettony Gullivant

CHAPTER ONE

How many villages still have their own police station?

You may well ask, How many villages these days have their own police station? I can't answer that one. I can only say that however many there are, Sputteridge was one of them. It had its own police station which was actually more of a police house, and its own policeman who was living there, a very nice man called Bob Jenkins.

Bob was quite a large man, and not in the first flush of youth. He combined authority with reassurance. I can confirm from first-hand experience that he is good at calming down exhausted tourists in their late twenties. People who only two days before have dumped their shit of a boyfriend. People who have then decided pretty much on the spur of the moment to take some of the holiday that bloody company had been owing them for so bloody long and drive down to Cornwall for a well-earned break.

But first things first.

When you google Sputteridge nothing comes up.

I know this because one of the last things I did before I lost the internet was to pull to the side of the road and google Sputteridge on my phone. And nothing came up.

Which was very frustrating because after the internet disappeared nothing came up at all.

It was late at night. I had somehow managed to miss Truro several hours ago. I was tired. Tired and lost, I admit it. I speculated that some malicious entity might have moved Truro.

I was lost, probably somewhere off the coast road south west of Truro. I had headed off a main road ten minutes before, lured by a (sort of) promising sign that read, 'Hotel, Good Fod, ½ mile'. At that point I had already driven for five hours and I really needed to find somewhere to sleep, and if there was Good Fod as well, so much the better.

There is nothing wrong with my ability to follow directions, but if they had moved Truro, moving the hotel must have been a doddle.

Eventually, as I say, I came across a faded little fingerpost which pointed down an even narrower lane than the one I was on. It bore the legend, 'Sputteridge'.

So I googled Sputteridge hoping to find Accommodation (with or without Good Fod, I was desperate by now) and nothing came up.

There had to be somewhere to stay in a village on the coast in Cornwall, I reasoned. And if there wasn't, I would stop the car somewhere in the centre of the village. I would slide the car seat back and close my eyes. Some warm-hearted local with a spare room, giving their faithful old dog a last-thing-before-bedtime-so-please-don't-wee-on-the-carpet-again walk would see me. And take pity on me.

It wasn't the best plan I had ever come up with but it was, at least, A Plan.

I followed the even narrower lane and after, oh, maybe ten seconds, I saw the internet break on my phone.

After another couple of minutes grey stone cottages loomed out of the darkness on each side of the lane. I silently thanked my guardian angel. I also silently apologised for the hard time I had been giving her for the last few hours. A little way further on and the lane arrived at the village square and oh joy, a pub which looked as though it might have rooms.

Oh less joy, the pub was closed. No matter. I would knock on the door until someone opened it, or until I died, whichever came first.

And that is how I ended up in a police cell for the night.

** ** **

Bob also cooks a delicious bacon sandwich (apart from the bread, which was a bit chewy) and makes a wonderful cup of tea.

The cell was at the back of the house but we sat at the large wooden table in Bob's kitchen to eat our sandwiches.

'I'll make the bed up in the cell in a minute,' Bob said. He looked at me shrewdly. 'You haven't actually told me yet what you were doing here Miss, creating a disturbance in the middle of the night.'

I forgave him the Miss on account of the bacon and the tea, and told him about Truro being moved and the false promise of Good Fod. About finding the fingerpost and almost immediately losing the internet. He watched me carefully. I guessed, wrongly as it turned out, that over the years many a crook had had his falsehoods exposed by that shrewd gaze.

'And I can honestly state that I have no falsehoods for you to expose' I concluded nervously.

'I beg your pardon Miss?' Bob said, slightly shocked.

'Er.' I could feel myself blushing. 'I'm telling you the truth Bob, honestly.'

'Mmm.' He nodded, chewing thoughtfully on a piece of bread. 'I think you are.'

We both filled a moment of silence by taking a drink of tea. Then Bob said,

'I'll show you where the bathroom is and then while you're...' he blushed, '...you know... I'll get the bedding sorted out.'

'Thank you. I am sorry I've caused you all this trouble.'

'It's no trouble Miss. We can sort the paperwork out in the morning. Or maybe we'll just forget about it, that's probably the simplest.'

'Thank you.'

'You're welcome.'

** ** **

Assistant County Lord Lieutenant Peckler sighed. He often felt that the whole world had been specifically designed to torment him and moments like this only reinforced his opinion. Although he had been born without sufficient neural connections in his cerebral cortex for a functioning sense of humour, he had just enough of them to allow him to recognise flippancy when he was being bashed around the head with it.

He was supposed to be treating this... document... as though it were a factual record. As though these trivial recollections of someone who was clearly a half-wit - not just a half-wit, but a woman - were somehow of value. That was the problem of course, he thought bitterly. If you try to take the hysterical jottings of a woman as fact, this is what you end up with. He swallowed more coffee and looked longingly out of the darkened window in the general direction of his home. The coal fire that warmed his office was beginning to die down. Peckler dragged his attention back to his work and ploughed on...

✳✳ ✳✳ ✳✳

So far anyway, I have only ever slept in the one police cell, and I can fully recommend the experience. I slept wonderfully, and woke to the sound of birdsong. The small barred window high in the wall above me let in a golden ray of sunshine. I felt amazingly refreshed.

Bob knocked politely on the door, and I pulled the bedsheet over my t-shirt and waited for him to enter. Which he didn't. Eventually he knocked again, and feeling a little foolish I said,

'Come in.'

Bob pushed the door open and entered bearing a tray. On it were a pot of tea, a milk jug, cup and saucer, and a large plate covered in waffles, bacon, sausages, beans and tomatoes.

'I'll put these here' said Bob. He was clearly embarrassed, trying to look at me and simultaneously to look away. He placed the tray on my suitcase. 'When you've finished you can … you know…' he blushed '… Get dressed, and join me in the kitchen. You're not gluten-intolerant are you? Do you take sugar in your tea?'

'No. I mean, I don't take sugar and I'm not gluten-intolerant.' I looked at the breakfast tray. 'Wow. Thank you Bob this is so kind of you. Umm… I don't suppose you've got any brown sauce have you?'

Bob looked slightly crestfallen, and I hastened to reassure him. 'It doesn't need brown sauce though, it looks so nice. By the way how am I going to open the door?'

He looked at me oddly. 'You turn the handle and then pull. How would you normally open a door?'

'Isn't it locked?'

'Why should it be?' He smiled vaguely, and left me to my breakfast.

** ** **

The cell was joined to the kitchen by a short passageway. When I entered the kitchen with my tray I found Bob sitting at the kitchen table. A woman was also sitting at the table. She was a similar age to Bob, and was I guessed of Asian heritage. She was tall – I could see that, even with her sitting down – but was of much slighter build than the policeman. They both looked up as I entered. Neither of them looked very happy. Bob motioned for me to join them at the table.

'Is everything ok?' I asked. 'I am very sorry about last night. I was so tired and -'

'It's all right,' said Bob, forcing a smile. 'This is Mrs Ponch. She's our local magistrate.'

'You've got your own magistrate?'

'Of course. This is Cornwall. It's all to do with devolution.'

'Devolution of Cornwall?'

Bob looked shifty. 'Yes.'

'Oh. I must have missed that.'

The woman also smiled – a sort of apologetic smile, I thought – and stood up, and we shook hands. When she stood I could see that her coat was long and rather drab, like something out of the nineteen fifties. I do not usually make instant decisions about people but something told me that despite the coat, she shared a gentle honesty with her policeman. Nevertheless it was very obvious that both of them were deeply uncomfortable.

'Were you planning on journeying somewhere?' Mrs Ponch asked. 'Visiting someone maybe?' She had a deep voice which conveyed quiet authority.

It was not a question I had expected but I answered, 'Not really, no.'

'Only we might need you to stay here for a little while.'

My stomach churned. 'Has the publican decided to press charges?'

Mrs Ponch looked at Bob, as though for support.

'Yes,' he answered, with what seemed to be a certain amount of relief. 'I'm afraid he has. So it's important that you stay here.'

'Very important,' Mrs Ponch added.

'Yes. Very important. Just for a few days if that's all right.'

'A few days! What if it isn't?'

'I'm sorry?' Bob floundered.

'What if it isn't all right?'

'Er...'

'You'll be very comfortable,' Mrs Ponch said. 'It's just that we need you to stay here while we...'

'Sort out the paperwork' Bob finished.

'Yes. While we sort things out.'

'There's lots of things to do here,' Mrs Ponch added, in a rather ingenuous attempt at persuasion. 'It's a lovely area.'

'What exactly is he accusing me of?' I asked.

'Who?'

'The publican. What's his name anyway?'

Mrs Ponch looked at Bob, who looked vaguely around the room, as though seeking inspiration. Finally he said, 'Mr Window.'

'Mr Window?'

'Yes.'

'The publican's name is Mr Window?'

'That's right.'

I am a fairly spirited sort of person and now that the initial shock of apparently being in trouble was wearing off, this peculiar conversation was beginning to irritate me.

'Are you certain it's *Mr Window* and not his next-door-neighbours *Mr Door* or *Mr Ceiling* Bob?'

'I'm sorry?'

'What exactly is Mr Window accusing me of?'

'That's what we need to sort out' Mrs Ponch said. 'You have to understand that this is all quite new for us. What with... you know...'

'Devolution.'

She looked at me shrewdly. 'Yes. Devolution.'

'And where are you proposing to keep me, while you sort out Mr Window's accusation?'

'Oh, er...'

Once again Mrs Ponch looked to Bob for inspiration.

'Well the spare room's a lot nicer than the cell,' he suggested.

At that moment what I can only describe as a sound like a world-shattering fart ripped through the air outside. I am still convinced that the actual walls of the police house shook.

Mrs Ponch and Bob stared at each other.

'My Gods', said Bob. 'It's Victor Hugo.'

I know that I shouldn't interrupt myself here, especially at such a surprising moment in my day, but I feel that I should clarify something: As I learned later, what Bob had actually said was, 'It's Vic Terrugo.' Otherwise what is probably already a slightly odd – yet, I have also to say, absolutely truthful – account, would become bizarrely confusing. Conjuring up in your mind the image of one of the titans of French nineteenth century literature letting flatulence get the better of him on the Cornish coast.

But I digress.

Mrs Ponch and Bob leapt to their feet. Bob turned to me, and in some desperation said 'Promise you'll stay here.'

'I promise,' I answered.

Bob looked at me a moment longer, then hurried after Mrs Ponch who had already left the room, heading down the hallway to the front door.

I heard the front door bang, then tried to get my thoughts in order.

I failed.

Instead, I went and cleaned my teeth and washed my face. Then I spent a while considering the wildly unlikely idea that I had found a Cornish village which had not only its own policeman but also its own magistrate. And its own system of processing and administering justice. Other than the equally unlikely idea that they were all Cornish nationalists, or maybe a whole village of complete nutters, I did not have a clue what I had stumbled into. The thought of running to my car and fleeing flashed through my mind. But I am not one for running away, and this was too interesting a situation. Besides, both Bob and Mrs Ponch were innately reassuring. Nobody who means you harm is going to leave you free to have a wash and clean your teeth while they run out of the house. So hurriedly in fact that they leave the front door swinging open behind them, securing you in their property by the cunning ruse of getting you to promise you were not going to leave.

So I waited.

It was fully an hour before Bob reappeared, without Mrs Ponch. He had soot on his face and generally looked dishevelled. He was also clearly very tired.

'What on earth has happened?' I asked.

'Nothing.'

'Nothing? I don't think so.' I stood up.

'What are you doing?' Bob almost shouted, his face a mask of anxiety.

'I'm going outside to have a look.'

Wild panic chased the weary anxiety away from Bob's face. 'No! You can't do that!'

'Why not? You just said nothing has happened.'

'I know I did.'

I raised my eyebrows. Bob sank onto one of the kitchen chairs. 'All right, all right. I'll tell you everything. Just give me a minute. It's been a bit hectic.'

I sat down again. I looked at him closely and noticed a couple of holes had been burnt into his uniform. He put his head in his hands, and through his fingers he muttered, 'there's been an explosion at the kipper factory.'

I shook my head and stood up, and said, 'No there hasn't. There isn't a kipper factory. Tell me the truth right now Bob or I'm off outside.'

'All right! The truth.' He was almost sobbing. He looked up and regarded me for some seconds. 'I am going to tell you something very surprising, Miss. In fact you are probably not going to believe me and you'll most likely think I am a picnic short of a plank.'

'Huh?'

A series of farting sounds, much quieter than the first one but still loud nonetheless, rent the air outside. Bob shook his head wearily.

'For fuck's sake.' He dragged himself to his feet. 'Please don't go outside Miss, it genuinely is not safe for you. I'll be back as soon as I can. I'll tell you everything then.'

'Can I look out of the windows?'

'I suppose so.' His voice was weary. 'Make yourself at home, why don't you.' He trudged away and I wandered into the living room to see what I could see.

** ** **

That's the limit, Peckler thought. I can't cope with this drivel.

Peckler had ability, but it was within a strictly defined range. The methodical checking of accounts; comparing the performance of informant A against that of informant B who lived three doors down; monitoring death in custody rates, actual versus target. These were his strengths. Whereas analysing reports such as this...

To be honest, never before had he read a report such as this. Any man writing this sort of guff would have been weeded out long before he could have produced something for ACLL Peckler's eyes.

Peckler thought again of his dinner. Of his slippers, warming by the fire. He reached for his telephone and dialled a number.

He'd never liked Hugo Crean.

CHAPTER TWO

The view from the Police House

To be honest, there wasn't much to see. Well in a sense there was, because I was looking across the village square towards the pub, pale sunlight filtering down through a haze of fine dust and warming the golden stone cottages that made up the square. There was even a village shop a few doors to the right of the pub. A postcard rack stood outside its door and children's buckets and spades squeezed into a gap between the rack and some carefully laid out boxes of fruit and veg. This was unspoilt Cornwall at its best (apart from the dust, the lack of cars and the fact that everywhere was deserted).

And also apart from the five figures I saw hurrying out of the pub and towards a lane at the far end of the square to my right, all of whom were wearing what looked like hazmat suits.

** ** **

I have always been able to cope well with the unexpected.

For example, when I recently cut short my trip to our Thames Ditton office to give darling Jack a lovely surprise. I had quietly let myself into our apartment late in the evening and, somewhat to my surprise, found myself staring at my naked boyfriend tied up on the floor with some sort of gag in his mouth and a look of horror on his face. I reacted without panicking to a sound behind me, my years of martial arts training kicked in and within moments a perverted and powerfully-built intruder was lying next to my hogtied boyfriend, unconscious and with some pretty painful injuries. I might only be a five-feet four inch tall woman but I can handle myself. When I untied Jack I discovered the sordid truth, but I like to think that I coped well with the unexpected nature of the situation. I calmly suggested to Jack that he would move out that very night, helped him to drag his semi-comatose Amazonian-sized girlfriend with him, and calmly agreed with my now ex-lover that he would store most of his belongings in the communal waste bins and on the pavement until such time as he could arrange a more permanent home for anything that the rubbish collectors (and passers-by) left behind.

I think that I coped well with that situation, although it was I suppose the reason why I had decided at short notice to take a week's holiday exploring some of the Cornish beaches that I had known so well as a child. I wanted reassurance, I wanted to fill my head with warm memories of happier days when my parents were alive and I was a part of a loving family. I wanted to bury myself in the cosy certainties of the past because I no longer had any close family and at that moment of chaos I could not think of another way of finding some sort of comfort, other than the comfort of memory.

And that was how I had found myself in Sputteridge.

I sighed, decided to wait for Bob to return, and looked around the room. It reminded me of my school friend Amanda's mother's front room. It was quietly traditional. A two-seater sofa and a couple of small armchairs were placed around three sides of a low mahogany coffee-table that stood on a blue-patterned rug in the centre of the room. They faced an open fireplace on the far side that was brightened by a vase of dried flowers. On the mantelpiece above it a clock patiently ticked the moments away.

I made myself a mug of tea and was sitting on the sofa idly leafing through an old Madhur Jaffrey cookbook when Bob returned. He stared at me, hardly focussing, then gazed longingly at the tea.

'Sit down,' I said. 'You look exhausted. I'll get you a cuppa.'

Bob sighed and slumped into one of the armchairs. 'Thank you,' he mumbled faintly.

The tea helped to energise my new friend. Bob almost sounded cheerful when he said, 'No harm done.' He smiled weakly at me and then added, 'Not much anyway. No more than usual. By the time we've had a bit of lunch it'll be safe to go out.'

'There's quite a lot of explaining to be done Bob.'

'I know. And we still need to decide what to do about you, Bettony. Let's get some lunch. I boiled a ham the other day and there's quite a bit left, we can have that with some salad.'

** ** **

Reading through what I have written here I can understand why you might wonder how much danger I was in. I can only say that I never felt in any, at least at this point in the narrative. What had happened was bizarre and inexplicable but there is something in human nature which helps us to accept almost any situation, however extraordinary, and make the best of it.

In mine, anyway.

I saw no veiled threat in Bob's comment about what to do with me. It was a puzzle that needed to be solved. I sensed no need to escape.

At least, that was how I felt until I met Pierre DeLondon.

** ** **

Bob served up a generous ham salad and whizzed together a vinaigrette to go with it. He cut lumps off a loaf of bread that he modestly admitted to baking himself, and on which I politely avoided commenting. We chewed in silence for a little while, then Bob succeeded in ungluing his teeth and said,

'I'm really sorry about this but until we can get Mr Window's view of events and the charge he wants us to bring against you, I'm going to have to ask you to stay as our guest.'

'As your guest?'

To give him credit, Bob looked deeply uncomfortable.

'As a serving policeman I suppose you are aware of the laws of kidnap?'

Bob didn't answer.

'What were those people doing wearing hazmat suits Bob?'

'They're... testing a new sort of beachwear.'

'Beachwear!'

'Yes. It's for people who... want to go on the beach but have to avoid the sun. For health reasons.'

'They were hazmat suits.'

14

'Not really. The design is based on … er … hazmat suits.'

'I think you were actually going to tell me the truth, you know. Before that last emergency, whatever it was.'

Bob ostentatiously looked at his watch. 'Oh goodness me is that the time? I have to go. I've got a meeting in a few minutes. Look…' he shifted uncomfortably. 'It would really be a great favour if you'd stay here till I get back.'

'Where?'

'In your cell.'

'It's not my cell!'

'I know. I'm sorry. *The* cell. In *the* cell. Would you please?'

'Ok.'

I returned to the cell. Bob followed, carrying the remains of lunch. There were also a couple of takeaway boxes containing some cold curry and rice, which he explained was "In case I'm a little late getting back".

'What if I want to use the toilet while you're out?'

'Oh please, go ahead.'

'Won't the door be locked?'

'Only if I'm in there!' He attempted a chuckle. I wasn't impressed.

'I meant this one' I said flatly.

'What? The cell door? No of course not. Unless you wanted me to lock it of course. But you'll be perfectly safe.'

I give up, I thought to myself. This is too surreal. 'That's fine thanks. I suppose you want me to promise I won't run away?'

'Well yes, I thought that was already agreed.'

'Bye then,' I said coldly. 'You'd better get off to your meeting. With Mr Windows the publican.'

'Yes. Right. Bye then.'

I lay on the bed, looking at the ceiling of the cell and trying to figure out what on earth I had stumbled into. Some sort of secret research facility perhaps? If so, security was extremely lax. Nothing like the menacing set-ups that appeared in films. I couldn't believe that someone had taken a decision to replace a squad of tough, steely-eyed security men with Bob. After a while I got bored and wandered back to the living room. I had another look at the Madhur Jaffrey book, and perhaps inspired by it, went back to the cell and ate the cold curry. It was pretty good.

** ** **

It was late afternoon before Bob returned with Mrs Ponch. They were both clearly tired, but much more purposeful than earlier. Bob gazed sadly at the empty takeaway boxes.

'It was delicious,' I said cruelly. 'Curry doesn't come much better.' Then I saw the look of weary hunger on his face and regretted my meanness.

'So are you going to tell me what's going on here?' I asked, partly to hide my discomfort.

'Come and sit at the kitchen table,' Bob said. Still feeling guilty, I offered to make a pot of tea. My offer was gratefully accepted.

'The thing is,' said Mrs Ponch, 'we don't get many visitors.' She glanced at Bob. 'Actually, we don't get any.' She tried to smile again but failed and was left with a slightly vacant expression on her face, eyebrows raised and eyes wide open. I was far too polite to laugh, and in any case I was rather bemused at her statement. Bob took up the tale. He had rested his head in his hands, and his voice was a bit muffled.

'We like to keep ourselves to ourselves,' he mumbled. 'It's quite an important thing for us -'

'– Very,' interjected Mrs Ponch.

'– Very,' repeated Bob. 'It's a very important thing. For us.'

'It's all right,' I said. 'I won't tell anyone. There's nothing to tell, anyway, is there? Weird noises, a deserted village and a few people in unusual beachwear...'

They both shifted uncomfortably.

'You look like the sort of woman who can be trusted,' said Mrs Ponch, 'but who knows? What if we told you many strange things and at a later time you let something slip? By accident, or in a moment of jollity when your garden was down?'

When my garden was down...? Perhaps I had misheard?

16

'Please don't get us wrong,' Bob said. 'We're not going to hurt you or anything – '

'Oh goodness me no,' added Mrs Ponch. 'Nothing like that.'

'- But this has never happened before and we don't know what to do.'

He looked at me imploringly. Here it comes, I thought. The big reveal.

'We are what you would call aliens.'

He raised his head from his hands, and added, accusingly, 'Although we wouldn't describe ourselves like that. We could say that you were the aliens. We wouldn't though.' He glared at me defiantly. 'That would be rude.'

It was a measure of how strange this day had become, that such an explanation seemed to make sense. All I could think of to say was, 'You don't look alien to me Bob.'

'I might say the same to you Miss,' the policeman responded with some alacrity, his nerves clearly frayed. 'I might say, You don't look alien to me. What would you say to that?'

I had to acknowledge the logic of this. I stared at this creature, who so closely resembled a sturdily-built village policeman and yet was now claiming (with some corroboration, it has to be said, from the general air of unreality, the hazmat suits and the bizarre farting noises) to be a visitor from another world. 'Where are you from? And why are you here?'

'Sputteridge.' He looked at me challengingly. 'That is the name of this area on our planet. And we are here because of a slight error.'

Mrs Ponch was watching me closely. Once again, I was impressed by her personal authority.

'I suppose I had better set about explaining things,' Bob continued.

'Please.'

'It's like this. Imagine that you live in a block of flats.'

'I don't need to imagine that Bob. I do.'

'Oh. Er, good.'

'It's in Croydon though so we call it an apartment block.'

'Right. Anyway. You've been to visit a friend on the first floor. And you live on the fourth floor so you say goodbye to your friend, you step into the lift – ' at this point Bob leant forward and tapped the table in front of me, emphasising his words – 'and you don't move. And it sort of seems to you that the lift hasn't moved either. It hasn't gone forward, or backwards, or sideways. All that it has done is to move very slowly upwards for a few seconds. And when the doors open and you step out of the lift, you are in a world which seems identical in almost every way to the world you have just left –' tap tap – 'but it isn't. You have left your friend's world, where he lives'

'She'

'Pardon?'

'My friend on the first floor is a She. Not a He.'

'Are you taking me seriously Miss?'

'I'm sorry Bob, flippancy is just my way of dealing with all this. And you can call me Bettony. I'd rather you called me Bettony than Miss.'

Bob looked at me with all the frowning authority of the policeman that he wasn't.

'You have left your friend's world, and you are now in your own world, identical in every way, except –' tappity tap tap tap – 'except this is the world where you live, not him. Her.' He looked at me triumphantly. 'And that's what we do. Well sort of. We have understood how to travel between universes – bridge mind-blowing leaps between different versions of existence - by simply...' he finished his peroration rather lamely, 'taking the quantum lift to the next floor. Sort of.'

I stared at him, aware that I should make some sort of impressive response.

'Gosh.'

There was a silence while I digested Bob's news, and Bob opened a bag of crisps.

Some sort of silence anyway, crisp bags being quite noisy.

'This is something that I have heard about,' I said. 'The idea that almost identical worlds exist, worlds that split off from our own every time anybody makes a decision. And they all have identical versions of us in them.' A thought struck me. 'Is there another me, Bob? Here in Sputteridge?'

Bob shook his head and then swallowed his crisps.

'There might be another you somewhere else,' he answered. 'But not here. There's nobody here. Which is a bit strange, to be honest.'

'Have you met another version of you?'

Again he shook his head, less convincingly I thought.

'So how come you're here now, and what's this slight error that you told me about earlier?'

He shook his head a third time and sighed. 'I have to be honest with you Bettony, it's a lot more than a slight error. The semi-conductor holding three of the five intermediate phase quanta –' he ticked them off on his fingers – 'the Charmed Mellow Quellon, its antimatter equivalent the Offended Quellon and the yellow biphasic Bottom Up Quellon – has got a strange patterning on it, which Vic thinks indicates some kind of de-integrated photon shift at zero point minus five in the transitioning. Obviously that can't be right because it would have triggered an abort routine on the pre-transition run.' He must have noticed my blank look, because he shrugged and then added,

'If I'm honest Bettony, Fuck knows. We're up shit creek without a pedallo, good and proper.'

'Er...'

Apparently the Transition Vehicle (or TV, as Bob confusingly called it, leaving me with an image of an enormous old-fashioned television crammed with people) had been used three times previously. Each time a small fault had developed which had been put right on return to base. None of the faults were life-threatening, or even significant. The first one had involved the surprise appearance of a small lizard (no-one knew where from) which Vic Terrugo had named Walter and now kept as a pet. The second transition had left everyone with a headache and a craving for tinned oranges, and the third had triggered some sort of double transition which had put the TV in the same quantum space as itself but with a visible gap of about a quarter of a second, which Bob said was very disconcerting and reminded him of a party he'd been to in his undergraduate days. (I didn't pursue that one any further.)

'And then this time there was a tremendous jerk and a massive bang and we ended up here. And the really funny thing was that there was nobody here. It was a ghost village.

'Anyway, Vic and Kevin were able to set up a deflection zone. In other words they concealed road entrances so that anyone trying to find Sputteridge would simply get lost. Although in fact our AI surveillance cameras have only shown one person trying to get here in the three months since all this happened, and that was you Bettony. It seems that you were already lost and were not trying to find Sputteridge, a situation that we had not allowed for. Your mobile phone must have combined with some atmospherics to momentarily cancel the deflection transmission. You found the lane and you found us.'

Something suddenly became clear. 'So that was why I kept getting lost last night!'

'No Bettony, we've gone back over the video. You're just a bad driver.'

'Oh. And all the explosions…?'

'The Transition Drive is basically wrecked' said Mrs Ponch. 'Without it we can't get home. Kevin and Vic and Dildow have been trying to reconfigure it using locally sourced replacement material. As you can gather it's not going too well.'

'Dildow?'

'She's third engineer. You don't have any objection to women doing engineering work do you?'

'No of course not. Is Dildow her real name?'

Bob smiled smugly. 'Most of us have made use of your communications network to identify and adopt popular names that you would recognise as your own, to help us fit in if we have to.' His expression darkened for a moment. 'Only Kevin has refused and insists on keeping his real name. Hopefully he would just be viewed as a harmless eccentric.'

'I think he'll be ok. You mean our television transmissions?'

'No. Nothing so outdated!' Bob laughed. 'It's the worldwide system of formal and informal information sharing that you have. I believe you refer to it as Internet.'

There was a pause while I digested all this and tried not to smile. Mrs Ponch seemed to come to a decision. She stood. 'The Senior Officers' meeting starts in ten minutes, Bob, in the pub. I suggest you bring our young friend with you.'

There's this one thing about me, I hate being patronised, even by other women. (Which I suppose, technically, is matronised.) It sparks a rush of temper. 'Your young friend is called Bettony' I fumed, 'and she would appreciate it if you would use that word when you are talking about her. Especially when she's sitting right in front of you.'

Mrs Ponch raised her eyebrows and looked at me appraisingly. When she spoke her voice was not unfriendly. 'Bettony,' she said, 'please come over with Bob and join us.'

'Thank you. I shall.'

A smile flickered for a moment over her lips, and then she turned and left the kitchen.

'Good for you,' Bob said. 'She likes straight talking.'

'Good for her. Look Bob can you tell me what the set-up is here? Is Mrs Ponch in charge?'

'Mrs Ponch is the Officer in Charge, or what you would call the Captain. I'm the Chief Operations Officer, or what you would call, er…'

'The Chief Operations Officer probably. I'm no expert on spacecraft command structure.'

'It's not a spacecraft. It's a Transition Vehicle.'

'Whatever. Are you second in command?'

'Yes.'

'Good.'

'Vic Terrugo is Chief Engineer, or what you might call… anyway you get the idea. His brother Kevin is second engineer, and Dildow Thrust is third engineer.'

'We need to have a chat about which websites you've been using for names Bob. Carry on.'

'Uh huh. There are twelve of us in total. Of the remaining seven, four are alien life and society specialists, who have all decided against my advice to call themselves Dave. Even though two of them are women.' Bob sighed. 'They're academics Bettony. Highly competitive with each other. One of them identified 'Dave' as a common name, so they all went for it. Each of them claims that they found it first. Wankers. Anyway I'd never met them before this mission, for which I consider myself lucky. Then there's Nurse This the medic, and Wether Mapps, the software specialist.'

'That's eleven Bob.'

Bob's kindly face darkened as he added, 'And Pierre DeLondon.'

'Who's Pierre DeLondon?'

'Our Tactile, which is almost but not quite an acronym for Technical Community Team Interaction Leader, which is almost but not quite a human being as you or I might understand one. His job apparently is to make sure that we all work together to achieve our goals in a smooth, caring and mutually supportive yet robust environment, careful to reach out to each other and always aware that good team morale leads to great results in the exploration community. As far as I can see, the best way of ensuring good team morale would be to give the greasy bastard a robust kick up the arse and float him away on a rowing boat, but apparently I'm not allowed to do that. Not yet anyway.'

'Does every TV have a Tactile?'

'You must remember that this is the first Series Four TV and it is the biggest ever built. All of the Series Ones were automated, programmed to jump out, capture some images and immediately jump back. The first few never did. When the first Series One did return it was absolutely amazing, top news story for weeks. It brought back photographs of people! Admittedly with very surprised looks on their faces. And also an empty plastic bottle stuck to one of its feet. Imagine how we felt! We had proof that we were not alone in the universe Bettony! Or at least, in another universe. The Series Twos were one-person vehicles, highly successful but small, they allowed for some brief and very limited exploration. The Threes were a little bigger again, getting up to five crew for the last one. And now us. And based on how much the five-person crew argued with each other during their mission, the decision was made to create the role of Tactile. I suppose that it works in a way. We all get along ok because what unites us is hating the fuckwitted Tactile. Have you heard of mission creep?'

'Well yes but -'

'Right. Well that's Pierre. He's the creep on this mission.' Bob half smiled at me and looked shamefaced. 'Sorry Bettony, when you meet him you'll see what I mean. Do you have any questions?'

'I have so many Bob! Just for starters - How do we understand each other? Are you using a Universal Translator? What about food? Did you bring your own or can you manage to digest ours?'

'A Universal what?' Bob looked at me blankly. 'We learned English. What did you expect us to do?'

'Oh right.'

'And as for digesting your food, I can manage most of the wonderful menu at the Golden Bridge takeaway in Truro but not the spicy ribs. They seem to disagree with me.' Bob frowned and added, 'Wind. Which is a shame because they taste bloody gorgeous. I think they put just a bit too much chilli in them. And it's clever what you've done about the eggs – goodness me Bettony look at the time. We'll be late for our meeting.' He gave one last longing glance at the empty takeaway boxes and led the way to the door.

'And this meeting is taking place in the pub?'

'We use one of the rooms there, yes.'

'Great! So I get to meet the famous Mr Window.'

'Yes all right very funny.'

CHAPTER THREE

The Trouble with Meetings…

Bob pushed open the pub door and led me inside. I was greeted by the friendly smell of stale beer and looked longingly at the beer pumps on the bar. If these travellers had been here for three months, I guessed that any beer must be undrinkable by now. Probably, anyway. Oh well.

I followed Bob through the bar and along a short corridor which led to a door marked Smoke Room. Bob again pushed ahead of me, and I followed him into a smaller room. Four people seated around a table looked up at me. I smiled and tried to look more confident than I felt.

Mrs Ponch was seated at the head of the table, she smiled back and indicated an empty chair next to her. 'Take a seat dude,' she said. 'Introduce yourself to us and we will do the same to you.'

I sat down. 'I'm Bettony Gullivant I'm twenty nine I'm single and I live in Croydon I studied Art at college and work in marketing for a pet food manufacturer.'

Despite my best efforts the words came out in a nervous rush. They all stared at me. Then the man on my left spoke, and I turned and I realised that I was sitting next to a heartachingly beautiful Adonis. Golden hair tumbled carelessly onto his wide, muscular shoulders. His large blue eyes seemed to suggest laughter and fun, while his chiselled jaw radiated firm decisiveness.

I didn't mean to murmur 'Are you for real', just as he started speaking. It was nerves. His eyes widened slightly in surprise. He glanced at me with a worried look on his face and then said, 'I'm Kevin Terrugo. Protocol might dictate that I should not be here at all, as Chief Engineer Vic Terrugo is the rightful occupant of this chair, but yet still here I am in what you may think is a breach of SQUIRT regulations but yet which in reality is permissible on two counts the first being section nine subsection five of the command meeting procedure whereby a senior officer may delegate in excelsior to whomsoever he decides could meaningfully deputise on his behalf and secondly the senior Transition Vehicle commander namely in this instance the Officer in Charge has authorised this deputisation which is also authorised under section twelve subsection three of the senior officer command protocols.'

I laughed politely, thinking that this meaningless drivel was just this god's way of putting me at ease. No-one else did.

'Thank you Kevin' Mrs Ponch said. 'I think you meant in extremis rather than in excelsior but well done.'

The god called Kevin smiled self-consciously. There was some clearing of throats and then the man at the far end of the table, facing Mrs Ponch, spoke.

'Welcome to our community Bettony, and a special welcome from me, Pierre DeLondon. We are reaching out to you right now in a spirit of hearty friendship and look forward valuing to your contribution to our team.'

His voice was rich and deep and conveying firm yet friendly authority. He looked the opposite, a shifty individual who badly needed a bath. Very rarely do I take an instant dislike to anyone but I took an instant dislike to Pierre DeLondon. For some reason the way that he had emphasised the words *right now* had put me in mind of the worst kind of duplicitous politician.

Bob had taken the chair to Pierre's left, facing Kevin, and he seemed to be having some difficulty controlling himself. 'You know me,' was all he managed.

A quiet individual was sitting bolt upright next to Bob. Her dark hair sprung vertically upwards from her head for several inches, projecting an air of permanent surprise.

I'm Dave,' she said. 'Dave Potts. My speciality is integrative societal variance across quantum space and I am representing the science group. I'm also the darts club secretary.'

'Scientific community' corrected Pierre. Dave looked at him expressionlessly and then back at me. I wondered if there was just the suggestion of a twinkle in her eye. 'Sorry Pierre, I mean the scientific science community group.'

DeLondon frowned and was about to speak, but Mrs Ponch raised a hand to cut him off and said 'Thank you everyone. You have met me already Bettony, I am the officer in charge of our vessel. I'm assuming that Bob has identified himself to you as our Chief Operations Officer. This is one of our regular senior officers' meetings where we discuss progress – or lack of it – and any issues that have arisen.' She looked at me closely. 'And clearly you are the major issue of the moment.'

There was an uncomfortable silence. Someone cleared their throat. For the first time I began to understand my predicament. Was I their captive? They were hardly likely to let me wander off and risk me giving them away to some shady government organisation who might torture them for their advanced scientific secrets. My heart began to thump in my chest. I looked at Bob for reassurance, and he smiled and said 'It's ok Bettony, you're fine. We just need to work something out.'

'That's right,' Mrs Ponch added. She smiled with what I felt was a similar smile to the surgeon who met me before he operated on my knee. I waited for her to continue.

'Obviously we are in some peril here. We are stranded in your universe and until Vic, Dildow and Kevin here can come up with something, stranded we shall remain. We are also in possession of technology which for some reason no other society we have visited in any other universe has discovered. This makes our position all the more dangerous in two ways.' At this point Mrs Ponch seemed to abandon her rational discourse and raised the first two fingers of her right hand, giving me an obscene and in the circumstances somewhat surprising gesture. Then she used her left hand to pull down each finger in turn as she spoke. I quickly realised that Mrs Ponch was unaware of some of our more confrontational gestures and that she was simply ticking off the two points. 'One – we are clearly in danger ourselves because of who we are and what we know. (She pulled down her forefinger leaving her middle finger raised, now unintentionally giving me the finger.) And Two – we risk the danger of changing the entire course of your universe if our knowledge gets out.' She dropped her hand back to her lap and I relaxed slightly.

'If we were about to leave none of this would be a problem. You would have a fantastical story that no-one would believe, and have nothing to confirm it. The best you could hope for would be an interview on daytime television and maybe an article about you in the Daily Mail Online.

'Believe me Bettony when I say, we mean you no harm. We are not violent people.'

'Hear hear' said DeLondon, in a voice which radiated so much insincerity that it conveyed the complete opposite to what the actual words said.

Mrs Ponch frowned at him and then continued. 'Perhaps I should ask you what suggestions you yourself might have Bettony?'

I took a deep breath. 'Well obviously I can't leave can I?'

There was a noticeable relaxing of bodies around the table.

'What about your job?' Asked Bob. 'Won't you get into trouble?'

'Probably.'

Bob winced and shook his head.

'Look Bob, imagine that you have two alternatives.' I gave Bob the V-sign and noticed the corners of his mouth twitch. 'One – you get to spend time – even more time – with your colleagues in the large marketing department of a petfood manufacturer. Or two' – now I was giving Bob the finger – 'you get to spend time with people who are not just from a different planet but from a completely different universe. What would you choose?'

Bob nodded and allowed the smile to spread over his face. But it was Kevin who spoke.

'Technically we are from the same planet in a quantum-defined alternate reality, not a different planet. And it would be hard to justify the assertion that our universe is completely different from yours. Yes, certainly – '

'Shut up Kevin.' Mrs Ponch looked at me, searching my face. 'You mean you are volunteering to stay here with us until we can get our shit together?'

'Yes. What alternative is there? Actually Mrs Ponch that phrase–'

'Woop di doo,' Dave said, starting to get up. With the exception of Kevin the rest were leaning back in their chairs, all tension released. 'Problem sorted. Time for a celebration everyone?'

Mrs Ponch again raised her hand, and the room became still. Dave sat down again.

'Do you realise exactly what you are committing yourself to Bettony?'

'Probably not. I don't know what I'm going to do all day, or what you eat, although Bob seems to exist on takeaways. But you have my full commitment Mrs Ponch. If you'll have me I'm here to stay. And to help wherever I can.'

They were all smiling now. 'Welcome to our community,' said Pierre DeLondon, standing and reaching over to shake my hand. Surprising myself I grasped his hand and he shook it warmly - he had an unexpectedly firm grip - followed by everyone else.

'Shall I get something from the wine cellar now?' asked Dave eagerly.

But Mrs Ponch had no time to reply. The sound of a huge fart ripped through the room.

'Not me,' said Bob. 'Not had any ribs since last Thursday. Only one anyway. One box of four.'

'On your way Kevin,' said Mrs Ponch urgently. Then, more quietly as the huge muscular god stumbled awkwardly out of the room, 'see what they've cocked up this time.'

** ** **

'You have to understand that as our commanding officer Mrs Ponch works extremely hard and extremely long hours.'

Bob and I were sitting over a mug of coffee in the Police House kitchen.

'As a result, she hasn't had the time that the rest of us have to come to terms with your language. Both your verbal and your physical language. But don't underestimate her. She's a very intelligent woman and she has a very clear idea of leadership. It's one that I like. If you've done something well, she will tell you. If you do something that she thinks you could have done better she will let you know. But she's always very positive, very encouraging, and if she has to criticise it is always the action and not the person.'

I nodded my agreement. 'What's her real name? In your own language?'

'Zagretia.'

'Just Zagretia?'

'No of course not.' Bob looked at me as though I were an idiot. 'Zagretia Ponch.'

'Right… And the clothes?'

'She chose things that were dull, that would help her to blend into the background.'

'They certainly do that. Did you make all the clothes? Do you have some kind of simulator?'

'We bought them from a couple of what you call charity shops.'

'That figures. And that's another thing Bob. Where do you get your money from to buy things? Not just clothes but your takeaways.'

'I don't live on takeaways you know' Bob said testily. 'I do buy other things. You've eaten the bread that I baked and the breakfast I cooked.'

'And they were both delicious.' Half of that was true, anyway.

'Hmm' Bob grunted, mollified. 'You've put your finger on something there though Bettony. Hoppers have always taken their own food and drink. It's common sense. We don't know if what is food in another universe is poison to us and it's one less thing for us to worry about. But we've been here for three months now, all our supplies have gone. We've had to take a risk with your food. We analysed it all first of course and we couldn't see any problems, apart from eggs obviously although it's quite ingenious how you soak them in malted vinegar to neutralise them. Delicious too. What a treat.'

'You're really going to have to stop eating from chip shops and takeaways. Most people buy eggs raw from the supermarket, some people even eat them raw these days.'

Bob looked at me horrified. 'So you're another race that has evolved a way to digest eggbane?'

'I don't know what eggbane is Bob but I can only guess that we don't have it in our universe.'

'Oh yes you do! We could see it in our analyses.' Bob sat back, took a drink of coffee, and assumed the pose of an avuncular lecturer, which he favoured and which I have to say I was beginning to find a bit irritating. 'If you think about it Bettony it's obvious. The first creatures to develop external egg-laying as their preferred method of breeding faced a problem. Namely, they were producing nutritious and tasty snacks for other animals, and furthermore these snacks couldn't even try to run away or hide. So they had to find a way of deterring their predators, and quickly. The creatures whose progeny survived to produce their own eggs were the ones who had evolved to lace their ova with a genetic poison. Being genetic, it was harmless to themselves, but deadly to any other animal.' Bob leaned forwards again and tapped the table, which seemed to be a habit of his when in irritating-lecture mode. 'Now here's the interesting thing Bettony. Evolution being what it is, in every other universe that we have visited so far the predators also evolved to cope with eggbane – apart from a few harmless side-effects such as constipation and wind. But for some reason, this did not happen in ours.' Bob leaned back again in triumph. 'Something in your pickling process neutralises the eggbane. Otherwise, eggs are just about fatal to us, even when cooked. How weird is that?'

'It is strange,' I agreed. 'And I can't help noticing that you've moved the subject away from that of money.'

'Ah.' Bob's cheeks coloured in embarrassment. 'We steal it.'

'What!?'

'I know.' Bob looked at me imploringly. 'We haven't got any choice Bettony. It's steal it or starve.'

'How do you do it?'

'You have machines set into walls that release cash when someone inserts a piece of specially designed plastic into them. We just … fiddle with the … electronics.' Bob was blushing on top of his blush now, his voice mortified into a whisper. 'It's awful I know. But we haven't got any choice Bettony.'

It was agreed that I would move into the spare room at the police house. It was a nice room overlooking a rather brambly garden; it soon acquired a homely feel to me, which is to say that the various clothes and few possessions that I had brought with me and which I retrieved from my car were soon scattered around it. I am not the tidiest of people. I tried hard to keep the mess contained inside my room. Bob didn't complain. In fact he seemed to regard my room as my private sanctum. He always knocked on my door, even when it was open, and as I recall never once entered it. Bob's natural kindness was a great reassurance in the following days. He was a busy man, but he insisted on sharing the cooking 50-50 and always found time to talk to me, usually in the evenings when he was clearly tired. It was in the course of these conversations that he explained something about the nature of moving between realities.

'Have you ever put a mirror on each side of you,' he asked, 'or better still stood between two big mirrors?'

I smiled and nodded. 'Who hasn't?' I said.

'So you know that each mirror reflects the reflection in the other ad infinitum. You stand there and you see images of yourself stretching away into infinity. The images further away seem to get darker and darker, and they swing around much more if you move one of the mirrors even the tiniest bit.'

'Yep. I've played that game Bob.'

'From what we can tell, that's what the alternative realities are like. There are realities that are almost indistinguishable to ours, that mirror us closely and don't seem to be affected by changes that we make. And then other realities spread away in an infinity of tiny differences. Go far enough and those tiny differences accumulate into big changes, so that those realities which are further away seem to be wildly affected by even the smallest decisions that we make in our own. But here's something to send a shiver up your spine Bettony.' Bob leaned forward in his armchair and I could see it was tappy-time. 'Just as the reflections in the mirrors become darker, the further away they are, so the realities that are further away are more…' he seemed to search for the right description, and then said, '… more sinister.'

Bob was right. Something in his voice did indeed send a shiver up my spine. For a few moments the living room was silent. I'd like to say it was a silence broken only by the ticking of a clock – and there was the clock on the mantelpiece which had been doing the job perfectly until a couple of days before - but we had both forgotten to wind it.

'What do you mean by 'sinister'?'

'You may think that people can be a bit unpleasant, but believe me Bettony in some of the places that we've been to, what you might call Basic Human Nature is … dark. The innately kind response that we have gradually lessens as you move reality further away. It seems to become more difficult for people to take good-natured decisions, however much they appear to want to. Go far enough, and acceptable behaviour is very different to what you and I know. I mean, there are places where the Nazis won the Second World War, and further out still, there are places where there was never any need for a Second World War. And not in a good way. And sadly, for some reason that we haven't worked out yet, it is easier for us to transition to universes that are further away.'

'Where does your universe fit Bob?'

'You're asking the wrong question Bettony. You should be asking, where is yours?' He smiled again, and then said, 'And the answer to that one is, it's not far away. It's close enough. You're ok Bettony.'

CHAPTER FOUR

Good news and bad

It was decided that I should go shopping. Or in Pierre DeLondon's idiotspeak, that I should take robust ownership of the next out of area provision replenishment project. This was the good news; I had spent a couple of days kicking my heels and it felt good to be doing something. The bad news was it had also been decided, for reasons which I shall explain, that Wether Mapps would be joining me.

I had met Wether a couple of days beforehand.

Certain areas of Sputteridge were off bounds to me, which obviously made them very attractive. I tried to stay away from them, I honestly did. Especially Bay Lane at the far end of the village square. Even when I wandered over to it on a quiet afternoon I had no intention of pushing aside the 'Police – Do Not Cross' tape that cordoned it off, then creeping along the pavement on the shady side of the street. On the horizon I could see a thin strip of ocean, blue against a blue sky. An old brick-built public toilet block stretched across the end of the lane and blotted out much of the sea view. I wondered where the Transition Vehicle was –

'Well well well, what have we got here?' A sneering voice broke my reverie. I spun around and then instinctively took a step back, away from a greasy, leering individual.

'Somebody's not where they should be are they? I've been following you my girl. Naughty naughty naughty.'

As I may have previously mentioned, I really don't like being patronised. The heart-bumping fear that had been my first reaction was very quickly replaced by anger. Either Mr Greasy didn't notice this or it didn't worry him. His mistake, either way.

'You're in a lot of trouble my girl,' he sneered. 'A lot. Spying in a restricted area.' He pursed his lips and sucked in, making a strange hissing sound. 'Or you could be. I can make a lot of trouble for you. Unless you're nice to me. If you're really nice to me I can – ooof'

It was a move that I had practised dozens, probably hundreds of times in the martial arts class. I marvelled as I kicked forward at how Mr Greasy was actually making it easy for me, standing legs wide apart as he did. I pulled my foot back from between his legs and watched him slowly fold forwards. I was thinking of an axe kick to follow, swinging my leg upwards and then bringing the heel down hard against the back of my opponent's head, but they can sometimes kill and that would have been quite an extreme response; and anyway I saw Pierre DeLondon hurrying towards us across the square and stopped myself in time.

'Bettony!' he called. 'What are you doing to Mr Mapps? Leave that poor man alone.'

'She attacked me,' Mapps managed to croak. 'You must have seen her Pierre. All I was doing was trying to stop her from coming down here -'

'And the rest' I shouted. 'Tell him what you just said you greaseball.'

'Control yourself,' Pierre cut across me. He stood protectively over his stricken colleague and raised an arm, holding his hand palm-forward towards me. Shock had drained his face of colour and expression and he stared at me, eyes wide open. 'And kindly moderate your language as well. This may be how you behave in your universe but in ours we have standards of interpersonal respect.'

'Huh? Interpersonal respect? Are you kidding me? He just -'

'Not now Bettony.' DeLondon raised his other arm and began tapping on his watch. 'I suggest that you save your energy for an emergency council meeting that I am going to call - right now.' There was a pause while we all waited for something to happen. He tapped again at his watch and repeated, with some emphasis, 'Right now.' An electronic voice said, 'Your alarm has been set.' DeLondon looked at his watch in some surprise.

'Don't you want to know what he was saying?'

'No I don't, not at this moment and possibly not ever, not from you. Truth is a valued principle in our community and I am sure that Wether will give us a full account.' DeLondon tapped again at his watch and the voice responded 'That item is currently unavailable. Press five to choose an alternative or eight to cancel your order.'

'What? You can't just take his word!'

'Be quiet please.' DeLondon frowned in concentration as he tapped ineffectively at his watch, then said, deflatedly, 'Come on, I'll go and knock on their doors.'

DeLondon steered me towards the old toilet block. I wondered vaguely why we were heading towards this eyesore, but I was so wrapped up in my emotions that I did not pay it too much attention at first. I felt mixture of rage and, increasingly, fear. How could they possibly take this creep's word against mine? But what if they did? Mapps tagged along, exaggerating his limp I thought.

The toilet block was closed to the public. It said so in large print on notices pinned to the gents and ladies entrances. I was becoming increasingly suspicious of DeLondon; people who take other people into toilet blocks - open or closed to the public - rarely do so with good intentions, I thought.

There was a third door, marked Staff Only. DeLondon pushed at it. It gave a strange hissing sound as it opened and I looked into a high-tech interior. This was no ordinary toilet block.

We entered a small reception area. In front of us there were four doors set into a curved wall. There were childish crayoned pictures stuck to the walls. But the walls themselves were made of a kind of smooth pale green plastic. There were no sharp edges or corners anywhere.

DeLondon chose the second door on the left and pressed his thumb against a small glass rectangle set into the wall next to it.

Nothing happened.

DeLondon sighed in frustration and pressed a glowing red circle towards the bottom of the rectangle.

Nothing happened. DeLondon's face began to colour in embarrassment. I looked at Mapps and caught him smirking.

DeLondon lifted his wrist and touched his watch against the circle. He turned to me and said, 'I'm not great with electronics. I'm more of a people person.'

I nodded and tried to force a smile of encouragement. At that moment another door opened and Bob stepped out. Relief flooded through me.

Bob stared at us in surprise.

'Pierre? What on Abbuth is happening?'

'Ah, Bob. We need to call an emergency council meeting right now.'

'I rather think we do. What made you decide it would be a good idea to bring Bettony here?'

'She was making her way here when our friend Wether managed to intercept her. At which point she physically attacked him. I saw it Bob.'

'I find that hard to believe.' The ghost of a smile twitched across Bob's lips. 'He's still alive for one thing. But you caught her trying to get in here and you thought it would be a good idea to finish the job for her?'

'What else could I do?'

'Just about anything I reckon. Take her over to the pub and wait for us there. Anyway the cat's out of the barrel now isn't it? Where are you proposing to take her?'

'The Council Room.'

Bob shrugged his shoulders, gave me the tiniest of smiles and what may or may not have been a wink and disappeared back through his door.

Which left the three of us still marooned in the little lobby while Pierre struggled to gain entry. Eventually Mapps roused himself, bad-temperedly pushed DeLondon out of the way and swiped his wrist across the door. It whooshed open and Mapps led the way down a corridor in which all the walls, the ceiling and the floor were of the same smooth, somewhat tastelessly green plastic. Mapps caught me running my fingers over the flat material and smirked. There was something salacious in that smirk that really creeped me out. We passed doors on each side; each had a small plaque bearing bizarre hieroglyphics, and some supplemented these with more children's drawings. Finally Mapps pushed open a door on the left and the three of us entered a larger room.

I heard DeLondon mutter 'oh'. Four people were hunched over some paperwork on a table. They looked up at us and I recognised one as Dave Potts. I guessed that the rest were the other Daves, there was something generic about them. Another female Dave with curly hair stared hard at DeLondon and said, accusingly,

'We do have this room booked you know.' At this point Dave Potts saw me, smiled and said 'Oh hi Bettony.' I managed a little smile in return. Potts' eyes went to DeLondon and Mapps and she mouthed, 'You ok?'

I shrugged my shoulders.

Pierre was nonplussed. 'I, er…' He cleared his throat. He seemed more uncomfortable than ever in the company of the four scientists but before he could reply the door burst open again and Mrs Ponch strode in followed by Bob and a small, careworn man with a large head.

'I'm sorry people but we need this room.' It was a polite and friendly tone, but it also carried authority. As one the four Daves stood up, three of them collected their papers and headed to the door and the fourth put four glasses and a half-empty bottle of wine onto a tray and followed them.

'Wine?' Queried Mrs Ponch.

'I'll speak to them' Bob replied. He sighed. 'Again.'

'Sit please.' This seemed to be a directive to everyone; certainly everyone sat. 'Bettony, this is Vic Terrugo.' I nodded to the small man with the large head, bent forward slightly as though he had the weight of all the world on his shoulders. Could he really be the brother of the huge and muscular blond god? Vic gave me a slight, tense smile of reply. Mrs Ponch looked at me as though trying to find something within me. It was a very piercing look. I shifted uncomfortably in my seat. She said, 'Tell me what happened.'

I told her. She turned to Mapps.

'And what is your version Wether?'

The creep that was Wether Mapps repeated his earlier, lying version of events. Mrs Ponch squeezed the bridge of her nose with the thumb and forefinger of her left hand and stared at the table in front of her, deep in thought.

'If what you say is true Bettony, then this is clearly unconscionable behaviour by Mr Mapps. Equally, if you have the truth Wether, then Bettony is guilty of an appalling lie.' She continued to stare at the table. My heart was thumping. I wanted to earn the trust of these amazing people; I wanted to continue this astonishing adventure. More than anything, I wanted the approbation of Mrs Ponch and Bob. In the few days that I had spent in Sputteridge their honest, straightforward intelligence had already earned my respect and admiration.

'What did you see Pierre?'

'Well I was a distance away. I couldn't hear what was said. But I definitely saw the assault as our friend Wether described it.' A typically two-faced reply, I thought.

'We're in a Category Four universe Zagretia,' Mapps said. 'Surely you can't take the word of a Category Four occupant over mine?'

Mrs Ponch had raised her eyebrows at the use of her name. As Mapps finished she slammed her hand onto the table making everyone jump. 'Do not ever make a statement like that again Mr Mapps! You know that we do not judge.'

'But –'

'We do not judge!' Mrs Ponch's eyes blazed. 'Our TVs have found good people in every universe that we have visited thus far. It is true that the proportion changes in the different categories but nevertheless experience teaches us that the only thing for us to do is to consider each person on their own merits.'

'Sorry.' Mapps looked down, avoiding her eyes.

'I prefer to think of the situation like this. Bettony, you misheard what Mr Mapps had said. The assault occurred as Mr Mapps and Pierre have described, but you were reacting in what is an acceptable way in your universe. Particularly if you mistakenly thought that you were under threat. Still, you were completely wrong to abuse our trust in seeking to explore beyond the limits that we had imposed on you for your own safety. What do you say?'

It was pointless to protest against Mapps and DeLondon together. Feeling completely wretched I nodded and said, 'It is true that I should not have abused your trust. I'm very sorry.' I could feel tears welling up inside of me, which made me feel angry with myself. I forced them back and looked at Mrs Ponch.

'I'm very sorry' I repeated.

'Hm.' Mrs Ponch nodded, and stared at the table again, evidently considering what she had heard. Then DeLondon broke the silence.

'I think some robust team-building may be appropriate, Zagretia. We need to help foster a bond of trust between our two valued colleagues.' He looked smug, pleased with himself and what he was about to say. 'Can I propose that we ask Bettony and Wether to spearhead our next venture into Truro?'

It took me several moments to register what DeLondon had just said. I was thinking about what they all seemed to accept as a given – that I live in a Category Four universe. Whatever that was, it didn't sound good. I was shocked, to say the least. I thought about Bob's description of the mirrors and the darkening reflections. He had told me that we were close enough. But was he just being polite?

And then Pierre DeLondon's words sunk in.

'What?'

DeLondon smiled. 'I am proposing, Bettony, that we ask yourself and Wether to team together and buy ownership of our next venture into Truro to collect provisions, the day after tomorrow.'

This was bad.

What was worse, Bob and Mrs Ponch were both nodding their agreement.

CHAPTER FIVE

A clearer understanding with Mr Mapps — but what car to use? And when to go?

We used my car. We set off early morning. Bizarrely, Bob and Mrs Ponch waved us off, provoking vague memories of my proud parents waving me away to university. For one moment the old unreliable Renault seemed less than a blink away, my parents alive and well and not crushed to death beneath the wheels of the lorry whose driver was busily texting his wife's sister. I felt suddenly overwhelmed by intense sadness.

'Steady on Betbet' Mapps barked. I swerved around the telephone box, blinking back tears, back in the moment. Mapps patted my thigh. 'It's not really a woman's job is it, driving a car?' His hand remained on my thigh, which he began to stroke. 'Women are much better at other things don't you think?'

I checked my rear view mirror, made sure that my friends were out of sight, and pulled to a stop. Then I released my right hand from the steering wheel and in one smooth movement I twisted my body towards Mapps, brought my right hand around and used it to execute my own unique version of Tiger Claw on Mr Mapps.

Tiger Claw is one of the lesser-used martial arts moves, concentrating as it does on attacking the throat. Unless it is used in extremis it is not tremendously legal, and this is mainly because the most likely outcome of performing it successfully is the death of your opponent. Interestingly, the smaller size of a woman's hand seems to make my adaptation of it (which involves gripping the throat, rather than simply pulling back after a hard strike) more likely to have fatal results than, say, the larger width of a man's hand, which whilst it can still kill requires more accuracy to do so and when it grips tends to take hold of the whole of the neck rather than just the windpipe. It is easier for a smaller hand to wrap tightly around the windpipe. It is also an easier move to perform on men, who generally have prominent Adam's apples. A man's greater natural strength is also fairly irrelevant in these circumstances. They don't get the chance to use it.

But enough of the biology lesson. I practised this move many hundreds of times over the years, often on my usual, long-suffering Aikido partner Martin Copple. So my move on Mapps was accurate and efficient. (Thank you Martin. Those trips to the hospital were all worthwhile.)

Mapps was making strange gurgling noises as his Adam's apple was forced back into his windpipe, which was simultaneously being pressured from each side and pulled forward, and which he was clearly aware was about to be broken with some serious life-shortening consequences.

'Don't try to move my fingers,' I said, as I saw his hand move from my leg. 'I'll have plenty of time to kill you before you can do anything. You need to believe me here Wether, for your own safety. In fact what I might do is take your hand, break some of those little pinkies of yours, and then crush your neck.' I leaned closer into him, putting my mouth next to his ear, and whispered, 'So stay very still.'

Mapps stayed very still, apart from his eyes, which seemed to bulge out from his face. His hands rested on his own knees. He stared in front of him. His face had already turned startlingly red.

'Ok. I can see that we have established a good channel of communication, as Pierre would probably say. So let's agree on a few ground rules. First up, if you ever lay a hand on me again I will break it in such a way that you will never be able to use it again.' I tightened my grip on his neck just a little. 'Shatter some of the smaller bones. Probably push them through your skin so you can have a good look at them.' His face began to turn a strange shade of purple. 'You need to believe that I can do this Wether. Do you believe that I can do this?'

The gurgling sounds changed slightly, which I generously interpreted as his agreement.

'Next. If you ever call me BetBet again I will dislocate your shoulder and then break it in a uniquely painful way. Still with me Wether?'

Gurgle gurgle.

'And finally, and I think this is perhaps most important of all. If you ever think that you can take me by surprise and use your strength against me I shall kill you, but I shall do it quite slowly. And painfully.' Squeeze. Gurgle. 'I think I could get away with that. Self-defence. Probably take ten or fifteen minutes. By the end you will be begging me to finish you off. Still with me?'

Gurgle.

I released my hand. Mapps did not move at all. At first he didn't even try to breathe. Then his breath began to come in short choking bursts, as though he were still being strangled. I felt a slight concern; something in his throat had definitely crunched on that last squeeze.

Only a slight concern though. It was probably just a bit of ligament.

I put the car into gear and we moved off, away from Sputteridge, past the empty stone cottages and up to the crossroads where nearly two weeks ago I had changed the entire course of my life in search of Fod and a bed, and maybe a beach where I could have a paddle and try to forget about Jack, or at least come to terms with his deceitful concealment of his alternative lifestyle choice. I had had varying degrees of success in achieving these aims, but I had certainly managed the last of them, if not in quite the way I was expecting. Jack was of no interest to me now.

** ** **

My passenger remained in a state of frozen paralysis for almost all of the journey. His breath was very slowly becoming less of a struggle. By the time we reached Truro — which we found no trouble by the way — he was breathing fairly naturally and also tentatively moving his neck, very slightly left and then right. I found a car park, pulled into a space and cut the engine. I turned towards Mapps and he flinched, eyes beginning to bulge again in fear.

'See what I don't understand Wether, is how come an insect like you can come from the same universe as the rest of them. They seem to have a good-natured wisdom that barely exists in my own world. Even the Daves, in their own whacky way. And then there's you.'

He turned his body so that he could face me without having to twist his neck, at the same time trying to put as much space between us as he could in the small car. The only phrase he uttered, in a croaking whisper, was 'Can we get on?'

The rest of the expedition went reasonably well. We found a cashpoint and Wether managed to extract two hundred pounds from it. Then we wandered around, buying provisions from a list, taking them back to the car, going and buying more. Occasionally people looked at Mapps, who was still struggling with his breathing and clearly in some discomfort, but this was England and no-one was impolite enough to speak to us or enquire after his health.

By two o'clock we were heading back to Sputteridge, me having eaten at a lovely little coffee shop in the town centre. Mapps had declined my offer of a coffee, which was understandable as he was still having a great deal of trouble swallowing. I had even found a delicatessen somewhere that sold pickled eggs, they were not on the list but I bought them as a surprise for Bob.

I had made a few mental notes of the surroundings when we pulled off the lane and onto the main Truro road, and felt confident going back that I would find it again. Even so, at first I was convinced that I had taken a wrong turn (not an unfamiliar experience for me) and was approaching a T-junction not a crossroads. But then as if by magic both the lane to Sputteridge and the signpost suddenly reappeared. I headed down the lane and through the village, and as arranged I stopped against the 'Police – Do Not Cross' tapes.

Bob was waiting by the roadside. He greeted me with a smile and a mock salute and moved the tapes to one side. I trundled the car down the lane, followed its curve to the left and then pulled to a halt outside the toilet block.

'Everything go ok?' Bob asked.

''Yep' I smiled. Bob turned to Mapps.

'Are you all right Wether?'

Mapps gave a very quiet non-committal grunt then winced and headed into the building, leaving me and Bob to carry things inside.

Bob watched him go, then turned to me. 'What's up with him?'

I shrugged my shoulders. Bob frowned.

'Bettony, what have you done to him?'

'Nothing.'

'Nothing?'

'Not really.'

Bob looked at me appraisingly for a long moment, then said, 'Let's get your shopping into the TV. We'll use the kitchen storeroom.'

I still had not seen much of the TV, and was excited at the chance to see more. So the kitchen was quite a disappointment. It was towards the end of one of the other corridors, and it was quite a long walk, but – basically, it was just a kitchen which opened into an area with a couple of dining tables and chairs and some uncomfortable-looking easy chairs around the sides. There was a door at the end which led into a storeroom. Nowhere was there any evidence of an advanced alien civilisation, unless you consider a double oven with integrated rotisserie to be particularly progressive.

Bob saw me looking around. 'It's not great is it? And somebody leaves the oven in a real mess. I think it's the bloody scientists.' He sighed. 'You can see why I prefer to cook in the police house.'

We transferred the contents of the car to the kitchen and storeroom. The last box that I brought in had the jar of pickled eggs. I slipped the jar out when Bob was not looking and then held it behind me when he shifted the box onto a shelf.

'All done,' he said, and smiled. 'Time for a cup of tea don't you think?' Then, puzzled, 'What have you got behind your back Bettony?'

'Ta da!' I brought my hand out and presented my friend with the jar. He examined it and exclaimed delightedly,

'Pickled eggs!'

'It's a surprise for you Bob.'

'It certainly is! Wow these look posh. Thank you my friend.'

It was the first time that Bob had called me that. I swelled with pride. 'I thought you might want to take them back to the police house and have one as a treat now and then.'

Bob smiled again, looking like a naughty schoolboy. 'I could though, couldn't I? And it would be ok because no-one else likes them much.'

I nodded. I was smiling too, happy at his innocent delight.

CHAPTER SIX

I become a valued member of the team and take ownership of the out of area replenishment strategy

I was put in charge of doing the shopping.

This was not the doddle that it sounds. There were thirteen of us including me, and that's a lot of stuff to buy. And to keep buying.

Every few days I would drive into Truro, and each time someone different would go with me and do the embarrassing thing with the cash machine. Bob was most fun, and the one in whose company I felt most relaxed, but the regular trips were giving me the chance to become acquainted with other crew members. Some were more talkative than others. Dave Green for example explained at probably a bit too much length about Reinhold's Theory of Gum. The basic idea was fairly simple: Take any well-used street, and count the number of pieces of chewing gum stuck to the pavement over a fifty metre length. ('It needs to be fifty metres,' Dave explained, 'to give it statistical validity.') Dave called this the G-number. Compare this with the G-numbers for the same section of pavement in different realities. The G-number for a particular reality would give an accurate estimate of where that reality fitted into what Dave called the Response Spectrum, in other words how kind, or apathetic, or cruel, the average individual would be in any particular situation.

'For example,' Dave said. 'Imagine an old chuffer falls over in the street. At one extreme a group of concerned people gather around and do what they can to help. In another reality people just ignore him and walk past. At the other extreme somebody nicks his wallet and his shoes.'

'But I've seen more or less all three of those responses here on Earth,' I said. 'I was waiting for a bus in a city centre and exactly that happened. Someone collapsed. It was the middle of winter. A group of people gathered around, someone called for an ambulance, somebody else covered him with a coat.'

Dave looked interested. 'What happened?'

'Well, when my bus arrived forty minutes later the ambulance had still not arrived. Most people had wandered away but one person was still with the person on the floor.'

'Mmm. And the other times?'

'I was on holiday. An old woman was lying across the pavement moaning and everyone was just stepping over her.'

'What did you do?'

'Nothing.'

'Nothing!'

'It was a foreign land. I didn't speak the language. Somebody said she was a beggar. There were police around and I was expecting them to do something. Ok it wasn't my proudest moment but what could I do?'

'And the third?'

'That was on tv - on television Dave, not your transition vehicle. Don't look so startled. A youngster collapsed and some people stole things from him while they pretended to help him. It was caught on cctv.'

'Good Greeks.' Dave looked around uneasily.

'I think you mean good grief. Don't worry Dave, these are rare examples. I'm just trying to make the point that predicting somebody's behaviour based on the amount of chewing gum on a street is a bit too... prescriptive. And why chewing gum anyway?'

'It's an indicator of how thoughtless people are. And I'm talking about the average response. There will always be people who are not average.'

At this point Dave Green launched into an explanation about probability curves and normal distributions which I'm not going to repeat, mainly because I had no idea what he was on about.

'... and how kind or cruel this 'average' person is,' said Dave, rather over-emphasising the word average, I thought, 'determines how kind or cruel society is as a whole. Fancy a pint?'

'Desperately.'

Dildow, on the other hand, was quite guarded. I got the feeling that she did not trust me. She was polite, but unresponsive. I would have liked to talk to her about her choice of name but at no time did

I feel comfortable enough to raise the subject. I stayed polite. I quite liked her, and thought that in time, with care, I could overcome her suspicions.

The one who was hardest work - the one who gave me a stultifying headache which lasted long after the shopping trip - was Pierre DeLondon. His relentless artificial good humour was very difficult to cope with. His robust use of clichés made me want to scream. The less said about Pierre, the better.

There were a couple of people who did not join me on my trips. I guessed that Vic was too busy to be spared. Nurse This the medic was a good-looking but very quiet young man with a vague air of sadness about him. I wondered if he was considered too shy to venture out successfully. On the whole though, I enjoyed getting out. It was a beautiful early summer, Truro is a nice place to be, and it was a good way for me to get to know people. I wondered if that was at least part of its purpose. That was fine with me. I noticed that after our first visit Mapps did not join me again. In fact I saw very little of him. That was fine with me too. On the few occasions when we passed in the TV, his eyes burned into me with an intense hatred and I needed to remind myself that there was little he could do now. Or so I thought.

** ** **

What turned out to be my last shopping trip for a while was in the company of Mrs Ponch.

The streets of Truro were becoming more crowded with tourists now. Only a couple of weeks earlier most people had walked purposefully around. Now, everywhere was busier but the pace was slower. Shorts and t-shirts were everywhere and people sauntered, enjoying the early summer sunshine. I felt slightly embarrassed for Mrs Ponch who was still in her drab 1950s coat. I noticed a few people glance at her, some with pitying looks. Mrs Ponch didn't seem to notice.

'How are you finding your time with us Bettony?' She asked.

'I'm enjoying it.' We seemed to be skirting around the issue of Mapps, I noticed.

'Surely you must be missing your regular life? Friends, work, family? That sort of rumdiddly?'

'I'm sure I'll manage without seeing my friends for a few weeks. And I don't have any close family. I certainly don't miss work. All this is far more interesting.'

'Won't you get into trouble at work? You must have stayed beyond your holiday leave by now.'

'I resigned. I phoned them up last week when I was out with Dave Lanyard and said I'd decided not to go back.'

'You resigned! I'm so sorry Bettony, we really have messed you around. I've been so busy that I haven't given enough thought to the implications of you staying with us.'

'Honestly Mrs Ponch it's fine. I'd had enough of that place anyway. It was time for me to move on, even if - all this - hadn't happened.' I would have had to get away from everything that would lead me back to Jack, I didn't add.

'You're making a very useful contribution, you know. Each of these shopping trips has to happen and by replacing one of the crew you are saving us between two and three man-days a week.'

'Thank you.'

'Don't thank me Bettony! It is I who should be giving you the hows-your-father.'

'Um...'

'One of the early Series Twos didn't return, you know. A single hopper was piloting it. We have not lost all hope yet of rescuing him. But apart from that there has never been a problem with any of the previous staffed transitions. A couple of the very early automated vehicles never returned as well, but we were very much on a learning curse back then. We were always very careful, always learning from everything that happened. A staffed TV was not sent out until we were as close to being absolutely sure of its safety as is hubertly possible. It remains a mystery what happened to the Series Two. But we seem to have faced problems from the very beginning of this trip.

We have been stranded for nearly four months Bettony!' She shook her head. 'I never even knew you could still buy tinned oranges...'

'Bob told me about that.'

The warmth of the day and the bright happiness of the people around us seemed to free Mrs Ponch from some of her cares. 'Come on,' she said. 'Before we get the shit to take back let's get a coffee and a sandwich slap.'

'I think I'd better order it if you don't mind.'

I had been mulling something over for a few days, and inspired by Mrs Ponch's confidence I bought a map-book on the way to the coffee shop. I ordered our lunch and we found a quiet corner. Mrs Ponch watched as I found the page for Truro and opened the map book out on the table. She waited patiently as I peered at the map, not questioning me even when I exclaimed 'Bloody hell!'

Eventually she said, gently, 'Would you like to share your brainfart?'

'What got me thinking was the actual name, Sputteridge. It just doesn't sound Cornish. It doesn't sound like anything, to be honest. There's a place called Totteridge, in London, but that's hundreds of miles away.' I pointed. 'Here's Truro. And here's the road that we came in on...' My finger followed the line of the road. '...see?'

'Good Greeks.'

'There's nothing. No Sputteridge. No houses at all. Just open country.'

'So we haven't transitioned *to* Sputteridge...'

'That's what I was thinking.'

'Somehow, and from granny knows where, we must have brought Sputteridge with us.'

** ** **

Mrs Ponch called a senior staff meeting as soon as we got back. I did not attend these, but it didn't matter because I knew that Bob would not be able to resist telling all when he got home. (Yes. That's how it felt now. Home was a strange deserted police house which I shared with an alien from another universe.)

49

In any case it was my turn to cook dinner and tonight I was determined to shine.

I had a sneaking suspicion that one reason why Bob insisted on cooking every other meal, despite his heavy workload, was that his cooking (as opposed to his baking) was far better than mine. Not that he ever commented. However surprising the taste of the meal that I prepared, however unexpectedly crunchy or chewy it was, Bob was always very grateful, and was always determined to clear his plate, at whatever the cost to his digestive system or his teeth. But I knew. It was noticeable that whenever we treated ourselves to a takeaway it always seemed to be on one of those evenings when I should have been cooking. And when occasionally another crew member was invited to join us for dinner, it was always when Bob was cooking. So I had decided to try cheating, in the sense that I had used the shopping trip with Mrs Ponch to buy a copy of a cookbook of easy-to-prepare meals by a well-known TV chef. Unlike the ancient Madhur Jaffrey book which lived on the bookshelves, and from which I had made several explosive attempts at preparing Indian food, 'Frankie's Five Minute Feasts' were quick, simple, and did not leave room for confusion between a teaspoon and a tablespoon of chilli powder.

What I had forgotten of course was to check whether we had all of the easy-to-prepare ingredients.

We hadn't.

I definitely remembered buying the garlic. Mrs Ponch had expressed an interest in them at the time, commenting that they were one of her favourite ingredients and on Abbuth she grew the little buggers in her greenhouse. So if they weren't here in the police house they had to be in the TV's kitchen storeroom.

No problem. It was still early and there was plenty of time. I wandered over to the TV and found my way to the kitchen. Bob was sitting at one of the tables with Dildow and Kevin. The map book was spread out in front of them and Bob was obviously explaining things to them.

That was fine.

So was the fact that the two engineers were eating pie from a dish. I didn't mind that they were dribbling gravy onto the table, it was hardly clean in any case. I wouldn't have minded if they had dribbled it onto the map book.

What I minded though - quite a lot, to be honest - was that Bob was also eating the pie. Not just eating the pie, he had a large portion in his own dish.

He swallowed hastily. 'Ah. Bettony.' To give him credit, he looked very embarrassed.

'I've come to get the garlic' I said, coldly. 'For our dinner. Which I'm cooking. For you to eat.'

'Ah! Good! Garlic! Yes. I'm looking forward to... er... what is it tonight?'

Dildow stood, forcibly pulling Kevin to his feet. She must have spotted that all was not well and she was obviously not a fan of blood sports. 'We'll get going,' she said. 'Thanks Bob, we've got all we need.' She glanced at me. 'Good call on this Bettony. Come on Kevin.'

'Why are we leaving now?' Kevin asked. 'What about the pie? The scientists will be here soon. We can't just leave it.' He was still protesting as she pulled him out of the door.

Bob glanced at me and gave a hollow laugh. 'Just a quick snack before dinner,' he said.

A period of frosty silence seemed to be the best of the options available to me at that moment. I turned without replying and followed the two engineers out of the kitchen, then headed out of the TV. Bob caught up with me before I reached the square. He did not speak, but walked alongside me.

I was thinking how best to express my hurt and anger at his betrayal. I was putting together a really cutting remark that would wound him and yet also stretch him remorselessly on the cruel rack of guilt. One that would leave him in no doubt as to the hurt I was feeling at being let down by someone I had considered to be a true friend.

And while I was doing this something very weird happened.

It is very difficult to describe what it was but it felt as though a drunken foggy bubble had formed deep in my subconscious and then pushed its way into the more active part of my brain. Bob had started to speak but his voice became very slow and deep, repeating half of what he said in a sudden high-pitched catch-up every couple of seconds. Colours leaked out of the buildings we were passing, staining the air around us. I looked down at my arm and realised that Bob had grabbed it and was pulling me back towards the TV. The problem was that although my hand went with him, my feet had not moved. I watched my arm stretching and wanted to giggle – and believe me, giggling is not something I have done since I was 13.

'Now Bettony!' he squeaked suddenly, his voice high-pitched beyond idiocy. I pushed spongy, unresponsive legs and managed to move, feeling as though I were stretching like rubber and moving through unresponsive treacle. The closer we got to the TV the more that normality reasserted itself, although the door would not open automatically; Bob had to swipe at it with his watch, and when he did so his arm stretched slightly. But we got inside and then we were into the TV, Bob still pulling at me, my head still struggling to cope. I remember being in the entrance hall, then Bob pulling me through a different door, down another corridor, and into a large room lined by worktops. There was a single, small console in the middle of the room. People were still running into the room, diving to seats at workstations, tapping and touching screens in front of them. Mrs Ponch sat at the central console, watching them. A sudden convulsion took my stomach and I was sick all over her.

'Fuck sake,' she said in a surprisingly calm voice, wiping her hands at my lunch. Then, to Bob, 'Are you both ok?'

Bob took his head out of a waste bin, wiped his mouth and nodded. 'More or less. A bit of temporospacial displacement. We were outside.'

'Get to your station. You can empty that bin later. Bettony, shift your arse onto that stool and stay there.'

'Ok. Sorry.' I felt weak and was gently shaking but my head was clearing quickly now and being sick had settled my body. I went and sat at one side of the room and watched what was happening. It was amazing. The room was not brightly lit and the screens on the worktops glowed, although I had no idea what they were showing – it looked to me like a variety of amorphous shapes floating across one screen and onto the next, accompanied by strange symbols which I guessed were writing in these people's own language. Although Mrs Ponch was clearly in charge, everyone was following directions issued by Vic Terrugo, who moved constantly across the room from one workstation to the next. His face was solemn, his movements quick and with scarcely any noticeable panic. Occasionally he would call out instructions in a loud voice; sometimes each operator would shout out a response. At one point every screen was filled with his brother's handsome face, although Kevin's flaxen hair was sticking out wildly, giving the impression of him being electrocuted as he spoke. Mrs Ponch watched everything, occasionally pressing a few buttons on the arm of her chair or picking a piece of half-digested ham and cheese toastie from her clothes. She spoke rarely, and when she did it was usually to Bob, who would respond with a nod of his head or a few short words.

This was the first time that I had heard any of them speak anything other than English, which they did as natives. More or less. Their own language was quite guttural and reminded me vaguely of Welsh, their voices making sounds that had no home in the A to Z alphabet. After a while I could sense everyone starting to become less stressed. Vic was now spending more time at his own console. A few minutes later Vic said something, Mrs Ponch responded, and everyone sat back in their chairs. Dildow was sitting near to me, now she took a deep breath and blew out hard.

'What just happened?' I asked.

'Buggered if I know.' She shook her head. 'Unexpected transition. Looks like we've left your Sputteridge behind this time Bettony.' She tapped her screen. 'This cannot happen.'

Mrs Ponch stood up. 'Except that it did. Bob, you have control. I'm going to clean up.'

'I have control' Bob repeated, as Mrs Ponch left the room.

'Are we ok?' I asked him.

'Yes and no.' He looked at me. 'Yes, in the sense that we successfully completed a transition into a parallel universe. We seem to have left that bit of Sputteridge behind too, I'm buggered if I know where it came from. We should also have full tracking, which means that we can find our way back to your universe Bettony. No, in the sense that no-one says they initiated transition, which is sort of worrying, and also with things as they have been for the past few months we can't get you back yet. Whenever we've actually tried to initiate, something goes wrong.'

Sometimes when you look at a group of people there is some instinct that draws your attention to one person who is behaving differently to everyone else. I was sitting at one side of the room looking across at Bob, who was seated now in the captain's chair vacated by Mrs Ponch, and so everyone was within my field of vision. Everyone's body language was similar – some slight relief mixed with the remains of a certain amount of tension – with one exception. One person in that group was giving off different signals. This idea registered in my brain and began to permeate through to my consciousness; I was about to start actively searching the room – and then Dave Potts sat up very straight and pushed back from her console and said loudly 'Oh Gods.'

Everybody looked at her. She launched herself back at her control panel and brought her fist down on a red button, triggering a single muted dunk on a small bell somewhere.

'Somebody really needs to get that alarm fixed,' she said. 'We're in a Cuban Reality.'

And then it was all activity again. Hands back at screens, frantically pushing and manipulating the shapes on them. People calling out, apparently at random. Vic Terrugo, re-animated like some madman, running around the room from console to console. I had not realised that the wall at the far end of the room was a screen but suddenly it lit up, the entire wall showing what I guessed was a view of outside. There was no similarity to the world we had recently left, the one with buildings and roads and bacon and beer. This one was grey and desolate, lifeless rubble all around, and here and there the crumbling ruins of what may possibly once have been the wall of a building. There was no movement at all and it looked more like a photograph than a live feed.

'How long have we got?' shouted Bob above the noise.

'Somewhere like this? You know the figures Bob, twenty minutes safe tops,' Dave Potts called back. 'Then we're into the red zone.'

I realised that Pierre DeLondon was standing next to me, watching me.

'Are you all right Bettony?' He asked. There seemed to be genuine concern in his question. His gaze was unusually penetrative, as though a mask had half-fallen from his face.

I nodded. 'What's happening?'

When he replied his voice was calm, reassuring, just a tremor betraying his anxiety. 'We have transitioned into what we call a Cuban Reality. In some versions of our shared existence there was a standoff between two nuclear powers, back in the 1960s. I think that in your own world a nuclear war came very close to happening. Well in a few realities, it actually did. In those worlds the highest surviving lifeforms are insects. Nothing else. They are still highly radioactive places and exposure to them is…' he shook his head. 'Is highly time-limited. We think that is why some of our early unmanned probes never returned, although one made it back with some video of such a place. We have a small window now to get away before nuclear radiation destroys our equipment. After which, in due course it will…' He swallowed and coughed before taking a deep breath and finally adding,

'…it will prove fatal to us.'

He was doing his best to hide it but I could tell that DeLondon was genuinely scared. And that terrified me, although to be honest, right now being scared was pretty much the most obvious thing to be. Because these people had been trying for months to transition, without success, and now they had twenty minutes to manage it again.

I watched Bob, an oasis of calm among the frenzy all around him. Then I thought about the odd-one-out and began to look at each individual in the room. Dildow Thrust was sitting to my left; next to her was Dave Green. Next to them was an empty console to which

Vic Terrugo kept returning. At the far end of the room was Dave Potts and to her right, in front of the screen showing the barrenness outside, another empty console. Along the wall facing me was the greaseball known as Mapps and another console, one with two screens, to which DeLondon had now returned.

'This is weird,' I heard Dildow say. 'Something is trying to pull us away from here, back to where we came from.'

So who was it, I thought, as much to distract myself as anything. Who was the odd one out? I watched DeLondon with his two screens. I watched him lean forward and prod at one of the shapes. And at that moment the floor seemed to give a slight lurch upwards, Dildow called out, 'We're on our way', and once again the atmosphere in the room changed. The two Daves even started clapping.

Did you do that, DeLondon? I thought to myself. *Who are you?*

Mrs Ponch re-entered the room. I thought that she might have taken the opportunity to change into some sort of official uniform, but she was wearing a drab grey jumper and a very old-fashioned skirt that went as far as her lower calves.

'Report,' she said, taking over the chair from Bob. They repeated the 'You have control – I have control' routine, which I guessed was some sort of protocol.

'We managed another jump,' Dildow said. 'Don't ask me how.'

'First signs are good' Dave Potts added.

Mrs Ponch looked at her Chief Engineer. 'Vic?'

Vic was back at his consol. I saw that Kevin's handsome face was on his screen and they seemed to be arguing with each other, although Vic's voice was barely above a whisper. I was struck by the difference between the two brothers, one looking like a Norse god, the other resembling a large-headed human ferret.

'Vic!'

Vic Terrugo started, then turned to Mrs Ponch. 'Kevin will have confirmation for us in a couple of minutes. There's something… I don't understand.' He glanced at me, then looked away.

Mrs Ponch stared at Vic for a moment longer, frowned and then turned to look at the far wall. The screen had blanked out, but now

a new image began pixilating into existence. A familiar scene began
to take shape.

'Sputteridge!' I exclaimed.

Dave Green laughed. 'Yes and no. It's Sputteridge Bettony but
not as we know it.'

This was clearly some sort of in-joke among the techies. Dildow
and Dave Potts smiled and Dave Green sniggered at his own
humour. No-one else reacted except for a couple of tired sighs.

'It's a Sputteridge from another universe,' Bob explained. 'Looks
quite close to yours, Bettony...' he was staring at the two screens
behind DeLondon. '...very close, actually.' There was a note of
surprise in his voice. 'I'm guessing that we have full tracking.
Dildow?'

'Yep. First signs are good on that one Chief.'

'Tell me we are blanketed,' Mrs Ponch said.

'We're blanketed' Dave Green replied, adding, 'It looks pretty
quiet out there. Could be like the Cat Four we've just left. That's
weird if it's true - '

A loudish fart ripped through the air and all the screens went
blank. Then the lights went out as well and we were in total
blackness. I felt someone stumble past me... Someone? Or maybe
two people?

There was a lot of noise. Some people were still tapping away at
screens and keyboards; others seemed to be crashing into them.
Eventually it became quieter, then silent. Somebody sighed, there
was some disgruntled muttering and I guessed that this was not the
first time this had happened. Dave Potts' voice muttered, 'another
bloody language to learn,' and I think it was Dildow who answered,
to a couple of chuckles, 'think of all those extra swearwords though,
Kagh.'

Somewhere,   a   very   quiet   alarm   was   going
dunk......dunk......dunk......

'OK everyone out,' Mrs Ponch said. 'Vic?'

Silence.

A stab of light swept around the room and I could see that Mrs
Ponch had hold of a small torch.

'Vic?' she repeated.

But there was no answer, and no sign of the chief engineer.

** ** **

We all stumbled out into the corridor, led by Mrs Ponch's torchlight, and made our way to the light of the entrance hall. Outside seemed deserted and uncannily like the world we had just left - my world - and I wondered what had happened to the people who lived here.

Not for long though. In this Sputteridge, at least, the answer would soon become apparent.

'We need to locate Vic,' Mrs Ponch said. 'Bob? Buggering beachballs, where's Bob?'

The door to the entrance hall opened again and Vic Terrugo limped out. I looked at him and gasped. The Chief Engineer's shirt was torn. His left eye was already swelling and had clearly taken a hard knock. His right cheek was heavily bruised.

'Jupiter's Jockstrap,' exclaimed Dave Potts. In spite of the strange situation I thought to myself, *Where do they get these phrases from?*

Mrs Ponch looked at Vic appraisingly for a second. When she spoke her voice was empty of emotion.

'Report.'

Before Vic could respond Bob followed out of the same door, and behind him - in the heart-bumping flesh - Kevin. Kevin also sported a bruised cheek and I wondered briefly if the brothers had been fighting. But it was Bob who most caught my eye. He had bizarrely chosen this moment to swop his policeman's uniform for a bright yellow t-shirt and grey trousers. Mrs Ponch raised her eyebrows and Bob said,

'Got blood on the uni' boss. Breaking up a difference of opinion between these two.' He seemed very on edge. In fact I could not recall seeing him so nervous, although he was trying hard to conceal it.

'Vic.' Mrs Ponch repeated. 'Report.'

Vic passed a shaking hand over his brow. I could see blood on his knuckles.

'I think... we...' He shook his head and looked around desperately, finally turning to Bob.

'What do I say?'

'Just tell her the truth' Bob answered. 'Tell her you don't know.'

'It's true.' Vic turned to Mrs Ponch. 'I don't know.'

'What is it you don't know Vic?'

I thought to myself, How does he know what he doesn't know if he doesn't know it? And as if in response to my thought Bob half-laughed. But there was a certain steel in Mrs Ponch's question, and now she directed a glare of icy authority onto her Chief Operations Officer. Bob's smile immediately disappeared. We were all standing around her in the entrance hall like a group of naughty schoolchildren waiting for a telling-off from the head. Mrs Ponch turned to her third engineer. At no time did she raise her voice but her authority was absolute and I understood now why she was Captain.

'Dildow, get those chuffing lights back on. As soon as they are - and I mean immediately - there will be a senior officers' meeting in room five.'

Dildow responded in a series of pseudo-Welsh sounds but Mrs Ponch broke into her reply, saying 'Because we are not hiding anything from our guest. Because the chances seem to me to be very high that this is close to the Cat Four we have just left, with a concurrent language correlation. So until we establish that that is not the case we shall continue to practice our language skills even when Bettony is not here to appreciate them.' Dildow looked suitably burned and scurried away. Mrs Ponch stared out of the window for a moment, deep in thought, then said, 'Potts, you and Bettony go and scout. Immediate area only. Usual protocols. Explain them to Bettony as you go.'

Dave Potts nodded. 'Understood Captain. Come on Bettony.' I followed her out of the main entrance door leaving Mrs Ponch still issuing orders. When the door closed it cut the sound of Mrs Ponch's voice off completely and Dave breathed a sigh of relief.

'We're better off out here,' she said. 'It's safer when she's in that sort of a mood.'

Something was wrong here. Dave's voice was wrong. The light was wrong. Movement felt wrong. The beginnings of that realisation started to pull itself together in my head. Before it could coalesce into a thought I turned to look at the Transition Vehicle.

The old toilet block was gone.

** ** **

Where the TV should have been there was nothing but the view across a recreation field, then an area of rock leading down to the bay and out to sea. Something looked wrong with the sea, too. Panic began to well inside me. Dave looked at me and smiled.

'It's blanketed Bettony, they haven't done a runner. Clever stuff eh?' She broke off and frowned, then carried on, 'Burns the batteries though so as soon as you and I check things out it'll be switched off. Right then. What shall we check out first? How about the pub?'

The thought had almost formed now, but the well-brought-up daughter inside me butted it out of the way to say, *Shouldn't we be scouting, not going to the pub?* Which prompted an immediate response from the rest of me, *Come on, we need a pint.* (It was obviously the rest of me that won.)

And then the observation stubbornly forced its way through, and into my consciousness. My brain struggled to cope with the information it was being given, leaving me with a disconcertingly drunken feeling. Not only that - in some strange, indefinable way, I didn't want to move. I looked at Dave again, she had clearly spotted the same things and her frown had returned.

'Say something,' she said.

'When you speak your mouth moves very slightly before your voice arrives,' I said. 'You're very very slightly out of sync. Also there is no other sound anywhere which is really weird. And when I started to move there was a resistance which I don't know maybe comes from my head or my joints.'

I expected Dave to suggest returning to the TV or possibly to come up with a detailed scientific explanation, something with the

60

word Quantum in it quite a lot. Instead her lips moved, and moments later I heard her voice say,

'Cool. Let's get to the pub and we can down a pint while we think it through.'

Movement was strange but not impossible. Bizarrely, there was no wind yet every time I moved I was suddenly walking into a scorching hot gale which stopped as soon as I did, my hair taking several seconds to float back down to my shoulders. The sunlight was unnatural, bright enough but with a slight purple hue and carrying no heat. It was the total carpet of silence that was most unnerving though. I have heard recordings of people in anechoic chambers and was strongly reminded of them now, the deafening dullness of a complete lack of sound. I was also beginning to notice that however hot it was when we were moving, every time I stopped I began to get cold.

Dave suddenly pulled to a halt next to me.

'Will you take a look at that!' She exclaimed.

We were on Bay Lane, the narrow lane that led from the old toilet block (or the TV if you're being pedantic) into the square. The square itself looked very familiar - the old stone cottages, even the gift shop/general stores and the pub looked identical to those in the world we had recently left. From a distance however we had also seen several cars in the square, and I had thought at first that they were parked. As we got closer I realised that they were too far out into the road to be properly parked.

And anyway, each one contained motionless people, all of them as still as 3d photographs.

'And there.' Dave pointed to a family of frozen dummies outside the gift shop.

'This is seriously creepy,' I said.

'We could have a lot of fun here. Imagine how that tubby guy will feel when time restarts and he discovers his trousers are round his knees and his shoelaces tied together.'

'Dave...'

'Yeah ok I was only kidding. Come on. We could do with a pint.'

Dave led the way into the pub. There were a few people frozen around some of the tables and also a barman, statuesque behind the counter. She poked a finger speculatively into a glass of beer at the nearest table.

'Dave! What are you doing?'

'Scientific experiment Bettony.' She grinned. 'This is so odd. I can push my finger into the beer. At first it resists and it's viscous, like treacle. But then it goes all runny around my finger. Have a go.'

'No thanks.'

She pulled her finger out of the glass and licked it. 'Tastes ok.' She eyed the barman. 'I suppose we'll have to pour our own.'

'That's theft!'

'It's science Bettony.' Dave pulled a face. 'Might not be safe to drink though.' She looked wistfully at the beer pump in front of the barman. 'How about that? They've got Frakes' Steady Hand. All written in your English script, note, so we must be very close to your place. One of my favourite beers, Frakes. Nutty but with a hint of hops. Not too fizzy.'

'It's a good beer.'

'I can't stand fizzy beer.'

'Me neither.'

There was a pause. We both stared at the beer pump with the ache of longing.

'Let's just try an experiment. In the interests of science.'

'Go on then.'

Dave walked over to the bar. She lifted the hinged end section of the counter, edged around the barman and took two glasses from a shelf. She put them under a beer pump and pulled at it, grunting with the exertion. Her efforts were rewarded as a treacly liquid glooped out of the pump and she filled first one glass, then the second.

We found an empty table, sat down and looked at the two pints in from of us.

'You first Dave.'

She smiled. 'Testing out the dodgy booze eh? I've been to parties like this.'

'You sound like Bob.'

'He's a good bloke isn't he? We wind him up a bit but I don't think he minds.'

I didn't reply.

Dave lifted the pint to her lips. 'Here goes then.'

I watched her tilt the glass and suck the syrupy liquid into her mouth. Her eyes suddenly widened in happy surprise and she swallowed.

'Wow. As soon as it gets in your mouth it's just like normal beer.' She took another long pull and I followed.

About half an hour later I leaned back in my chair and surveyed the room happily. It was cold - very cold - if we sat motionless, but we had both perfected the technique of swaying slightly, which seemed to provide enough heat to keep us warm. It was easy enough to do this, and became even easier as we worked our way through the beer. It seemed that my brain was also adjusting to the tiny time lag between the sound and vision elements of speech, although that may also have been helped by the beer.

'Another?' Dave asked.

'No thanks. Three's enough for now. We need to keep a clear head.'

'You're right.'

We both sat in silence for a few moments, looking around the room.

'Maybe another half?'

'Ok.'

When Dave returned from the bar I asked, 'Why did Dildow call you Kagh?'

'It's short for Kaghendra which is my real name.' She pronounced the letters gh as a soft sound, like the Scots would the ch at the end of loch. 'The Captain prefers us to choose and then stick with a local name. The idea is that if we're out and about and get caught in a stressful situation we run less risk of accidentally reverting to our real names or language which could lead to complications.'

'And your world is just like Earth?'

'Abbuth we call it. Yes. More or less...'

'What aren't you telling me Dave?'

'Weeell... maybe we made a few good decisions along the way.'

She was not going to say any more, that was clear, so I changed the subject.

'Is Kevin always so wrapped up in his work?'

Dave looked at me, her face broke into a grin, and then I heard her laugh. 'Thinking you might help him to relax hey? Provide a bit of R and R for him?'

I smiled. 'He is... rather hot. Actually no. He's very hot. Actually he's probably the hottest bloke I've ever met outside of my fantasies.'

'Willing to give anything above the eyebrows a miss are you, if everything below them looks good? We've got a phrase for that in our language. Cabbeth sethen na bong curau cabbeth sethen na beng.'

'What's it mean? And stop smirking.'

'Well these little sayings never translate well do they? But roughly, it means what's in the pants beats what's in the head.'

My laugh was perhaps a little dirtier than I intended.

'I agree his looks are to die for,' Dave went on. 'And I can't say that I've never mentally undressed him. But he's a bore! He's a geek! I've never heard him talk about anything remotely interesting. In fact you could give him your Kama Sutra to read out loud and I could guarantee that within five minutes you'd be asleep. And not in a good way.'

'That's terrible.'

'I know. What a waste eh?'

We were silent, perhaps relaxed by the beer but suddenly morose, each of us dwelling on the appalling waste of rippling human muscle that Kevin represented. I stared into the remains of my beer. 'You all seem genuinely nice in your different ways.'

'Thank you.' Dave adopted a voice that was a good mimic of DeLondon. 'And I mean that most sincerely my friend speaking as a member of the caring and genuinely nice community. Our aspirations are to be even more robustly caring and nicer every day and I value your input.'

I laughed. 'OK apart from Pierre DeLondon, you all seem genuinely nice in your different ways. Oh and Wether Mapps. Which is a really stupid name and not a proper one at all. If anyone on our world heard it they'd think he was taking the piss.'

'Yeah I know right? Pierre's ok, in his own way. And sometimes - well I wonder what's actually going on in his head. More than we see, I reckon. But 'Wether Mapps'. I think you've already noticed the Captain's grip on English language and gesture is not quite as strong as it should be, so she hasn't clocked it. Bob must have done, he's a pretty shrewd bloke. But I suppose he either thinks it's funny or can't be bothered with such a dickbrain.' Dave shook her head. 'I didn't have anything much to do with Mapps until after the oranges thing. You know what us scientists are like, we tend to get a bit wrapped up in our own work. Did Bob tell you about the oranges?'

I nodded. Dave continued,

'Forced return to base, plenty of tinned fruit, then we were given the all-clear and the rest is history. Or mystery maybe, since we're so far off-chart.'

I told Dave about my experiences with Mapps. She reacted with shock to his various attempts to bully and assault me. When I got to the part where I set about him in the car she laughed and stared at me, eyes and mouth wide open.

'My hero! Good for you Bettony. Who would believe you could do that! I wish I could.' She shook her head. 'I can't believe he did all those things. I mean - I do, because I believe you - but people just don't behave like that where we come from. Or if they do, they are given some serious psychiatric help. Structured stuff that helps them develop a stronger sense of empathy and personal self-discipline...' She shook her head. 'How did he pass the screenings to get on the crew? ...And the Captain believed him and not you?'

'I think she found it difficult to accept what a member of her crew could have done.'

Dave raised her eyebrows. That's not like the captain I know. Still I suppose everyone has a Hercules heel.' She stood up. 'Let's have a bit of a wander then.' She smiled. 'I'm really glad we've had this chance to talk. I feel like I've made a new friend.'

'Me too.'

We wandered slowly around the village streets, taking care not to overheat. I peered through the windows of the Police House. It looked occupied although I couldn't tell who by. We completed our tour and sat on a bench in the square.

'What's going on here Dave? You're the scientist.'

She laughed. 'Not that sort of science Bettony! I'm a doctor of Alien Life and Society, or Alas in your language as Dildow kindly pointed out. I could hazard a guess at the amount of chewing gum on the floor in any particular category of reality, or why the different groups of people are distributed as they are around the village and their reaction to treading in the gum, but not why they aren't moving.'

'But you were working the controls when we were jumping. And you must have done some basic science? General stuff?'

'Working the controls is just basic navigation. Mostly I'm just doing what Dildow tells me to. It's true though, I've done some subatomic theory. You have to pass that to qualify for this gig.' She shook her head. 'Not a clue about this though. I'm afraid it's way out of my league. Dave Morland might have a better idea, he's got a brain the size of a planet and he did quantum stuff as an optional postgrad course.' Despite saying this, she went on, almost to herself, 'It's like time has frozen. That would possibly account for some of the things we've seen...' She was silent, thinking, then said, 'Come on. Let's get back to the TV. See what Dave and Vic have got to say. I need a pee anyway.'

We wandered back across the square and down the lane. It seemed odd looking ahead of me, knowing that the Transition Vehicle was directly in front, yet seeing only the view across the recreation ground, past the swings and slides and out to sea.

'Still amazed?' Dave asked.

'It really looks like it's not there.'

Dave laughed. 'Come on.' Then she stopped and said, 'Oh.'

I had a horrible premonition of what she was about to say. 'Dave?'

She was waving her arms around now, taking a few steps forward and then back.

'Dave! It's gone hasn't it?'

'It must be here somewhere. Ok. Time for a scientific experiment.' She picked up a large stone and threw it hard, in front of her. The stone slowed rapidly after it left her hand and travelled weirdly slowly. We watched for several minutes. It was a strange sight as the stone seemed almost to be floating in the air, its movement soon barely noticeable. Nevertheless, it was describing a wide arc directly through where the Transition Vehicle should have been.

'Shit.'

'This must have happened before. Tell me it has.'

'Bettony, I can indeed tell you that this has happened before but I'd be lying.'

Eventually the stone hit the roundabout in the playpark behind, and several seconds later we heard a strangely dull clang.

CHAPTER SEVEN

A safe refuge...?

We were back in the pub. Dave came out of the toilets grimacing.

'You ok?'

She shook her head. 'You don't want to know. Well yes you do obviously. I'm going to tell you anyway... You know how the beer is so gloopy until it's in your mouth?'

'Uh oh. I think I can see where this is going.'

'Yep. It's sort of the other way around when you pee.'

'Eugh.'

'That about sums it up. Ah well no harm done.'

'What do you propose?'

'I dunno. We could stick to the whisky although to be honest the Frakes is so nice and the weird peeing experience is not that much of a problem -'

'I really meant, what do you propose we can do to get the TV back?'

'Oh that. Well to be honest the best that we can do is sit tight and wait. I've got a single-burst emergency beacon but is this really an emergency yet? There's food here, and some high quality liquid refreshment. Chances are they'll have a trail and when they get sorted out they'll be able to find us.'

'You're not that bothered are you Dave?'

She grinned. 'I could think of worse places to be marooned. We'll stick a sign up in front of where the TV will appear saying we're in the pub, although to be honest they'll probably look here first -'

There was a dull, muffled snap from the general direction of the door. I turned to see a spider-web of thin cracks spreading jerkily out across one of the windows next to it. What looked like a small ball of fire pushed out from the central point of the slowly spreading pattern and headed towards Dave's chest. It was doing so however at a speed that was barely walking pace. Dave saw it and stepped to one side, watching curiously as the small ball of fire hurtled unhurriedly past her and pushed itself into the wall next to the door to the toilets. The beginnings of a cloud of plaster began to form around it. Dave raised her eyebrows but before she could speak two more cracks sounded and two more small balls of fire headed in our general direction.

'I think we're being very slowly shot at,' she said. 'Probably best if we vacate the premises by the back exit, molto expresso.'

I shook my head. The old familiar burst of anger had driven any fear away. 'Plenty of time to dodge bullets at that speed and I want to see who's firing the gun. In fact I want to do more than that.' I smiled. 'And how many people can truthfully say that they've dodged a bullet?'

The pane of glass began very slowly to separate into randomly shaped pieces, none of which seemed to understand what gravity was all about. They started to spread out in what I thought was quite a beautiful pattern, and then to decide without any haste that the laws of physics were probably ok and worth a punt. Some had started out their flying career heading upwards but all of them now displayed the beginnings of a trajectory that would eventually head them towards the ground.

'That is stunning,' I said. 'Do you realise Dave that we are probably the first people ever to see something like this?'

'Can we move please?'

'Hang on. If we just go now this glass will hit these people in their own timeline and cause some serious injury. We need to do something.'

'Spoken like a Cat One. Ok, what do you propose?'

I lifted a chair, held it in front of me as though I were a lion tamer, and hurried towards the window. I could feel the heat of movement on my face and hands.

'Steady!' Called Dave. She was doing the same thing, but moving more slowly. The glass was still fairly focussed and it wasn't too difficult to knock its course away from the frozen occupants of the bar-room. We dropped the chairs, which once released fell in slow motion towards the ground, and moved as quickly as we dared towards the door.

'That's going to cause them some confusion' Dave said. 'Shots in a quiet Cornish village and chairs that suddenly leap across a room to defend the people in it.'

Dave pulled the pub door open and led the way out into the cold glare of daylight. Halfway across the square a figure was walking towards us, a pistol in his right hand.

'Mapps!' I exclaimed.

He saw us at the same moment that we saw him. He raised the gun again and fired twice more. Flames blasted twice from the end of his gun, followed moments later by two loud retorts, but the bullets suddenly appeared two metres in front of it, vortices of air swirling around behind them, still travelling quickly in straight lines but slowing fast. By the time they were halfway towards us they were almost as slow as the ones that had burst through the pub window. Mapps looked at them, then looked at me with something approaching horror on his face. He turned and ran. I started to hurry after him but Dave managed to grab hold of my arm.

'He won't get far.' She said. 'Not at that speed.' She continued walking towards the fleeing Mapps, still gripping my arm and resisting my attempts to hurry.

I soon realised what Dave meant. Mapps had not even reached the far side of the square before he collapsed to the floor. Then the muffled blanket of silence that surrounded us was pierced by the horrible sounds of his screaming.

** ** **

We need to pause here for a moment. Hopefully you have been interested in what I have to say and I have managed to convey to you something of the excitement of my adventures so far without presenting you with anything too shocking. With a bit of luck you'll be keen to find out what happens next. But if you want to stay unshocked, flip forward to beyond the next set of asterisks, about a page or so. I am going to describe what condition Mapps was in because (1) that's how he was, and (2) it affected what happened afterwards. It's not nice though. Believe me, I was there. I still have the nightmares. Move on now. You have been warned.

Mapps was writhing around on the floor when we reached him, clearly in agony, clutching at his face. The backs of his hands were burned and criss-crossed with blood where they had cracked open. He was still screaming, and I guessed that in his pain he had reverted to his home language.

'What is he saying?' I asked Dave.

She shrugged. 'It's not Enceldic and I don't recognise it as any Abbuthian language. Doesn't mean it's not. But if it is I don't recognise it.'

We reached down and tried to pull the screaming man's hands away from his face. He resisted hard, but for one moment I saw eyes that seemed to be nothing more than bloody holes. The face, like the hands, was charred and bloody.

'Look at his clothes,' Dave exclaimed. I nodded. They were also blackened by heat, and there was a sickly smell that was a mixture of scorched cloth and burnt flesh.

She patted her pockets, then pulled a silver tube from one, about four inches long. 'I don't know that anyone has ever used one of these except in tests, but I'd say that this is definitely an emergency now. Wait here with him.'

She headed steadily across the square. It seemed to take ages before she disappeared down the lane towards the bay, towards where the TV should have been. A couple of minutes passed, filled only with Mapps' sounds of distress. He was tiring, and the screams had subsided now to a pathetic whimpering. His hands still flapped in front of his face.

Dave reappeared, accompanied by the slight figure of Nurse This and Bob, still wearing his badly-fitting yellow T-shirt above grey trousers. Bob and the medic carried a stretcher between them and Dave was now lugging a large medical bag over her shoulders.

In the end the medic managed to press some sort of metal device against the top of Mapps' arm, sedating him. He was manoeuvred onto the stretcher and Bob and Dave carried him unconscious back to the Transition Vehicle. It stood once more at the end of the lane, a shabby council building that I was very grateful to see again.

** ** **

I was asked to recount my experiences to Bob, while Dave talked in a separate room to Mrs Ponch.

'Triangulation,' Pierre had explained. 'That's what we're after here. It's a robust procedure. Basically Bettony it means that neither of you influences the other, and mistaken impressions are not reinforced.'

'Triangulation between two points,' murmured Dave. 'Binary triangulation.'

'Biangulation,' said Dave Morland, who was part of the group jostling around to greet us in the reception area. Mapps had already been hurried away to a sick bay somewhere.

Bob had directed a withering glance at the two scientists. 'Come on Bettony. We'll get together with the boss and Potts afterwards and compare notes.'

Bob listened without comment as I described what had happened, tapping from time to time at an electronic pad. He kept looking at his pad, avoiding my eyes, and seemed distracted. When I finished he explained events on the TV.

'Vic and Kevin had a bit of a set-to. If they hadn't been brothers it would probably just have been an argument. Luckily I found them and managed to pull Vic off Kevin -'

'You pulled Vic off Kevin?'

'Like I say, brothers. We then had a pointless senior staff meeting where no-one had anything useful to say, we went back to stations in the control room and pretty soon afterwards there was a dither, like you get when an aircraft hits turbulence. Everything still seemed ok until Dildow Thrust says, New Coordinates. Then all hell breaks loose. It hadn't felt like a jump but more like an adjustment but we know we've lost you and can't track back. Someone asks for a software status and then we realise that Mapps is missing. The Boss puts a general call out for him but he doesn't answer. If he was in an

72

uncontrolled area of the ship when there was the adjustment he could have been killed -'

'Like when we were outside! I knew that was more dangerous than you were letting on.'

'- but no-one could go and check in case we jumped again. Then we get Potts's emergency signal and we can get back to you.' He stood up. 'Come along, we'll join Potts and the boss.'

They were in the next room to us, seated at a table which also had four empty chairs around it. When we went in I had the impression that they had been talking and then stopped suddenly, but Mrs Ponch smiled and waved us to two of the spare seats. At her request I repeated my story, Bob all the time checking his pad and giving little nods of confirmation. When I finished, Mrs Ponch frowned and pursed her lips, staring blankly at the table, deep in thought. No one interrupted the silence. Eventually she stirred, took a deep breath and said, 'Thank you Bettony. It's always interesting to get two different impressions of the same series of events, although I have to say yours and Dave's were remarkably consistent.' She smiled. 'Perhaps you had less to say about the beer.'

Emboldened by her smile I asked, 'What do you think is going on out there? Has time stopped?'

She shook her head. 'Time would not have stopped completely, that much we can be sure of. Light is a wave-like movement-chain of subatomic particles, and movement requires passage of time. If time had stopped, there would have been no movement of light particles and it would have been dark. Similarly you would not have had the opportunity to dodge a bullet because there would have been no moving bullet to dodge.' She tapped the sleeve of her old coat and said, 'Vic and Mr Morland please, meeting room three.' I heard her voice echo outside. Dave Morland appeared after a few seconds.

I had had little to do with Morland so far. He was fairly tall, of a similar height to Dave Green. His build was heavier than Green's, but lacking muscle and although I guessed that like all the Daves he was late twenties, he was already developing a paunch. His dark hair was long and parted in the middle. Think early seventies George Harrison, but without the facial hair and a bit heavier. He had a strange mannerism, tending to avoid eye contact for much of the time and then looking at you deeply and intensely, but not in a way that made you feel uncomfortable: As though you had suddenly stirred some puzzled thought. He favoured a loose check shirt over a t-shirt, and jeans that had seen cleaner days.

It was a couple of minutes before Vic pushed his way into the room and took the last empty chair. He looked a mess. His left eye was now completely closed, his nose had swelled to a comical size and like the bruise on his right cheek it was turning blue.

At Mrs Ponch's request Dave and I told our story yet again. Mrs Ponch repeated her suggestion that we had visited a place where time had slowed considerably but not stopped, looking at the newcomers as if hoping for a discussion, but she had barely finished when Vic spoke. His high-pitched voice sounded nasal and he was having trouble pronouncing his words clearly. He said, tersely,

'We've shifted agaid. Dot a full transition. It's like Bettody and Potts' reality was ad udstable equilibriub. Please do dot ask be how we edded up dere because I do dot doe. We've just booved off it like we did last tibe. Back to her place I tink' - he glanced at me. 'Dat's all I cad cottribute here. You ought to be askig yourself what Bapps was up to. Cad I go dow?'

It wasn't quite a challenge, but it wasn't far off. Mrs Ponch remained her calm, unflappable self, and yet I felt waves of restrained anger radiating from her.

'Thank you for your time Chief Engineer,' was all she said. If Vic noticed the ice in her voice he was ignoring it. He rose to his feet and shambled his way out of the room.

'Perhaps you can be more forthcoming Mr Morland.'

Dave Morland looked everywhere except at our faces. 'I'd go with the unstable equilibrium bit. If we're randomly banging around there's just as much chance of landing in an unstable state as a stable one. However briefly.' He suddenly fixed his eyes on Mrs Ponch. 'Which sort of raises the question Captain, why are we apparently banging around at random?' He paused. Not for effect, I thought, but because he was trying to capture his thought and express it with words. 'And that raises another question which you might think is almost the same. But it isn't. It's completely different. Why are we banging around at all?'

There was the slightest of nods from Mrs Ponch.

'I agree that somehow we stopped long enough to launch Bettony and Dave into a temporally misaligned reality,' Morland continued. 'It's interesting that the written script in that reality appeared to be English although that's really only a supposition.' He turned his gaze now on Dave Potts. 'Persuasive, but insufficient evidence for a conclusion.' Point made, he turned back to Mrs Ponch. 'I also agree that the temporal difference was one of velocity, not direction of entanglement. The purple edge to the light which Bettony observed could represent a longer wavelength which supports that theory. The heat of movement could be explained by friction caused by the resistance of air molecules obeying their own laws of movement; similarly the dissipation of heat when movement is stopped could be argued to be consistent with that idea although that would require more work to confirm. It's interesting also that when our friends were waving the chairs around they pretty much responded as you might expect, yet once released began to obey the laws of physics of their own universe. Similarly thank goodness the bullets.' I felt the gaze directed at me now. 'It is almost as if the objects from that universe borrowed our own laws when in close proximity to you, but gradually surrendered them the further they moved away. To hazard a guess from your description of the bullets, at an inverse exponential rate, although that's just intuition.' Morland smiled. 'And we know from many results that we cannot rely on intuition. It's fascinating though. And it opens up a whole new area for research, maybe even one that could throw light on the interconnectedness of quantum-separated states of existence.'

There was a stunned silence.

'Nice one Dave,' smiled Potts.

'Reckon you owe me a pint,' Morland responded, looking down at the table.

'Reckon I do.'

'Thank you Mr Morland.' Mrs Ponch regarded the academic closely. 'I suspect that there is something else occupying your thoughts.' There was the twitch of a smile at the corners of her mouth. 'Please feel free to share with us, as I'm sure our friend Pierre would have me say.'

Morland half-smiled, looked across Mrs Ponch to the wall by her side, then glanced at Bob. He gave a slight shake of his head.

'It's trivial and it doesn't make sense,' he said.

And that was all. Mrs Ponch's mixture of encouragement and authority could get nothing more from him. Bob could offer nothing very constructive either, except to suggest what he called a trial jump, to which Mrs Ponch frowned but did not reply. The meeting broke up soon afterwards.

'Isn't he a dream,' Dave Potts said, looking at the back of Dave Morland's head as he disappeared down the corridor.

I looked at her, surprised. 'He's not quite Kevin, is he?'

Dave reddened, then replied, 'You can have the muscles Bettony. It's what's above the eyebrows that really interests me. Anyway he's not so bad bodywise.'

I looked at Morland and decided Dave must have it bad. 'You kept that quiet Dave. Does he know how you feel? Have you told him?'

Dave shook her head. 'He's out of my league Bettony.'

Really bad, I thought. 'You could always try.' I raised my voice. 'Hey Dave Morland.' Morland looked around but continued walking and almost cannoned into Bob, who had stopped just in front of him in the corridor and was peering abstractedly at the ground. 'Got time for a coffee with me and Dave here?'

Morland looked at Dave Potts and his face also reddened. 'Yes ok,' he mumbled.

The three of us found our way to the kitchen, further down the same corridor. I went as if to sit at the table, but as the two blushing Daves joined me I got up again and went over to the worktop, leaving them seated together. An embarrassed silence settled fug-like around them. I wondered how often they had sat together as a pair, rather than in a group. Less than once, I thought.

'We were wondering what it was you didn't want to tell Mrs Ponch,' I said, finding a couple of mugs that weren't too dirty. I rinsed them out, spooned instant coffee into them and filled the kettle.

Morland visibly relaxed at the introduction of a topic of conversation. 'Oh it was nothing really. Just an observation that didn't fit the facts as stated.'

Dave paused, and we looked at him expectantly.

'Vic's knuckles,' he said, as though this explained everything. He looked at us both, settling his eyes on Potts, reddening again, then looking at the table.

'Brothers eh?' I grinned. 'I don't have any myself. How about you Dave?' I was actually asking Potts, trying to get them to talk to each other, but Dave Morland was still staring at the table and it was he who answered. 'I've got two older sisters,' he said. 'They used to dress me up. I didn't like that.'

'What as?' Asked Dave Potts.

'Once when I was asleep they dressed me up as a baby. They glued some sort of baby clothes onto me so I couldn't get them off when I woke up.'

'How old were you?' Dave asked.

'Sixteen.'

'Sixteen?-!' Dave Potts laughed.

'I'd been to a party and I was a bit drunk. Bettal was back from Uni and Demmy had driven over from town to see her. Mum and Dad went nuts.'

'What happened?' Dave asked.

I never found out what happened. I set the two mugs of coffee down in front of them. 'I'm going to go and have a look at Mapps,' I lied. 'See you two later.'

I'm not sure what the expression was on Dave's face when she looked at me. I like to think it was one of thanks, although it could have been blind panic. Hard to tell under that deep crimson blush.

I closed the door and almost fell over Bob, who was on his hands and knees examining the floor opposite.

'Oh it's you Bettony. Look at this.' I joined Bob on the floor and looked at where he was pointing. There was no defined edge between the walls and the floor but at the point where the curve between the two was sharpest I could see a thin crack, about five inches long. Bob heaved himself to his feet and walked a few paces back towards the meeting room. 'Now look here.' I got down on hands and knees. Another crack, about double the length of the first.

'Is this serious?'

'What do you think? We're in a craft that has jumped more than any other craft ever. These could be serious stresses in the actual fabric of the thing.'

'How many more are there Bob?'

'I don't know. I only spotted them when we came out of the meeting room.' He joined me on the floor and pulled a penknife from a pocket. 'Watch this.' He opened the blade and pushed it down the crack. It disappeared up to the hilt of the knife. 'We need to get this logged. I'll get Dildow onto it. Not much point in asking Vic right now, you saw what state he was in. And I don't want to interrupt Kevin.'

'Should we tell Mrs Ponch?'

'All in good time. Let's get some idea of the damage first.'

We headed back to the reception area. Bob told me to take the leftmost of the four corridors and check for cracks. 'It's as good a place to start as any,' he said. 'I'll go get a layout chart. The first thing we need to do is to map out where all the cracks are. We'll meet back here in a few ticks.' He swiped open the two doors to the left and disappeared into the more central of the two. I wandered into the other.

The leftmost corridor was staff quarters and sick bay. It was deserted. I wandered along, scanning for cracks. At first glance the corridor was clear, but I got down on hands and knees and soon realised that although they were smaller and fainter, there were more here than in the corridor with the meeting rooms and the kitchen. All of them traced a rough line along the angle where the wall and ceiling joined and the curve was sharpest. I reached the end of the corridor and looked at the closed door of the sick bay. I wondered what state Mapps was in, behind the door, and what treatment he was getting. Then I turned and crawled back along the corridor, seeing more of the cobwebby splits as I went.

Bob re-entered the reception area just as I did. He was out of breath, holding a large touchpad in his right hand. 'That took a while' he said. 'You'd think these things were made of gold. OK then. Find any more cracks youngster?'

I nodded, and told him what I had found. He raised his eyebrows. 'Lead on then. Let's get to work.'

I had spent ten minutes on my first examination of the corridor but Bob was quite meticulous in logging the cracks, and this time it seemed never-ending. I started yawning. It had been a long and very eventful day and I was very tired. At some point Bob disappeared for five minutes, returning with coffee and my favourite tuna mayonnaise sandwiches, which we shared. I was so tired I could hardly eat. My brain was barely functioning. When we started again, my eyes began to close, however hard I tried to force them to stay open. We had not even made it halfway down the corridor when I heard Bob's voice calling me from what seemed a long way away. I jerked back to consciousness and realised I had fallen asleep.

'You look shattered,' Bob said. He swiped at a control panel next to the door I was leaning against and it whooshed open. I half-fell into the room. Bob laughed. 'It's a spare room. Get on the bed and go to sleep.'

I was too tired to argue. I dragged myself onto the narrow bed, lay back, and was gone. The last thing I remembered was the sound of voices in the corridor outside, and the light dimming.

My sleep was not to last long, though.

CHAPTER EIGHT

Coffee Time

I was woken by the door whooshing open and simultaneously the lights turning up. I wondered vaguely where I was. Then Bob entered carrying a mug. He managed to get into the room before the door closed again and only spilt a few drops from the mug.

'Bloody doors. Never give you enough time. How are you?'

'Tired still.' He had finally swopped the tasteless yellow t-shirt for a dark grey shirt with a collar. It looked like he had bought the shirt in slimmer days. I rubbed my eyes and sat up. He smiled. 'Coffee.'

I took the mug from him, sniffed it. 'Sugar?'

'Ah, yes, sugar. You need the energy. We've got work to do.'

'What work?' It all felt wrong, like it was still the middle of the night. 'What time is it?'

'It's four am.'

'What? Four am? Don't you sleep?'

The door whooshed open again and Mrs Ponch joined us. 'So this is where you've hidden her,' she said. Bob turned, surprised.

'She needed rest Captain.'

Mrs Ponch went and sat in an easy chair facing the bed. She looked at her Chief Operations Officer for several long seconds, as though trying to read his mind.

'Is there something you want to tell me Bob?'

Bob stole a glance at me, then his shoulders sagged dramatically. 'I wanted to get it all together before I came to you.' He flopped into the second of the easy chairs and outlined what he knew about the cracks.

Whilst I slept he had gone through much of the TV, although not yet all of it. There were cracks in every corridor and every room, although none as bad as the ones he had first shown me.

'Most are very faint. More like cobwebs. You'd never see them if you weren't looking for them.'

'And you asked Dildow? What was her assessment of the damage?'

Bob pulled a paper notepad from his pocket and consulted it. 'She wanted to see how the cracks spread throughout the ship,' he read out. 'She was worried that they were indicative of a divergent-flag cusp catastrophe relating to stress fracturing.'

This was bad news. At the time I had no idea what that last sentence meant (and to be honest, after a lot of googling I still don't). But it was obviously bad news, I could tell from the way Bob said it and from Mrs Ponch's instant reaction. She held the sleeve of her drab old coat next to her mouth and said quietly, 'Privacy override. Personal call Ponch to Thrust immediate urgent confirm immediate urgent presence required guest quarters room three.'

Less than a minute later Dildow Thrust was stumbling bare-footed through the door, hair wildly dishevelled. She had clearly just woken up. I wondered if she slept in the baggy white t-shirt. Probably not in the jeans though.

Dildow sat on the edge of my bed and looked at Mrs Ponch. 'This about the cracks?'

Mrs Ponch nodded.

Dildow rubbed her eyes. 'I think we should involve Vic.' She looked at Bob but it was Mrs Ponch who replied.

'Vic already has more in his dish than he can eat. We need you to step up to the table now Dildow.'

There was a moment while Dildow worked out what her senior officer meant. I wondered whether to interpret but Bob caught my eye and shook his head. Mrs Ponch went on,

'You think TV structural integrity may be on a cusp catastrophe manifold?'

Dildow nodded. 'That's my guess. But it's only a guess from what Bob showed me.'

'It's a good one though. What is your best guess of asymmetry and bifurcation values?'

Dildow shook her head. 'No idea. When Bob told me what he'd found I started looking back through the transition records to get some base data. I thought that would be a good starting point for any analysis and would give me enough information to define and calibrate the catastrophe model. But...' She shook her head again.

'But?' Asked Mrs Ponch.

'A lot of it seems to be missing.'

'Missing!' Mrs Ponch exclaimed. 'The transition records are missing?'

'Not all of them. But quite a lot. I haven't had time yet to go through them all. I don't understand. Vic would normally run and record a check after each transition so perhaps the data has only just been corrupted.'

'Maybe Dildow's right and we should involve Vic,' Bob suggested. Mrs Ponch looked at him for a moment and once again I was struck by her personal authority. Her control of this discussion was absolute, without being in any way aggressive or alienating, without her even having to raise her voice. 'Dildow, go back to bed and get some sleep. We will talk again at eleven of clock in the morning. Bob, I order you to go back to your quarters and get some rest. You are no use to this operation if you make yourself ill. Join us at eleven in the Council Room.' She looked at the two of them. 'Now!'

Dildow and Bob dragged themselves to their feet and left. Mrs Ponch remained a moment longer and looked at me as though about to speak. Then she seemed to change her mind, wished me a bloody good night's rest, and followed her two officers out of the room.

There was a bathroom unit at the far end of the room. I tipped the coffee into the sink, refilled the mug with water from the tap and took a long swig.

I think I was asleep before I hit the bed.

CHAPTER NINE

What's in a dream?

I was dreaming about Bob dressed as a waiter, I didn't know where we were except that somehow I knew we were outdoors. He wore a long apron over black trousers and carried a whisky glass and a tuna sandwich on a silver tray. For some reason there was also a bottle of brown sauce on the tray. There was a tea towel over his arm. His hair was slicked back and he looked like something out of the 1950s. He was looking away from me and I called to him. But when he turned, the face was wrong. The leering face was Pierre DeLondon. Its mouth opened and an inhuman sound came from it, starting as a high-pitched wail, falling in pitch, and then repeating.

I shouted in my dream, a cry of fear, and as I woke up I realised that I was still calling out, making a quiet, strangled sort of noise. I looked around the grey outlines of the dimly-lit room in panic, gradually becoming aware of three things - that there was no Bob, with or without Pierre DeLondon's face; that I still felt achingly tired; and that they must have fixed the alarm. It seemed to be both inside and outside the room, a sound that started fairly high and then dropped in pitch, repeating after a few moments.

'Lights up' I called. Nothing happened. I tried a couple more times, then scrambled out of bed and found a light switch in the wall, still vaguely disoriented, wondering for a moment if my shouting had set an alarm off. Then consciousness took control of my senses and I decided to go out and investigate. I found a button to open the door, stumbled into the corridor, and almost collided with Nurse This.

'Sorry' he said, 'emergency call.' He ran down the corridor and I followed, curious to find out what was happening. We went out into reception and then took the corridor to the kitchen, pushing past three of the scientists to get into the room. Dave Green and Dave Lanyard tried to peer into the kitchen but it was Dave Potts who forced her way in behind me.

The first thing I saw was Bob's back, and for one moment I was reminded of my dream. But then he half-turned and it was obviously Bob, with Mrs Ponch standing to his left and a bewildered Kevin next to her.

Next to Kevin, sitting at the same chair he had occupied the previous day, was Dave Morland.

Except that he was slumped, rather than sitting, his skin ashen grey and his head lolling back against the chair. My tired brain registered the fact that his eyes were open.

For the first time in my life I looked into the glazed, dry, sightless eyes of death.

There was a shriek of agony from beside me and Dave Potts launched herself forward. She managed to push Bob away but Kevin caught her easily before she could reach the dead man. She was still screaming as Kevin picked her up, flailing wildly at him with arms and legs as he carried her out of the room. Even after the door closed I could still hear her.

Nurse This was beside Morland now. He checked a couple of things on the body, turned to Mrs Ponch and shook his head. There was no doubt in my mind what that meant.

'There's nothing more you can do here,' Mrs Ponch said to him. 'Bob can arrange to have the body moved.' She turned to her second in command. 'Chill down the guest room next to Sick Bay and use it as a temporary morgue.' Bob nodded and went over to a communications panel on the wall. I heard him asking for Pierre DeLondon as Mrs Ponch resumed her instructions to the medic. 'Give Potts something to calm her down. Nothing strong please, I need her active today. Something like Peridown Five, I'm sure you know better than me what to use. Keep her in her quarters until I arrive. And stay with her.' She looked hard at the medic. 'Stay with her until I personally tell you that you can leave. Understood?'

He looked at her, surprised, but repeated, 'Understood.'

She turned to me. 'Go with him Bettony. You also stay with Potts until I tell you otherwise. That is a command not a request.'

I nodded, then followed the medic out of the room, checking my watch as I went. It was not yet eight o'clock. No wonder I felt so tired.

Kevin had already carried Dave Potts to her own room and was still holding her, restraining her, when we arrived. Dave's struggles were less frenetic now and I guessed that she was tiring against his gentle but implacable resistance. Possibly she was simply beginning to accept the truth of Morland's death.

Nurse This took a small half-round object from a pack attached to his belt. He briefly touched it to Dave's temple. She became limp immediately and Kevin laid her gently onto her bed. He looked at her tenderly for a moment, then at Nurse This and me. He muttered awkwardly 'I have much to do,' and left.

** ** **

Nurse This was a quietly good-looking man of slight build, not that much taller than me. He was quiet to the point of shyness, and we had barely spoken to each other before now. My natural gregariousness and curiosity took over now (ok I mean I'm nosey), and I tried to encourage him to open up. At least talking to him would help me stay awake, I thought.

It was difficult to get a conversation going. He would smile and nod and give good-natured but monosyllabic answers to my questions. I persevered, asking about his home life and his work, and gradually discovered a likeable man whose shyness hid a thoughtful intelligence. His qualification did not have a direct parallel, at least not in my very limited experience of the medical world. From how he described it, it was a sort of cross between a paramedic and a General Practitioner with a fair amount of psychology thrown in. It was his first big posting, he said.

'Didn't it worry you?' I asked. 'The danger?'

He shuddered a little at this, but shook his head and said 'Not really. Seeing a world that is so like your own but it's not your own. It's so... strange. Coming into contact with creatures that look just like you but they're not...' he realised what he had said and focussed back onto me. 'I'm sorry Bettony you could take that the wrong way. I wasn't thinking of you. I didn't mean that you're a creature. But you are different aren't you? To the rest of them?'

I decided not to be offended. 'How?'

He frowned. 'I don't know.' He looked like he was struggling to put his thoughts into words. Eventually he said, 'You look like we do and you sound like we do but...'

'...But I'm not one of you?'

He raised his eyebrows, considering the implications of what he had said. 'Goodness. That sounds awful. Some of the Cat Nine worlds have seen genocide perpetrated on less. I need to think this through more carefully.'

Something inside me warmed to his quiet, fumbling honesty. A change of subject would ease his embarrassment, I thought. 'Why do you call yourself Nurse This?' I asked him. 'It's not actually a name, you know.'

'Isn't it? I've got to admit I didn't spend much time doing the name assimilation work and a friend suggested it.' He paused. 'Well... a colleague more than a friend... Hum. It was Mapps.'

'Ah. I did wonder.'

'I did a quick check across your communications network and it recognised nurse this.'

'I think at least one of your colleagues made a similar mistake. "Nurse This" is a phrase that might be uttered as a prelude to violence.'

'Oh.'

I could imagine Mapps laughing at his little joke. 'What's your real name? On Abbuth? I think some of your names work on Earth. Zagretia Ponch sounds more or less ok and Kevin is actually a name that we have.'

'Is it?' He looked at me, astonished. Then he said, hopefully, 'My actual name is Strikken Flange.'

'OK that's a non-starter. We'll have to come up with something else.' I thought for a moment about famous doctors. 'How about William Hartnell?'

'William Hartnell. I don't see myself as a William.'

'How about Will?'

'Will... Hartnell.' Strikken rolled the words around his tongue. 'It sounds good.' He smiled. 'You can call me Strikken though Bettony. If you want to.' As quickly as it had appeared, his smile vanished. 'Sorry. Ignore me.'

I want to though, I thought.

On the bed, Dave Potts stirred, then groaned. Will-or-Strikken took her pulse, holding his fingers against her wrist. He said, quietly, 'How are you feeling Dave?'

'Extremely sad. I can't believe...' She sat up, holding her hands to her face, looking wretched. 'Just can't believe' she repeated. 'How did he - how did he die?'

Will-or-Strikken looked at me, then said, 'I only saw him for a moment. I still have to do the autopsy.' I wondered what he wasn't saying, but Dave seemed not to notice.

'He was always so healthy', she mumbled. 'So full of life...' She flopped back onto the bed and closed her eyes again. Will-or-Strikken looked at me and smiled. Secure in his professional role. 'She'll be back with us soon now.' He said.

The door opened and Mrs Ponch entered. After a few enquiries about Dave's health she looked at Will-or-Strikken and said bluntly, 'Mapps is gone.'

I was shocked. 'Gone! That's impossible.'

'Impossible or not, he's not in Sick Bay and we've scanned the TV and he isn't anywhere else either.'

Will-or-Strikken was shaking his head. 'I'm sorry but he was in no condition to move.'

'You're sure?'

Strikken scratched his head. 'Apart from anything I had had to sedate him. He was in agony from those burns. And his internal organs were beginning to fail. I had him hooked up to a Drick.'

'When did you see him last?'

'I sat with him until six yesterday evening, then checked him at eight, at ten, at midnight and at three am. There was a slight but a noticeable deterioration each time. My next check was to be a few minutes ago. I was expecting to have to put him on full life support at some point today.' He sighed. 'I didn't think there was much hope of survival, to be honest. Let alone of him getting up. And certainly not of him being able to harm another crew member.'

'Mmm.' Mrs Ponch squeezed the bridge of her nose with the thumb and forefinger of her left hand, deep in thought. Dave stirred again and seemed to notice her for the first time.

'How are you now Dave?' Mrs Ponch asked.

'Oh, hello. Not too bad. I'm sorry about that. I... I lost control.'

'It's understandable.' Mrs Ponch's voice was unusually gentle. 'We've all lost a good friend, and I think perhaps you were closer to him than any of us.'

'How did he die?' Dave asked her.

'Hmm? You mean Mr Morland?' Dave nodded. 'We're not sure right now.' Will-or-Strikken started to speak, but Mrs Ponch cut him off and changed the subject. 'You may be interested to know, Dave, that for gods know what reason we have somehow transitioned back to your frozen world. It seems to have happened around two am. So I think there is a high chance that if Mapps is anywhere, he is here. It's too much of a coincidence that the last time we were here, Mapps disappeared, and now we arrive at this unstable equilibrium again and once again he goes missing.'

'But he couldn't have -' Will (I'm going to call him Will from now on. It's what he wants and as you'll find out, things are going to get confusing enough as it is) was cut short by Mrs Ponch.

'He apparently did!' It was rare for her to raise her voice, and now she lowered it again. 'I accept what you have told me, and common sense tells us that an Abbuthian would be dead by now.' She lowered her voice further, so that it was barely a whisper. 'This is not to be repeated by any of you - but I would ask you to consider that his ability to recover may be different... if he is not Abbuthian.'

There was a silence, as we considered the implications of this.

'It would certainly explain a few things,' Dave said.

'What a dreadful thing to happen,' Will murmured, more to himself than to anyone else. 'Although yes, I agree it would explain some of his actions. But even so, with those injuries...'

'Why? -' I began. But Mrs Ponch cut short any further discussion. She was nodding, as though she had arrived at a decision. As though an agreement had been reached, if only with her own misgivings.

'This situation is rapidly escalating,' she said, 'and I don't have the luxury of spare crew to deal with everything in the way that I would wish. Otherwise I would not ask this of you. But I need you Dave, and you Bettony, to get back out there and hunt Mapps down. Bettony, I think there is plenty of evidence to suggest that you can handle yourself well in a physical how's-your-father. I also think that you and Dave work well together. Dave, do you feel up to this?'

Dave nodded. 'I do.'

'I understand how you will feel when you find Mr Mapps. But we have ways of handling wrongdoers and I ask you to respect them.'

'Of course.' Dave looked vaguely surprised.

'Good.' She stood and headed for the door. 'I'll meet you in Reception in five minutes.'

Will also left. We had a quick wash in Dave's room. I wanted to grab a coffee from the kitchen but Dave shook her head. 'If Mrs P says five minutes she means five minutes.'

We made it in time, just. Even so Mrs Ponch was waiting for us. She gave us each an emergency beacon. I thought how tense she looked.

'No guns then?' I was picking up on her nervousness and it was a flippant comment, but she took me seriously.

'We do not carry heaters,' she said. 'And in any case -' She broke off as a door swooshed open and Bob lumbered out to join us.

'Hi ho,' he smiled. 'I wondered where you two had gone.' Turning to Mrs Ponch, he added, 'What's the plan boss?'

'Dave and Bettony are going to do a little searching for us.'

Bob's face was a mask of concern. 'No way. Out there? Searching what for? Absolutely not.'

I was beginning to get to know Mrs Ponch now and I was aware that she did not like to be defied so directly. A trace of annoyance was beginning to replace the tension in her face. 'There's a good chance that Mapps -'

'Oh no!'

I'm not sure that Bob meant to be so blunt but Mrs Ponch's eyes blazed at him.

'I beg your pardon?'

'It's not safe. He's already tried to kill them.'

'This is not open to discussion!'

Even Bob, consumed with worry, must have noticed the iron will and the anger in Mrs Ponch's reply. Still, he tried again.

'I'm going with them.'

'You are not!' Mrs Ponch struggled to keep control of herself. 'I need you here. If I could have spared you to join them, I would have asked you to go, without them. I know the risks and so do they. This is a dangerous time for all of us.'

For the first time since I had met him I saw anger flare in Bob's face. I felt embarrassed, watching these two confront each other. But there could only be one winner in any confrontation with Mrs Ponch. There was no door for Bob to slam, so he stomped away, the electronic door whooshing closed behind him.

Mrs Ponch turned to us. 'Go quickly now,' she urged. 'Or as quickly as you safely can. I will remain here for a few minutes until you are out of sight.' She spoke into the sleeve of her coat, and her voice boomed throughout the corridors and the entrance hall. 'Ponch to all staff. Emergency meeting in the Council Room in fifteen minutes.' Then, turning back to us - 'Go!'

We headed out into the strange half-world. Once again I felt the weirdness of movement and of deadened silence, the violet-tinged light, my senses screaming at me that this was not a genuine reality.

'Do you think Mapps is out here?' I asked Dave. She shook her head, then said, 'Where else could he be though?' She sighed. 'We have smartpads back on Erce but we were not allowed to bring them with us. Pity. We could probably have tracked him if he'd got his pad on him.'

'I don't think he could have walked out of the TV. We both saw the state he was in.'

Dave did not respond, so I went on, 'There are a lot of things that don't make sense to me.'

'Such as?'

'How would Mapps have got the TV back here? How come Vic or Dildow or Kevin didn't notice?'

'What was it that lovely Dave spotted on Vic's knuckles?' Potts replied. I wondered whether she had even heard me, but then she turned and said, 'And don't you think that Mrs P was rather keen to get us away from the TV as quickly as possible? We've got a lot to discuss. Let's slowly go and find breakfast. We can cook something up in the pub.'

I wondered how much time had passed in this world since our last visit. I was soon to find out. It was immediately obvious that things had changed. There were different cars and different people dotted around, in different places to yesterday. In the distance, I could see a small clump of people frozen in time as they clustered around the entrance to the pub. We headed towards them, careful not to move too quickly, taking as direct a line as we could, edging around the holidaymakers and locals who were scattered in our path, all of them paused in their daily activities.

We had become less concerned about the human statues that populated this frozen world and we were giving them less space as we passed, almost brushing past them as we made our way along the side of the square and towards the little crowd around the pub door, half-guessing but curious to find out for sure what was happening.

And then I screamed.

I'm not a great one for screaming, in much the same way that I don't giggle. Women laugh, in my opinion. If you are over thirteen and you giggle, or you scream, you should book yourself onto a course on self-assertiveness. If I'm reading a novel and come across a woman who is pathetic enough either to giggle or to scream, the book usually ends up being deleted immediately or if it's a hard copy, used to start a bonfire, or as emergency toilet paper. But I hope you agree, I could be excused for transgressing some hard-won claims to equality in the name of pure, abject terror. If I ever read this account, I shall try and forgive myself and resist the temptation to tear the pages to bits, and I only ask that you do likewise.

I was aware of my own voice, echoing shrilly around the dull silence, and of Dave Potts turning and staring. First at me. And then... well...

At me.

There are no words to describe the feeling of recognising that the person you are physically next to is yourself. It was not just that the hairs on the back of my neck that were standing up, I felt as though my whole body had been electrocuted. I felt, momentarily, less than a complete person. I felt robbed of my own identity. Deep down, I think we all believe that we are unique and maybe this is a conceit but it is how we are. I still cannot think of anything more shocking than to be suddenly shown that you are not.

I even had on the same clothes, although I was carrying a linen shopping bag with A Present from Cornwall etched into it beneath a vague image of a beach.

'Cool,' said Dave. 'Not sure about the bag though.' Then, grabbing my arm, sharply - 'Don't run Bettony! Remember where we are. Stay still. Take some deep breaths but do it slowly. Breathe slow and deep. You knew this could happen. Relax. Enjoy it.'

Her composure had an immediate effect. I took a deep breath, let it out, then a couple more, slow and steady. I could feel my pulse returning to normal.

'Wow,' I breathed. 'This is so weird.' Then, as panic dissolved away, 'I wonder what's in the bag? ...Fudge? I don't believe it! What on earth am I doing buying tourist fudge?'

I inspected myself. It was nothing like looking in a mirror. I hadn't realised how big my nose was, or that one eyebrow was slightly higher than the other. Also I hadn't realised how small five feet four was. I must have gotten used to most people being taller than me and didn't notice it much. I was walking slowly around myself now, telling Dave what I saw.

'You're being too hard on yourself,' Dave replied. 'You look fine.'

'At least I'm slim. And I hold myself quite well don't you think? Decent posture?'

'Ok that's enough. Come on. You'll still be here when you get back. I want coffee and breakfast.'

We managed to pick our way carefully around the rubberneckers outside the pub but there was police tape across its door, and a stern-looking constable standing close in front of it. It would have been impossible to get in without picking him up and moving him, which would have been unfair on him and physically extremely difficult for us without dropping him. The window to the left of the policeman had been freshly boarded up and there were two holes that had been smashed into the stone between the window and the door. Mapps' last two shots, I thought. Both were circled with chalk.

We made our way around to the back of the pub where a man in a suit was opening a door, obviously about to leave, but frozen into the role of a polite doorman for us.

'Come on,' Dave said. 'Let's have a goose.'

'I think you mean a gander. A goose is something else Dave.'

We edged around the doorman and wandered down the passageway that led past the toilets. I followed it as far as the door to the bar and went in. Tables and chairs had been pushed away from the wall closest to me. A bullet hole had been punched into the wall to my right, at head height. Its centre was deep and had gone through the plaster and into the brick behind it. The hole had clearly been widened in an apparently successful effort to chip the bullet out. There were two more similar holes a couple of feet higher up, spaced several feet apart.

There had been a cursory attempt to clean the room but it was still quite a mess. When I walked in further my shoes scrunched on a mixture of brick and plaster and bits of glass that had not been swept away.

A clattering came from the passageway. I looked around and realised that I was on my own. I headed back to the passageway and followed the noise to a door marked Staff Only. My pulse quickened as I pushed the door open but I need not have worried. Dave was standing in front of a cooker, layering bacon into a frying pan that sat on a gas ring.

'Watch this,' she said. She backed away from the hob and as she did so the gas flame started to change. It kept the same overall shape but resolved down into something that resembled a circular ring of tightly dancing filaments, each one stiffly flicking and twitching against the next. 'Weird eh? It starts to obey its own universe's laws of dynamics as I move away from it. It's almost as though I am radiating my own universe's rules, a few feet all around me. Just like Dave said.' She suddenly looked sad, then made an effort to recover herself. 'It'll have to be instant coffee. I can't be arsed with that machine in the bar. Talking of which, can you stand a bit closer to the kettle please Bettony?'

We ate bacon sandwiches in the small room the other side of the bar. The top half of the door into this room was frosted glass; the words Smoke Room were still outdatedly etched into it. There was carpet in here and the chairs were more comfortable. I remembered the room from my first meeting just a couple of weeks before. Dave looked longingly at the beer pumps behind the counter.

'What I really want to do,' she said, 'is to get very drunk. But that's going to have to wait for another time. So. Before we go and look for Mapps, we both want to understand some of what's going on. Agreed?'

'Agreed.'

'Good. So. As Dear Pierre would say, what is our agenda?'

I answered, 'Gullivant's agenda items as follows: Heading: Stuff I don't understand. Bullet Point One: How the hell did Mapps manage to make good his escape, when Will is pretty clear that he was in no state to do anything except die? Two: As I said before, how could he have piloted the TV here without Vic, Dildow or Kevin noticing?'

'Will?'

I explained about Mapps' little joke and Strikken Flange's choice of a new name. Dave sighed.

'It all seems to fit a pattern with that creep,' she said. 'Maybe he is some kind of imposter. Bullet point three - as I said, what was it that Dave Morland had noticed about Vic's knuckles? Four: Were we imagining things or did Mrs P really bundle us out of the TV? And if so why?'

'Five,' I continued. 'Although this is probably less urgent right now. I would like to understand how time moves here. And Six - and I think this is the most important item Dave - How come I've never noticed my high cheekbones when I look in the mirror? They're defined and they're wide too - I'm a bit of a looker aren't I?'

Dave laughed, for one moment her old self. 'Get some specs Bettony, your mirror's fine.' She became serious again. 'OK. Item one.'

'Item one.' I wasn't looking forward to this. 'How much did you hear what Will said about Dave Morland's death?'

She stared at me. I could almost see her brain fitting the pieces together. 'I didn't. What did I miss?'

I told Dave what Will had said about Mapps not being in a fit state to have harmed a crew member, and the way that Mrs Ponch had prevented him from saying any more.

'So... they both think that Dave was killed?' She was staring more intensely than ever. 'He wasn't ill?'

'No.'

'Why wouldn't Mrs P want us to know that Mapps had murdered Dave?'

'No idea. Maybe she thought Will could have been wrong and she didn't want to spread mistrust. Or fear.'

Dave's face had hardened. 'Evil is an infectious thing isn't it? Because what Mapps did was so very wrong but right now I want to do to Mapps exactly what he did to Dave.'

'What if it wasn't him though Dave? What if Will was right: Mapps was too ill to do it -'

'- And Dave really was murdered. Wowza.' Dave stared at me. 'Somebody else on the crew killed him?'

'Correct. Which sort of ties in with item two...'

'How did Mapps get the TV back here?' Dave pulled at her bottom lip. 'If it wasn't Mapps it could have been Vic, Dildow and Kevin. No. That's too ridiculous for words. Four imposters out of a crew of twelve. And where on Abbuth are they coming from? How come no-one has noticed? How come they got through all the vetting before we were selected? Ye gods. Paranoia central.'

'Ok Dave, try looking at it from a different angle. Why would someone want to be here?'

We both thought about that one. Neither of us had a clue. Eventually Dave broke the silence.

'Look I know what we said and I know it's early but I can't help thinking that a pint would help.'

'Fair enough.'

She returned with the drinks and I complemented her on her skill at pulling a good pint. Her face relaxed into a smile.

'You say the nicest things Bettony.'

'So where's Mapps?' I asked. 'Or maybe, should we be asking, what happened to Mapps?'

'Good point. Either way, I dunno. At least we can go and have a look for him in a bit.' She took a deep draught of her beer, sighed, and said, 'Oh that's better. Ok then, how about this as an answer to your Why Here question: Mapps was hiding something away here on his last visit. He spots us, thinks we're following him and decides to eliminate us. Fails, and hurts himself badly in the process, but maybe once he's back on the TV he exaggerates his symptoms to give himself somehow the chance to get back here and recover his stash.'

I smiled. 'It's amazing, the effect one drink of beer has on you Dave. That could work. It relies on Will not being a very good doctor, but it's possible.'

'You forget that Mapps is from another universe. Maybe he either shows injury in a different way or he recovers more quickly.'

'And he still needs to find a way of fooling the engineers, but let's assume that you're right. So why would he want to get back here almost immediately to recover something he had only just hidden?'

'No idea.' She pulled at her lip again. 'But it's not almost immediately is it?   At least a day has passed here. Enough time for somebody else to pick up his stash and hightail it, leaving something else in its place? A replacement for Mapps to collect? Payment maybe?'

'Makes sense I suppose, and you described it very dramatically. Have you been reading Raymond Chandler by any chance?'

'Maybe.'

'Also, it depends on someone else having a TV. Bob told me that only your world has them so if you're right, Bob must be wrong. If not, everything that's happening is all originating from Abbuth, in which case Mapps is also from Abbuth, and we're back at square one... How did he recover?'

'I agree there are a lot of inconsistencies. I just can't think of anything else.'

We both stared into space, mulling over Dave's idea. Finally she said, 'Next item, what had Dave noticed about Vic's knuckles?' Potts glanced at me. 'Do you think Kevin's the other imposter?'

'He could be I suppose...'

'Do you think that's all an act? All that nerdy awkward stuff? And his own brother hadn't spotted the impersonation?'

'Honestly Dave, I don't know. You must know him better than me.'

'Not Kevin or Vic. This trip was the first time I'd met either of them.'

I shook my head. 'You should have seen the way he laid you down on the bed. So gentle. I can't believe he's the murderer.'

'Hmm. Anyway, could he really pilot the TV back here without Vic knowing?'

'So it's Vic then. Or Vic and Kevin together. Brothers together.'

'In which case Dildow would have spotted something so she would have to be in on it as well. Or for that matter so would Bob or Mrs P, they're both qualified transition pilots. So we're back to the first square on the dartboard and they're all imposters or something, which is ridiculous. What was the next item again?'

So we passed on to the next part of the puzzle, and missed resolving the one which, if we had approached it with cold logic and simply concentrated on that part alone, would have given us answers that would have saved us both a lot of pain and trouble.

'Was Mrs Ponch really trying to push us out of the TV? It felt like that.'

We agreed it had felt like that but neither of us could explain why she would want to do it. We couldn't make any progress on either of the last two items either: Dave's knowledge of quantum physics was considerably better than mine but still limited and we agreed to disagree about my cheekbones.

We resisted the temptation to have a second pint and headed out to look for Mapps, and whatever he may have hidden.

CHAPTER TEN

Walking through a photograph

We reasoned that if Mapps really had managed to hide something it would not be far away. Our first excursion into this world had started almost as soon as the TV arrived; we had spent around half an hour in the pub before Mapps launched his attack, so at the very most anything that he had hidden could be no more than fifteen minutes' walk away. We agreed that leaving something in a building would have been risky. For all Mapps knew, time may have resumed its flow here before the something could be collected. Someone from this world could have found it. So logically, he must have left it -whatever it was - concealed outside somewhere.

As I pointed out, it would have made life easier if we'd known how big it was - whatever it was. And as Dave pointed out, well obviously.

We had encountered Mapps when he was pretty much in the centre of the village square. Four routes led into the square, one at each corner. Bay Lane led back to the TV and curved away to the left, continuing its curve beyond the TV and then sweeping back to the right and downhill to the beach around the bay. We thought Mapps was unlikely to have used this route as it seemed to be regularly used by holidaymakers, making discovery likely, and in any case he would have risked being picked up by the TV's external cameras. At the far end of the village square, to the right of Bay Lane, was a short terrace of large Victorian houses. At right angles to these and forming the third side to the village square was another, longer row of much older terraced cottages, stone-built, of which the police house was one. A short track, leading away from the corner where these two rows of houses met, quickly narrowed to become the coastal path. This was a well-worn path but was my favourite for what we were now calling Mapps' Stash. Past the police house, the next corner yielded a narrow lane between high hedges, signposted as a dead end. This was Dave's favourite. Neither of us thought the fourth exit, next to the pub and leading out towards Truro, was likely. It would easily be the busiest route.

Incidentally, if you're visualising this, notice the wooden bench in front of the row of Victorian B&Bs. It looks so lovely, shaded by that tree, yet it's actually a right mess. Some very big birds must sit in the tree that shades the bench. You'd think somebody would do something about all those droppings.

But I digress.

We chose my guess first. I would like to say that this was after an intelligent and rational discussion, but it was actually because the coin landed heads.

At first the grass-covered track was wide enough to take a car but it quickly narrowed, the grass thinned and the ground became stonier. Within a few yards we were beyond the hedges that screened off gardens on each side. Fifty yards further, the track began to climb, gently at first and then increasingly steeply so that after a few minutes we were looking down on the bay to our left and out to sea. It was a strange sight. The water, like everything else in this peculiar world, was solid and immovable. Waves were caught in mid-fall as they lurched towards the beach, paused precipitously in the air. Children were playing in the shallows and the water they were splashing hung around them in chains of droplets of all sizes.

It felt like walking through a photograph.

There were few places to hide much of anything. The path was cut into what was rapidly becoming a cliff, with a steep drop to our left and the ground rising above us to the right. We passed occasional cuttings and crevices that Mapps might have used, and we carefully examined each one.

Which is how we came to find Mapps himself.

What I found first was a small area, not completely flat but climbing less steeply than the land around it. It widened out into the cliff on my right. A bush had colonised this little area, as had some fizzy drink cans and a couple of plastic sandwich boxes. And a shoe.

The shoe was half hidden behind the bush. Thinking that it might be a decent place for a Stash, I left the path and climbed towards the bush. This was when I realised that the shoe was attached to a leg, which in turn was attached to the rest of Mapps.

'Dave!'

She hurried over and we both looked down at the lifeless body of the software specialist. Some of the bandages had pulled loose, and his skin showed as hideously charred and torn as I remembered it. But also, something heavy - a rock, I guessed - had been bashed at his skull with some force. It had not been an equal contest and the skull had lost, and caved in.

I'm afraid you'll have to imagine the rest. The mixture of blood and brain. The thought of it still makes me retch. We were both sick, both of us on our hands and knees. Eventually Dave gathered herself enough to say,

'I'm actually quite pleased that I don't feel glad to see that.'

'Who did it?' I asked.

'Whoever he was meeting here?'

'Do you really think he was in any condition to climb up here on his own?'

'How else would he have got here?'

Neither of us could make sense of what we had found. We agreed to head back to the TV and let Mrs Ponch know. Someone stronger than us would have to carry Mapps' body down the side of the cliff. I had my misgivings about going back so soon, when Mrs Ponch had been so keen for us to get away, but Mapps could not be left here.

** ** **

We met Bob on Bay Lane, heading away from the TV and towards the square. He was clearly worried about something and his expression did not lighten much when he saw us.

'You two are back quick,' he said. 'She's not going to be pleased. Everything ok?'

I told him what we had found.

'Bloody hell,' he said. 'This gets worse. What was the bugger doing up there? You did right coming back. Show me where he is and I'll get him down.'

'The path's pretty narrow up there,' I warned him, 'and it gets pretty steep. We were thinking it would need two people and a stretcher.'

'I'll be ok. Show me the way.'

Bob had no trouble navigating the path. I realised that he was very light on his feet for such a big man. Dave had started off several yards behind us, and dropped further back as we ascended.

We reached the wider area containing the bush and the body and it was left to me to show Bob where Mapps was. He dragged the lifeless corpse into the open and checked around the surrounding area. Potts was watching from a little way away, looking strained. I wandered over to her.

'I think I've worked out what Dave Morland meant about Vic's knuckles,' she whispered. She glanced at Bob who was looking at us. She looked grim. 'It doesn't make sense though.'

'Everything all right?' Bob called out.

Dave forced a smile. 'It's fine.' Then, under her breath to me, 'Tell you later. Keep your distance from him.' She stepped away again, already starting her way back. I nodded, not going with her, watching the gap between us widen. Tired as it was, my brain had also begun to piece a few things together. Perhaps it would be more accurate to say, had collected together a few inconsistencies.

Bob lifted Mapps' body easily onto his shoulders and hurried back to the path. 'What was all that about?' He asked.

The inconsistencies had not yet solidified into anything that made sense. I needed more time to work things out properly. All I could think of to say was, 'I'm not sure. From what Dave said, she thinks Vic could be behind this.'

'Vic!' Bob laughed. 'I'm not sure he's strong enough to carry this one up here.'

'She wants me to keep my distance from him.'

'Dozy woman.' Bob stepped in front of me and began the climb down, his right arm securing Mapps' body across his shoulder.

'Come on. Potts is getting away.' He called to her, but Dave seemed
not to notice.

CHAPTER ELEVEN

We find out if Bob can keep up with Dave Potts, and I discover how odd the engine room is.

Bob tried hard to keep up with Dave, but the gap between them steadily widened. Eventually he stopped, dumped Mapps' body unceremoniously onto the path, and flopped down next to it.

'I need a break,' he said. He was sweating profusely. 'You keep going youngster. There's a real danger that they'll lurch out of this reality like they did the last time. It's not stable. The last thing you want is to be marooned here.'

'What about you?'

'Better one of us gets back than none. I should be ok. Leave me your emergency beacon. Worst comes to the worst, they should be able to find me again. I can't just leave Mapps here for somebody in this reality to stumble across.'

I edged carefully around Bob and passed him my beacon. He examined it, then pulled his small notebook and a stub of pencil from his trouser pocket. He scribbled furiously into it, tore the page off, and passed it to me.

'Here,' he said. 'Give this to Vic. It's the beacon's signature, it'll make it easier for them to find me. Don't worry, you can trust Vic. Whoever did this, it's not him. He can be a moody bugger but you can trust him.'

The paper was covered in indecipherable squiggles. I stuffed it into my pocket and looked again at Bob. Sweat was still standing out on his forehead and he had his eyes closed.

'Are you sure you're ok? You're not having a heart attack or something?'

He laughed, but did not open his eyes. 'I'm all right. Just getting too old for these sort of games. Go on. Get going while you've still got time.'

The rest of my journey back was uneventful. I moved as swiftly as I dared, always aware of the risks of going too quickly. When I crossed the square I barely glanced at the frozen me as I passed. It was with some relief that I saw the TV suddenly appear as I neared its position, and then I was inside and feeling much safer.

I had half expected Dave to be waiting for me but the reception area was empty. I headed for the control room, but it too was empty apart from Dildow, who was gazing at a screen and biting her thumb. She turned and stared at me.

'Want something?'

Bugger. What should I do? 'I need to give something to Vic,' I said. She frowned, and I added, 'It's a note from Bob.'

Dildow shrugged and pointed to a door in the far corner. 'He's through there. Up the stairs, knock on the door at the top, wait for them to answer it. Good luck.'

The stairs were metal steps which led up to another door. This one was red, with large black hieroglyphs written on it. I knocked. No-one answered.

I knocked again.

Nothing.

I pushed the door open and found myself in a large room full of benches, all of them covered in tubes and wires and small pieces of highly polished metal. There were lots and lots of small mirrors, all angled differently. Each piece of equipment was held in place by clips and clamps. Some of them were flat on the benches, others held suspended by stands made of fine polished metal. The room itself was huge. I guessed that it covered most if not all of the width and length of the TV. Small farting noises came at random from tubes on different benches. Some tubes that farted then broke from their clamps, flipped into the air and splintered. I saw one of them break a small mirror as it landed. A couple simply disappeared in mid-air, which left me somewhat stunned.

I don't know what I had expected the engine room to be, but certainly not a nightmarishly disorganised shambles like this. Something where a couple of big cylinders hummed impressively maybe. Lit by the glow of a powerful but well-contained nuclear reaction. There would have been metal walkways above it all with the engineers - wearing white coats - holding computer pads and tapping importantly yet calmly at them. And it should by rights have been underneath the rest of the TV, not above it. In all the sci-fi movies that I had seen the engine room was downstairs, like engine rooms were in ships. Maybe I just hadn't seen enough movies.

Kevin was working at a bench near me. He was wearing blinkers, like horses do, but I thought that still looked incredibly hot, possibly in a slightly pervy sort of way. He looked up, confused, then said quietly, 'You can't come in here.'

'Hoi!' Vic was less polite. He was further inside the room and also had a pair of blinkers on. 'Stop looking at things! Get out!'

'I've got a message for you from Bob.'

'What message? What are you talking about? Get out of here! And keep your eyes down!'

'It's his emergency beacon coordinates.' I held up the piece of paper. Several more tubes farted and splintered. Kevin moved towards me, reaching out to take it, but Vic darted across the room and grabbed at it first. He looked at it, then at me.

'Ok you've delivered it. Now clear off.'

The red mist came down. 'No really,' I said. 'There's no need to thank me.'

I headed back to the red door. Vic was saying something to my back but I was too angry to listen. This door was made of a heavy metal, and extremely solid. Unlike the ones downstairs it was one of the old-fashioned sort that swung shut, allowing the disgruntled door-closer every opportunity to vent their rage.

I vented my rage as hard as I could and was reassured by the satisfyingly loud clang that echoed down the stairwell.

** ** **

Dildow was still on her own in the control room. 'Don't take it personally,' she said. 'He's like that with everyone. It's stress.'

'You heard then?'

'I heard the door slam.' She smiled. 'The rest was pure deduction.'

'Where is everyone?'

'Dunno. Meeting maybe?' She checked her watch. 'It's nearly lunchtime so you'll probably find a couple of the scientists in the kitchen. They normally manage to get in there before the rest of us. Were you looking for anyone in particular?'

'Dave Potts. Or Mrs Ponch.'

'Sorry.' She shook her head. 'You could try the captain's private office or the Council Room. Are you ok Bettony?'

'Yeah... I just watched something disappear. This tube sort of jumped in the air and then... it sort of went.'

'Ah! They let you in did they? It's their own fault then.'

'The door was open.'

'Was it? Oh of course, the warning is in Enceldic. You weren't to know. Sorry, I should have said not to go in. I was too wrapped up in this.' She waved a hand vaguely at the screen. 'Don't worry, it's ok. You won't have damaged anything. It happens a lot. It's not important.'

'Really?'

'Well... not very. Think of it like this Bettony, that tube may not have been there in the first place, so it didn't actually disappear at all. It couldn't, could it, if it wasn't there?'

'Oh. But...'

'It's a quantum thing.'

'Ah. Right.'

I think Dildow could see that I was struggling with what she said, but to give her her due, she tried again. 'A lot of the tubes contain sub-atomic particles which may or may not be there.'

'Huh?'

'When you looked at one you would have crystallized the position of the particle inside it, and if it wasn't there but it was in the tube, then obviously the tube wasn't there either.'

'Er...'

She tried again. 'You know that thing about quantum physics, a quantum particle does not actually exist in a particular place. It may do, or it may be somewhere else, or it may alternatively be in a third state of being in either one or the other place. We can't tell which of those three states it is in. Only by the act of looking at it do we make its position definite. The paradox of Humdinger's Cat, we call it, after the physicist Gerhardt Humdinger who lost his cat and then claimed he never had one in the first place. The TV is powered by the balancing effect of displacing our BEC but we attempt to guide it with a cumulative nudge deriving from hundreds of individual quantum paradoxes, all pulling together.'

'Ah yes.' It seemed to be the right thing to say. It was either that or asking who Becc was. Dildow's sister, maybe?

'Or it would be if we could get it to work. Did you look at much?'

'Mmm.'

'That may have made Vic a bit crosser than usual.' She smiled again. 'Still, no harm done. Probably. Too late now anyway. It's fine Bettony.'

'I understand the last thing you said there Dildow. I'll go and find the kitchen. If it's still there.'

'By the way those cracks aren't a problem. It was a bit of a false alarm. The substructure is stable, it's just the modules stressing a bit. Worth checking though.'

** ** **

Hugo Crean stretched languidly, took another sip of coffee, and let his eyes wander around his small, slightly tatty office. The occasional sound that echoed down the corridor outside and through his open door told him that he was not quite alone in the building, but at ten thirty in the evening it felt that way.

Peckler's phone call had arrived during the dessert course of his dinner. Crean had betrayed none of his true feelings — the genial, charming veneer came easily to an ex-Hinton man — but he recognised the act of random viciousness from his superior for what it was.

And yet, and yet…

He was so pleased now to have received that call. The evening was fast becoming fascinating.

Nevertheless, Hugo was getting increasingly worried.

Some of this is extremely important, he thought. Obviously the woman hasn't got a clue what she's on about but neither does a mirror know what it does. It simply reflects. You still see the image it produces.

Bettony Gullivant is a mirror, reflecting things from a scientifically advanced civilisation that is far beyond anything we could even dream of. I can't let this get out. People will learn too much.

The Regency are all about power. They're like a disease. All the trade missions that they send out, all the foreign aid they give to those poor little nations - it's all just a cover for stripping their minerals for our factories. For extending Regency power and making those little countries vassal states. In all but name they become part of the Regency empire. If the Regency somehow use the vague but quite astonishing pointers in this report to develop something powerful...

No. I can't let this get out.

Also, Crean was getting to like this woman. In his society, women did what they were told. They respected their husband (even when the man didn't merit any respect). Their goal, they were told, was to support their man. Behind every great man there's a good woman.

This woman was different. She had strength. She was independent. Crean admired that. And her flippant humour found a ready echo in him. It was something that he tried to hide, of course. His sense of humour had landed him in plenty of trouble over the years. Crean envied the free expression she gave to her personality.

He wondered whether it was possible to fall for someone you had never met...

No. He absolutely could not let this get out.

I poked my head inside the kitchen but it was empty. I didn't want to walk in on a private meeting so I wandered back to the guest room that I had slept in and lay on the bed. For the first time since my adventure had started I felt lonely. Now that the TV had taken to lurching across realities my new home in Sputteridge had disappeared. I looked around the bare little room. Stop feeling sorry for yourself, I thought. I tried to focus instead on what was playing out around me, and the inconsistencies that were beginning to accumulate. Each of them, considered separately, meant nothing. Together they did, but the conclusion was too ridiculous to be taken seriously. There was something else as well, some thought that nudged at my consciousness and then bobbed away whenever I tried to get hold of it.

And what exactly had Dave Morland worked out about Vic's knuckles? If Dave Potts could figure it out, why couldn't I?

It was quiet in here. Peaceful. And I was so tired. I closed my eyes.

Vic's knuckles...

I realised that I was in the Council Room, watching Mike Potter give a presentation on the latest Happidog product. He was pointing to a slide showing a tin with a picture of some bloodied knuckles on it. 'Fish,' he said. 'It needs more fish.' Adding fish was Mike Potter's answer to everything. Cat food, dog food, any brand, whenever sales started to flag Mike knew it was because the product needed a higher fish content. 'The blood from the knuckles makes a delicious gravy' he added. 'It tastes of mayonnaise.'

It was one of those silly stand-up meetings, based on a trendy idea that people pay less attention if they're sitting down, so instead of making the meeting more interesting - making it shorter, for example - all the chairs are taken away. Mrs Ponch was there, and so were Bob and Dildow and Kevin and some people from Happidog Sales. Everyone was sporting bruises.

I woke up with the realisation of why Vic's knuckles were important. It locked the inconsistencies into a solid pattern. Dreams could get things wrong though, I told myself. Think, Gullivant! You have to be sure about this. I forced myself to remember events, as clearly as I could. Now that my brain had made the connection it all seemed to make sense, but unfortunately I still had no idea what that meant. It was not a solution in itself, but another puzzle. If this was what Dave Morland had spotted, was it really enough to cause someone to kill him?   No prizes for guessing who that would have to be though...

It was ridiculous.

** ** **

I was wandering back to the kitchen when there was one of those ground-juddering bumps which I now recognised as a transition. The kitchen door swooshed open and assorted scientists and engineers, led by Dave Green, burst out, all of them hurrying past me as they headed for the control room.

'Bloody thing always seems to happen at the wrong time,' he said. 'Right in the middle of lunch...'

'Bettony!' Dave Potts looked surprised. 'Where have you been?'

'Asleep.'

We stood to one side as everyone passed.

'You got back ok then,' Dave said. 'You could've let me know. I was starting to get worried.'

'I couldn't find you. Look we need to get to Mrs Ponch. I think I might have worked out the business about Vic's knuckles. But -'

'Yeah...' she looked uncomfortable, then said, 'I've already done that. I need to get this beacon back to stores and then get onto the nav station. Let's catch up later. I think Mrs Ponch will want to talk to you when things have quietened down a bit. Er... did Bob get back with Mapps?'

'I don't know. I left him my beacon. He said he was finding it hard going. I think he overdid it trying to keep up with you.'

Dave smiled. 'Right. Look I have to go. You may as well get something to eat and drink while it's quiet in there.' She patted my arm. 'Glad you're ok.'

111

'I am but we need to talk. I'm beginning to think I can't trust anyone.'

'OK. Understood. Later.'

She was about to hurry away, but I stopped her and said, 'Bob gave me a note for Vic which he'd written the coordinates for the beacon on. So Vic could find him again if we transitioned.'

Dave frowned. 'Oh. Right. I'm not too sure, you know – '

Mrs Ponch's voice boomed urgently through the corridor. 'Potts to nav station immediate!'

Dave dashed away, calling, 'See you later. Get some lunch...'

** ** **

I got some lunch. Beans on toast, butter soaking through the toast, the beans covered in tomato sauce. Instant coffee with milk. I ate among the abandoned detritus of half a dozen unfinished meals. I'm not saying that I was bored but I was halfway through reading the contents of the baked bean tin when Dave Lanyard wandered in.

My Truro shopping trip with Dave Lanyard had had its awkward moments. One such had been her surprise at what she saw as the lack of social responsibility shown by all concerned (including me) when we had a coffee. It was Dave's first trip outside of Sputteridge, and it showed.

'Go and get a table,' I had whispered as we queued at the coffee shop's counter.

'Why?'

'So that we'll have somewhere to sit.'

'There's a table there' she said, in a loud voice. She pointed.

'There's only that one left,' I hissed.

'What about the people in front of us?' Dave was still talking loudly. 'They will want somewhere to sit too.'

'The old boy who's being served now - that's his wife over there.' I made a slight movement with my head and swivelled my eyes.

'Are you ok Bettony?'

'Yes! Keep your voice down.'

'Why? What's wrong with your eyes?'

'Nothing! I'll explain later.'

A family joined the queue behind us, mother, father, and two teenagers. The two younger members of the family were physically present although their phones were clearly sucking whatever was left of their brains out of their heads and spewing it into the internet. The mother and the two zombies went and sat at the empty table.

'Well look at that. These people in front of us are going to have to stand. Isn't that thoughtless?'

The mother was staring daggers at Dave. I began to hope that, against all the laws of physics, a large hole would open up beneath me and swallow me.

'Dave,' I whispered, 'it's the way people behave.' I added lamely, feeling as though I was apologising for the whole human race, 'I'm sorry.'

'So it isn't usual for you to get a coffee and then go and find a table? Wouldn't that be the socially responsible thing to do? Why go and sit somewhere when you don't have anything to eat or drink? Especially if you are denying other people the chance to find a seat?'

'Mmm.' Try the distraction technique, I thought. 'Are you having anything to eat?'

'What about anyone who comes in on their own?' Dave persisted. She lowered her voice to a loud stage whisper. Possibly the couple sitting in the furthest corner of the coffee shop might now be struggling to hear her. 'They will never get a seat. It's not very thoughtful behaviour, is it?'

Possibly be struggling. Possibly not. The coffee shop seemed quieter, suddenly. People were looking at things in that distracted, I'm not really listening to you, I'm looking at this very interesting sauce bottle sort of way.

'I know it's not great and I'd rather not do it,' I whispered. 'But if we don't and everyone else does, we'll never get anywhere to sit either.'

'So co-operation breaks down when faced with the possibility of immediate short-term personal loss. But the loss is only there because you expect someone else to behave badly, either through selfishness or because they themselves fear that another person in turn will behave badly. It's like a chain reaction of bad behaviour. This is fascinating Bettony. It's game theory at its crudest. The Prisoner's Dilemma, I think you call it. In their attempt to avoid the worst outcome for themselves, everyone ends up with a bad outcome. Best Gain Win is our nearest equivalent model of social conduct.'

'Dave please keep your voice down! People are looking at us!'

'Are you all right Bettony? You're sweating.'

There had also been the incident at the "Ten Items or Less" aisle in the supermarket, but I won't go into that. Nor the business in the car park. Dave had seemed happily unaware that her observations of socially-accepted selfishness were causing me any concern, or putting us into any sort of danger of reprisal from those who were enraged at having their selfishness pointed out to the world in general by someone with a loud voice and - even worse - what sounded like a foreign accent.

She was quiet for a while on the drive back to Sputteridge. Then she said,

'Do you think that what lies behind your society's acceptance of these selfish behaviours is ultimately an irrational fear of physical violence? Or just a desire to avoid confrontation?'

'I need to concentrate on driving Dave. Can we talk about this later?'

'Oh sorry. Yes of course. What a fascinating day. Thank you Bettony. Hasn't it been exciting?'

'Sort of.'

'Why don't your people realise that if they co-operate, everyone wins? A slightly smaller slice of a bigger cake is more cake than a bigger slice of a smaller cake.'

'Later. Please don't talk about cakes.'

'Sorry. What a great day though. So much to write up. This could be the basis for a research paper. You're going to have to explain a lot to me. Why was that man who came into the delicatessen allowed to jump to the front of the queue and take the last cream sponge simply because he was a surgeon who had operated on the foot of the son of the woman behind the counter? Are surgeons more important than everyone else in your society? He certainly seemed to think that he was. Can we stop for a pint on the way back? Sorry I'll shut up. So many questions Bettony! What an exciting day!'

Now, Dave Lanyard spooned instant coffee into a mug and came to sit opposite me while the kettle heated up.

'Want to come and see what we do in the labs?' She asked.

'Aren't you all doing things in the control room?'

'Not all of us. I'm like first reserve now that Dave Morland...' She left the sentence unfinished.

'I really need to talk to Mrs Ponch.'

'It's probably not a good time, right now. Come and have a look at the labs.'

'Yes... ok - I mean, thank you Dave, I'd be very interested.'

Dave made her coffee. She led me back to the small entrance hall, then down the second corridor from the right. I knew that this was the science corridor and that the labs were down here, but this was the first time I had visited them.

'We each have a general interest in alien life and society,' she explained. 'And we all had to have some basic understanding of subatomic theory to qualify as crew members. But we also each specialise in different disciplines. I'm chemistry, Dave Green is biology, Dave Morland is - was... physics, and Pottsy is what you might call a quantitative sociologist. She's also in charge of the gin still and she runs the darts club.' She smiled. 'By the way, it was me who realised that taking the name Dave would help us to fit in, you know. Pretty neat eh?'

Each of the scientists had their own generously-sized private office. We walked past these to the labs. Three of the four office doors were open, and I glimpsed rooms that had bookshelves and a desk with a screen on it. They were in varying states of chaos. I guessed that the closed door would have opened onto Dave Morland's room.

Dave Lanyard stopped at the next door on the left.

'This is the chem lab,' she said, and led me into a room that was nothing like the chemistry labs I remembered from school. There were none of the Bunsen burners or glass bowls that I half-expected. Instead, metal boxes ranging in size from coffee maker through filing cabinet to upright fridge-freezer filled the room. The smaller ones sat on benches, the rest on the floor. Some of them had what looked like binoculars attached, presumably allowing the user to peer inside.

Dave went over to one of the smaller ones and pulled open a flap on its front.

'This one is my favourite,' she said. 'It can analyse co-mineralisation of organic and carbonated silica residues across realities.'

'Oh.' I tried to look intelligent. 'Wow.'

'No mucking about Bettony! Start to finish in ten minutes. Fifteen tops.' She looked at me expectantly. She was obviously expecting a positive response.

'That's... pretty quick.'

She nodded, gratified. I wandered over to one of the larger cabinets.

'What does this do?'

'That's the fridge. Pilsners on the top shelf, IPAs and Guinness next one down. The rest is just science stuff.'

The physics lab was just as disappointing. Instead of machinery that looked capable of generating huge electromagnetic forces, maybe even things you could touch to make your hair stand on end, there were more metal boxes. I have to say that Dave's explanations of them sounded exciting at the time, although as I had no idea what she was on about I have forgotten all of them. The biology lab smelled like biology labs everywhere but was more interesting, in the sense that it had things to look at and also a couple of mice in a cage. Given what I was learning about the generally high moral standards of the Abbuthians I was surprised by the mice.

'Do you experiment on these?' I asked.

'Good Greeks no. They were in a pretty bad way when we found them so Kagh and I nursed them back to health. We've released them into Sputteridge a few times but they always find their way home.' She bent down to the cage and her voice rose a couple of octaves, as people's voices everywhere do when they talk to babies or pets. 'Don't you coochicoochies. You come-di home-di.' Her voice returned to normal. 'That one's Henry the Eighth and this one's Amber Lynn.'

'That's an interesting choice of names Dave.'

'We wanted to give them something historical from your world. Luckily I'd heard an audio transmission about one of your historic dictators.'

'We call them kings and queens. Are you sure her name's not Anne?'

'I did a quick name check Bettony. It was definitely Amber. Anne Lynn must be someone else.'

Henry the Eighth and Amber Lynn. A psychopathic monarch and a porn star. It's a mind-boggling combination but I'm sure it would have worked on some level. And maybe, it wouldn't have left him with enough energy to do all that beheading. The mice shuffled over to her and Dave cooed at them for a few more seconds. Then she said, 'Fancy a beer Bettony?'

More than anything I wanted to talk to Dave Potts and Mrs Ponch, but I daren't interrupt whatever they were doing.

The floor juddered again as we took the beers back to Dave's office. 'Wonder where we are now?' She mused. 'No doubt we'll find out.'

'Doesn't it worry you?'

'Not really.' She smiled, briefly. 'Not that. We'll get home in the end and we'll get you home too.' (Why did I feel bad when she said that?)

'Violence worries me though,' she went on. 'We're not used to it. There's something happening here that's...not right. People don't hurt people on Abbuth, let alone... you know.' She moved a pile of papers off a chair. 'I don't think Dave M was ill... Anyway. Come in Bettony, take a seat.'

She had been trying for a while to arrange a time to question me about her day in Truro and I could not really stop her now. I had been avoiding it because her intelligent but naive questions exposed many flaws in the human personality and for some reason made me feel vaguely responsible for all off them.

'It's not all bad,' I said as I finished the beer. 'I ruptured an Achilles a couple of years ago and had to go around on a pair of crutches. When you do that you discover the kindness inside most people. Opening doors for you, stopping cars so you can cross the road. Offering their seats to you.'

'That's interesting.' She thought for a few moments. 'Can we try that?'

'How do you mean?'

'Well to be honest it's more Kagh's area than mine. I bet she'd be interested though.' Dave began to get more excited. 'It could be a development of Reinhold's Gum Theory. Something like, How many times in a specific situation do people help you? This is spunky Bettony!'

'Spunky...?'

Dave Lanyard's excitement was building. 'Reinhold based his original theory on observations from the first automated TVs. He had to. It was all the data he had. It was ground-breaking! And it has held up. But now we're in a position to take those old remote observational theories and blast a new dimension into them! It would need two people of course. One with the crutches and one measuring... no! - Not measuring - recording! A recording to facilitate peer group review!'

Dave was getting very excited, although I could see practical problems in her new idea. Pierre DeLondon's voice, rather muffled, suddenly burst out of the ether.

'How do I switch this on?' There was some muttering in the background, then DeLondon said, more clearly, 'It is green.' Another pause, and more muttering, then I heard him say, 'Would all members of the transition community make their way to the Council Room please. It's gone red now. Is it meant to do that? ...Which one? This one? Oh that one.'

I counted myself a member of Pierre's transition community so I joined Dave and everyone else in the Council Room. This would be where Mrs Ponch revealed what Dave had told her, I thought. Where the murderous traitor got their just desserts.

It was going to be interesting.

But when I got to the Council Room everything was wrong. A few people were sitting down but the rest of us stood around the edges of the room. Mrs Ponch stood at the far end, looking uncomfortable. Bob stood to her left, DeLondon next to him. I stared at Dave Potts, who gave a slight shrug and shook her head.

There was a little awkward whispering but the room fell silent as Mrs Ponch started to speak.

'You all know what has been happening,' she said. 'Unexpected transitions, like the one we've just navigated our way around. Things that we could never have imagined when we set off on our inaugural Series Four transition. The tragic death of Dave Morland, from what we are not yet certain. The shots fired by Wether Mapps at either Bettony or Dave Potts, seemingly with the aim of actually injuring them. A situation that I am pretty sure none of us will ever have experienced, or probably even countenanced. The injuries that Wether Mapps sustained, his apparent escape and the discovery of his battered body outside. Unconscionable events that have left us all gobsmacked... He used an armament! We have no idea how Mapps got tooled up - that's a whole bag of potatoes on its own - but he did and he used it. And here's the meatball salad: It's disappeared. The armament has gone. And what we have to find out is, where? Where has it gone?' She subjected each of us in turn to her piercing gaze.

'Where has it gone,' she repeated, softly.

'Isn't it still out there?' Dave Potts asked.

'I brought it in,' said Will. 'I put it in the Med bag when I was outside.'

'Shouldn't you have given it to Bob or Mrs Ponch?' Asked Dildow.

'He did.' The Officer in Charge's discomfort visibly increased. 'I am one hundred cents sure that I put it away in my room. Locked it away in a draw.'

The silence took on a stunned quality.

'One hundred cents sure', Mrs Ponch repeated. 'The whole Canadian dollar.'

'Somebody broke into your room? One of us?' Dave Green articulated what I suspect everyone was thinking. I noticed Dildow glance at me.

Bob spoke, his voice solemn. 'So unfortunately people what we have to do now is to ask you all to stay here while we search your rooms. Personal rooms and offices.'

'Even yours?' Challenged Dave Potts.

'Even mine.'

'And labs?'

'And labs.'

'And the engine room?'

Bob looked at her for a long moment. 'Vic will search the engine room if we haven't found something first.'

Dave looked across and caught my eye. Bob was still watching her. He also glanced at me. I kept my face expressionless.

'Pierre and I will carry out the search,' continued Mrs Ponch. 'Bob will stay here with you all. This may take some time.' She looked distraught. 'I am so sorry everyone. We all prize the value of trust. It is an unshakeable value. I realise that I am betraying that value with what we are about to do. I am so, so sorry. But someone has behaved in a way that is far outside our accepted norms of behaviour...' She took a deep breath and started again. 'We shall unpick this, I promise you. And we shall have you all home safely.'

DeLondon and Mrs Ponch left the room. In what must have been a prearranged move Kevin went quickly and stood against the door by which they left, and Bob by the one at the other end of the room, where we had entered. The rest of us simply waited. Vic sat alone in the centre of the room, tapping his foot on the floor. Will went and sat next to Dave Green and Dildow. He looked deeply unhappy. I noticed that Dildow kept glancing at me, the old suspicion back in her eyes. Dave Potts and Dave Lanyard both stayed by my side, and I was extremely grateful for that.

** ** **

It took less than half an hour for DeLondon and Mrs Ponch to return. When they did everyone stared at them. I think what they were staring at mostly though was the clear polythene bag that Mrs Ponch was carrying. It looked like a lightweight food bag but it was being weighed down by the heavy pistol inside it.

'Dave?' Three Daves looked at her. 'Mr Green, I want you to do a DNA analysis on this. I know it's outside your usual work but I think it should be simple enough?'

'Yes. Yes I can do that.'

I shall ask Pierre to oversee you, so that there can be no doubt about the validity of your results. I shall be in my private quarters. Bring the results there. How long will it take?'

'About ten minutes.'

'Good. Thank you.' Mrs Ponch looked around the room. 'Please bear with us for another few minutes everyone.' She left, followed by Dave Green and a very sombre DeLondon. Kevin and Bob resumed their positions.

'Bloody hell' said Dave Lanyard. 'Where do you think they found it?'

'Dunno,' Potts replied. She looked at Kevin and then at Bob, his solid frame planted squarely in front of the door preventing any attempt at an exit. 'I've got a bad feeling about this though.'

It was fifteen minutes later when Mrs Ponch returned, alone. We all looked at her - the three engineers, the two scientists, Will, Bob and me. As I've pointed out before, stress can bring an odd flippancy out in me. I was put in mind of some sort of tacky quiz show, done in extremely poor taste. Who murdered Mapps? Step forward Bettony Gullivant, you are this week's weakest stooge.

But it wasn't my name that Mrs Ponch uttered.

'Dave would you come with me please?'

Lanyard looked at me. Panic was written all over her round, honest face. But it was Potts who stood up, shook her head, and ruffled my hair as she went past. Bob left his post at the door to follow her.

'Thank you everyone.' Mrs Ponch's voice sounded tired. 'Please return to your stations. Or your labs. Or wherever...'

The stunned silence carried on even after the door closed behind Bob. Vic's eyes flitted continually across all of us, but nobody moved. Eventually Will came over to join Dave Lanyard and me.

'Are you two ok? Do you want me to give you anything?'

We shook our heads and Dave roused herself. 'No thanks Will. Want to come with me Bettony? I'm going to feed the mice.'

'Ok.'

We walked back to the biology lab in silence. Dave pushed the door open and said, 'I don't believe that. I just don't believe it! Do you Bettony? She must have touched the armament when you first caught up with Mapps. Don't you think?'

'Neither of us touched it Dave.'

'So you think she took it?'

'No. Definitely not.'

'So how did her DNA get on it?' Dave walked over to a shelf and took down a tub of pellets. She sprinkled them into the cage.

I didn't give an answer, mainly because I didn't have one. And I didn't go to talk to Mrs Ponch. What could I tell her that Dave Potts hadn't already?

Nothing made sense any more.

** ** **

Mrs Ponch put a few changes into place. We were each given a thin metal bracelet which was a simple location tracker. Dildow reprogrammed the information screens around the TV and in staff quarters so that anyone could see on a sort of map of the TV where everyone was. An awful intrusion, said Mrs Ponch. But until we could be sure that the situation was fully resolved all possible steps would be taken to protect staff.

The trackers were also simple heartbeat monitors. Should they fail to register a healthy beat, an alarm would be sounded on all screens throughout the TV. (I realised this also meant if anyone took their bracelet off the whole ship would know immediately.) Mrs Ponch personally interviewed Dave Potts; whatever was said in those meetings was not passed on to anyone. Dave herself was being kept

122

in her room, Mrs Ponch and Pierre DeLondon were the only people allowed to see her or take her food.

Vic managed to get the TV back to the Sputteridge that I had come to think of as home, although I felt safer using the guest room and did not return to the police house. We were there for nearly a week before we juddered unintentionally back to the frozen world. It gave me the chance for several shopping trips, but now I was always accompanied by Pierre DeLondon. They were uneventful, but I struggled to enjoy them and despite DeLondon's attempts to reassure me - or maybe because of them - was always uneasy in his presence. The trips became more of a chore and less something to be looked forward to. There was also the added tension that the TV may not still be there when we returned to Sputteridge. DeLondon and I always took a couple of beacons but the thought of having to spend any more time than absolutely necessary in that creep's company was not one to fill me with joy.

Dave Lanyard on the other hand became a true friend. We ate together, and after her working day was over we chatted and played board-games. I taught her backgammon and Carcassonne, both brought back on shopping trips, and soon she was beating me at both. Sometimes Will joined us; his quiet and relaxed company was heartening in a way that DeLondon could never be. Dildow was more suspicious and would barely even say hello to me.

At least Henry the Eighth and Amber Lynn were on my side. If I had food for them.

Lanyard and I took it in turns to feed the mice. When it was Dave's turn to do the feeding I generally went with her. As I became more used to the labs the machines in them began to interest me more. I imagined these machines were way in advance of what we had on earth. (That was purely down to my ignorance though. They could have been way behind and I wouldn't have known. But they were on an alien vessel and most were made of a shiny metal, some even had small flashing lights, so logic told me they had to be advanced. One of them even went beep.)

'What does this do Dave?'

I had wandered over to the nearest metal box and reached out idly to twiddle the controls. Dave looked round from trying to feed Henry and Amber equal amounts.

'Don't touch it! Sorry Bettony I didn't mean to make you jump. That's the axial MALDI-TOF mass spectrometer. Kagh brought back an egg from your crazy frozen world and Dave Green's been doing an iterative eggbane analysis on it. You wouldn't believe how long it takes. It's still got a couple of days to run -'

'Aaah!!'

'Bettony! Are you all right?'

'Yes!' However crazy my idea, there was no longer any room at all for doubt. The proof was, as Mrs Ponch would say, The Whole Canadian Dollar. It didn't explain Dave's prints on the gun, but there would be some explanation for that. There had to be.

'It wasn't the fish! Mike Potter was wrong!'

'I'm sorry?'

'I need to get to Mrs Ponch. I'll explain on the way. Come on!'

I knew that Mrs Ponch's private quarters were close to the control room, which meant going back to reception. Before we were there I had told Dave the essence of what I had just - finally - realised. It took barely one sentence.

Bob was standing in reception, gazing out at a vaguely purple-lit landscape. He half-turned, then resumed staring outside.

'We're back here again,' he said. 'Sometimes it makes me wonder if we've died and this is Hell. What are you two up to?'

'Dave's offered to show me the control room,' I lied.

'You've seen it haven't you? Anyway I'm sorry, but after your little incident in the engine room last week I'm afraid the control room, the engine room and the access corridor to them are all out of bounds. You can't go down there.' Bob shrugged his shoulders. 'Sorry youngster it's out of my hands.'

'I can though, can't I?' Said Dave.

'Not right now, no.'

The door to the staff quarters and sick bay swished open, and Vic appeared, manhandling Dave Potts before him. Potts had some sort of tape over her mouth and her hands were tied behind her back and she was struggling. Vic stopped dead and looked at the two of us, his mouth open. His eyes rested on Lanyard. 'What the fuck? Not another one.'

'Oh balls,' Bob said. He tutted, and shook his head sadly. He was still perfectly relaxed, almost apologetic. 'Really out of my hands now, Bettony.' He turned to Vic. 'Fraid so. Another one.' He waved his arm vaguely at me. 'Or two counting this one. I could possibly have thought of something if you'd taken a bit longer sunshine, but it's unlikely. We'll have to make it up as we go along, for a while.'

Potts was still struggling to get away from Vic, who was hanging on to her. Bob strolled over and casually punched her in the stomach. It didn't look like a hard punch but she folded over onto the floor, gasping for breath. But in doing so, Bob had moved away from the exit doors and Dave Lanyard ran to them. Before Bob could stop her she was outside. I started to follow her but I was too slow, Bob's arm shot out and grabbed the back of my jumper, tightening it around my neck and choking me.

'Don't run!' I shouted to Lanyard. 'Remember Mapps!' She stopped. When she looked around at us her face was red, but it could have been a lot worse. She turned away again and set off down Bay Lane at a brisk walk.

'That's one problem solved then,' Bob said. He went to the control panel next to the doors and looked at it, then turned to Vic. 'Change this Vinny. Make sure she can't get back in. I can always come back for her if I need to. And just make sure that you jump out of here smartish. Think you can manage that?' There was contempt in his voice.

Vic nodded. All of his tetchy attitude had disappeared. When he looked at Bob the only thing I saw on Vic's face was fear. 'Keep working on getting this thing to Erce,' Bob went on. (He pronounced it earchay.) 'It's what you were trained for. You've been acting like a fucking failure so far. If you can't do it these two can be Plan B, maybe the other one as well if I can catch her. But if you can't pilot this thing to Erce don't bother coming back when we force Ponch to do it. You know what'll be waiting for you.'

He grabbed Dave with his free hand and pulled us both outside. He was holding the ropes that bound Dave's hands behind her back and this bent her forwards and off-balance. Bob - I'm going to have to call him that for a little while longer - was walking quickly and Dave was continually stumbling, held upright only by his grip. I could feel the heat on my face. I was grateful I had a woolly jumper on; rather than making me hotter, it shielded me from some of the heat that the brisk walk was generating. We were marched down Bay Lane and diagonally across the square, past the police house and towards the dead end. A couple of times I tried to turn and twist out of Bob's grip. Neither was successful. After the second Bob said 'Do that again and I'll knock you out and carry you.'

I believed him.

'I shouldn't be here at all really,' he said. 'All this is well below my pay-grade. Trouble is, somebody's got to sort things out. It's turning into a right fucking mess.'

We were dragged down the dead end about thirty yards, towards a crudely-shaped metal box. It was tatty and about the size of a family car. It looked like a small version of the sort of containers that get carted across the world on ships and stuck on the backs of lorries.

'That's the missing Series Two!' Dave exclaimed.

Bob did not answer. He tightened his grip on my top, making it difficult for me to breathe. 'I'm going to release you,' he said. 'If you try to escape I'll kill her' - he pointed to Dave. 'It's your choice.' He released me and then just for good measure punched me in the stomach. It didn't involve much effort for him but like Dave had done, I collapsed to the floor. It felt as though all the air had been forcibly ejected from my entire body. Not only that, my stomach muscles were refusing to suck any more in. I lay, gasping like a fish on land, fighting to stay conscious. By the time I had recovered enough to crawl onto my hands and knees Bob had entered the metal box and reappeared with a length of chain. He looped the chain around the ropes tying Dave's hands and then wound it around a tree trunk and secured it. This took him a little while. By now I had got my breath back and was able to stand.

Got to try this, I thought.

I knew I could do it.

I had seen men bigger than Bob be knocked out by some very thin opponents in the dojang. Only ever by one type of kick though. It was technically the most difficult kick, but it focussed a huge amount of power. I was flexible, I was well-coordinated, and it was a kick that I had practised a thousand times. Never with the intention of knocking anyone out - least of all someone as big and thick-set as Bob - but this was the moment.

Reverse turning kick, heel to the side if the head. Specifically - and to be successful it had to be very specific, and very accurate indeed - to the temple.

I knew that I could do it but everything had to be perfect.

I focussed my concentration. Relaxed my muscles. When Bob approached me I was fully in the zone, completely relaxed. I waited until he was barely six feet away and suddenly flung both arms in front of me, swung them a little way to the left, then pulled them in the opposite direction, twisting arms and shoulders clockwise with as much force as I could. Both feet were still planted on the floor and I held them for as long as I dared, twisting my shoulders, tightening my body. Then I let my right foot lift behind me and at the same time bent forwards at the waist.

I straightened my right leg as it began to move. I made sure that my foot was horizontal, leading with the heel.

The elastic power that I had forced into my body released into my right leg, which spun around. My foot quickly gained height, pivoting upwards as I swung my head down almost to ground level. All the time, I was accelerating the rotational speed of my right leg as much as I possibly could.

I had spotted Bob's temple before I started. (Spotting here is a technical term, a bit like what dancers do when they spin although with perhaps more serious consequences.) I was looking at the ground just in front of my nose when I felt my heel connect with the side of his head with all my weight, all the power that I could put into it.

'Owaar.'

Wrong sound. That was the sound of someone who was still conscious.

I regained my feet as quickly as I could but the problem with any sort of kick is that recovery takes time. Recovery from a reverse turning kick takes longest of all. By the time I was back on my feet Bob was staggering slightly but lumbering towards me.

I had connected just a fraction late. Just a couple of inches behind the temple. Enough to hurt him but just hurting this man would never be enough.

Got to keep trying. I did a fast little shimmy, desperately resetting my feet for a front kick to the opposite temple.

Bob used those moments to completely close down the space between us, and swung his fist.

I had not even lifted my foot before I felt a piledriver explode into the side of my own head. A dark purple fog suddenly blocked out my vision, here and there green and red pinpricks of light were firing. I realised my body was completely limp and that I was falling to the ground but just for good measure another piledriver buried itself into my stomach.

Before I lost consciousness completely I heard Bob's voice. 'Nice try youngster that was very good. But you know what they say, A good big 'un will always beat a good little 'un.'

CHAPTER TWELVE

In which I discover Erce. Or at least a bit of it.

Consciousness came slowly. First there was the pain in the head, not unlike a really bad hangover. Then I tried to move and discovered that my stomach muscles were badly bruised. Or maybe my ribs. Or maybe both.

I took it one step at a time. I concentrated on breathing. This was harder than it sounds and uniquely painful but eventually I had it under control and I opened my eyes.

I was lying on a small hard bed in a completely white room. The walls and the floor and the ceiling were all brilliant white. There was no natural light and the strip lights that were set into the ceiling were too bright and there were too many of them.

I closed my eyes again.

Eventually I forced myself to stand up and examine the room I was in. I realised with a shock that the walls were padded. The door was too, although there was a small piece of reinforced glass in the top half. I was not surprised to discover that the door was locked. There were small glass spheres, about a centimetre diameter, set into each corner of the ceiling. They may or may not have been cameras. There was a small metal table with two metal chairs each side of it, all of which were screwed to the floor.

I was very thirsty.

There was nothing to do so I lay back on the bed and tried to rest.

It was pretty obvious that I was not in the Series Two. This room was too big. And it was highly unlikely I was back in the TV. So the only conclusion was that the man looking like Bob had taken me back to Erce.

And hopefully, I thought, also taken Potts, because the alternative to that was not good.

I must have drifted back to sleep. The sound of the door opening woke me. I opened my eyes and watched the Bob-man enter the room and sit at one of the chairs.

'Had you fooled didn't I?' He said. He had changed into a dark, well-tailored suit and leather shoes, white shirt and a pale blue tie.

I did not bother sitting up. I closed my eyes against the glare and said, 'Not really.'

'No? When did you begin to suspect?'

Don't tell him about the eggbane, I thought. Right now I had very few cards left to play but that was definitely one. If he could give himself away to me, he could do it with others.

'You're fatter than Bob. His clothes don't quite fit you. And that yellow t-shirt was a mistake.'

'Ouch!' He smiled complacently, then went on, 'That idiot Vinny didn't let me know what the creep was wearing. We couldn't get hold of another uniform and there was too much blood on his.' My stomach lurched when he said that. 'Anything else?'

Confuse. Hide the truth in a mist of half-truth. Right now words are your only weapons. Use them carefully. Make him feel uncertain. Get inside his head.

I opened my eyes and propped myself up on one elbow. 'You can look like someone but you're still a different person. Everything you do is slightly different. The way you move. The phrases you use.'

'Mmm.' He sounded doubtful. 'Nobody else picked anything up, I'm pretty sure about that. And no-one has noticed Vinny.' He leered. 'Of course you'd spot more things because you were living with him.'

I ignored the inference. 'Who's Vinny?'

I was not making any progress in denting his confidence but perhaps because of that he was happy to share information.

'Vinny Schsheltsky. Currently appearing as Vic, the clueless senior engineer who doesn't know his arse from his elbow. What phrases?'

'You called me Youngster. Bob never did that.'

'One thing. That's not much.'

It was a strange conversation. So light. And yet... So much menace.

'Can I have a drink?'

'Soon. Come on youngster. I don't want to hurt you if I don't have to. I don't get much of a kick out of that sort of thing.' He sighed. 'Mind you there are plenty here who do.'

'Bob wouldn't call Mrs Ponch "Boss". And you kept calling the TV a craft. I dunno... it just sounded wrong. So many things did. Just little things that didn't mean anything on their own but taken together... And that thing when we were outside, about giving me a note for Vic. It was some sort of message wasn't it? They didn't need any coordinates to get back to us the first time, when Dave set off her emergency beacon.'

He nodded. 'Well done. Written in Vinny's home language of Ruslan.' He laughed. 'Bet you thought it was their lingo eh?'

'What was that all about?'

'Ha!' Perhaps I was beginning to get through to him and he needed something to prove his intelligence to me. Or perhaps he was so confident that he thought it didn't matter. 'I needed time to get back here and get some DNA onto the gun. We had already located all the doubles of most people on the Q-craft - sorry youngster, that's the TV, I'm going to have to get used to saying that aren't I? As far as we can tell based on the guy who was piloting the little Series Two, and what Vinny got back to us, DNA for the same people across universes is more or less the same. Your kid on the ... *TV* ... wouldn't have been able to spot the difference anyway. So I told Vinny to do a little jump. Just to give me time.'

'So he's not that clueless?'

He laughed. 'He can manage those little half-jumps. That's about his limit.'

'Can I have a drink of water please?'

'Not yet. Tell me about the blood on Vinny's knuckles.'

'I don't know your name. Tell me your name and give me a drink and I'll tell you about Vinny's knuckles.'

He could move swiftly for such a big man. He reached out, took my arm with one hand and wrenched my middle finger back with the other. It was excruciatingly painful.

'Thing is, youngster, I don't do deals. Except this one. You tell me what I need to know and I won't break your fingers. All of them. Both hands. Deal?'

I nodded. I was determined not to cry out but the pain was so intense I couldn't speak.

He let go of my hand, half-smiled and raised his eyebrows. 'Well?'

I nursed my hand. Gathered myself. 'When you first made your appearance - after all the lights went out which I'm guessing was a part of it in some way - Kevin had got a bit of a bruise. You hadn't got anything. But Vic had got blood all over his knuckles. So unless he had been hitting himself something else had been happening. Someone else had got bloody. So you were lying.' I stopped myself from saying any more.

He nodded, then sucked his cheeks in. My finger was throbbing. When I tried to move it pain shot up my arm. At least it took my mind off the pain in my ribs and my head.

'Mmm.' He sighed. 'Devil's in the detail eh?'

'Is that why you killed Dave Morland?'

'Partly.' He spoke as though the death of an honest and harmless man meant nothing to him. 'He'd obviously spotted something and he was obviously suspicious of me. I was pretty sure he didn't trust me or he would have shared his thoughts in the little get-together with Ponch. I couldn't take the risk. Then when you and Potts were with him in the kitchen I guessed he was telling you what he knew. Couldn't hear though. Bloody doors are too thick.'

'So all that stuff about the cracks in the floor...?'

The Bob-man laughed. 'Could've been right for all I knew. It was just lucky for me. It gave me an excuse for being there.'

A thought occurred to me.

'When you came into my room that night...'

'Ah yes. I was going to kill you.' So calm. So matter-of-fact. 'In fact I'd put something useful in the coffee. I guess you don't take sugar in coffee?'

I shook my head. 'And Bob wouldn't have forgotten that.'

'Yeah I realised from your reaction. More detail eh? I didn't even need to poison you, I could have killed you like I did Morland. But Ponch chose that moment to wander in. Made me wonder if she was watching you but just as likely she was watching me, so I had to go back to Bob's quarters. Play the part of the reliable Number Two. Truth was, I was absolutely knackered and I fell asleep until the next day. I'd had a busy day you know and then I'd had to carry Mappsy out and dump him up the cliff before I had a go at you.'

'When did you kill Dave Morland?'

'Yep, I'd had to get that done as well. When you were counting the cracks.' He laughed. 'He was in the physics lab. I told him Ponch wanted to see the four of us in the kitchen, I think he was a bit suspicious but he went along with it and I coughed him there. Made life easier for me.'

'Why the kitchen?'

'To confuse things.'

'And moving Mapps made it look like he was the killer.'

'Got it in one.'

'Was he dead when you moved him?'

'Dunno. It didn't really matter. He was lifeless and he didn't struggle. And after I'd used the rock he definitely was.' The Bob-man laughed. 'I thought the rock was a nice touch' he added.

I felt sick.

'Isn't Mapps one of your lot then?'

'Mapps? God no. He was just a decoy. You're very clever at this aren't you? I come here to ask you things and I find it's me answering all the questions.'

I pulled my arms under my body. 'I've answered all of yours. You did say you'd get me a drink and tell me your name.'

'Mmm.' He stood up. 'You can call me Sir.' He rubbed the side of his head. 'You've given me a bloody headache with that kick.

Think about that while you're waiting for a nice glass of cool, clear water.'

** ** **

It was three hours before the Bob-man returned. My ribs and my head were feeling a bit better. My finger wasn't.

He brought a glass of water with him, sat at the table and placed it in front of him.

'Come and sit here.'

I sat opposite him. This is one of his games, I thought. Don't play it. Ignore the water.

'So tell me the sort of phrases that the sainted Bob would use. What does he call Ponch?'

'Her first name is Zagretia. He tends to use that or a diminutive of it, Zetia.'

'I hope you're telling me the truth here youngster because if you're not it will be very painful for you.'

'I am. Ask Vic - Vinny.' Part of it was true, anyway and hopefully Vinny wouldn't know about the rest. If the Bob-man called Mrs Ponch Zetia, surely that would rouse her suspicions? Confirm what Dave must have told her? If it did, of course, and he made it back again, I would have consequences to deal with. But I guessed that plenty of consequences were on their way, whatever happened.

He snorted. 'Vinny? That dipshit wouldn't notice if they were talking Sepanish.'

'Sepanish? - Spanish?'

'In this world it's Sepanish. You can drink the water you know.'

I tasted it gingerly, then swallowed quickly. The glass was small and barely contained two mouthfuls. My body absorbed the water and cried out for more.

'So in this world you basically speak the same language as us? Do you call it English?'

'Looks like it, more or less. Anglish. It made fitting in on the - TV - that bit easier. I'd have been nutted if they used their own gibberish but good old Ponch came to the rescue on that one.'

134

'If Vinny's so useless wouldn't you have been better off replacing Mrs Ponch and leaving Vic there to operate the TV to her commands?'

'Yeah... No. Putting aside the fact that we didn't know Vinny was going to be so out of his depth... Women in this world know their place which is either the kitchen or the bedroom. Looking after their man. That's how it is and that's how it should be. Even if we could find Ponch's double - and we did try, believe me, we trawled all the ghettos - what use would she be? What's she going to do, cook her way to power?' The Bob-man shook his head at the idiocy of my question. 'What is the most powerful weapon on your world?'

'Er... I don't know.' Cold rage had replaced blood in my veins. 'Nuclear bombs, I suppose. No-one's supposed to have biological weapons but ... I don't know. You're asking the wrong person. And I'm only a woman you know. These things are way beyond me.'

'Mmm. Main energy source?'

'It's a mixture these days. It used to be coal, then oil, now there's more renewables.'

'You're going to have to explain what you mean by renewables to me at a later date. I've been told your society harnesses the power of nucular explosions to make electricity. Pulling tiny atoms apart to release huge amounts of power. Why didn't you mention that?'

'It's used less and less. I think people are too worried about accidents. I just work in the marketing department of a pet food manufacturer, you're asking the wrong person.'

'I know. But you're all we've got.' He smiled. 'Almost all we've got. You're definitely a lot more talkative than the other buggers.' His smiled widened. 'They tend to do more screaming.'

Don't let him see your fear. 'Why do you want to ask me about our world?' I managed to keep my voice steady.

'Just curious. Could come in useful, you never know.' He changed tack. 'What did those cute little Abbuthians think about Mr Mapps?'

I was already livid over the Bob-man's misogyny; now I felt another wave of anger. 'I couldn't believe they took his word over mine.'

'What's that then? Who did?'

I explained how I had first met Mapps, and DeLondon's insistence on backing him up.

'That guy sounds a complete fan.'

'So he's not one of you? Even Mrs Ponch believed him. Or she seemed to.'

'Ah well she's a woman, what do you expect? She's not even white.'

Any moment now, I thought, the top of my head is going to crack open and steam will come pouring out. Somehow I managed not to react.

'You said Mapps was a decoy. Wasn't he one of your people?'

'You like to live dangerously don't you?' He reached out and took my arm but just gave the wrist a gentle squeeze. I tried not to flinch. I'm not sure I succeeded. But then he let go and leaned back. His smile broadened again. His was the sort of ego that liked to be appreciated. 'A bit of research about who we could take out of the *TV* without too much impact on things, then some work on identifying a double from somewhere nasty. One of my agents picked him up on one of his little Q-Craft's trips. I wanted someone to distract attention.' He tapped my wrist in a gesture not unlike Bob's when he was in lecture mode. 'As a matter of fact this guy was also a software bod and he fitted in better than we could have hoped.'

'And he distracted attention from you, Vic and Kevin?' A bit of a shot in the dark there. It didn't work.

'You know, like a magician?' Waves his right hand around and while everyone is watching it the left hand does the trick? Mappsy was my right hand man. Vinny was the left. Or he should have been if he wasn't so useless. I could see what you were doing there by the way. And since it doesn't actually matter what you find out I'm going to tell you. Kevin is the real deal.' The Bob-man enjoyed the effect of this on me. 'No replacing that numpty. No need. We could've replaced Vic with a five-legged cat and he still wouldn't have noticed.' He stood up. 'Right I'm off to bed. It's gone midnight and I need my beauty sleep. And I've still got this bloody headache. Give me your watch.'

There was no point in trying to resist or even to ask why. I gave him my watch. He looked at it briefly then dropped it to the floor and ground his heel into it. He headed for the door.

'You get a good night's sleep,' he said. The door swung shut behind him. The lights stayed on.

** ** **

I slept, in spite of the lights. I was very tired. At some point – I guessed that it was the next day but had no way of knowing – a man in a white nurse's uniform brought in food and water. At some point, I was taken for a toilet break. Time passed. More food, more toilet breaks. No change in the lights. Measured by the number of meals they gave me, a couple of days must have gone by before the Bob-man turned up again. The ribs, head and finger were all beginning to improve.

'They looking after you?'

'Could be worse. How's the head?'

'I'm glad to say that apart from the odd twinge it has cleared up. Let's talk about your world.'

We talked about my world. The Bob-man asked about population, how it was spread across continents, and the shape of the continents. I was asked to draw a map of the world which I made up. I was shown a map of Erce which was basically the same as Earth, and my damaged finger was given a squeeze and I was told not to lie. I was asked about minerals and mining and sizes of armies and which countries were the most powerful. After the map incident, the Bob-man accepted my answers, even when I said that I didn't know, which was my answer to a lot of his questions.

As he left he rubbed his head and said, 'Here's something for you to think about youngster. No-one has ever done anything like this to me before and lived.'

'Am I really that valuable to you?'

'Right now, yes.'

Two days later he returned and asked the same questions again. Each time I saw him, he wore a different suit. They were all well-cut and expensive-looking, always with a white shirt. This one was navy

137

blue and he had matched it with a yellow tie. He brought with him a man in a long white coat who took blood samples. When the man had gone I said,

'It would be nice if you would tell me your name, you know.'

'I'm not nice though youngster. Put your shoes on, we're going to meet some very important people.'

He led me out of the room and down a long white corridor.

'What is this place... Sir?'

'It's a mental health institute. We use it for the politicos.'

'Politicos?'

'People who get too interested in politics. It's not good for your mental health. They get cured of that here.'

'You mean your opponents.'

'Not really. There aren't any opponents to speak of. We get a few, bound to, but we flush them out.'

'So even people who agree with you get the treatment if they get too involved in things?'

'There's nothing really to agree with. We chop and change. At one time everybody had to accept the same religion and we controlled who became priests. Then there was a period when we went in for common ownership.' He sneered the words. 'That was a joke. Everybody owned everything but of course we looked after it all for the masses. Now, we're in favour of people working for themselves and even running their own businesses - subject to our rules of course - and if they can't afford to buy healthcare or education or whatever, that's too bad, they get what they've earned enough to pay for. That's a surprisingly popular idea with the majority of people. They think they've got quite a bit and they can see folk who are poorer than them and that makes them feel good. It doesn't really matter what system we choose. When one feels used up, we just move on to another. As long as people do what they are told that's all that matters. It's what most people want. They want to feel there's a reliable system and they want to know there's someone worse off than them.'

'Who does the telling?'

'We do.'

'We?'

'The ruling class.'

'And how do you get to be a part of the ruling class?'

'Born into it usually. Occasionally men force their way into it.
It's always better to have powerful men...' he searched for a phrase.

'Inside the tent pissing out rather than outside pissing in?'

The Bob-man smiled. 'Yes! Nice phrase youngster. I shall
remember that. You make it up?'

'It was said by an American president.'

'See? There you go. Your world is no different to ours. People
are the same.'

'It is different. Large parts of it are anyway.'

'Oh is it. And I suppose you're lucky enough to live in one of
the different bits?'

'I am actually yes. People can vote for who they want.'

'And let me guess, these men who they vote for, are they all part
of the ruling class?'

I didn't answer.

'Well? Did they all go to the same exclusive schools? The same
few colleges?'

'Not all of them. Some are women anyway.'

'But are they all from the same families? Generation after
generation?'

'Some of them aren't.'

'And whoever you vote for, nothing really changes?'

'Yes it does. It must do. Some things do...'

'You know what youngster, we need to talk more about your
world. I've got a feeling I could learn a lot.' The Bob-man pushed
open a door into a reception area. A group of younger men in
uniform were standing around talking. When they saw him they all
turned and stood stiffly to attention. They saluted.

It was a salute to make my heart sink. Not quite the same, but
close. Very close. The right arm was bent slightly at the elbow, and
the hand was clenched into a fist. It was still sickening though.

The Bob-man led me outside. I looked across parkland. There
was a faint reddish haze and the air had an acid taste. We headed
towards a large car parked just in front of the building. It was a

curiously old-fashioned vehicle with a long bonnet and boot and a lot of chrome.

'Get in the back.'

I got in. There was a large man in a cheap suit in the front passenger seat and a familiar figure in the back.

'Bettony!'

'Dave! Are you ok?'

She nodded. A huge grin split her face but it showed up wrinkles that I hadn't seen before. She looked thinner and was black under the eyes. I bet I do too, I thought.

'Ok cut the hen-clucking. Silence from now on unless you want to do the rest of the trip in the boot.' The Bob-man had got in the driver's seat. Dave and I looked at each other and smiled. We didn't speak though.

We had both learned about the Bob-man.

** ** **

There were no seat belts in this car, which felt very odd. It floated like a sponge over the country roads and rolled around corners sending us sliding across the wide, leather back seat and into each other. It wasn't long before I began to feel nauseous. After a few miles we joined a dual carriageway and the Bob-man immediately pulled into the outside lane which was coloured a faded red. I guessed it was a reserved lane, there were quite a few smaller cars on the road but none in our lane. He accelerated hard. The car's engine roared.

'Oh I do love to do this,' he said. 'I must be an old softy at heart.' He turned to his passenger. 'What do you say?'

'Sir.'

The Bob-man looked at me in his mirror. There was almost a Bob-like twinkle in his eye.

Almost but not. There was vicious menace there too if you looked closely.

Soon the huge bare fields on either side gave way to heavy industry. Some areas were endless low warehouses. Others were covered in thick metal pipes that eventually linked up to tall chimneys belching a variety of thick coloured smoke into the air. An hour later we were driving through the centre of a city, still on the dual carriageway and the car's speed unchanged. I looked out at closely-packed apartment blocks, fifty or sixty floors high. Some were bridged high-up by crude walkways. Several of the walkways had collapsed, leaving stubby projections of concrete. For a while a river ran beside the road, slow-moving and almost black, its surface stained here and there a bright orange. Then suddenly we were out in the countryside again. In time, the road simply tapered into single carriageway and began to wind its way between small woods and hedges. The fields here were small and the car's vents blew fresher, cleaner air onto our faces. The traffic had been thinning for a while; now we were the only car on the road.

The Bob-man suddenly clutched at his head with his right hand. 'Hell's teeth,' he said. The car veered across the road and with an effort he pulled it back with his left hand, still holding his right hand to his head.

'You ok sir?' Mr Cheap Suit asked.

'Yes.' He rubbed the side of his head, and drove on. A minute later he gasped, and his right hand returned to the side of his head. 'No. No I'm not. Hell.' He drove on for a few more seconds, right hand pressed against his head and the car slewing all over the road. Then he said 'Aaah.' It wasn't loud but it was unnaturally high-pitched and it conveyed a lot of pain. Suit was looking at the Bob-man in alarm. We all were. We watched his left hand leave the steering wheel to join his right but before it could reach his head he slumped forward and to the right, wedging between the big steering wheel and the door.

The car bounced off the road. Suit was making a grab for the wheel but the Bob-man had trapped it with his body. Suit wrestled at the wheel and didn't see the tree directly in front of us.

I did.

'Down!' I yelled at Dave. We both ducked down and moments later were propelled into the luxuriously padded backs of the front seats as the car slammed into the tree, then seemed to pivot and twist and spin, ending on its roof and sliding through bushes.

It all seemed to last forever and yet take no time at all. Dave and I were thrown around, colliding with bits of car and each other among the cacophony of screaming metal and shattering glass and tearing wood.

Then there was stillness.

At first all I could do was listen. I did not lose consciousness but it took time for my body and my brain to start functioning again. For a while I half-lay, half-sat on what had been the roof, propped against the side of the car. There was a hissing coming from somewhere and the sound of a wheel still turning. Apart from that, complete silence. Eventually my brain fired up and I realised I needed to get out. Mr Suit looked at first glance as though he was trying to climb through the shattered front windscreen, but he was dead. If he wasn't, with his neck at that angle, he needed to be in a circus. The Bob-man was barely visible among all the metal that crushed into him. I could smell a strange mixture of oil and petrol and tortured metal mixed with crushed wood and leaves. Next to me Dave started coughing.

'Come on' I said, trying to pull her with me as I scrabbled my way across the car. The window on my side was smashed to pieces. She began to crawl after me and we dragged ourselves out of the car, then further down the bushy slope into which it had plummeted. I managed to put twenty metres between myself and the car before I collapsed onto soft grass. Dave pulled herself along next to me.

'You ok?' She asked.

'I think so. Everything seems to be working and no real cuts. Bit shaky though. You?'

'Same. Amazing really.'

'One advantage of being small. The car rolled around us.'

She laughed. 'Did it? Those seats helped.'

'Yeah.'

'What just happened?'

'He's been complaining of headaches on and off ever since I landed the kick on his head. It's possible I did more damage to him than he realised. If I caused an internal bleed it could take this long to build up pressure and give him a stroke. Or it could've been nothing to do with that. But I live in hope.' I rolled onto my back and looked up at grey clouds. Felt wet on my face. 'Great. Just what we need. It's raining. Come on Dave we need to keep moving.'

We staggered on, making our way down the slope and into a wood. By now the delayed shock was setting in, I was shaking badly and barely conscious. We were into a river before I even realised. One moment I was on dry land, the next I was paddling water, then I was out of my depth, being pulled along by the current. It took my last reserves of strength to make it to the other bank. I managed to lift myself out of the water and flopped onto muddy ground. I was cold and completely soaked and the shaking was becoming uncontrollable.

'Dave!'

'I'm here Bettony.' She was just to my left, further up the bank. Her face looked ashen. At any moment she was going to collapse. I managed to get onto hands and knees, then pushed myself upright by an act of will and we stumbled a few metres up and on to dryer land. Dave dropped to her knees and I wanted so badly to join her. Instead I managed to blurt out, 'Can't stop here. Too wet. Die of cold. Too open. Be seen.' I pointed across the field. 'Barn. Dry. Out of sight.'

'Uh.' Dave managed to nod. We reeled across the grass like a pair of drunks but we got to the old building and pushed our way through a gap in the walls and almost fell onto a fire being tended by a bundle of rags, somewhere inside of which must have been a very thin man.

I saw him stare at me in shock and then I passed out.

CHAPTER THIRTEEN

In which I find out if all the inhabitants of Erce are bad.

I gradually became aware of the heat of the fire. Apart from the crackling and spitting of burning wood there was silence. I opened my eyes and looked around. We were both lying on some old sacking, Dave next to me, both of us close to the fire. Her eyes were still closed.

My left arm was numb from being trapped under my body. I sat up and rubbed it. My clothes were still damp but they were drying in the heat of the fire. The shaking had stopped.

The bundle of rags was sitting across the other side of the fire, looking at us. 'Just fancy eh? Needing the central heating on in June. Arctic winds, that's what it is.' His voice was thin and high-pitched. Cultured.

Frightened.

'Whatever next' he added.

I nodded.

After a while he broke the silence again.

'Are you boys in some sort of trouble?'

'Girls.'

'Pardon?'

'We girls are in some sort of trouble.'

'Girls!' He stared.

'Ok women.'

Another long silence. Eventually he said, 'Women in trousers eh? Whatever next' and half-smiled.

Silence again. To break it, I said, 'I'm Bettony. This is Dave.'

'Those are men's names.'

'It's a long story.'

He nodded. Apparently that was all the explanation I needed to give him.

'Who're you?' I asked.

'I seem to remember that a long time ago I was Benedict.'

Benedict! Benedict Erwin! It had to be.

So the rumours were true. No wonder Sir Edwin had looked worried the last time Hugo had seen him. It had been his yacht, of course; that was well known. The story was that it had been stolen.

But Sir Edwin himself? Crean shook his head. Impossible. The man was the living embodiment of the Regency.

Crean often thought about Benedict, and his mysterious disappearance some years ago. That was put out as a boating accident, of course. But a boating accident could mean anything. When someone disappeared people never enquired too much. A lot of people disappeared. A lucky few returned. They were different though, the ones who returned. Quieter.

It didn't pay to be too inquisitive.

Crean wondered if Benedict ever understood the value of their friendship at boarding school. Without Crean's muscular protection, he was sure that Erwin would have fallen victim to the grotesque bullying that was almost encouraged by the Masters as a form of sport. Character-building, they called it. It revolted Crean. Benedict had arrived at Hinton aged fifteen, an outsider to the boys who had long since formed their own friendship groups. He would have been an outsider from day one though. Quiet-natured, intelligent and sensitive, everything about him was the opposite to what Hinton sought to develop in the boys who were destined to be the future leaders of Angland. The packs of boys eyeing up the harmless-looking new-boy reminded Hugo of wolves, watching a small animal that had wandered into their territory. It would not be long before they attacked. Without really knowing why, Crean had gone out of his way to openly befriend Erwin. No-one would harm the new-boy if he was under Crean's protection. Hinton had its bullies, who went around in groups. It had its fighters - large boys who simply loved to hit other boys. It even had the odd crazy boy, who if attacked would stab and bite and use any weapon that was to hand. But no-one messed with Crean. Not unless they wanted a lengthy spell in the San, and - worse than this - the humiliation of being watched by everyone else as they sprawled, bloodied and semi-conscious and usually tearful, before being dragged away by unsympathetic teachers.

The strange thing was, the friendship that developed became a very strong one that benefitted them both. Hugo's natural kindness found encouragement, and flourished. He learned to balance force with compassion.

He owed a lot to Benedict Erwin.

He had to read on, now. He had to learn what had happened to his old and very dear friend.

** ** **

'But you're not Benedict any more?'

He smiled again, sadly. 'As you can see, now I am nothing.'

Dave stirred. She looked around for a moment, eyes wide, then sat up.

'Bettony. Who's this?'

'This is Benedict. How are you?'

'I'm ok.' She moved arms and legs experimentally. 'Yep. Ok. Ow! More or less. A bit bruised.'

'How do you do Dave?'

'Hello Benedict.'

The sound of dogs barking, very faint, broke the silence.

'It's ok' Benedict said. 'They were closer a while ago.'

'I suspect they'll be back.'

'Are you so important? Women in trousers though, I suppose you have to be.'

'We should go,' I said. 'We don't want to get you into trouble.'

'They won't be back for a while. They didn't even get as close as the river and I doubt they could track you across that. Lucky for you it rained, it makes things even more difficult for them.'

'How long were we out?' Dave asked.

'Quite a while. I took the liberty of making you comfortable on the furniture -' he indicated the sacking - 'and built the fire up.'

'Thank you.'

'You're very welcome.' He reached beside him and picked up a plastic box. 'Would you like something to eat? Freshly cooked rabbit on a bed of chickweed salad. Delicious spring water to wash it down with.'

We both politely declined.

'I think you should, you know. There's plenty to go around. Such a big and beautiful rabbit, I felt so guilty depriving him of his life. But needs must when the devil's a driver, as they say.' He held out the box. 'Take some.'

The smell of cooked meat made me realise how hungry I was. He nodded, as though he could read my thoughts. 'Honestly. Today is a good day for provisions and summer's advent enricheth the ground, as the poet says. You won't be taking food from my mouth.'

'Thank you.'

Dave and I ate and drank. The sound of the dogs was becoming fainter and fainter. Little by little we all began to relax. If you're expecting me to say, *The food was surprisingly good* at this point I'm afraid you're going to be disappointed, but it was well-cooked and filling and there was plenty for the three of us.

'Why do you live like this?' I asked. 'You're obviously an educated and intelligent man.'

'Intelligence is not always an advantage in our society is it? For much of my childhood I was *home schooled* - this phrase was emphasised as though it were a naughty admission. 'My mother wanted me to understand and appreciate the wealth of culture and learning we still have. Hardly any of it is taught, a lot of it is actively suppressed. Father was a district administrator so she was able to do this. But I learned to question things.' Benedict flashed his eyes mischievously. 'To think for myself. Some people can hide such instincts and fit in. But I never learned that most important skill of all: I was never very good with people. I never understood how to be one of the chaps, one of the crowd. Eventually it just seemed safer to... live like this.'

'That is so sad.'

'Thank you Dave. But I have so much. All the flora and fauna. Time to think. Space to relax in. Clean air.' He poked at the fire. 'I do miss having someone to talk to though. So don't feel guilty about taking my food. Feel pleased that you have given something much more important to me... your company.'

The light was fading. When dusk turned to night Benedict took some sacking and went to sleep at the other end of the barn, 'To give us some privacy' as he put it.

Dave and I talked in low voices and described our separate experiences after the Bob-man knocked me out. Dave told me the Bob-man had to make two journeys in the Series Two, which was only designed for one person and was very cramped. Sputteridge in this world is a highly fortified place, she said. No houses, and no pub, but a lot of soldiers and various large guns all pointed at the gap where the TV would be. Someone there had checked me and pronounced me all right. We were then both injected with something, to keep us quiet the Bob-man had said. Dave remembered us being put in his car before she passed out. When she came round she was in a room at the "Mental Health Institute".

'How did you get on with Bob's look-alike?' Dave whispered. I described his sadism. Dave nodded. 'Same here,' she said. 'Same finger. He must enjoy doing that.' She flexed her hand tentatively.

'Past tense I think now Dave.'

'Yeah.' Dave paused. 'They found the emergency beacon that Mrs Ponch had given me.'

'When did she give you that?'

'When we had our little private talks. I told her what I thought Dave Morland had worked out.'

'Ah yes... I got there in the end Dave. I'd watched him eat my mayonnaise. And missed the importance of it! It took ages for me to remember that mayonnaise's got egg in it and you lot can't eat eggs. And then the blood on Vic's knuckles...'

Dave laughed mirthlessly. 'Well we can eat eggs, it just kills us.' She nodded at some private inner thought. 'Yeah, the blood on Vic's knuckles. It didn't really mean that much on its own did it? Just another of those little things that didn't make sense. Hardly worth killing someone for, was it?' She added bitterly. She took a moment to compose herself, then went on, 'Mrs P was already on to what you call the Bob-man. It's true what you said, he looked like Bob but he talked and behaved very differently. I reckon he was fatter too. How on Abbuth he thought she wouldn't pick all that up, I don't know.'

'Well Mrs Ponch is just a woman. You couldn't expect her to be clever enough...'

Dave looked at me for a moment, then chuckled quietly and shook her head. 'This is a crazy world. They measure a person's intelligence based on whether they're a man or a woman or even the colour of their skin. They seem to think the paler your skin, the cleverer you are. How weird is that? And what does that make Dave Green? His skin's nearly black. By their measurement that should mean despite having a higher degree in mathematical biology and winning the Corngreave Yalta prize for his work on stochastic DNA variation, he's some kind of half-wit.'

'Mmm.'

'Even so this joker must have had a strangely high view of his abilities if he thought he could pass himself off as Bob.'

'I wonder where Bob is.'

'Me too.'

And how he is, I thought. Please let him be alive.

'Mrs P was also becoming suspicious of Vinny,' Dave went on. 'And she trusted me enough to tell me she thought the armament was a set-up. I don't get how they identified my DNA on it, I can't believe Greeny is one of this lot. I've known him for years. That man is definitely the Bollie Sneggs we all know and love.'

'You have some great names you know.'

'Says the woman who thinks Kevin is a cool moniker.'

'That's not the name, Dave, that's the body.'

I told Dave about how her double's DNA was used.

'Sheesh.' Dave dropped her voice to an even quieter whisper. 'She gave me two beacons though Bettony. She said she had a bad feeling. She gave me the standard one and a miniature one. They only found the standard one.' She smiled. 'The Bob-man wasn't the only one who could do distraction.'

'Where did you hide it? Actually don't answer that I'm not sure I want to know... So we've got a beacon?'

'Yeah. We have the means to escape from this place. The trouble is, the TV will only transition across realities. Not across distance. So we need to get back to Sputteridge before we set the beacon off.'

'And hope that Mrs Ponch has sussed Vinny out and ... what? Replaced him with Kevin? Or Dildow?'

'Or does the transition herself? She's a qualified engineer too. I reckon all the problems come from Vinny being out of his depth and Kevin too much of a rule-follower to challenge him. Once they remove Vinny they'll be ok.'

'That makes sense. But when? How will we know?'

'Dunno.' Dave shook her head.

'And if Sputteridge is as heavily guarded as you say, even if the TV turns up - then what? All we'll have done is the Bob-man's job for him.'

'Yeah... that also makes sense.'

We both stared at the fire.

'What about the Series Two?' Dave said. 'Maybe we could use that. It might not be so heavily guarded. If we've got the beacon it doesn't matter where we end up. As long as we can use the beacon they'll be able to find us.'

'Can't we use the Series Two to get home? - To get to your home, I mean?'

'In theory, yes. But I would need to be able to understand the transition logs, compensate for where we are and then program the co-ordinates with one hundred per cent accuracy. That's a bit beyond my nav skills. It's going to be much easier to go to some random place and then set the beacon off. Kevin should be able to entangle the Series Four with the Series Two and bring it home.'

'Huh?'

'Connect the two machines so that at the quantum level they are effectively one. So that what happens to one happens to the other.'

'I've no idea what that means but it sounds good. How do we get into the Series Two? It must have a lock of some sort.'

'There's an emergency access mechanism. Basically you just twiddle two of what look like retaining nuts on one of the edges.'

'I like this idea more and more Dave.'

'We still need to get back to Sputteridge.'

'This is a different country in many ways but the geography will be the same. We both know this place. If we can work out where we are, at least we shall know which way to go.'

'We can hardly hitch a lift though. And we'll still need to eat and drink.'

Our conversation was becoming increasingly slow. By now there was just a dull glow from the remains of the fire. Benedict had begun lightly snoring.

'If we can work out where we are we might be able to figure out how to get to Cornwall.'

'Could be a long walk.'

'At least it's a plan... Dave?'

She was asleep.

Before long we both were.

** ** **

I was woken by Benedict tugging at my arm.

'You need to wake up,' he said. 'We haven't got very long before they find you.'

I heard the dogs again. They were still a fair way away.

'They seem to be very persistent. Sooner or later they will cross the river. Even if they don't pick up a scent they'll have a look in the barn. Bound to. Here drink this.'

I swallowed a surprisingly tasty liquid which Benedict said was a stock, made from the bones of last night's meal. He must have been awake for a long time. Dave was awake now as well.

'Can you tell us where we are?' I picked up a stick and started to scratch out a rough map of Britain on the dusty floor. 'We need to get here -'

'No!' Benedict stopped me and rubbed the outline away with his foot. His voice was panicky. 'Don't tell me where you're going.'

'Huh?'

'If you don't tell me then I won't be able to tell them.'

'So you're pretty sure they will come here?'

He didn't answer.

'And... they will know that we've been here - how? From the reaction of the dogs?'

A small nod. 'I think that's quite likely.'

'So you're in big trouble. They'll probably think you know stuff about us even when you don't so you'll be put through a lot of pain just to make sure you've told them everything.'

No response.

'Benedict!'

'It was my choice.'

Dave reached out to take his hand but he instinctively drew away from her. She said, 'You're a good man Benedict.'

'Thank you. You need to move.'

'How long has this been your home?' I asked.

'A while.' He made a strange dipping movement with his head. 'The farmer was... known to my father so he leaves me alone.'

'Come with us.'

'I'll be fine. I'll find somewhere until all this calms down and then I'll come back here.'

'As you said Benedict we are important. I'm really sorry but I don't think this will all calm down. I don't think you will be able to come back here safely. Not for a long time. They'll find you and want to find out all you know about us.'

'Ah well. Our fate doth run so contrary to our will.'

'Nice words. You're coming with us. What do you say Dave?'

'Absolutely. We're not going to leave you.'

'No. I would only slow you down. And I don't know where you think you could go that's safer than here...'

'Trust me. There is somewhere. I'm being very honest here Benedict, if you came with us it would give us a much better chance of survival. You can find food for us. You know the layout of the land. We've got a long journey ahead of us and neither of us has a clue how to skin a rabbit. If you come with us we'll be more likely to get away.'

He sat on the floor, ignoring me. 'There's nowhere to get away to,' he muttered.

'Yes there is. There really is. A nice place where you will be safe and not have to live in a wreck of a barn.' I sat next to him. The barking of the dogs was getting louder.

'You must go!' There was an edge of panic to his voice.

Dave came and sat the other side of him. 'Not without you,' she said.

We were like that for several minutes, the three of us sitting side by side, silent and motionless, playing a strange game of chicken. The dogs sounded quite close now. Benedict began picking feverishly at his rags. Finally he stood up and said, 'You are both very silly. I'll see you safely away from here.'

'I shall take that as a Yes,' I replied.

'Take it how you want.' He poured the rest of the stock into a plastic bottle, picked up a few pots and pans, some wires and a bottle of water and stuffed everything into a small sack. He slung the sack over his shoulder and headed towards a gap in the far wall of the barn.

'Come along then.'

He led us away from the sound of the dogs, down a hill and across grassy fields. The river had wound its own leisurely way around the hill and was in front of us again now. Benedict led us down to the bank where a rowing boat was tied under an overhanging willow. He untied the rope that secured it.

'Get in.'

He manoeuvred the boat out to the centre of the river and allowed it to drift downstream, making gentle movements with the oars to keep us pointing the right way and central in the stream. 'Another crime to add to your list,' he said. 'Theft of a rowing boat.'

'We're not criminals.'

'You are now.'

** ** **

153

We drifted through woods and between overhanging trees and bushes for several hours. Eventually Benedict steered the boat to a bank.

'We're about four miles from the barn in a straight line. Although nothing happens around here in a straight line.' The truculence had gone from his voice. He didn't seem like someone who could hold a sulk for very long. 'The river runs across open countryside from here, but we can follow the tree line overland for a fair way, either north or south. We can tie the boat up under these bushes. No-one should spot it for a while. I suppose it all depends on which direction you want to go.'

'Thank you Benedict.'

'Thank you Benedict.'

'Hmm. You'd better explain where you're going then and why it's so safe.'

We sat for a while on a fallen willow trunk. Once again I found a stick and drew out a crude map of southern Britain on the ground. I pointed at Cornwall.

'Cornwall, yes, I know it. We used to go on holiday there when I was a child. Though why you should think Cornwall is safe...' He looked from one to the other of us. 'You know it's a reserved area? In fact more so than around here. It's red all the way from the Tamar ferry.'

This may not be a good time to reveal either the full extent of our ignorance or our ultimate destination, I thought.

'Do you know Truro, Benedict?'

'Truro?... oh Tre-Uro. You do have an unusual way of pronouncing certain words, you know. I have noticed that. Are you foreign? ... Ah, I see. You mean to escape over the sea.'

'Sort of.'

'Are you spies?'

'No.'

'Do you mean harm to Angland?'

'No! Certainly not!'

'It's ok. I'm not sure you could do it much more harm than the Regency is already managing. If any.'

'We're not spies.'

'But you are foreign?'

'Not really.'

'Methinks the lady doth too much confusion sow.'

'It's difficult to tell you everything Benedict. I promise that we will, as we gain your confidence.'

'Hmm.'

'We have trusted you with our lives,' Dave said. 'Will you in return trust us now?'

'With my life?'

She shook her head. 'Why not just trust us?'

Benedict stared at her. 'What an unusual suggestion. And yet... yes, why not indeed. I cannot remember the last time I met anyone in whom I would feel comfortable placing my trust. You are clearly fugitives and quite important ones at that, but despite that, I do feel drawn to trusting you. Or maybe because of it. How bizarre... What a strange twist my life is taking.' He sighed. 'Tre-Uro is a long way. With me here to slow you down it could take all summer.'

'With you here to help us at least we'll get there,' I said.

'And am I permitted to know what happens in Tre-Uro?'

'Nothing happens in Tr... Tre-Uro itself. We're aiming for a small village further west, along the coast.'

'I see. From whence you hope to reach your ship and flee to safety.'

'Sort of.'

'Hmm.'

'Can you tell me where we are now?'

Benedict took the stick and pointed to an area vaguely north of what I would know as Southampton. Or maybe Bournemouth... Or Portsmouth. Somewhere in that lower middle bit anyway.

I didn't do much geography at school.

'Better get going then. South I think will suit us. To start with, anyway.'

We let Benedict set the pace. It was slow. At first he refused our offers to share the carrying of the sack, but eventually he gave in. It wasn't heavy but carrying it seemed to tire him, so Dave and I took turns, refusing his offers to take it back. Every so often he would reach down and scoop up some weeds or sticks and push them into the sack. No-one spoke much.

We stopped mid-afternoon, in a small copse. By now we were walking across open ground but we were following the line of a shallow valley. For anyone to see us they would have to be pretty close. There were no houses visible, and no roads.

Benedict scooped a shallow hole. He arranged bits of dead grass and some of the twigs he had collected, and nursed a fire into life. He placed larger sticks to form a square and rested a small pan on them. The weeds and stalks went into the pan along with a little water and some of the stock. It took a while but eventually we were taking turns to spoon a sort of vegetable soup out of the pan.

The success of his meal seemed to give Benedict confidence.

'We shall soon approach the limits of my empire,' he said. 'After that I only have a rough idea of the land. We shall have to rely on the sun for our direction. We shall be more at risk of discovery. There are many weeks of peril ahead of us, ladies.'

He wandered away to set snares.

'Ladies!' I huffed.

'Easy Bettony. Remember what sort of a society he comes from.'

We lay back and stared at the sky. Somewhere a bird was singing; there was no other sound.

** ** **

Benedict rejoined us and we rested for a while. I commented on his boots, which were strong and expensive-looking, if rather tatty.

'I do all my shopping at the bespoke commercial outlet to the east of my mansion. Only those without style would refer to it as a landfill site. I think it serves a lot of the restricted zone, so it is the repository for the unwanted items of many people of privilege. It's quite astonishing what people no longer wish to keep.'

By now the fire had died down; Benedict checked his snares - which were all empty - and pushed them back into the sack. We were about to head off when I heard the distant buzz of a small plane. We hid in the copse, watching the skies. After a while it came into view, a single-engine effort, old-fashioned in its design. It was ponderously slow and flying at about five thousand feet. After a short while it headed away north.

'Well well,' Benedict said. 'Whatever next.'

We walked for another few hours. This was traditional English rolling countryside, although with less habitation and much less traffic than the England I knew. There were plenty of woods and copses dotted around. Plenty of places to hide if the plane came back; I had no doubt it was looking for us.

We kept off the roads as much as possible. They were no more than narrow, winding lanes but we had no wish to meet anyone. Sometimes this meant following the line of a hedge across a field, arriving at undergrowth that was too choked with brambles and bushes to continue, and having to retrace our steps. It was all very tiring, and the soup had been a small meal. Hunger gnawed at my stomach.

At least the weather was improving. There was a very light breeze, and the clouds had thinned and mostly gone, leaving us the warmth of a late evening sun. Eventually we stopped in one of the many woods we had been fighting our way through. Benedict nursed a fire into life, set his snares, and we ate another meal of vegetable soup.

It probably wasn't the best night's sleep I've ever had, but it wasn't bad. I must have been very tired. When Dave and I woke Benedict was preparing another soup - this time with pieces of roast rabbit meat. We ate, did our best to hide any trace that we had been there, and set off. I heard the plane again, not long after. The sound was faint and soon faded away completely.

We trudged on, through woods, across fields, occasionally down narrow lanes. Every so often Benedict would drop back, stooping to examine plants and pulling some up to add to the sack.

'It's going to be a vegetable lunch again I'm afraid,' he said. 'At least we had a nourishing breakfast to set us on our way.'

We stopped for lunch on the edge of a small field that was almost completely surrounded by trees. It had been sunny and warm all morning; the sky was clouding over again now, but it was still bright. Birdsong occasionally broke the still silence. Benedict wandered away to check his snares. After a while a lark announced itself. I stretched out on the warm grass and stared at the sky. I love lark song. I love staring at the sky.

In another world I would have thought all this was beautiful.

In another world it would have been.

'What do you think our chances are?' Dave whispered, after a while.

'Low.'

'Me too. If we're going to have to survive on weed soup we won't last long.'

I watched clouds scud across a patch of blue, closing it out. 'I feel really guilty about getting him involved with us.'

'I know. He's so lovely isn't he? He seemed to be quite content in his little barn.'

'He wasn't though.' Benedict had moved through the trees in a half-circle and come up behind us. He was so close that he made us both jump. 'He wasn't content at all. He had relaxed into a self-indulgent sadness of missing out on an imagined world where culture is celebrated and gentle people can be trusted. Left on his own, little by little he would probably go mad, if the winters did not claim him first. Don't confuse my resigned acceptance with contentment.'

'Jimminy Krankie, Benedict! Please don't creep up like that. My heart is only so strong.'

'Sorry Dave. That was wrong of me.'

There was an awkward silence.

'Let's tell him,' Dave said. 'Let's tell him everything.'

Benedict looked at her. 'You should agree between yourselves first that that is the right thing to do.'

'We're going to have to tell you sooner or later,' I said. 'May as well be now. But I warn you, it's going to sound crazy. You're going to think we're nuts.'

'Oh dear. I had begun to think that you were both rather sane.'

'Draw on that belief, Benedict. You're going to need it.'

We gave him a potted summary of ourselves and how we had arrived at Erce. He listened, expressionless, and then reached out and prodded my arm.

'It's strange,' he said, 'you feel real enough. You promise me all that I crave for; magical entry to a world where freedom and learning are held dear, and difference is celebrated. But I don't think you're a figment of my imagination. And the plane sounded real. And the dogs too.'

'We are real Benedict.'

'The Bob-man, as you describe him, sounds like Regency Lord Lieutenant Slepwood.'

** ** **

Slepwood! Crean whistled quietly to himself. No wonder the old sadist hadn't been seen. There had even been the odd rumour about Slepwood having been 'disappeared'. Crean had never believed that. This made a lot more sense. And this slip of a girl had done it! Hugo Crean glowed with vicarious pride.

** ** **

'If you really did cause Slepwood's death then no wonder the police guard are after you. My word. Perhaps you should have let me continue to believe you were spies. And your spacecraft is in a village near Tre-Uro that isn't actually there? But somehow it is?'

'We probably haven't explained it too well.'

'Hmm.'

'Will you stay with us?'

'Oh yes. Despite the fantastical nature of your tale, our low chance of success and the limited range of our cuisine. This is all so curious that I am agog to discover its conclusion.'

'That sounds like the plane again.'

'Yes. And it sounds real. So we should withdraw to the shelter of the trees.'

We headed back into the undergrowth.

159

'You know, I have feared a descent into madness for some time.'

'We're real Benedict.'

'No-one but myself to talk to. And often I don't even listen to what I'm saying.'

'We're real.'

'Does a madman know that he is mad? Ouch!'

'Sorry. I wanted to make the point that a figment of your imagination wouldn't punch you in the face.'

'Owww.'

'Steady on Bettony.' - This from Dave.

'It's ok Benedict, I didn't hit you very hard. Oh... Here, use my hankie.'

'This blood certainly looks real.'

'Yes. Sorry. But there you go. Er. Keep my hankie, and if you start to doubt your sanity pull it out and look at the blood.'

'Hmm. Or I could just feel the bruise.'

'It's only a scratch. Honest.'

** ** **

We reached the edge of the wood and I looked out at a meadow, dropping away in front of us towards a railway line. The tracks approached us from behind a bank of trees, supported across a shallow valley by an embankment, and by a bridge at its deepest part. A lane wound its way down the hill to my left and then curled to the right under the bridge.

'What line is that?' I asked.

'It must be the Solsbury to Escanceaster line.'

There was a distant chuff chuff of a steam engine.

'Is it a heritage line?'

'A what?'

'A steam line.'

'Well yes, I suppose so.'

'So it's a steam line run by enthusiasts? We call them heritage lines in my world.'

160

'I realise that you're talking what sounds like Anglish, Bettony, and indeed I fully understand each individual word. It's just the sentence that I'm struggling with.'

The steam train heaved into view and we stepped back into the wood.

'Is Escanceaster a village?'

'Hardly. It's the county town of Devonshire.'

Escanceaster...Exeter. He must mean Exeter. My heart began to beat faster.

The train was pulling trucks. Many of the open ones were filled with coal. Some appeared to be empty.

'Are all your trains steam powered?' Dave asked.

'Yes. Of course.'

'So this is the main line?'

'Indeed it is. Probably three or four trains an hour.'

The train thundered past, following the line as it curved away to our right.

'Does the line finish in Escanceaster,' I asked, 'or does it carry on?'

'Well it continues to Sutton Plymouth... ah. I think I can follow you now. Yes. The line itself goes as far as Penzance, in the far west of Cornwall. And of course on its way it passes through Tre-Uro.'

We watched the train disappear into the distance.

'It would certainly save a lot of time,' Benedict said. 'But I think the authorities would be somewhat suspicious if we turned up at Solsbury station asking for tickets. We cut distinctive and easily recognisable figures, all three of us. Especially me. Well, especially all of us actually.'

'I saw this old film once,' I said. 'These people were escaping from somewhere, and they jumped onto a train from a bridge.'

'And did they break their legs?'

'No.'

'I think the key word there is, Film.'

'You saw how the engine was struggling to cope with the gradient. If we follow the line of the tracks, sooner or later we'll come to a bit where it really slows down. We need somewhere where there's a bridge over the tracks for us to climb down from.'

'I may have to say goodbye to you at that point. I fear your athleticism far outstrips my own.'

'No you won't! We're not going to leave you Benedict.'

'Hmm.'

'I have to say I'm with Benedict on this one,' Dave said. 'I admire your optimism, but...'

'Can we at least follow the tracks?' I said. 'At any rate we know they're going in the right direction.'

There was a bit of mumbling and grumbling but we set off along the tracks. I thought about "Flight from Justice" (1948, Starring Bill deLain and Monica Treves, Dir Hubert Wimly, Slough studios) and also about that episode of Thomas the Tank Engine where Big Gordon struggles up the incline. I had to admit, it wasn't an exhaustive exploration of the risks attached to jumping onto a moving train.

✳✳ ✳✳ ✳✳

We walked alongside the line for much of the day. The few trains that passed us were easy to hide from; they were noisy and slow, announcing their presence long before they appeared. We didn't see the plane again. Benedict refilled our water bottles from a small brook that we passed, promising to boil the water before we drank it. The line passed a single station, a small village affair that was easy to avoid.

We didn't find a suitable bridge.

The evening meal was vegetable soup again, and although Benedict had pulled different weeds up, it was a broadly similar taste. My stomach was beginning to knot up at the thought of more soup. At least we had scrabbled a cabbage and a few potatoes from fields as we passed, so it was reasonably substantial.

The next couple of days were much the same, although the weather was becoming noticeably warmer. My woolly jumper joined our various possessions in the sack. We followed the rail tracks as they picked their way through a landscape of gently rolling hills.

162

Cuttings were usually wooded, giving plenty of cover should a train come past. Embankments were more exposed, we left the trackside and walked along the bottom edges of these. On one occasion a cutting deepened into a tunnel. We scrambled up the bank and had to risk using several miles of lanes as we struggled to regain the route of the line, but although we occasionally heard a tractor at work in a field, neither it nor any cars passed us and we saw no-one. We skirted around a couple more village stations without too much difficulty.

I asked Benedict about Angland, which seemed to include the areas covered in our world by Wales and Scotland. The total population was around twenty million, he said. Some areas were reserved, which meant that only those who were born there could live there. Those above certain grades within the Regency could visit, and some owned large houses set in acres of grounds. The most exclusive were the red zones, of which Cornwall was one. Anyone who was found there without permission was sent to a re-education facility. Often people never returned.

'So your father is pretty high up then?'

'Yes. I am a child of privilege. Can't you tell?'

We were probably getting too confident. Without thinking, we had followed the rails into a wide, open field at the bottom of a shallow valley. We were half-way across when we heard the now-familiar sound of a steam engine.

This one was approaching at speed.

There was nowhere to hide. There were hedges on each side, but they were easily a hundred metres away. Helped by the gradient, the train was hammering along. We ran towards the hedge to our left but had covered barely half the distance when I glimpsed the engine heading into view.

'Down!' I shouted. 'Get down!' We dived into the long grass.

They can see us, I thought. If they look - and they have to look - if not the driver, or the guard, then somebody, sitting in a window seat in one of those carriages - they will look and they will see us, dark shapes against the pale grass. They could hardly miss us.

Someone will have seen us.

The train thundered past. It didn't stop, of course it couldn't, but it didn't need to. A report of three suspicious-looking people, passed on at the next station; and who else could we be? The search parties would soon be here.

We waited until the train had disappeared into the distance before we picked ourselves up.

'Oh dear' said Benedict.

'Maybe they didn't see us' Dave suggested. But the tone of her voice said, maybe they did.

We agreed it was safer for us to assume they had. We headed away from the tracks, followed the line of the hedge as far as a gate, climbed it and walked along a lane for a few hundred yards. We headed into a wood, all the time moving further away from the railway.

There were noticeably more woods in this version of England, and few main roads. (The dual carriageway, and the one across which the Bob-man had spread his car, were the only ones I had seen). There was no traffic noise. The lanes were narrow and seemed to be little-used. Hardly surprising, I thought, if the population was a third or less of the Britain I knew.

We found a stream, took off our shoes and socks and stumbled along it for half a mile. We had a vague idea that this might throw any dogs off our scent. Then we rested on a bank, rubbing life back into our cold, numb feet. That was when I heard the plane.

My heart sank.

We waited, while it droned overhead. It seemed to make a couple of passes and then disappeared into the distance. A single dog barked somewhere. It was most likely a farm dog, but it still set the nerves jangling.

'Time to move, methinks' Benedict said.

We kept under cover of the wood for as long as we could, then followed a line of trees that ran alongside a lane. We were still trying to regain the railway line, and could even hear the occasional train in the distance. What use was the railway line, I thought, when following it left us visible from the air for so much of the time? But we had no other plan, and it was still leading us in the right direction.

We kept under cover as much as we could and headed back towards the west, towards the sounds of the trains.

That was how we came across the trucks.

There was a long line of them in a siding, some made of metal and open to the elements, some taller, wooden and covered with tarpaulins. Somewhere up ahead, at the front of the trucks, a goods engine coughed steam and smoke into the air, waiting for its turn on the main line.

Benedict managed a thin smile. 'No need for gymnastics from a bridge then.'

'We don't know what direction it's going to go,' I pointed out.

'It's either going to be towards Escanceaster or away from it' Dave answered. She peered along the track. 'The engine's pointing in the right direction so I'd say that gives us a better than evens chance. It's make your mind up time anyway. I don't know much about steam engines but that one seems to be about to go.'

'Look at this!' I pointed at the side of a truck. Chalked in capital letters was "PZ". 'Penzance?'

The back two both had the same marks. The ones in front of them were marked, "S/Plm". All of this section were the wooden type.

'It's got to be Penzance,' I said, 'and those in front are for Sutton Plymouth.'

'Makes sense to me,' said Dave. 'But it really is time to move. Either that or we watch it go.'

There was a clanking of metal, as the slack between the trucks was taken up. Far ahead, the steam engine began chuffing and coughing frantically. Very slowly, the trucks' wheels began to turn.

Dave pulled the tarpaulin back and climbed into the wooden truck at the back of the train, and between us we helped Benedict. He seemed to have no strength to manage on his own, but he was surprisingly light and was quickly manhandled (or rather, womanhandled) into the truck. The train was not so much picking up speed as gradually losing the ability to remain stationary; by the time I clambered in the truck was moving at a slow walking pace.

The truck was maybe a quarter full of packages of various sizes. We made ourselves as comfortable as we could and Dave pulled the tarpaulin back over us. It was threadbare. Light filtered through it, and also between the gaps in the planking that made up the truck's wooden sides.

I felt a huge sense of relief. After so much trudging along it felt good to rest, knowing that we were moving steadily and unseen towards our goal.

I picked up one of the parcels.

'Parkers of Penzance,' I said. 'Assorted nails.'

'Beautiful words,' Dave replied. 'In fact never have the words "assorted nails" sounded so welcome.'

'Shouldn't there be a guard's van? I asked.

'This is Angland,' Benedict replied. 'On a paper of authorisation somewhere, there is probably a statement to the effect that this train has a guard's van attached. So there is indeed a guard's van. It's just that you can't see it.'

** ** **

I'm not going to pretend it was a comfortable journey. We started off sitting on the truck's bare wooden boards, feeling every bump and vibration. After a while we rearranged the parcels, which absorbed some of the sharper jolts, and sat on them.

We had plenty of time to make the best of things. The train often trundled along at little more than walking pace, and rarely went faster than about twenty miles an hour. There were also a lot of stops in sidings, presumably while faster trains went past. But we were moving, and from what we could see of the stations we passed, moving in the right direction. By the time we got to Exeter/Escanceaster it was dark. We were stationary for a long time, but eventually the train pulled away and continued its leisurely journey.

We reached Plymouth. Once again we endured a long period when the train did not move. I guessed by now it was the early hours of the morning. I had managed to doze, briefly, a couple of times, and was slipping into another light sleep when I heard footsteps. It was too dark now to see my companions, but I could sense their alertness and their fear as the footsteps approached. The goods yard had been noisy when we first arrived, but now it was quiet and the stillness of night made the sounds seem louder and more threatening.

Somewhere nearby a steam engine fired up. It sounded small, even compared to the one that had brought us here.

The man (and it would have been a man, in this world) stopped a few feet away from us. There was the clank of metal against metal, then the clash of a heavy chain being released. The footsteps became fainter. The little steam engine coughed into life. I risked a peep through one of the many gaps between the wooden planks and watched the other trucks roll slowly away, leaving ours and the one in front.

'They've uncoupled us' I whispered. 'They're moving the rest of the trucks.'

The trucks moved about fifty metres and then stopped again. A workman appeared from behind them, walked halfway towards us and manoeuvred a huge iron bar by the side of the rails. Points, manually operated. I watched the rails next to him shift their position. He was wandering away from the points when two men approached him. I heard one of them say,

'Is that the one o'clock freight from Solsbury?' The voice was authoritative.

The workman nodded.

'Open up the trucks' the voice commanded.

'Oh dear,' whispered Benedict.

'We might be ok' I said. The workman went to the last truck - the one nearest to us - and pulled back the tarpaulin. A torch was shone into it, then he replaced the tarpaulin. They moved on to the next truck and then each truck after that, moving steadily away from us. I watched the two men stride away and approach a third, who was standing watching them.

'Anything?' The third asked. His voice carried clearly on the night air.

'No sir.'

'We'll have to get the dogs. If they got out here the dogs will pick up their trail. And get me a list of everywhere that train stopped between here and Semley. Hell! They could have got out anywhere, these things go so slow they could have jumped off while it was moving. If we can't pick anything up here or at a stop we'll have to walk the dogs back along the tracks.'

Pushed by a small engine, a single passenger carriage was slowly approaching us on a line that curved in from the right. It crossed the points and came to a halt just as it touched the truck in front of us. Someone jumped down from the engine and coupled the carriage to our two trucks. We began to trundle out of the goods yard. All three of us were peering through slits in the planking. I looked across seven or eight sets of tracks to a small brick building, its windows bright against the darkness. It stood alone among the tracks. The light from the building fell on three men standing just in front of it. They were deep in conversation and didn't even look up as we passed.

'That was close,' whispered Dave.

The train chugged along at a steady pace. Soon we were passing over a wide river. It could only be the Tamar, and that meant we were on target for Truro. With every mile I began to relax a little more. Unlike the last one, this train didn't pull over into a siding every few miles. At this time of night there probably wasn't another train to pull over for. Time went on, the sky began to lighten, still the little train chugged along. The line cut through thickly forested hills, then open countryside, briefly along the coast, and then back inland. I tried to work out where we were, and failed. My eyelids were becoming very heavy. Dave and Benedict both looked asleep. I thought it best if one of us stayed awake, but after all the stress of the day it was getting difficult. I thought it would help if I just rested my eyes for a few seconds...

The truck bashed into the one in front, jolting us awake. Bright daylight shone in through the gaps in the planking and the tarpaulin. We had stopped in what looked like a goods yard. I looked out of the back of the truck, up towards a road bridge. It looked vaguely familiar. From one side of the truck I could see the sea, and quite close by a small hilly island, tapering upwards to a peak on which sat a stately home.

My heart sank.

I recognised St Michael's Mount. This was Penzance.

We had overshot.

CHAPTER FOURTEEN

Thursday Market

We scrambled out and dodged among the various engines and trucks, keeping as many of them as possible between us and the railway buildings which were to the seaward side of the yard. There must have been people somewhere but we didn't see anyone. We climbed a grassy bank, hurried across a lane, and slid down another bank.

The land in front of us was marshy and uncultivated. It looked impassable. We were out of sight of the goods yard and even the lane now, but sooner or later, I thought, we would have to climb back up the bank. There was no other way.

'Listen to me,' Benedict said excitedly. 'I know somewhere we can go, close to here. There is someone whom we can trust.'

'Trust with our lives?' Asked Dave. 'Because that's what it would be. And it would mean putting someone else in danger.'

'We can trust her with our lives.'

'Why not just set off for Tre-Uro?' I asked.

'Because we have no food, we have run out of potable water, I am sure that you are both as hungry and thirsty as me, and above all I am reaching the limit of what I can physically endure. Compared to how far we have travelled, the remaining twenty or so miles to Tre-Uro is nothing much. We ought to be able to do it in a day. But it is more than I can manage. She will offer shelter, allow us time to regain our strength and give us food and water for the last part of our journey.'

'How far away is this person?'

'She lives just this side of Thursday Market. It should be straightforward enough to get to her house without being seen.'

Thursday Market? I thought I knew this part of Cornwall, but I had never heard of such a place.

Excitement had given Benedict new life and we were too tired to argue. He led us along the bottom of the bank, close to the edge of the marsh, keeping the lane above us and to our right. A second lane ran from left to right in front of us; we crossed this close to where the two met to form a T-junction. We dropped back down, this time to dryer land and Benedict led us to our right, back over the railway line and below the road bridge I had seen from the truck. Our lane had swung right to cross the tracks, and was heading towards the sea which was now only a few yards in front of us. Once over the bridge it turned back to the left to run alongside a beach. We were still keeping to the bottom of the bank and for a while the ground on this side of the lane became marshier again. After two hundred metres it dried and hardened, and joined a track. We followed this to the left, inland, between high bushes, for another few hundred metres.

All the time Benedict was becoming more and more animated. He stopped next to a small gate. Beyond it, a path led through a garden of thick, high flowers to a thatched cottage. He was grinning with delight.

'We're here.' He could have been unveiling the eighth wonder of the world.

'Benedict are you sure about this?'

'I am absolutely sure. Come along.'

An old woman appeared from the side of the house, carrying a garden hoe.

'What do you want? Clear off.' She waved the hoe. 'There's nothing for you here. Go on clear off. I've got a telephone and I'm going to call the guard. Then you'll be sorry.'

This is not good, I thought. But Benedict was still smiling.

'Hello Nanny.'

'What - no. Who are you? ... It can't be.'

Recognition spread across the old woman's face and tears welled in her eyes. 'Benny!'

'Hello Nanny' Benedict repeated. He took two steps forward, and then the effort of will with which he had been holding himself together relaxed, and he collapsed, exhausted.

CHAPTER FIFTEEN

Between us, Dave and I carried Benedict into the cottage. Once again, I was surprised at how light he was. The old woman fussed around us. We took him into her living room and laid him on a sofa. She covered him with a blanket and left the room. He was coming round when she bustled back in with a mug of hot liquid. She plumped up cushions and raised him so that he could drink. His hand was shaking badly and he spilled some of the hot liquid onto the blanket and his clothes.

'Oh my poor Benny. What have you been going through? My poor boy. What have they done to you?' She twittered. She was unable to stay still, constantly rearranging the cushions around him, adjusting the blanket, dabbing at the drops he spilled with her handkerchief.

'I'm all right Nanny, I'm just very tired. I'm not as fit as my companions here.' He smiled at us. The look his nanny gave us was less than friendly.

'Does your family know you're here? Perhaps I should contact your father.'

'No!' Benedict's voice, naturally high, seemed to rise another octave. The strength of his reaction startled her. 'Please don't do that. My friends don't have papers nanny. There would be trouble aplenty.'

This time she looked at Dave and me with deep suspicion. Before she could speak, Benedict added, 'I haven't seen my father for - quite a while. He may not be overly understanding of our plight.'

'Oh Benny. What sort of people have you fallen in with.' It was a statement not a question. Hello? I thought. I am here you know?

'Nanny, may I introduce Dave - David - and Bettony. They are my good friends. They are people of the highest integrity.' Adopting the self-mocking tone that I had heard him use before, he added, 'We are *having an adventure*, nanny.' Turning to us, he said, 'May I introduce my former nanny and my eternal rock, Mrs Colshaw.'

'How do you do?' Dave said. I held out my hand. She ignored it, sniffed, and said to Benedict, 'I think a hot bath and some clean clothes is what you need. Perhaps these young men could help you to the bathroom. Whilst you're bathing I shall prepare a meal. You look half-starved Benny.'

There was no offer of anything for either Dave or myself. Resentment bubbled inside. 'Would it be asking too much for a glass of water?' I said.

The look of disgust returned to Mrs Colshaw's face. 'First things first. Make yourselves useful and help poor Benny to the bathroom.'

We manoeuvred Benedict up steep, winding stairs.

'Young men?' I said. 'We're not exactly flat-chested.'

'In Anglish society women neither wear trousers nor have short hair,' Benedict said. 'Modesty is all-important. Nor do they behave as you do. I made the same mistake myself, remember.'

We left him at the bathroom door.

'I'm not sure about this,' whispered Dave.

'Me neither.'

We found Mrs Colshaw in the kitchen.

'There's glasses up there.' Up to her elbows in flour, she nodded at a cupboard. I took two glasses and Dave and I filled them twice, gulping the water down.

'You should be ashamed of yourselves. The state he's in.'

'That's how we found him.'

'A likely tale.'

'He's been living in an old barn.'

'How dare you!' She turned and poked a wooden spoon at me. 'How dare you make up lies like that? His father is Sir Edwin Erwin.'

'Ask him yourself.'

'Oh don't worry I shall. And then we shall see. Oh yes indeed young man. Then we shall see.'

We left her to her foul thoughts and sat in the living room. It was a clear sunny day; the only sound was the singing of birds. The sweet smell of garden flowers drifted through the open window.

'We need to get out of here as soon as we can,' Dave whispered. 'The first chance she gets she'll be reporting us.'

'Agreed, although I'm not sure she's really got a phone. As long as she's here I think we're ok.'

'See if she'll feed us then but either way...'

'Yes.'

** ** **

Benedict went straight to the kitchen after his bath. A conversation which started in hushed tones was soon being conducted in raised voices. It wasn't that it was easy to hear what was being said; rather, it was impossible not to.

'Why are you covering for them? I bet you don't know what family they're from. They both have funny accents. They could be egypsies for all we know. Or even worse. Scottish. Or from Leeds or somewhere. Here to steal whatever they can.'

'Nanny they were speaking the truth. They really did find me in a barn. Hand on heart. I give you my Nannybenny promise. And anyway Iain Maclane is Scottish. You like him.'

'He's the second son of the Duke of Glasgow! That's different. He's got breeding. He's not going to murder us in our beds.'

'Why would they want to do that? And anyway if they wanted to murder me they have already had plenty of chances.'

The voices dropped again, and then Benedict joined us in the living room. He looked very different. He was wearing cream trousers and a sky-blue shirt buttoned to the neck. His hair, washed now, was brushed into some sort of order. His face, free of ingrained dirt, was ashen and very thin.

If they were his own clothes, he had lost a lot of weight since he last wore them.

'I suppose you heard all that?'

We nodded.

'Most of it probably,' I said.

He sighed and sank into a chair. He looked exhausted. 'She's just overprotective. She'll be fine.'

Dave said, 'I think we ought to be moving on.'

Benedict shook his head. 'You can of course, if that's what you want to do. I really don't have the energy to join you. She will come around if you give her time. In a few days we'll all feel better and she...' he closed his eyes. 'She'll be fine.'

Mrs Colshaw and Benedict ate in a small dining room across the hall. In spite of Benedict's protests, Dave and I were given two small bowls of stew and dumplings to eat in the kitchen.

Very small.

Luckily the stewpot was half-full and we were able to tuck into seconds. And thirds.

We were instructed to help Benedict back upstairs after dinner and help him to bed. At the doorway to the spare bedroom he managed a smile and said, 'It's ok I can manage.' We made our way back to the kitchen and offered to help clear away.

'I don't need your help.'

'Thank you for the stew it was delicious,' Dave said.

'Close the door on your way out.'

Dave looked stunned. 'We don't have anywhere to stay.'

'Well you should have thought of that before you turned up. I've only got one spare room.'

I sighed. 'Come on Dave. We'll find somewhere.' I looked at the old woman. 'We'll be back tomorrow.' Before she could reply I added, 'Benedict will be expecting us.' I turned towards the back door, lifted the latch to open it and realised I was on my own.

'Dave?' I looked around.

Dave hadn't moved. All the colour had gone from her face. She was swaying where she stood. Greeny yellow spittle bubbled from her lips. Emotions flickered across Mrs Colshaw's face, first disbelief and suspicion then alarm. She was saying something. I ran back and helped Dave as she staggered towards the sink, reaching it just as her body convulsed and a stream of bile projected from her mouth. There was a couple of seconds' pause, another heaving vomit and despite my efforts to support her, Dave collapsed to the floor. A thought hit me.

'Did you use eggs in the stew?' I asked the old woman.

'Not in the stew, no.' The aggression had gone. She was defensive, now. 'There was some in the dumplings of course...'

'Oh no. She's - allergic - to eggs.'

'Eggs? I've never heard anything so ridiculous. Why didn't you tell me? If this is a trick...' But there was worry in the old woman's voice. Dave's eyes were closed, her body jerking.

'Help me get her to a chair or something.'

Between us we got Dave back into the living room and onto the sofa. Mrs Colshaw looked at me.

'What should we do?'

'I don't know.'

'What do you mean you don't know?' Then, a few seconds later, 'You said Her'.

'It's a long story Mrs Colshaw. Not now please.'

At this point Dave's body convulsed into the foetal position and began jerking again. It did this for far too long, finally stopping and leaving her limp.

'Oh god.'

'Is she - is she...?'

I felt for a pulse. It took me a while but I finally found one. It was very weak. I timed it against the mantlepiece clock but it got fainter and fainter, until it wasn't there at all. I looked at Mrs Colshaw. She must have read the shock in my face because she pushed me out of the way, straddled Dave's inert body and thumped hard on her chest, then gave her the kiss of life. She did this three times. By the end of the third cycle the old woman was exhausted.

'Do what I've just been doing,' she said. 'I can't...'

I did the best I could. I did it for five more repetitions, then Dave gave a small cough, groaned, and said, 'Please don't kill me Bettony.'

I laughed as a wave of relief and shock hit me. Even the old woman's face cracked into something that could have been mistaken for a smile. I rolled off Dave and fell on the floor.

'Thank goodness you knew what to do. She would have died, if you hadn't.'

'I was a nurse before I became a nanny.' It would have been an exaggeration to say that she was warming. But she was less frosty. We both looked at Dave, resting now on the sofa. 'I'll get some blankets,' she said. 'You'd better stay here and keep an eye on her.'

'Thank you.'

'You've got a lot of explaining to do young man.'

'Can we do it tomorrow please?'

She grunted, which could have meant anything. I decided it meant Yes.

I slept on a rug on the floor. After the past few nights it was something of a luxury.

** ** **

Dave was asleep and breathing comfortably when I woke, early the next morning. Benedict was already dressed and sitting in the dining room reading a book. Through the open window came the sound of a hoe scratching against stony soil.

'We can talk,' he said. 'Nanny is in the garden. She won't hear us if we're quiet.'

'How much did she tell you?'

'Dave's had a bad turn...?'

'Worse than that.' I explained about the eggbane and described what had happened.

'How peculiar... So she knows that Dave's a she and not a he.'

'We need to come up with a plausible story Benedict.'

'Hmm.' He stared into the distance. 'Do you know what this reminds me of? Are you familiar with the plot of Epiphany Eve?'

He must have guessed from my blank reaction that I wasn't.

'It's a play by the great Willard Shakespeare. Proscribed of course, like all his works, after he was denounced as being a deviant subversive and a plagiarist. A bizarre judgement on a genius who lived five hundred years ago, but there we are. His masterpieces are thought to be subversive, and in truth like all works of genius they probably are. They lead us to question and to dream, both highly dangerous pastimes in a repressive society. Anyway, the plot of

177

Epiphany Eve centres on a young noblewoman who is washed ashore on a strange land after a shipwreck, and dresses as a boy to find work with the local Duke. Naturally she falls in love with the Duke, who of course thinks he is in love with someone else. All is well in the end, of course...'

'And how does that work for us?'

'Use your imagination Bettony! Dave is a girl dressed as a boy...'

And that was how we came up with our story. Dave was a Sepanish noblewoman and I her servant. A cruel shipwreck had left us destitute. In fear of - as Benedict coyly put it - our safety, and in order to pay our way, we disguise ourselves as two young men and enter service with Benedict, the son of a powerful knight. Benedict soon discovers Dave's secret and they fall in love. But Benedict's father has already arranged a marriage for his son! We run away, heading for a ship that will take us to Spain (or Sepana, as Benedict called it) and happiness for the lovers. The journey is more arduous than we thought which explains Benedict's state of health. Being Sepanish also explains Dave's problem with eggs, because as everyone knows, foreigners don't eat proper food.

'And you think she'll believe all that?'

'Believe me, she will. She used to read novels all the time with that sort of a plot. Making Dave Sepanish is a neat twist. Angland is currently in negotiations with Sepana, the idea is to form an alliance which will act like a pincer on the dreadful Farnch. So the Sepanish are not only romantic foreigners, at the moment they are also the good guys.'

'But we don't look Spanish!'

'How many sepanolls do you think nanny has seen?' Benedict permitted himself a wry smile. 'I think it's more plausible than the aliens from another universe ploy.'

We agreed that Benedict would drip-feed this plot to Mrs Colshaw. I was to show deference to the two lovers - obviously, being of low birth, I would have to - and be ready to warn Dave as soon as she was in a state to understand what I was on about.

Dave woke, late morning. By then, Benedict had clearly begun to share his story with Mrs Colshaw. She was already treating me as something of a peer - after all like her, I was a Favoured Servant. And not just any old Favoured Servant - the Favoured Servant of a Contessa! I was allowed to prepare a nourishing soup for "my lady", Mrs Colshaw breathlessly giving useful advice which I was happy to follow because frankly when it came to making nourishing soups I didn't have a clue. Pillows appeared, Dave was propped up. Mrs Colshaw fussed around her. I would have preferred a few minutes alone with Dave to warn her, but I didn't get the chance.

'If there's anything that I can do, my lady,' she said. Dave looked at her in astonishment, then at me. Has she gone nuts or have I? Her expression seemed to ask.

'Master Benedict has seen fit to reveal your status to Mrs Colshaw, my lady,' I said. I tried to nod surreptitiously, and to convey in my expression that she should play along. That's too much info for one nod. The look that Dave gave me back was a mixture of surprise and alarm. In other circumstances it would have been hilarious. Fortunately her experience had left her so drained that she didn't speak, she simply stared.

'If you will allow me to say so my lady, you are making a wise choice. Ben - Master Benedict is a young man of great honour. It was my privilege to nurse him from infancy.'

Dave gawped at Mrs Colshaw, then leaned back and closed her eyes.

'Please try and eat my lady.' I held the bowl under Dave's nose. 'Mrs Colshaw must take the credit for this delicious soup.'

The old woman glowed. 'I'll leave you alone,' she whispered. She curtsied and tiptoed backwards out of the room.

'Jupiter's jockstrap,' Dave muttered, eyes still closed. 'Has everyone else gone crazy or is it me?'

'It's you Dave. This is all just a dream.'

'Huh?'

'Just kidding.' I explained Benedict's plan while Dave sipped at the soup.

'What a lot of tosh,' Dave whispered. 'She'll never buy that gruff.'

'Guff, not gruff. She will. You saw her just now.'

'I think I prefer the old version. That was just rude. This one makes my skin crawl.

'Indeed my lady.'

'Oi. Enough.'

'Yes Contessa.'

'I'm not always going to be so feeble Bettony. You'll pay for this one day.'

'Indeed.'

'Right.'

'My lady.'

'Sheep's teeth!'

Dave managed half of the bowl. The effort seemed almost too much for her. 'So this is what it's like when you ingest eggbane,' she said. 'I've often wondered.'

'Once you're up and about, Benedict has a plan to get us to Sputteridge.'

But Dave was asleep again. I checked her pulse and crept out of the room.

Benedict's plan involved the sea. He had spent a lot of his youth in Thursday Market and like the privileged son of any baronet had had plenty of opportunity to learn how to sail. He thought there was a good chance that his father's boat would still be moored over on St Michael's Mount. We could use it, he said. Sail through the night and be in Sputteridge before light.

It was likely that whoever was after us would have guessed where we were headed, so all the roads and paths into Sputteridge would be watched. Coming in from the sea made sense.

'Won't someone notice it's missing?' I asked.

Benedict laughed. 'We are talking about Sir Edwin Erwin. My father's boat has its own slipway on the east of the island and its own boathouse, facing out to sea. No-one would be able to see anything unless they sailed directly in front of it. Once we get it into the water we can lock the boathouse doors again. No-one will know it's gone. First though we need to check it's still there and it's seaworthy.'

Benedict had a variation of his plan for Mrs Colshaw. The Sepanish ship would be waiting for us a few miles south of the Lizard (or the Heel, as he called it), ready to take us to the Contessa's ancestral home near the beautiful city of Sattanda. Once they were married he intended to write to Sir Edwin, seeking forgiveness. He was sure this would be joyfully given, the union of two powerful families being a happy sign of the wider alliance between the two countries.

'You've got a real knack for stories. You should write plays yourself Benedict.'

'Ah, the benefits of an eclectic and unconventional education! I'm afraid the straitjacket of what is politically acceptable would crush my soul.'

St Michael's Mount is a tidal island. Twice a day for roughly five hours, when the tide is low, it's possible to walk across to it. Mrs Colshaw found the key to the boathouse and Benedict and I went over early in the afternoon. The old woman was completely sold on the story. Her eyes glowed with delight when she handed the key over.

'I do feel guilty about lying to nanny,' Benedict said. 'But needs must. And it is a reasonable approximation to the truth. We are trying to flee, after all. We are unlikely to be challenged. If we are leave the talking to me. I have my papers and I am the son of Sir Edwin. There won't be a problem.' I believed him. Unlike Dave, he was recovering quickly. There was a strength to him which I had not seen before. Colour had returned to his face, which already seemed to be putting on weight. (This was natural to Mrs Colshaw. Obviously a man would recover more quickly than a feeble woman.) With good health, he was also standing straighter. I realised he was taller than I had first thought.

'This whole area is owned by the Patterwill-Smites,' Benedict said. 'Sir Gernful is an old schoolfriend of my father's. They never came here much and I doubt if that's changed. The house on the Mount will probably be empty.'

It was a strange experience, walking over the causeway to St Michael's Mount. In this world the island was not a National Trust property, it was a working settlement ruled over by a privileged family. There was a shabbiness to the cottages that clustered around the harbour and I could see sheep here and there on the grassy slopes. Benedict led the way confidently towards the eastern side of the island. The locals we passed around the harbour were poorly dressed. I expected them to challenge us but they avoided our eyes.

'Did you see that?' I whispered. 'That man actually tugged his forelock to you. He actually grabbed hold of a lock of his hair and pulled at it! And I'm fairly sure he wasn't taking the piss. I've never seen that in real life before.'

'I'm afraid that's the world we're in Bettony. I vaguely remember him from years back - he must have recognised me. There's the boathouse.'

We crossed a meadow to a wooden building at the water's edge. The Mount rose away to our right, the stately home sitting on top of it. It was a very still day. Gentle waves lapped at the rocks. A hazy sun shone through thin, high clouds. It was stunningly beautiful.

Benedict unlocked a door at the back of the boathouse. A strong smell of seaweed and damp stale air hit me. The boat was rather larger than I had been expecting. Dragged out of the water and resting on some sort of wheeled support, it seemed to almost fill the boathouse. The wheels fitted onto rails that ran down into the water near the huge doors at the front. Benedict edged around the boat and waded into the water. He unlocked the doors and pushed them open. Light flooded in. He looked over the vessel.

'Seems ok at first glance,' he said. He smiled. 'What do you think?'

'It's a boat all right. It's... big. It's got a cabin! Can you sail this on your own?'

'Yes.'

Benedict clambered onto the boat and began to examine it. I followed him onboard and had a look at the cabin. Everywhere was very dusty.

'Is it still seaworthy Benedict? Don't they need... oiling or something? When was it last used?'

'It only needs to get us around the Heel to Sputteridge. It'll be fine for that.'

Benedict poked around the boat. After a while he declared himself satisfied. He locked the boathouse and we returned to Thursday Market.

** ** **

It was almost a week before Dave was fully recovered. Benedict used the time to prepare the boat for a return to the sea. He found charts on board, and plotted our route.

'It's lucky that we're heading east,' he said. 'The prevailing westerly wind will speed us on our way. If we wait for the right weather conditions we should make six knots or more, which by my reckoning means we should take a little under six hours. Ideally I'd like to take her out for a trial but caution forfends.'

'Her? When did "it" become "she"?'

'She's capricious, needs looking after, needs controlling... of course she's a she.'

'Are you pulling my leg?'

'Maybe.'

'The trick is not to grin while you're doing it. It gives the game away.'

As far as Dave was concerned, the downside of her recovery was that Mrs Colshaw insisted on dressing her in a pale pink, calf-length dress. It was something that more befitted the Contessa's social status. Benedict thought it must have belonged to another of her ex-charges. It was certainly of very high quality.

'Does she keep clothes for all of you?' I asked. 'That's a bit weird isn't it?'

'I feel a complete idiot in this' Dave said.

'You look beautiful' was Benedict's only comment. He blushed. So did Dave.

It was true though, I reflected. Dave's shock of hair had lengthened and sat around her head and neck. In a ridiculously old-fashioned way she did look nice in that dress.

'I've never worn anything like this,' she said. 'It's like something out of the history books. It gives me the creeps.'

Now that Dave was up and about again we were all impatient to be away. But the still, fine weather continued. There was no wind. Benedict used the time to teach us how to help set the yacht up for the sea. On different days either Dave or I would accompany him to the boathouse. When we did, we dressed in the same male clothes. We were similar height and build and as long as no-one looked too closely we would pass as the same person. If the police guard were looking for three people we would give the impression that there were two of us: That Sir Edwin's son had a manservant to help him.

On the morning of the tenth day of our stay a few gusts of wind blew up and then almost immediately died away. An oppressive stillness settled. Benedict returned from his latest trip to the boathouse looking shaken. He called Dave and me to the garden, and whispered,

'We need to get away. I've just met Roland Pilch. He's been in the guard since I was a child. He was so pleased to see me. He asked me if I've seen three fugitives. They look like tramps, he said, but they're Farnch spies. The guard have been searching for them for a while and now they're going to conduct a house search around here. Starting tomorrow. They will come here, I have no doubt of that.'

'How far will we get on these few bits of breeze though?' Dave asked. 'Will it be enough?'

As she said this a gust returned. It was stronger than the last, although again, it quickly died away.

'I fear that before long it may be too much.'

We gathered our few possessions together and told Mrs Colshaw of our plan to leave.

'Are you sure?' She asked. 'It looks as though we're building up to some bad weather.'

'We have no choice I'm afraid nanny. Needs must when the devil's a driver.' Benedict explained about the searches that would happen the following day.

The pattern of gusts of wind continued, with each one stronger than the last. The gaps between them became shorter, and a strengthening breeze persisted in the gaps. A bank of clouds built low in the west. Despite the worsening weather Benedict insisted that we wait until it was dark. Without papers, he explained, even Pilch would have to detain us.

There was a tearful farewell of Mrs Colshaw. Even I felt my eyes welling.   Benedict promised that he would write at the first opportunity, which I thought was a sadly clever way of putting it. If we were successful, he would never have the opportunity. And if we were unsuccessful… well, he would still not have the opportunity.

** ** **

Crean sighed, and rested his head in his hands. He would have to re-write it, of course. Destroy this copy and print off an edited version. Crean had met Benedict's nanny a number of times and was very fond of the old lady. It would be risky, particularly if Codename Wellbeck managed to get another message out. But he could not possibly allow any harm to come to Mrs Colshaw. He had already worked deep into the night, preparing a very edited summary of the transcript for ACLL Peckler. He had made a particular effort to phrase it in the dry language that his senior so loved. Crean had also managed to locate the source document on the central data store, and using Peckler's own authorisation (he had cracked the ridiculously easy password Peckler1 some months before for his own use, the man was semi-literate where computers were concerned) had established that no-one else had downloaded the document. He would edit it and reset the date and time to the original before re-saving it as the source.

Crean would take no chances. He checked his watch: Three thirty am. He needed to get ahead of the game to give himself time for everything. He wandered down to the kitchen, made himself another strong coffee and took it back to his office.

Peckler would see his hours worked, of course. The Sentinnat watched everything, even themselves. The desk guards monitored arrivals and departures. But Peckler would probably see that as evidence that he had finally started to take his work seriously.

Which was sort of true.

Crean picked up the document and continued to read.

CHAPTER SIXTEEN

In which I discover what it is like to sail in bad weather

At least the thick, dark clouds that had rolled across the sky foreshortened the summer evening. We set off at ten, by which time there was a very dull gloom. Dave and I were once more in our regular clothes.

We made our way quietly back down the lane and past the cottages that formed Thursday Market. Some of the houses were in darkness; the rest had lights glowing behind closed curtains. We kept to the shadows. We had made this journey a number of times in the past week but it was very different in the gloom. I was grateful that we had Benedict to lead the way. We passed down an alleyway and found our way down the steps that led onto the beach.

The causeway that linked the Mount to the mainland disappeared into the sand nearby, close to the looming mass of a large rock. For most of its length, it was slightly raised above the level of the sand and rocks around it. The tide was going out and the sea level had fallen to the point where it had receded from the causeway but still covered the ground on either side of it. Had it been a calm night, our feet would have stayed dry. As it was, the wind drove water across the causeway and across us. It wasn't easy to see the causeway in the darkness. We had to move slowly. By the time we got to the Mount the three of us were soaked.

Benedict led us to the left, along the shore. We skirted across a stony beach, in front of the dark mass of cottages that straggled alongside the harbour. Once we were past them we climbed onto the meadow. Away to our right, the stately home at the peak of the Mount was also in darkness. Benedict unlocked the small access door and we crept into the pitch-darkness of the boathouse.

The yacht was ready to sail. Benedict splashed his way to the big doors at the far end of the building and unlocked them. They were sheltered from the wind which was blowing from the back of the boathouse, and swung gracefully open. It was so dark inside that I could only hear his movements. I couldn't see him at all.

'A few slight changes to our plan,' he said. 'First, I'm going to have to reef the mainsail. That means I shall fold part of it back onto itself. Running full sail in this weather would wreck the sail, the mast and probably the yacht herself. Reefing the sail will allow us to catch a lot of the wind and make good time. It's going to be a bit hairy while I do that. You normally do it before you hit a high wind, and we're not going to have that luxury. Dave, you're going to have to drop the keel yourself. That's got to be the absolute first thing that you do. I'm not running a jib, the wind's too strong.

'Next, we can't try to use the lifeboat in this weather. When we get to Sputteridge Cove I'm going to run the yacht onto the beach. I'll probably have time to lift the keel myself but Dave, be ready for my call. You know what to do. And we shall need to get off pretty quickly because chances are, she will fall on to her side.' Our original plan had been to paddle quietly ashore in the yacht's small lifeboat. Benedict had intended to set the yacht to head out to sea, which we thought might confuse our pursuers.

Benedict said we should rope ourselves to each other before we climbed onboard. He grinned. 'We are breaking all the laws of sailing, my friends. As the great man said, we are in as desperate an execution as that is desperate which we would prevent. But we shall triumph!'

His voice in the darkness was calm and impressively authoritative.

I was terrified.

We clambered onto the yacht, Benedict released a rope, and the trolley, with the yacht resting on it, rolled forward, down the rails. The boat floated free, out into the gloom, and Benedict used a long pole to push it out of the boathouse and into the gathering storm.

We began to lurch wildly. 'Put the keel down Dave,' Benedict shouted. Dave had already found her way to the metal wheel at one side of the yacht. She began frantically turning the handle attached to it. I could feel the yacht become more stable as she did this. Then she hurried to join us.

We knew what to do. Benedict had rehearsed us so many times over the past few days that we could probably have done it blindfold. Lucky really, because on this black night that was almost the case. Lift this, pull that. Pull hard on these ropes to help lift the mast; secure them to that metal hook; secure the mast with these pins. Help Benedict to hoist the big sail by pulling on more ropes. As soon as we were clear of the boathouse the wind ripped across us, making the yacht rock violently. We carried out the tasks we had rehearsed, then loosened the rope that held us together. Dave and I were both falling and sliding. Dave scrambled for the cabin, and I got to the steering wheel just behind it (boats are really not my thing) and hung on to it for dear life. Benedict had clipped himself to the boat. The wind had gripped hold of the sail and was forcing the vessel over at a crazy angle onto its side. We're going to sink, I thought. Benedict waited for each gust of wind to blow itself out, then worked on the sail until the next one hit. Eventually he managed to tie part of the sail back on to itself. The yacht was still keeling over sickeningly but it felt more stable. With a look of triumph he unclipped himself and came surefootedly to take the wheel from me. I dropped down and joined Dave in the little cabin in front of me. I was shaking so much I couldn't speak. The cabin was below the outside level, with portholes on either side, but we could look back up to where Benedict was wrestling with the wheel. He was little more than a shadow above us in the darkness. He had managed to tie another rope around himself. He showed remarkable balance, seeming to anticipate the boat's wild movements and constantly adjusting his stance with apparent ease. At one point he looked down and I made out the whiteness of his teeth as he grinned at us.

'It'll get worse when we're out of the Bay.' He was shouting at the top of his voice; we just about heard him.

'I do believe he's enjoying this,' Dave said.

I can't describe that journey in any rational way. At no time after the first few minutes until it was over did I think any of us would survive it. It certainly had different parts, although none of them was good. At first the wind was almost blowing across the boat, from right to left. Despite this, somehow Benedict made the vessel go in the direction he wanted. When we first set off I thought the waves were big, but after a few minutes we were out of the shelter of the Mount and they took on a new power, crashing over the side of the hull and throwing spray forwards. We would rise on waves, then lurch sickeningly down them, push forwards and repeat the process. All the time, the yacht was ploughing through the water at a ridiculous angle. Dave and I didn't so much stand on the floor of the cabin as lean against it. We were moving very quickly. Most of the time the sail was straining at the ropes that held it to the mast; occasionally it would sag and flap limply for a couple of seconds, as though it were resting, until the next force of wind took it. I expected the mast to snap at any moment. Yet during this second part of our journey Benedict remained almost still. Heavy rain began tearing down onto him. After what felt like a lifetime, but must have been a couple of hours, the swell increased yet further and became more erratic, hitting the boat from different angles.

There was a sudden crash as the beam bearing the sail swung from left to right. We were changing direction. I guessed that we were passing Lizard Point, the half way mark on our trip. Occasionally now a wave would seem to come from the wrong direction, meeting us head on, forcing the boat almost vertical before it plunged back down into the next valley of water. It was a terrifying experience and it was all happening in a light so dim that it made the waves still more threatening. Slowly we gained shelter from the Lizard, which was now a land mass protecting our backs from some of the fiercest of the weather. Benedict guided us more to the left. (I'm told that sailors might refer to this as North, or possibly, Port.) I knew from what he had told us that now he was aiming us towards the lighthouse at the head of the Falmouth estuary. He swung us to the right (starboard, east), and we began to sail closer in, hugging the dark mass of the coast. I wouldn't say that the weather was good here, but it was noticeably less violent.

We had been at sea for around four hours by now, and I was pretty sure that the yacht was sitting lower in the water than when we set off.

A short time later we watched Benedict loosen the ropes that were securing him and fasten one of them to the wheel.

'Time to get roped up,' he called. We went out into the wind and rain and stood by Benedict as he steered towards land.

How he decided he had found the right cove I do not know. He had studied the charts until he had memorised them, but what good is a chart when you only have the odd lighthouse and a few scattered village lights to guide you? A lot, is all I could hope, because now we were heading towards a small grey gap in a looming mass of dark cliff. A few weak lights flickered in the gap. Benedict instructed Dave to raise the keel little by little, waiting for it to graze rocks before she lifted it further. The movement of the vessel became more unstable as she did so. Soon, I felt the underside of the yacht scrape against the seabed, run clear again for a few seconds, then judder to a halt. Benedict passed lifebelts to us and slipped one on himself. Pulling us after him he lowered a rope ladder over the side. I almost lost my footing as a large wave lifted the yacht and propelled it forwards a few more metres.

'Now's a good time,' he shouted. 'Come on before the next big one hits us.' He almost jumped over the side, dragging us after him.

The shock of the icy water took my breath away. We were out of our depth, heavy in our soaked clothes but held up by the lifebelts. We all began swimming furiously towards the shore. Another wave lifted us on its swell and carried us a long way forwards, then started to drag us backwards with it. We could get our feet on the rocks and sand below us now though, and managed to resist most of it. The wave dragged sand and pebbles past us. When it went it left us in shallows.

'Must press on,' Benedict called. His voice was failing him. I realised that however easy he had made it look, the efforts of the past few hours must have exhausted him.

Up to us then, I thought. 'Come on Dave,' I shouted, and we launched ourselves forwards, dragging Benedict with us. It seemed ridiculously easy but still Benedict was urging us on. I soon learned how precious every inch gained was. It was too shallow now for the next wave to lift us; instead it was breaking when it hit and it smashed us to the ground, beating us down in a turmoil of water, sand and seaweed. Its power forced a mixture of grit and seawater into my nose and my mouth. I just about managed to resist the urge to try to breathe until the wave was spent and I could finally cough out, then breathe air again. Dave was on all fours next to me. Benedict was sitting down, coughing. I dragged them up and urged them on. The next wave hit us almost immediately but it was a weaker one, we were still standing after its onslaught and although the sand was sucking us back our progress was easier.

We were over the worst. Still roped together we stumbled onto harder ground. We stopped to recover for a few moments.

'Must keep moving,' Benedict said. 'I shall seize up if we don't.'

Encouraging each other, shaking with exhaustion and cold, and soaked to the skin, we dragged ourselves to our feet. We ditched the rope and the lifebelts and picked our way carefully to our left. We felt our way over rocks and boulders until we were against the cliff, under the path that in another universe had led up to Mapps' body. Keeping tight against the cliff we edged inshore. Dave had not seen much when she was pulled from the TV to the Bob-man's car but she thought all the focus was on the other side of the cove.

Suddenly, away to our right across the cove a bank of high-intensity lights fired into life. We dived behind a rock. The lights were illuminating the old toilet block. Rifles began to fire but the block - the TV - immediately disappeared.

'My god' Benedict gasped. 'Did I just imagine that?'

'That was our lift home' Dave said. 'Maybe Vinny got his act together after all.'

'At least they got away,' I said.

'Did you see that? It... It wasn't there. It was, and then it wasn't.'

'It's ok Benedict. It's what happens.'

The lights stayed on. We waited. At least here in the lee of the cliff we were out of the wind and rain. Soldiers were running around in front of where the TV had been.

'Could be a good time to move,' I said. 'If they're all over there they won't be around the Series Two.'

We crept on. There was no village here, in this world Sputteridge did not exist. We found our way across open rocky ground to the field that in my world ran along the back of the row of stone houses where the police house was. We were protected from sight by a hedge. We crossed the field and pushed through the hedge onto the narrow lane that I desperately hoped housed the Series Two.

And there it was, no more than five metres away from us. No mistaking the square hulk of the shipping container. Nor the soldier leaning against it, sheltering from the weather, smoking a cigarette.

The soldier had his back to us. Benedict calmly walked towards him. He had picked up a large branch. The soldier heard nothing in the tumult of the storm. Benedict brought the stick down hard on the soldier's head and watched him collapse to the floor. He turned to us.

'Shall we?'

CHAPTER SEVENTEEN

Out of the (cold, wet) frying pan...

Dave fiddled with two bolts that looked as though they were part of the shipping container's structure. The end of the container suddenly hinged outwards and the three of us crammed into the TV's tiny space. Dave pulled the door back into place. Lights triggered, blinding us at first after the gloom we had become accustomed to.

'My goodness,' Benedict whispered. 'So it's all true. There truly are more things in all the heavens than our dreams can hold.'

We were in a small space containing a desk and chair. The desk had switches and instruments and screens not unlike those I had seen in the control room of the larger TV. Dave squeezed onto the chair, Benedict and I wedged behind it. She pressed a few buttons and the middle one of three screens in front of her burst into life. Strange shapes drifted across it. She moved her right hand over the screen and at the same time flicked a couple of switches.

'Fingers crossed,' she said. 'I used to practice on one of these at the training centre so we should be all right.' The TV juddered. Dave checked all three screens, running her hands over them, pressing buttons, flicking switches.

'When do we take off?' Benedict asked. 'Because I'm not sure how long we've got before that fellow regains his wits.'

'You certainly gave him a good whack Benedict,' I replied. 'I think we're discovering a whole new side to you.'

'Hmm. As the poet says, Needs must when -'

'When the devil's a driver. Yes I know. And remember it's not a question of taking off, we're slipping across to a nearly identical universe... which I'm sort of hoping has just happened?' I directed this as a question towards Dave. Her smile told me I was right.

'Let's see where we are.' Another flick of a switch and the screen on the right showed our lane. Street lamps lit it against the wind and rain. Pinkish light filled the sky from the direction of the village square. A young couple staggered towards the TV, arms around each other, oblivious to the weather.

'Good heavens,' Benedict whispered. 'It's all real.' Squeezed next to each other behind Dave's chair, I could feel him shaking.

We watched the couple approach. Dave moved a small dial and a distant thumping noise filled the TV.

'Sound,' she smiled.

'Is that dance music?'

A loud groan cut over the thudding beat, followed by the sound of someone vomiting.

'Darren!' The girl said. 'Some of that went on me jeans.'

'Berrer pull em off then luv.'

'Ooh Darren.'

Dave shuddered and went through the routine with the screen and the switches again. The image of the lane outside dissolved and then reformed. The street lights were gone. There was no pinkish glow and no thumping music.

'Let's try this one,' she said.

'This is more than my mind can take' said Benedict. 'Have you just sent us careening across time and space a second time?'

'Sort of. Not time, and not space. And not really careening. Apart from that, yes.'

The TV was becoming noticeably warm. With all the water dripping out of our sodden clothes it was also rather humid. After ten minutes we tentatively opened the door, then took it in turns to strip our outer clothes off and squeeze the excess water out of the door before putting them back on. Benedict politely closed his eyes when Dave and I peeled off our outer clothes. We weren't going to bother doing the same for him but he was so embarrassed that we had to.

We watched the screen for half an hour. No-one appeared. We thought it best to explore during daylight but after all we had been through there was no way that Benedict and I could stay squeezed behind the chair. It wasn't raining here, and there was little wind. We decided a cautious walk outside would be ok. Dave tried to warn Benedict about the blanketing that would cause the Series Two to disappear as we walked away. It was still funny though, watching his reaction.

** ** **

We followed the lane back down to another Sputteridge village square in another world. In the blue-grey of early dawn, everywhere looked peaceful. The air smelt fresh and clean and perfumed with the scents of flowers.

If you counted the brief trip to Darrenland this was now the fifth version of Sputteridge that I had experienced. But this one was different. It was real, not frozen. There were going to be real people here living real lives, unaware that they were almost copies of other people in other worlds doing almost the same thing. And each one of them thinking they were unique. The idea stunned me.

The clouds had rolled away, or maybe they had never been here, in this reality. The first bird began announcing its presence. There was still a chill to the air. I was cold in my damp clothes. Maybe that's why I was shaking.

'Things to take note of,' Dave whispered. 'No vehicles. What can we infer from that?' It was a rhetorical question. Before I could work out an answer, she went on, 'No road signs or markings either as far as I can see although interestingly the roads are metalled. The pub is still there. That's good for two reasons. One, it is indicative of a certain level of social and technical achievement. Two, with a bit of luck we should be able to get a pint.'

'With no money?' Muttered Benedict.

'There are sometimes ways of getting round that problem, Benedict. Notice the shop. It's where we expect it to be but I see no evidence of holiday goods. Doesn't mean there aren't any, maybe they'll be brought out once it opens. But still... I wonder if there's a place of religion. And a school?'

'There's a bakery Dave. Over by the corner with Bay Lane.'

'Excellent.'

'What does a bakery signify?' Benedict asked her.

'It signifies that we can look forward to tasting some pies.'

195

'Exactly how long are you proposing we stay?' I asked. 'We need to get back to the Series Four and warn Mrs Ponch about Vinny.'

'Well... I suppose you're right. But we'll have transition logs. Once things are sorted, we'll be able to get back here. Do some serious research. Taste the pies.'

'That sounds a much better plan.'

'We need to do a bit of work before I set the beacon off. It's important that we don't wander into an invisible Series Four when people are watching. If it gets too busy here we'll have to find another reality.'

It was getting noticeably lighter. We decided to head back to the Series Two and reappear later in the morning.

** ** **

I can't describe what the next four hours were like but I won't forget them easily. We took it in turns to sit down, ten minutes at a time for me and Dave, and despite his protests, thirty for Benedict. He had been incredible on the yacht, but now his efforts caught up with him. He was clearly exhausted. The time not sitting was spent squeezed together behind the seat. It was impossible for those standing to avoid pressing the sitter against the console but even so, sitting was better than standing.

The Series Two had a supply of water, for which we were all very grateful. It also had a very efficient heating system. It's not that nice having your clothes dry on you but it's better than staying wet.

At eight o'clock we left the increasingly foetid air of the Series Two. As soon as Dave secured the door the metal container disappeared from sight.

'Safety first,' Dave said. 'Plenty of battery life.'

We flexed our stiff limbs and headed away from Sputteridge, retracing our steps across the field and towards the cliff.

The field was there, where it ought to be, but it was very different. The ones I had known up until now were grassed and bounded by hedges. This was open, and was divided into haphazard little strips, all of which had been planted with different crops. When Dave saw this she frowned and became quiet.

Our plan was to make it look as though we had walked along the cliff path. We found our way to the cove, walked across it to Bay Lane - an unmade stony track in this reality - and wandered back into the village.

There were a few people around. We greeted them with cheery smiles. They smiled in return, but stared at us and didn't speak. They were dressed oddly. The women wore long skirts that almost reached to the ground, the men were in coarsely-made jackets and trousers. Everyone seemed to wear heavy boots. The bakery was still closed but the friendly smell of hot bread wafted around us.

'So far so ...ok,' Dave said. 'We're supposed to do a reconnaissance first to check things like clothing and behaviour. We were told at training, if it doesn't feel right it probably isn't.' She paused. 'I'm not too sure about this place. The research potential here is massive, but...' She came to a decision. 'Maybe we should get back to the TV and find somewhere different.'

Our progress was blocked by a large, wide man.

'Welcome to our little town,' he said. He had a deep voice and, bizarrely for someone living in a version of Cornwall, a strong Geordie accent.

'Thank you,' Dave said. She explained, with surprising duplicity I thought, that we were down from Bristol and had set off for an early-morning walk along the coast from our lodgings.

'It's a long way from Bristol,' the man said. 'I hope it's worth it. The last time anyone did come through here on holiday was nearly two months ago.'

I smiled. 'It's so beautiful around here. Of course it's worth it.'

The man seemed pleased at this. Still tense, though he was trying to hide it.

'What time does the bakery open?' Asked Dave. The man stared at her. His mouth dropped open.

'What must you think of me? You must have eaten hours ago. Please, accept our hospitality.'

From this point on I began to feel increasingly guilty. No-one looked destitute here but they were clearly not rich. Even so, it seemed that generosity towards strangers was important to these people. The man knocked on the baker's door and paid for a large pie, then led us to his house and introduced us to his family. His wife was a thin woman. She looked miserable, but not from any recent bad news. She just looked unused to smiling. She greeted us and sat us in the kitchen. The man introduced her as Bectedil, and himself as Northman.

Bectedil cut the pie into four. One each for the three of us, one for Northman. The pie was still hot. It smelt delicious. Two small children stared at us and at the pie. With some pride, Bectedil opened a jar and showed it to us. It was tea. Very stale tea.

'My husband bought this when he was last in Plymouth. It is from Chinwah. Real tea.'

A response was clearly expected.

'What a wonderful thing,' Benedict said.

She measured half a teaspoonful into a large pot and filled it with warm water from a range, stirred the pot and immediately poured the result into pewter mugs. It was foul. The pie on the other hand was superb.

The three of us ate our pie. The man stared at his. He turned to his wife. 'How...?' He left the question unfinished. I watched her shake her head and turn away. The man sagged. There was an uncomfortable silence. We stopped eating.

I instinctively felt that his emotion was real but hers was not. She's acting, I thought.

'My boy did cut himself deep two days ago,' he explained. 'My wife washed the cut but the yellowness did set in. Next she used herbs to draw the yellow but...' He paused. 'The redness arrived. The doctor at Falmouth did give us a lotion to apply.' He shook his head and took several moments to compose himself. 'And now the redness is reaching up his arm. He has a fever and has become weak.'

Dave looked at me. 'Sounds like sepsis.'

'You are a doctor?' The man asked.

Dave took a deep breath. 'Yes. Perhaps I may be able to help.'

I stared at her. What on earth was she doing?

'We have no money to pay you.'

'You have paid me already, in kindness and hospitality.'

He looked at her for a long moment. He's not stupid, this man, I thought. It takes him a while but he gets there. He's a smart man.

Eventually he said, 'Will you look at Mickale?'

Dave nodded, then stood and followed the woman out of the room. We sat in silence. The man stared at his pie, untouched in front of him. The stairs creaked and we heard footsteps across the room above. The silence continued. After a couple of minutes they returned.

'I left my pack outside your town,' Dave told them. 'I'll go and get something that may be useful.'

There was pathetic hope in Northman's face.

'I can't promise it will work,' Dave went on. 'But there is a chance.'

The man stood. 'I'll come with you.'

'No!' Dave paused, then said, 'there are things I need you to do here. Boil a clean cloth in water and then pour the water into one of these -' she indicated the pewter mugs. 'Let it cool, then use the cloth and the water to gently clean the wound again. Do you have salt?'

'Salt?' The man looked surprised. 'A little.'

'Show me.'

The woman took a pot from a shelf. It was the size of an eggcup.

'Add it all to the water as you boil it. It will hurt your son but it will help to clean the wound. One of you will need to hold the arm to keep it still while the other does this. I shall be back soon.'

She left quickly before they could argue. The couple looked at each other. The man said to Benedict,

'She is very young to be a doctor.'

Benedict could be authoritative when he wanted to be. He wanted to be now.

'She is my personal doctor.'

They should have been impressed. Instead they both stared and Bectedil said,

'A woman? For you?'

Benedict could be very quick to grasp things. He looked outraged. He nodded towards me.

'For my wife!'

They were both embarrassed. They looked at me with new respect, and for some reason at my stomach, as though that explained everything.

The woman selected a cloth and a pan and the man went outside, returning with the pan full of water. Dave was gone a while and the couple had carried out her instructions before she returned. She was carrying a bag over her shoulder. She glanced at Benedict and me, then went with the woman upstairs. Silence returned. A few moments later, we heard a feeble wail. The man's eyes opened wide, and he stood. But now there were footsteps coming down the stairs and Dave led Bectedil into the room.

'She did press something against Mickale's arm,' the woman told her husband. He looked at Benedict as though for confirmation that this was expected. Benedict nodded.

'It is a new procedure,' he explained. 'It is quite usual in Bristol now.'

'In Bristol!' Bectedil exclaimed, awestruck.

Dave pulled a roll of bandages from her bag.

'He will continue to feel weak for a while yet,' she said. 'But the pain should ease very quickly and his fever should start to fall within the next couple of hours. By this time tomorrow you should be seeing quite a lot of improvement. He must rest for at least a week though, however well he starts to feel. Change the dressing on the wound once a day. Do what I've just done and make sure you wash the wound gently with boiled salted water.'

She gave the bandages to Bectedil. 'We don't have any more salt' the woman said.

'I'll have to get some from somewhere' Northman said. 'Somehow.'

'It's ok. The bandages have got... salt... in them. The important thing is to boil the cloth and the water. Make sure -'

She was interrupted by an insistent banging on the front door.

Northman answered the door. There was urgent muttering in the hallway. He returned leading two men.

The first of the two was thin and balding. 'That's him!' He pointed at Dave, then dramatically backed away. Northman stared at her, then turned to the thin man. 'Have you been drinking again?' He asked suspiciously.

The man shook his head. 'I've never been more sober. I haven't touched a drop for weeks.'

'So why can I smell drink on you?'

The man looked furtive. The second new arrival said,

'Why are they dressed like that?'

'They say they're from Bristol.'

I thought, *They say...?*

The man stared at us, fascinated. 'What are they doing here?'

'They say they're on holiday.' Northman turned to his wife. 'Tell me again what she did,' he said.

'She pushed a shiny thing against Mickale's skin. It made him scream.'

'What's all this about?' Benedict was doing Authoritative again. Northman turned to him and indicated the thin man.

'He says he saw your doctor disappear. He says she's a spirit.'

Benedict must have guessed what had happened. He paused a moment too long.

'See?' The thin man said triumphantly. 'He doesn't deny it!'

'Of course I deny it. It's hard to know what to say to something so stupid.'

'Show me what you used.' It was a demand not a request. Dave put her hand in her bag, making the two visitors cringe. They're enjoying this, I thought. If this place had a cinema they'd be front row for all the horror films. She pulled out a metal instrument. It was about half the length and width of a mobile phone and twice as thick. She held it out to Northman but he backed away.

'That's it'. Bectedil had put as much distance between us and herself as she could. She was dramatically pressing herself against the back door. 'She pushed it into Mickale's arm. It went all the way in until it disappeared and he screamed and screamed and his body shook and his eyes became the eyes of a demon -'

'Enough woman!' Northman shouted angrily. 'We heard him. There was no screaming. You were calm when you came back downstairs. Stop your silly stories.'

'She's a spirit,' Bectedil breathed. 'They all are.'

'I've had enough of this.' Benedict stood. Come on, we're leaving.'

'Get back!' The second visitor grabbed a poker and held it out. 'This is iron. Touch this, demon, and you will perish!'

Benedict reached out and grasped the poker.

'What enchantment is this?' Screamed the thin man. 'They can even withstand the force of iron! They must be truly evil indeed!'

Better than the cinema, I thought. For them anyway. Maybe not for us...

'Sit down' Northman said. Benedict sat. Northman looked at Dave. 'Use it on her.' He nodded at me. 'Use your... Bristol magic on her.'

'It is not magic.' Dave raised her eyebrows, then said to me, 'Pull your sleeve up. Sorry about this Bettony. I mixed some painkiller into the antibiotic and also something to bring the fever down. You might feel a bit woozy.' She pressed the instrument against my skin and I felt a brief tingle.

'Shit.' she whispered. 'Sorry. Nerves. Shit! Again! You've just had a treble dose. You'll be ok though. Hang in there Bettony you're in for a bit of a ride.'

Northman turned to his wife.

'Is that what she did?'

'Aye but...' Bectedil glanced at the visitors. 'But first she did laugh an evil laugh and horns sprang from her head and there was a crack of thunder and a flash of lightning -'

'Woman! Remember I was here! There was no thunder and no lightning.'

'You don't remember that because these two had enchanted you,' said the second visitor slyly.

After the tingle I felt nothing at all for a few seconds. Then a wonderful relaxing warmth crept up my arm and began working its way gently through my whole body. I started to realise how amusing the whole situation was.

Northman was watching me.

'How do you feel?' He asked.

'Pretty damn good. You should try it.' I suddenly felt very hungry. 'Don't you want your pie Norm?'

'What?'

'I'll take that as a No.' I reached over and grabbed his plate and began shovelling food into my mouth. Northman watched me, then said to his wife,

'Go and see how Mickale is.' He looked at her, then said, 'No. Wait here. I'll go.'

He left the room. There was an uneasy silence. Nobody moved. Except for me, eating. A light-hearted quip should break the ice, I thought.

'You know your problem?' I said to the thin man. He looked at me, eyes wide. 'Your problem is, you're a tit.'

There wasn't the round of laughter that I had expected. It's probably worked though, I thought, my little joke. They're all chuckling inside. Job done, I went back to my pie.

Northman returned. 'He looks calm,' he said to Bectedil. 'It's possible that the fever is fading, as well.' He seemed to reach a decision. 'Who did you tell about this?' He asked the thin man.

'Nobody!'

'Well that's not true for a start,' I said. 'He's obviously told Mister Chirpy there.' I pointed at the second man.

Northman frowned.

'Who did you tell?' He repeated.

'Nobody! I saw Herbert and he said he'd come along to help destroy the spirits -'

'Herbert!' I laughed so much I coughed some pie back onto the plate. 'Herbert Chirpy. Chirpy Herby. Woops. 'Scuse me. What a silly Herbert. Hahaaa...'

There was more talking which I guessed was going to be pretty boring so I turned my full attention back to the pie.

I realised that Northman - or Big Norm, as I now thought of him - had taken my arm and was kindly helping me up the stairs. I was helped into a large room with a bed and some chairs in it. I was vaguely aware that Benedict and Dave had also been kindly helped into the room, as well as the thin man and Herby Chirpy. It all seemed perfectly reasonable. I subsided onto the bed and allowed the wonderful relaxation to overwhelm me.

Any moment now, I thought, I'm going to fly around the room. I can feel it. That'll surprise them.

** ** **

I woke with a very dry mouth and a headache. It was still light.

'How do you feel?' Asked Dave.

I sat up. The room span. I lay back.

'Thop.'

It wasn't what I had meant to say but my tongue felt very thick and dry and it was all that I could manage. To be honest, my brain felt pretty much like my tongue. It more or less summed me up though. Dave lifted my head and held a mug of water to my lips. Some of it went into my mouth.

'Sorry. That was my fault.' Dave dabbed ineffectually at the spilt water, looked around, then whispered, 'He's giving us a day. To see if the boy recovers. If he does then it's proven: We're from Bristol, I'm your doctor and that guy's a drunk. We can go and they get their arses kicked. If he doesn't then we're all three of us spirits and we'll have to be destroyed.'

'No probbem then... How do they dethtroy thpiritth?'

'Fire. It's the only way apparently.'

'Oh. Courthe.'

'Yeah. Fingers crossed.'

'Can I have thome more of that thtuff?'

'It's a bit moreish isn't it? No. That wouldn't be a good idea even if I had my bag. Which I don't. Northman's got it downstairs.'

'What time ith it?'

'Must be mid-afternoon.'

'Why are you whithpering?'

'They're over there. The two blokes who are accusing us.' Dave nodded behind her and I saw the two men sitting on hardback chairs watching us. 'From what I can gather Northman is the main man around here. What he says goes. Even so he can't rely on these two to keep quiet and he seems to understand what a mob can do when it gets fired up. So they stay here too. Until it's decided, one way or the other.'

'Can I have thome more of that thtuff?'

'My bag's downstairs.'

'But I want thome.'

'I know.'

'Pleathe.'

'Northman's got my bag.'

'Pleathe.'

'No... He's not a bad sort, Northman. He's trying to deal with this the best way he can.'

'Pleathe. I want thome more of that thtuff. Pleathe give me thome more of that thtuff.'

'Go back to sleep Bettony.'

'Can I have thome more of that thtuff first?'

'No.'

** ** **

Next time I woke it was still light. No Dave though. I sat up. I didn't feel great but this time I felt like a human being. Benedict was asleep in a chair next to the bed. The two men were watching me.

There were voices outside. The door opened. Northman entered first, Dave behind him. Dave was smiling. Northman was glowing.

'Good morning sir, madam.'

Dave said, 'The patient is sitting up and taking soup.'

'His fever has gone. The redness is dying back. My son is going to live.' Northman was on the verge of tears. His face suddenly became full of anger. He strode across to the thin man and slapped him across the face with such force that the thin man sprawled onto the floor.

'If there's evil in this room it's in you,' he shouted. 'You and your sister...' he turned to the other. 'And what exactly did you see, tell me?'

The one called Herbert shook his head. 'I didn't see anything! It was Snoe. Snoe said he'd seen the man - the woman - disappear.' In his panic a thought seemed to occur. 'He said he'd seen the man turn into a woman -'

He was cut in mid-sentence by a slap to his face. He was more solidly built than the thin man but was still knocked to the floor.

'He's a drunkard and a liar' Northman stormed. 'And you're just a liar. You're the laziest pair in this town. Two days each - no! Five! - Five days each labouring for Widow Eames. Starting today.'

'But I need to tend my own strips'

'You never tend your own strips! Your slovenly idleness holds the whole town up!' Northman was shouting now. He was furious. 'I've put up with the two of you for too long! Five days each working for the widow. And I will come and check on you myself. I am putting you both on a last warning. If your husbandry does not improve your strips will be taken away from you.'

He was staring at them, panting with fury. Dave went over to him and said quietly, 'Can I have a word?'

Northman looked at her and nodded.

'In private' Dave added. The two of them left the room. As soon as Dave and Northman were gone, the man called Herbert turned on the other.

'You and your drunken lies. See what you've done. What will we eat without our strips?'

'I'm not drunk! I don't drink. I haven't touched a drop for weeks -'

'Oh yes? What's this then?' Herbert pushed his hand into the thin man's jacket pocket and pulled out a small metal flask.

'I didn't know it was there!'

Herbert tossed the flask into the middle of the room. The thin man turned to scramble after it but Herbert jumped on him and began punching him. At that moment Northman returned. He hurried over, grabbed the two of them and cracked their heads together. My God, I thought. He's killed them. But they both rolled around, clutching at their heads. Northman picked the flask up and uncorked it. He sniffed at it and grimaced.

'You're going to tell me where you got this from Snoe, because we both know this is utestengt.' He turned to us. 'This is the explanation of what happened. We call it Yannather because in time it kills the mind. Before that, it causes people to see what is not there.' He bowed. 'I am deeply in your debt. You have saved my son and in return I almost took the word of a Yannerthric over yours. I am ashamed.'

'All is good that ends well,' Benedict replied.

'As long as you take my advice' Dave emphasised.

'It is done already. My mother is with him now. She moves in with us today.'

Northman wanted to give us breakfast but we all wanted to get out of there as quickly as we could. He insisted on taking us to the pub where he bought us more food and ale. The food was not as good as the bakery, but it was still very good. The ale was very weak, thank goodness. The pub itself was basic. It had a wooden partition, about four feet high, instead of a bar. Behind the partition beer barrels sat end-on on wide shelves. Each barrel was fitted with a small tap, low down on the front. When the barman wanted to pour a glass of ale he held it under the tap, turned the tap and let the beer dribble into it. There were wooden tables and stools, sawdust on the floor and even a spittoon. It was the same room but very different to its counterpart in the frozen world. I found that disorientating.

It was close to midday before we set off. It was a hot day. Northman had offered to get word back to our lodgings that we were ok. Benedict readily agreed to this, then found it impossible to describe accurately where we were staying. It was agreed that we would be fine, especially since we had told the landlord of our lodgings that we were likely to be away for a night. We set off along the coast path, heading east.

'You handled that well Benedict,' I said.

'Hmm.'

'That was a close thing,' Dave said. 'It was all my fault too. I should have got us out of here more quickly. And I should have been more careful going back to the Series Two.'

'You saved a life Dave. Possibly more. No need to apologise for anything.'

'Is he still following us?' Benedict asked.

'Yep. So don't go too fast Benedict. He'll struggle to keep up. Especially without his Yannather to keep him going.'

We absolutely needed to keep Snoe following us because while he was here he wasn't poking around near the Series Two. It might be hidden from sight but it wasn't hidden from prodding. Something solid that you can't see would be direct evidence of interference from the spirit world. It would be watched. We'd never get into it and since calling the Series Four here was too dangerous, we'd never get away. It surprised me that Snoe hadn't gone straight back there. Dave pointed out that his alcohol-fuddled brain had probably only registered her disappearance, not the glimpse he must have had of the TV.

'What was the secret conversation with Northman about?'

'Oh. There was something not right about the infection. It had set in much too quickly. I didn't think Bectedil was genuinely worried either. Put the two together and you've got a suspicious situation. While you were flying with the fairies I managed to get out of the room a couple of times on the pretext of checking Mickale. I used the time to talk to Northman. His eldest daughter died last year of the same thing, a cut that went bad. Turns out that Bectedil's not the mother of any of them. Their real mother died in childbirth a couple of years ago.'

'Heavens. So this Bectedil was poisoning them?'

'It looks that way. We don't know do we? In these sort of societies people die of things that we would easily cure. But it looked suspicious. Anyway I've got a feeling that what I said was enough for

Northman. I can't see that marriage lasting much longer. Much longer than today probably.'

'So the comment about the mother...'

'I suggested he bring someone in to keep a close watch on Mickale. And on Bectedil, come to that. She's Snoe's sister, by the way.'

'That explains what Northman said about Snoe and his sister. Yeuch. Why would a decent man like Northman marry somebody like that?'

'I suppose he needed someone to be a wife and mother. Life is hard in these places Bettony, and much much harder for a single parent. And there may not be a lot of choice for a middle-aged man.'

'Why did you say we came from Bristol, Dave? What made you choose Bristol?'

'Oh!' Dave smiled, a little smugly I thought. 'So far, we've found that whatever world we investigate - however many things are different, however many places are bigger, or smaller, or maybe not there at all - for some reason, there's always a large town or city called Bristol. Always. We don't know why. Maybe it's something to do with the geography of the place. In fact Gumple and Frith in their publication "A Theory of the Size and Importance of Bristol Cities" suggest it's some kind of inter-quantal node. Why are you sniggering Bettony?'

'No reason.'

Dave eyed me suspiciously for a few seconds, then added, 'Anyway, I thought it was worth a punt.'

'He's flagging again,' Benedict said. 'We need to slow down some more.'

It looked like Snoe didn't have any water on him and it was a hot day so we led him towards a stream and pretended to drink from it. Thanks to Northman we had our own bottles of weak ale. We didn't want to risk the stream. It was far from its source and possibly downstream from a load of cattle. We were less bothered about the effect it would have on Snoe. For Snoe's benefit we rested in shade for much of the afternoon. By early evening we had only covered around six miles and Snoe looked like he was ready to go home. Dave and I started jumping about and laughing, which kept his interest for a while. We were able to move fairly quickly for the next two hours. At that point Snoe sank to the ground, leaned against a tree and appeared to fall asleep. We went a little further, then edged around him in a wide semicircle. Either he was being attacked by an invisible herd of spirit pigs or he was snoring very heavily.

We hurried back towards Sputteridge.

** ** **

It was late dusk when we got back. We pushed our way across fields and undergrowth to avoid the village itself, but there was no need. Everywhere was still and quiet. We got to the Series Two and squeezed ourselves inside. Once again, we were very grateful for the Two's seemingly endless supply of clean water.

'We'd better get going,' Dave said. 'Late evening, it's not a bad time to arrive somewhere.' She did the thing with the screens and the buttons and I felt the slight judder of a transition. Immediately, Benedict and I started to float towards the ceiling. The TV began to make strange groaning noises. Dave flicked the cameras on.

'There's nothing there!' She cried. She flicked and switched and the TV plummeted heavily to the ground. I plummeted heavily to the ground as well and Benedict plummeted heavily onto me.

'Cameras are rebooting,' Dave said. 'At least we're on solid ground.'

'Except for Benedict,' I groaned. 'He's on solid me.'

'I'm most awfully sorry,' Benedict said. He carefully picked himself up. 'Are you all right Bettony?'

'Give me a minute. I'm checking.' I realised there was wet underneath me. At first I thought it was blood. Then I had a moment of calm, just a few happy seconds after I realised it wasn't blood and before I understood the implications of it being water.

'Dave are the cameras back up yet?'

'On their way... boy that was a fright. The TV's taken a bit of stress. Six seconds in the vacuum of space! I bet that's a record.'

'Cameras Dave?'

210

'Any second now Bettony. Yep, here we go... Oh.'
'We're in a river right?'
'Not a river.'
'A sea? A lake?'
'There's a lot of water around. How did you know?'
'Because it's getting in. It's sloshing around me. How deep is it?'

'Hang on... about six inches.'

I checked myself, starting with the important stuff and then working outwards. Despite the fall and the squashing by Benedict I seemed to be ok. A bit damp but ok. I gathered myself and Benedict helped me up. I looked at the screen carrying the images from outside.

'Wow.'xxxxx

Dave had angled the cameras so that they were pointing towards the cove. Instead of hedges, fields and maybe houses, there was a flat expanse of water reaching out to the horizon. The cliffs on either side of what had been the cove were still there, but they were further apart and looked lower. They framed what was a small bay rather than a little cove. Closer to us, poking over the waterline, the wrecked shells of buildings showed where Sputteridge village square had been. Some of them were still recognisably houses. Others had been reduced to a few tumbledown walls.

Dave was flicking switches and moving her hands over the screens. I'm no student of human nature but I know panic when I see it.

'What's wrong?' I asked.

'I think I've wrecked the TV. They're not built to withstand six seconds in a vacuum, and then getting smashed to the ground was the straw that broke the camper's back. It wouldn't transition with holes in it, the failsafes would kick in. Even if water hadn't got in and damaged the circuitry.'

Dave leaned forward onto the desk and put her head in her hands. Her shoulders were shaking. Her voice became muffled. 'That's the end of our little adventure I'm afraid. I've wrecked the TV' she repeated. 'And I've wrecked our chances of getting home.'

Benedict reached over and put his hand on her shoulder. 'If we hadn't had you to help us Dave we'd still be stuck on Erce. I would be wasting away in my barn. Bettony and you would probably be in a re-education centre by now. Or worse. You must not blame yourself. I've been having the most exciting time of my life and I've met two wonderful friends. And I'm not giving them up easily.'

Dave turned and looked at him. Her eyes were wet. 'You were relying on me.'

'You're a behavioural scientist Dave, not a navigator' I said. 'You've done amazingly to get us away from Erce. And we're not beaten yet. We've still got the beacon.'

'Take a look at where the Series Four would appear. It would be submerged. The failsafes on a Four are much more sophisticated than on a Two. They wouldn't allow it to transition. We're stuck here. No escape. Oh and by the way we're not blanketed any more.

'Basically this thing is knackered.'

CHAPTER EIGHTEEN

What to do?

We did the sort of useless things that you do when there's no hope. We tried to see how big the cracks and holes were, and discussed stuffing jumpers into them. We talked about fixing the circuitry, as though any of us had a clue what it did. Or even know if there was any. We stared at the water. We stared at the screens; at the wreck that was Sputteridge.

Dave turned the cameras around. We saw by the fading light of dusk that we were on the edge of the ocean. There was no hedge and no track. I guessed that the soil which had covered the fields around here had all been washed away. As in other worlds, the ground gently rose behind us. Here, it formed one side of an estuary. The lane towards Truro sat on the other side of the estuary; it rose spookily out of the water, beyond the gloomy wreckage of the pub. That was the lane that I had found my way down, I thought. It was where my whole adventure had started.

Where my life had changed.

Eventually we pushed the door open and splashed our way towards land. The first thing that hit me was the heat. Dusk had faded into darkness now, but the temperature must have been well over thirty centigrade. It was humid too. The water was cool, but as soon as we were on dry land I began to sweat. Dave had found a torch on the Series Two. We needed it as we navigated our way uphill. We found a grassy bank that was sheltered from sight by trees, and lay down. There was a time when I might have thought about all the insects creeping around in a place like that. Those days were long gone. I fell asleep almost straight away.

** ** **

It was the heat that woke us, early the next morning. Thick clouds hid the sun but trapped its warmth. We looked down at the village. The tide had gone out a long way in the night and the village square was visible. Our TV was a metal canister resting bizarrely among rocks.

'If we time it right,' I said, 'what are the chances that the Four could answer your distress call and get us away?'

'Looking at this, quite good I think,' Dave replied. 'I don't see -
'

She was cut off by the sound of an engine. Instinctively we retreated further into the trees. A strange vehicle was making its way down the lane. It had four massive wheels that supported a crude metal box, open to the sky. Looking down on it from our vantgate point, I could see at least six people sitting in the box. At the front, someone sat on a raised bench, holding a large steering wheel. At the back a heavy-duty exhaust pipe pointed upwards, chugging thick diesel fumes into the sky. It all looked bizarrely home-made.

The vehicle was moving at around twenty miles an hour. It was heading straight for the TV. It crossed the edge of the square, then slowed and lurched crazily over the rocks. It stopped next to the TV and everyone climbed off. I could see now that they carried spades and pickaxes. We watched in silence as they pushed and poked at the TV for several minutes. There was a discussion between several of them, then they raised the axes and the spades and we could hear clanging as they battered away at the TV.

'They'll never get in with those,' Dave murmured.

She was right. We watched for about half an hour while the people bashed at the TV. They were becoming increasingly bad-tempered, hitting wildly at the vehicle and smashing rocks at it.

'Hello,' Benedict said. 'What's this?'

A car was making its way slowly down the lane. It had blue and yellow stripes and there was a police-style light on top. It made its way across the square and stopped. Two large uniformed men got out and walked over to the TV. The people with the axes and spades had stopped their efforts and watched them arrive. A discussion began. It started quietly, and then became more animated. People started waving their arms about. One of the uniformed men started prodding his finger at the chest of an axe-holder.

'It looks like this will end in Tears' a man's voice said.

We all jumped and spun around. A late-middle-aged couple were standing behind us. Both were wearing jeans, the man had a long-sleeve shirt on and the woman a t-shirt. They smiled, a little uncertainly.

'Sorry,' the woman said. 'We didn't mean to make you jump.'

'Who are the people with the axes?' Dave asked.

'Scrap-gatherers from Falmouth probably,' the woman said. 'We've seen them here before. Never seen that tractor-thing though.'

'Are you Walkers?' The man asked. He looked uncannily like the barman who stood frozen in time when Dave and I had first had a pint in the pub. I don't know about the barman but this version spoke with a lot of capital letters.

Dave nodded. 'Are they dangerous?' She asked, looking back at the escalating row in front of us.

'They're Best Avoided. We've got Dogs, so we feel Safe. And the mobile signal's quite good around here. We had to call the Police out a couple of months ago. The dogs were going Crazy. It was two in the morning but they were here in a Few Minutes. It helps if you served in the force for Thirty Years.'

It was said conversationally, with a smile, but it felt vaguely like a warning. Or more likely, a Warning.

'I wonder what that metal box-thing is,' the woman mused.

The chief axe-holder was shouting at the police now. We could hear his voice, although not the words. One of the police pulled something out of his pocket and pushed it at the axe-man and there was sudden silence. We watched the axe-man fold over and collapse to the ground.

'That's going to Hurt in the morning,' the man muttered.

The other scrap-gatherers backed away. Their body-language was still aggressive. One of the policemen spoke into something fixed to his uniform. They both pulled guns and pointed them at the scrap-gatherers who dropped their spades and axes and raised their hands. Their colleague was still lying face-down on the rocks, not moving. One of them lowered an arm to point towards him, and as he did so one of the policemen shot him.

We saw him lurch backwards before the crack of the pistol reached us. Dave, Benedict and I watched him drop to the ground and gasped in horror. The couple seemed unmoved.

'I said it would end in Tears,' the man said. On the beach, the man who had been shot rolled around shouting what must have been obscenities for a few seconds, then lay still as a policeman went and stood over him.

'That's one less then for a while,' the woman said. 'It won't stop them coming back though. It never does. They're like ants. You need to destroy the nest.'

'Are you All Right?' The man asked. I realised that I was shaking. 'Why don't you come back and have a cup of Tea with us?'

'It's probably best if we left now,' the woman added. 'The boys won't want any witnesses.'

They introduced themselves as Rob and Carol. Shocked, we let them lead us away through the trees. On the far side of the wood was a high hedge with a gap cut into it, filled by a heavy wooden gate. The man pushed it open and we found ourselves on a well-tended lawn bordered with flowering plants and shrubs. A 1930s-style brick-built house stood in front of us. Two alsatians hurtled towards us, tails wagging.

'You're ok while We're here,' Rob said. Like his earlier comment, it was innocent enough on the surface.

Carol locked the gate behind us, then led the way to the house.

'She's the Keyholder,' Rob smiled. Carol also smiled. She unlocked a door and led us into a large kitchen. It was wonderfully cool. She bustled around, making tea, offering cakes, while the man sat with us at the kitchen table. My first impression was that they were lonely. But Rob's questions were very probing. Where did we come from? Where were we staying? Where were we walking to? We explained that this was our first time in this area and were suitably vague. Carol was impressed that we came from Bristol, such a beautiful city she said.

Rob beamed. 'I was stationed there for Two years,' he said. *Uh oh*, I thought. 'It was a Long Time Ago,' he continued. *Phew.* 'First posting in the Force. A bit of an Easy Ride, I was Lucky.' He peered closely at Benedict. 'What did you say your Name was?'

'Benedict.'

'No. Your Surname.'

'Erwin.'

'I thought I recognised you!' Uh oh again. 'Are you by any chance related to Sir Edward Erwin?'

'I am. I'm his son.' *Quick thinking Benedict!*

'What a Great Man! And what an Honour to have his son visit our Humble Home!'

Rob's manner changed completely. Close questioning masked by geniality gave way to obsequious praise of the Great Man. Apparently it had been Rob's Honour to receive his Gallantry Medal from Sir Edward shortly before his Retirement.

It involved eating a lot of cake, but we negotiated another ninety minutes without too many problems. When we stood to leave Rob saw me looking at a photograph on the kitchen wall. It was an old black and white one of Sputteridge in all its glory. A group of shy children were standing in front of one of the stone cottages.

'That's my old Grandad,' he said, pointing to one of the children. 'Back in the Day. It's a Shame, what happened. But there's Nothing we can Do. The Earth warms and it Cools. We're ok up here anyway. Nothing we can do about it,' he repeated firmly.

'You don't go in for that global warming rubbish do you?' Carol asked.

'What global warning?' Benedict asked innocently. Of course, I thought. He wouldn't know.

'Carol!' Rob misinterpreted Benedict's reply. He was offended on our behalf. 'Of course they Don't. They're not Communists!'

Carol was deeply embarrassed. She hadn't meant to suggest that we did, of course, it was stupid the things people believed, all that rubbish some nasty people used for their own perverted reasons... We reassured her that we weren't insulted and managed to get away without too much more trouble, although with a lot more cake. They led us back into the humid heat and down through their manicured garden to the gate. We heard it lock behind us.

'What lovely people,' I said loudly. 'Quite a tale to tell Sir Edward.'

'What was all that about global warnings?' Asked Benedict.

'Just keep walking,' I whispered. 'Nice and fast.'

CHAPTER NINETEEN

What's in a name?

'Isn't that a strange coincidence,' Benedict said. 'In another world someone who looks like me seems to have a father called Sir Edward Erwin. And my father is called Sir Edwin Erwin.'

'It's not strange,' Dave replied. 'It's all to do with degrees of distance. It would be strange if it didn't happen.'

Benedict looked at her blankly.

'It is a very creepy experience though,' I said, 'meeting yourself.' I told Benedict about my experience in the frozen world.

He shuddered. 'Creepy indeed.'

We reached the edge of the wood. The Series Two still sat on the rocks. It was deserted, everyone had gone. There were a few marks on the metal but no evidence of any real damage. The tide was coming in although the square with its ruined buildings was still mostly dry.

'We can't use the beacon now,' Dave said. 'There's too much water where the Series Four would appear. We'll have to wait until the next low tide. Sometime this afternoon I guess.'

We were unsure what to do. If we stayed in the wood and Rob and Carol found us again it would be difficult to explain. If they had the dogs with them there was every chance that they would find us - and if the dogs found us first it would be painful as well as difficult. But heading on, over the bay, would make getting back without being seen tricky. In the end we decided to explore the ruins. If we were seen we could say we were just sightseeing. Hopefully we could find a building where the first floor was strong enough to support us and there were enough walls to conceal us. The obvious candidate was the old pub, but unusually for her Dave wanted somewhere else. Somewhere nearer to the TV's transition point, she said. We crossed the square and began paddling into the incoming tide as we wandered onto what was left of Bay Lane. I didn't mind. It was steamy hot; at least the water around my feet provided a little coolness.

The cottages along Bay Lane itself had been pummelled by the sea. Most were reduced to a few tumbledown walls. Those that still clung on to bits of their first floor had either lost their staircases or looked too unsafe. We settled on a wrecked stone cottage, near to the corner of the square. It was a good thirty yards or more from where we were hoping the Series Four would appear but it was the best we could get. I realised that we were close to where I had had my altercation with Wether Mapps. I looked down the ruined lane, slowly submerging beneath the incoming tide. That confrontation seemed a world away.

Well of course it was a world away. Several, hopefully.

** ** **

This cottage's stone staircase had lent extra support to some of the floor above. At least a third of it still existed. There was enough wall to hide us from the landward side, and the seaward side had collapsed so we could watch out for the Series Four's arrival.

The heat was oppressive. Thank goodness Rob and Carol had filled us with tea; we had no water with us and we were all sweating profusely. The Two wasn't that far away but none of us wanted to risk being seen going into it. We certainly didn't trust Rob and Carol. Thick clouds covered the sky, it was impossible to tell where the sun was but we could roughly guess the time from the water level. We were in for a long and thirsty wait.

Time passed very slowly. I watched the sea gradually maroon us. One by one the stone stairs disappeared under water. I reflected that if there had been a heavy swell the waves would certainly have soaked us and could possibly have dislodged us. Luckily the sea seemed to be as tired as I was. Any waves were sluggish, as though the water itself was exhausted.

We all dozed in the heat. When I awoke the tide was already beginning to ebb. A couple of the stairs above the water level showed wet, marking its limit. It had got maybe halfway to the first floor. I looked around the wall, back towards land. The sea reached inland, still covering the square. I was struck again by the strangeness of it all.

Dave and Benedict were both awake. Nobody said much. We were all tense. If Dave's emergency beacon failed, we were stuck on this world forever.

** ** **

Eventually the tide went out. Dave pulled a small tube from her pocket, twisted one end and threw it towards the place where the Series Four had been.

'Here goes everything,' she said.

The tube arced through the air, gave a loud *crik*, and disappeared.

'Whatever next,' Benedict said.

'Next, we wait' Dave answered. 'And hope.'

We watched the space where we hoped desperately the Series Four would appear. All the time, the tide edged further out.

It must have been an hour later when I heard the lorry. That was bad enough. Then I made out a car's engine as well.

We looked at each other in alarm. Dave and Benedict had crept alongside me and we risked another look around the wall. A police car similar to the one we had seen in the morning approached down the lane. It pulled to one side at the far end of the square and stopped. It seemed agonisingly close to us. Behind it a large lorry slowed, but did not stop. Its engine revved noisily as it pushed on, past the car and over the rocks until it was next to the Series Two. A thick metal tube projected upwards at an angle from the back of the lorry with a heavy chain swinging from it. At the end of the chain was a huge hook.

'They're going to load the Two on the back of the lorry,' I said.

'Come on Mrs P,' Dave whispered. 'We really need you to turn up now.'

We looked back at the transition point. It was still empty.

Three workmen climbed down from the lorry's cab. Two policemen got out of the car and went over to join them. The

221

workmen climbed onto the back of the lorry and struggled with another heavy chain. They seemed to be asking the police for help. They didn't get any. It was too far away to hear what was being said but I reflected that Pierre DeLondon would not have been happy. Members of the lorry community and members of the police community were clearly not working as a robust team.

Eventually the workmen manhandled the second chain off the lorry and began dragging it towards the Series Two. This chain had several separate lengths, all with a hook at the end and all joined to a short central section. It took another five minutes for the workmen to pull the separate sections of the chain over and around the TV and secure them. One of the men walked back to the lorry's cab, passing the policemen. As Rob might have said, Words were clearly Exchanged. The workman climbed into the lorry's cab and moments later its engine fired into life, spewing blue smoke upwards from a vertical exhaust pipe attached to the back of the cab. The chain hanging from the end of the tube began to lengthen, dropping the hooked end to the lorry's floor. A workman climbed onto the back of the lorry. He pulled the hooked end off the lorry and towards the chain that had been secured to the TV. The two were fastened together. There was some shouting and now all the chains began to tighten. We watched in dismay as the TV was slowly pulled over, onto its side, then dragged towards the lorry. Then there was a loud *Twonggg* and one of the hooked ends flew off the TV, almost decapitating a policeman. The workmen clearly enjoyed that. There followed some heated discussion between the police and the workmen. Eventually the hook was reattached and the operation started again. The back of the lorry began to squash down towards its wheels, taking more weight as the TV got closer; the cab started to raise. The chains tightened further and began to pull the TV upright again. The Series Two lifted a few inches into the air, knocking against the back of the lorry.

In a few minutes the Two would be secured onto the lorry. I looked again at the transition point, it was still empty.

Then I stared and hope drove my desperation away.

There were still a few tiny waves pushing tiredly towards the transition point, but they seemed to hit an invisible barrier and splash backwards.

'Dave,' I said. 'I think it's here.'

Dave and Benedict looked around.

'Look at the water.'

Immediately they both brightened.

Behind us, there were shouts from the group gathered around the lorry. In our excitement we had moved away from the cover of the wall.

'They've seen us,' Benedict said.

'Come on,' Dave said urgently. She hurried down the stairs followed by Benedict and me. We were on the open lane now, visible to all. I could hear shouting behind me. The policemen were running across the square towards us. We ignored them and ran towards where the Four had to be. I remembered our experience in the frozen world, when Dave had confidently told me about blanketing only for the TV not to be there. I prayed that we were right. That it would be there this time. A loud crack echoed from behind us and a splinter of stone sprung from the wall to my left and flew past my ear. Then two more cracks and I saw Benedict fall. Dave was in front of us, she had reached the Four and I saw her disappear into its blanketing. I stopped and put my arms under Benedict.

'Just go,' he said. 'Death is sucking the sugared -'

'Not gonna happen mate.' I pulled him upright. 'Save the speech.' We staggered on. Dave reappeared and ran back to us. The policemen were built for comfort rather than speed, but the gap between them and us was closing fast now. Bullets were spraying all around. I was in a trance that was a strange mix of energy, terror and euphoria. Something hard hit my left arm. I felt Benedict's body jerk as another bullet punched into him, and then the Four was suddenly in front of us, Dildow holding the door open. We threw ourselves inside and collapsed in a heap on the floor.

Everything was chaos. There were people all around. I was shouting for Will, even after I saw him bending over Benedict. I watched Kevin pick Dave up and hurry away, Will following. I think

I was still shouting. I was vaguely aware of a stabbing pain in my left arm, and that Dave Green was tying something around it which certainly wasn't easing the pain. Green leaned over me and touched something against my temple and a relaxing darkness quickly spread through my mind and my body...

CHAPTER TWENTY

When I woke I was in guest quarters, room three - the room where Slepwood had found me, that night he had wanted to kill me. I took a sudden deep breath of panicked consciousness and sat up. A pain shot through my arm, the room spun alarmingly and someone eased me back down.

'Welcome back to our community.'

'Oh god Pierre why did it have to be you?' The words came out before I could stop them. I opened my eyes again and tried to focus on the greasy face above me. 'I'm sorry I shouldn't have said that.'

'It's perfectly understandable Bettony. You're probably still in shock.'

'Yes. Yes that's it. Shock. That's what it is. How's Benedict? How's Dave?'

'Dave is fine. Will has operated on her and she is going to be fine. He is currently tending to our new colleague and he is confident that the young man is going to be fine as well. As are you.'

'Me? What do you mean?'

'You received a wound to the arm.'

'I did? I don't remember that.'

'Will has assessed you and determined that yours is the least serious wound. All is well, Bettony. You just need to rest now. He will operate to remove the projectile once he has completed his work on your new colleague.'

I gasped. 'You mean I've got a bullet in my arm? Which arm?'

'The one with the bandage and the blood I assume. Perhaps I shouldn't have mentioned that yet. I thought you may have noticed.'

I looked in shock at my left arm. My sleeve had been rolled up and a white bandage wrapped around my forearm. Quite a lot of it was stained red.

'Wow. There's a bullet in there?'

'That seems to be the consensus of medical opinion.'

Why couldn't the man ever just say yes or no, I thought to myself.

'Has Mrs Ponch spoken to Benedict or Dave yet?'

'Both of your colleagues were anaesthetised immediately after your return.'

'You mean, No they haven't?'

'Indeed.'

'There's a TV show on Earth called Don't Tell Me Yes And Don't Tell Me No. You should go in for it Pierre. You could win a nice holiday or a barbecue set. In fact you'd be nailed on.'

DeLondon looked alarmed. 'I'm sorry? Nailed on to what?'

I sighed. 'This is important Pierre. I need to talk to Mrs Ponch. Urgently.'

'As the crew's Technical Community Team Interaction Leader, I can assure you that I have your best interests at heart Bettony. What you need right now is rest. In fact I wonder whether I could prevail on Mr Green to give you a boost of Peridown.'

I raised myself as far as I could on my good arm. 'Pierre. This really is very important. I really need to speak to Mrs Ponch urgently.'

DeLondon looked at me for a few seconds, considering, and then tapped at his watch. 'Zagretia, Bettony would like to speak with you.'

Washed out as I was, it struck me how much Pierre's confidence in dealing with electrical gizmos seemed to have improved.

His watch gave a loud PIP, then a tinny voice said, 'THAT FUNCTION IS UNAVAILABLE AT PRESENT. PLEASE PRESS RESET.'

OK maybe he shouldn't be so confident, I thought.

'PLEASE PRESS RESET PIP PLEASE PRESS RESET PIP PIP PLEASE PRESS PIP PLEASE PRESS PIP PRESS PIP PRESS PIP...'

Several long minutes later Mrs Ponch entered the room.

'Bettony. It's good to see you again. How are you feeling?'

'ARE YOU SURE YOU WISH TO CONTINUE? ALL YOUR DATA WILL BE LOST.'

'I need to talk to you Mrs Ponch.' I glared at DeLondon. 'In private.'

'Bettony, you can speak in front of Pierre.'

'PIP'

'It's all right Zagretia. I'll withdraw.' DeLondon smiled and left the room, accompanied by a tinny voice saying, 'You have selected Swedish. Vilken typ av kaka vill du beställa?'

I tried to lever myself up again - but once again a sickening pain shot up my arm and I collapsed. Mrs Ponch pulled a chair up and sat next to me.

'You're going to have to rest that arm,' she said. 'Chill your jets for a while.'

'I need to talk to you about what I've learned. It's important. Really important.'

She nodded, and considered me for a few moments. 'Go ahead.'

I left a lot of the details out and concentrated on Bob being replaced by Slepwood, Dave Lanyard's escape, our abduction to the mental health facility and what Slepwood had told me when I was there. I told Mrs Ponch about Vinny, and Mapps, and why Slepwood had killed Dave Morland. Mrs Ponch's face remained impassive, although she grimaced when I repeated his comment about "the others" screaming. When I finished she stared thoughtfully into space for a moment, squeezing the bridge of her nose with the thumb and forefinger of her left hand.

'There have been rather a lot of unexplained absences,' she said. 'You, Bob, Dave Potts, Dave Lanyard. I was beginning to wonder when I would be the last person on this Transition Vehicle.'

'Vinny must know the game's up,' I said. 'He was the one who helped Slepwood get me and Dave out of this TV. He must realise we'll tell you what happened.'

'True. We don't want him doing any more damage...' She stared at the floor, then muttered, 'I've had my suspicions of Vic for quite a while.' She spoke into her sleeve. 'Pierre can you find Vic please? It seems our suspicions were correct. I'm still with Bettony. Bring Vic and Kevin here.'

'Pip. Thank you for trying to contact me. I'm not here at the moment but your message is very important to me so please - Hullo? Sorry Zagretia. Message received and understood. Collecting them now.'

Mrs Ponch's expression was unchanged. Perhaps there was the faintest of sighs. Then she turned to me and spoke quickly and quietly.

'What I'm going to tell you now must not be repeated to anyone. Not to anyone Bettony, not even Dave Potts and especially not to your new friend. Are you comfortable with that?'

I shook my head. 'No. Sorry Mrs Ponch. I'd find it impossible to keep things from Dave after all we've been through. And Benedict deserves to know at least some things. He's given up his world to help us. In fact just now he very nearly gave up his life.'

'Mmm.' She squeezed the bridge of her nose again and frowned. 'A very honest answer.'

A silence followed. My arm was throbbing. Whatever the Peridown was, it was wearing off. I was starting to feel sick with the pain. Eventually she said, 'Talk to me before you speak to Benedict. Some areas have to be off-limits with him. I'm going to tell Dave everything anyway, so you're free to discuss with her. Deal?'

'Deal.'

'Ok.' She took a deep breath. 'At an organisational level, we had begun to suspect that our very exciting search for other lives - other civilisations in other, alternative realities - had stirred up something of a hornet's vest. It started rather alarmingly, with a couple of unexplained disappearances of key staff at the research facility. Then a couple of other people began to behave very oddly. Then one of our top researchers was found dead, having apparently topped themself.' Mrs Ponch looked deep into my eyes. 'I know that this awfully sad thing happens not infrequently on Earth but it is exceptionally rare on Abbuth. We have a very well-funded health provision which covers mental as well as physical well-being. When someone is unwell they can quickly and easily access medical care without the shame or guilt that for some reason people sometimes seem to experience on Earth.

'We made a detailed examination of the unfortunate individual, with the intention of discovering more about their illness and hopefully preventing it from happening to others in the future. In the course of this examination we discovered some very subtle but unmistakeable differences in a few sections of their RNA/DNA sequencing. We probed further. Bettony, I'm sure you learned at school about the role of polymeric RNA macromolecules in controlling gene expression.'

'Huh?' *Try and look intelligent,* I told myself.

Mrs Ponch didn't seem to notice my blank look. 'Completely by accident, one of our researchers spotted an unusual instability in cytosine, which you obviously know is one of the nitrogenous bases of messenger RNA.'

'Well...'

'I know what you're thinking.'

'You do?'

Mrs Ponch smiled. 'Obviously cytosine is inherently unstable!'

'Yes. Hahaha.'

'Well here's the surprise Bettony. Despite the instability there was a complete lack of spontaneous deamination into uracil!'

'Gosh.' *Keep smiling knowledgeably Gullivant. She's bound to stop talking soon.*

'We probed further.'

'I'm not surprised.'

'Eventually we chased the anomaly down to the subatomic structure of the nitrogen itself. I know you must be very interested in the detective work needed to get there but you'll have to contain your impatience on that one Bettony. I'll cut to the chaste. This body - apparently of our valued colleague - was not of our universe! There was no other possible conclusion. To quote your scientist John Holmes, eliminate the impassable and all that remains, however unfortunate, is the answer.'

'Um...'

'The only explanation open to us was that this poor dead bugger had been brought to our universe and substituted. No doubt whoever did it made use of one of the lost TVs. The unfortunate individual had probably been killed in their own world and then their body brought to Abbuth to cover the disappearance of their twin, who we suspect had been abducted.

'We were gobsmacked. We knew that several of the early transition vehicles had gone missing. Was it possible that one had fallen into the hands of a malign power? One which had the sass to use it against us? Somewhat belatedly we introduced security protocols. Against our better nature, we set up a new department, specifically to look for narks.' She looked at me unhappily. 'This was very difficult for us, Bettony. It goes against the concept of Trust, which is one of our deepest instincts and a fundamental pillar of our society. When I left on this trip, the individuals who had apparently begun behaving oddly were already being closely watched. Mr Mapps' erratic behaviour had been identified a while ago but I requested that he be allowed to join the crew. If we watched him carefully, I reasoned, he might lead us to other, cleverer narks. At the very least, he was proof that someone with authority at our facility was not the dude they appeared to be.

'As regards the TV, what you've told me about Vic clears some confusion. I had begun to suspect that all was not as it should be with him. Bettony, you need to understand, Vic Terrugo as he calls himself has always been a rather - spiky - individual. I must fess up as well to placing too much reliance on Kevin spotting if something was wrong. That was an error. Vic was making too many mistakes. Mistakes that the real Vic would never have made. Transitioning us to a reality where we were shot at - apparently by tooled-up people who were waiting for us - was a desperate move. He tried to pass it off as bad luck. But... it didn't feel right. Your explanation makes it all very understandable. Clearly, he was so badly genned up that he didn't realise the safeties would kick in and arse us out of there before we took any damage.'

'Didn't you suspect Kevin?'

'Suspicion is not something that comes easily to us! But no, I have known Kevin for a long time. For someone to copy his very... individual... personality to such a fine level of detail would have been... exceptional.'

'Is there anyone else you suspect? What about Pierre?'

Mrs Ponch shook her head. 'Pierre is another individual I place absolute trust in.'

Oh Mrs P, I thought. I said, 'Did you spot the change in Bob?'

'I did and so did Pierre. It fitted all the boxers. Sudden change of behaviour. Strange change of vocabulary. He also looked... heavier. I know Bob's not the slimmest of people but even so... Some of those shirts were surprisingly tight. So I decided to keep a close eyeball on Bob.'

'That's why you walked in on us? The night when I was using this room?'

Mrs Ponch nodded. 'And why I hurried your and Dave's arses out of the TV. It was for your own safety. Even then Slepwood, as you call him, managed to give me the slip and get out after you. Once I had sussed the situation, it was obvious you weren't safe. You know Bob so well, and with the heightened sense of suspicion that your people have, compared to us, you'd be the first to notice something was wrong. They would know that. They would want to remove you as a priority.'

My mouth went dry when I asked, 'Have you found the real Bob?'

'I'm afraid not. Goodness knows what reality they have hidden him in. Not Bob and not Dave Lanyard. But I won't give up on them Bettony. We'll find them. At least now we can work from what you've told us and use the transition logs to locate Dave Lanyard.'

'Bob's here somewhere.'

'Come again?'

'Somewhere on this TV. Think about it, Mrs Ponch. We know what Slepwood told me. Vic smuggled Slepwood into the TV, they grabbed Bob when we transitioned to the Cuban Reality, and with Kevin's help Bob was abducted and Slepwood in that horrible t-shirt took his place. But they didn't have time to get Bob off the TV, not in the few seconds they had. They had to hide Bob somewhere on board. And with Kevin involved, I'm guessing he's still alive.' Hoping he's still alive, I thought. 'They can maybe fool Kevin with some story but he wouldn't tolerate murder.'

'You may well be right.'

The Westminster chimes bizarrely started up from a panel next to the door.

'Come in Pierre,' Mrs Ponch said.

** ** **

I was surprised at Vinny. Instead of the combative and prickly individual he had been, the man who preceded Kevin and Pierre into the room was bowed and beaten. We stared at each other for a long moment.

'What's your real name?' Mrs Ponch's voice was light and reasonable when she spoke to Vinny although the bluntness of the question stunned him. It also surprised Kevin, who looked at his commanding officer in astonishment.

Vinny made one last attempt at bluffing.

'What do you mean? You know my name. Vic Terrugo.'

Mrs Ponch spoke next in Enceldic. Vinny stared at her. It was obvious that he hadn't a clue what she'd said. Kevin looked as though he was about to answer, but Mrs Ponch held up her hand to silence him. She spoke again. Again, Vinny said nothing. Now she turned to Kevin, who answered immediately. He turned to Vinny and was now clearly asking him a question in Enceldic. Vinny looked at him blankly, then tried to edge around him, towards the door. Mrs Ponch was talking to Kevin again. A look of complete disbelief crossed that rugged, handsome face. Vinny suddenly tried to dash for the door. DeLondon moved to cut him off. There was no need. A huge muscular arm shot out and lifted the little man off the ground by his collar.

'Bettony, you must forgive my rudeness in lapsing into our home language but I had to make a point to Kevin. Bettony?'

Blackness was descending across my eyes. I heard DeLondon say, 'Good Greeks look at the blood' and then a glorious relaxation took both pain and consciousness away from me.

** ** **

'Wake up Bettony.'

'   '

'Bettony! Wake up!'

' .No. '

'You must wake up now!'

'Don't wanna.' I wished the voice would go away. Sleep is such a wonderful thing, I thought. Cosy, warmmmmmm...

'I was probably a bit heavy on the Peridown,' the voice said. Then another voice said,

'Aren't you going to say hello?'

I recognised the voice and thought, *That's different. That's worth waking up for.*

I forced my sluggish brain into consciousness and managed to open my eyes.

'Bob!'

He was smiling at me. His face was thinner and he looked tired but he was okay. And it was definitely Bob. Even in my groggy state I could tell that. I thought about trying to get up but I'd already changed my mind on that one before Will was gently putting his hands on my shoulders and shaking his head. I saw a drip bottle next to me, a tube leading into my right arm. There were fresh bandages on my left arm and it felt numb.

'It's good to see you again Bettony.'

'Are you ok Bob? Bob you wouldn't believe what we've done. Where we've been. What I've seen.'

'We've got some catching up to do old friend.' It warmed my heart to hear Bob call me that.

Will said, 'You lost some blood Bettony. I had to sort Dave and Benedict out first so you had to wait longer than I wanted. It's all ok though. They're both fine and so are you. I've removed the bullet from your arm and stitched you up. In a couple of days' time you'll be as good as new.'

I was in the white-walled sick bay. There were two other beds in the room. Dave was asleep in the one opposite, Benedict was sitting up in the one next to me and smiling.

'Our remarkable adventure has taken quite a turn for the better,' Benedict said.

'Wait till you see this thing,' I said. 'It's a bit better than a ship to Spain eh? I'll -'

'No you won't.' Bob cut me short. He put his hands on the end of the bed. 'Not yet anyway.' He turned to Benedict. 'You need to rest,' he said. Turning to me, he added, 'And you need to let him.'

'Can't we have a quick chat?' I asked. Bob smiled, shook his head and pulled on the end of the bed. It was at this point that I realised it was on wheels.

'See you soon Benedict,' I called as I was propelled out of the door and back to guest quarters, room three, drip-stand and all.

I was fully awake now.

'At least you can tell me what happened to you,' I said to Bob. 'It'll help me stay awake. That's what I have to do, you know. Will said so.'

Bob laughed. 'It's good to see your adventures haven't affected your curiosity Bettony.'

** ** **

I was right about the swap. Vinny had given Kevin some rubbish about the TV being full of imposters and Bob being their leader. During the blackout they had "freed" Slepwood, and the three of them had grabbed Bob. I was also right that it was because of Kevin that Bob was still alive. They had bound him and taken him to a little storeroom at the far end of the engine room. It was Kevin who had brought Bob food and water, and after they had finally convinced him of the truth it was Kevin who had led Mrs Ponch and Pierre DeLondon to him.

'What about Dave Lanyard?'

'Kevin has transitioned us onto the frozen Sputteridge. No sign of her yet but Dildow and DeLondon have gone out looking for her.'

'Pierre?'

'It's ok Bettony. He's a bit of a pratt but he's no spy. So tell me what's been happening to you.'

Bob was sitting in the armchair. He picked a tray up from the floor with a plate of meat pie and a glass of something interesting on it.

I repeated my story while Bob ate, drank and refused my requests to share his meal. (He was kind enough to describe the taste of the gravy though.) This time I included all the details. Apart from the overly detailed descriptions of his pie, Bob made a good audience. He gasped when I told him about how I had launched my kick at Slepwood, and almost succeeded with it. He winced when I described how Slepwood had bent my finger, and winced some more when I told him about the car accident. He expressed astonishment at the idea of a steam-powered railway, and laughed at the idea of Dave Potts in a dress. When I finished he shook his head.

'You did amazingly well Bettony. And you've discovered some extremely valuable information. Not least, confirmation that this Regency has got hold of some of our top people. That's extremely concerning. The idea of our scientists being tortured for what they know is dreadful, and so is the thought of these Regency bods getting hold of their knowledge.'

Dildow entered the room to an unlikely fanfare of Westminster chimes. Behind her, looking rather heavier than the last time I had seen her and with her curly hair wildly out of control, was Dave Lanyard.

** ** **

Lanyard had made the pub her base, eating and drinking her way through its contents. When she had eaten all the pies she moved on to ready meals at the gift shop/general stores. She found some paint and a brush, daubed I'M HERE I'M IN THE PUB on a big sign and propped it in front of where she hoped the TV would appear.

'We'd probably have guessed you were in the pub' Dildow said to her. 'The funny thing was though Bettony, she wasn't there.'

'I'd gone for a walk. I was bored silly. It's lovely countryside once you get used to how weird everything is.'

'Weren't you scared?'

'What of? I knew things would work out and you'd find me in the end. The weather was permanently ok. I knew where to get good tasty food and some excellent beer. I borrowed some paperbacks from the gift shop. I quite enjoyed the Mettlesham Manor Murder Mystery. And I read my way through all the Love For a Dashing Duke series of romances without being sick once.'

'You're remarkably laid back Dave.'

'It comes from doing chemistry Bettony.' She smiled. I wasn't sure if she was pulling my leg. 'Anyway look, I need a shower. And I want to see Henry and Amber.' Lanyard smiled again and gave my hand a squeeze. 'It's good to see you again Bettony.'

'You too.'

'Henry and Amber and their babies,' Dildow said.

'Aw no, how wonderful...'

The door swished shut, cutting their voices off.

'That's the next thing then,' Bob said. 'An infestation of bloody mice.' He stood up. 'I'm off as well for a decent night's sleep. Get some rest Bettony. This business isn't finished yet.'

Whatever was happening the next day, I wasn't included in it. I felt the familiar judder several times, telling me that the TV was making transitions between realities, but no-one came to explain. Will came to see me a few times. He said he needed to check my hydration level but we ended up just chatting. A couple of times he brought me food and drink. He was interested in how backward Northman's reality was, and agreed with Dave's enthusiasm for more research into the causes. He was impressed with Dave's use of what he called the Series Two's first-aid kit, although less so with her giving me a triple dose of the painkiller. He insisted on running tests to check I hadn't suffered any long-lasting ill-effects (I hadn't). In the evening he wheeled me back into sick bay, where Dave was now awake, and where the four of us had a very enjoyable talk. This mainly consisted of Dave, Benedict and I competing to relate either the funniest or scariest events we had experienced. For some reason Will also found the idea of Dave in a dress hilarious, which half-amused and half-annoyed her.

Reliving our adventure in this way put all three of us in good spirits. I wondered afterwards, when Will had dimmed the lights and left, whether this was his intention. What could have been a lasting trauma, if badly handled, had become an experience - on the whole - to be treasured.

** ** **

The following morning Will pronounced me well enough to be up and about. Whatever they use in their medical treatment, all I can say is, it works fast. I had thought about having a look at Henry and Amber, but found myself in one of the meeting rooms, drinking coffee with Will, Bob, DeLondon and Mrs Ponch. The only evidence of Will's surgery on me was a clean, thin bandage around my forearm. There was no pain and no numbness. I had full use of my arm and my fingers.

'We have a serious dilemma,' Mrs Ponch said. 'We know from what you've told us Bettony that some of our people are being held - probably being tortured - by the Regency. You have also been able to confirm our suspicions about narks within our facility on Abbuth.

'Under normal circumstances we'd report back to Abbuth and give respect to the decisions made by those we have elected to lead us. We can't do that. With unknown narks at large, it's likely that any plan would be leaked back to Erce. And we've already lost a shitload of time. Those people have been missing for months. Let's not forget also that Kevin's brother is one of them.'

She looked around the room.

'So it's up to us.'

She explained the daring plan that she, Bob and DeLondon had come up with. It was mind-blowingly risky.

The plan depended on Kevin and Dildow getting the Series Two back into commission. Between them, they thought they could do it in a couple of weeks.

Kevin now had complete control of engineering. Freed of Vinny's bumbling leadership, he had quickly resolved the problems around transitioning. From what I could gather, Vinny had accidentally entangled the dark matter in a large area of one of the

237

Sputteridges with some Booze Eisenstein Condensation in the ships core. (If that makes sense to you, maybe you could get in touch and explain it to me. Actually no. Please don't. I have a mental image of gin fumes swirling around a sealed glass jar. That's good enough for me.) Bob explained the effect of this as being like a small fishing boat that snagged its nets on a thick elastic band tied to a heavy load of scrap metal at the bottom of the sea. It meant it was hard to steer and hard to move and the elastic was always wanting to pull the boat back to one place, even if it ended up there sideways-on. Perhaps unsurprisingly, the place where the tangled-up dark matter belonged was what we referred to as the frozen world. Carried to Earth, Bob said, the dark imprint of Sputteridge had interacted with energy from our own reality. Effectively it had clothed itself in the fabric of our own universe to generate an unreal Sputteridge on Earth, acting as a brake on any attempt by the Series Four to transition away. Once it did manage to stumble away, the Four was most likely to be pulled back to the frozen world.

'So without any dark matter the people on the frozen world have had to make do without ... shadows and stuff,' I said. 'That must have been really weird.' They stared at me. *Pass it off as a joke then change the subject.* 'Ahahahaha... If it was so easy to sort out why hadn't Kevin done something before now?'

'If you want the answer to that one you'd better ask Kevin himself,' Mrs Ponch replied wearily. 'If you do though, make sure you've got a jotter, you'll want to take some notes. There will be a lot of procedures and regulations quoted. In fact you might want to take sandwiches. Allow for at least a couple of hours out of your life that you'll never get back.'

Bob's idea was to physically move the Two to an area close to where the Mental Health Institute would have been, then transition to Erce. He would bluff his way into the building as Slepwood and find a way of collecting the hostages together, then use the Two to get them back to the reality where the Four was, and safety.

'I can see a few obstacles,' I said. 'Perhaps the most obvious being, Slepwood's dead.'

'You've told us how secretive they are,' Bob replied. 'Our analyses of societies like that shows we've got a good chance of bluffing that one out. Either no-one will know or when they see me they'll assume it was another piece of disinformation. And he was a lot heavier than me. People will look at me and think the weight loss was all part of the injury.'

'He wore expensive suits! The smartest I've seen you Bob is in that policeman's uniform!'

'I can get measured up back on Earth. You can advise me what to buy.'

'We're hoping that Benedict will be able to guide us to the right place for transitioning,' DeLondon said. 'Obviously it's his choice whether or not to become a full member of our community, and even then our esteemed medic here will need to give the go-ahead. But Will thinks our new friend will be fit to be a full and active team member by the time the Two's ready for use.'

Was it only me whose skin was creeping?

'How will you get the Two there?' I asked.

'On the back of a lorry' DeLondon replied.

'What?'

'When we rescued you, it was a bit of a faff for Kevin to entangle the Four with the Two,' Mrs Ponch explained. 'It was his first time unsupervised and the Two was at least a hundred metres away. That's quite a distance, especially for a rookie.' She looked sheepish. 'He managed it though. However, er... he accidentally entangled the lorry as well.'

'Wow. And the workmen on it?'

'They managed to jump off before it transitioned. When it was bouncing up and down. They were probably a bit surprised though.'

'Yes I bet they were.'

'So anyway we've got the means of getting the Two to the right place. If Benedict decides he wants to help us it'll save a lot of buggering around.'

'Benedict can also coach me on speech patterns,' Bob added, glancing at his captain.

'Absolutely nuts,' I said. 'I'd better come with you.'

'Why?'

'I don't know the layout of the place that well but I know it a lot better than you do, which is not at all.'

'That's a constructive suggestion,' DeLondon said. 'Having Bettony there would also enhance your validity Bob. If challenged you would be able to say you'd been searching for her and finally found her.'

'Nobody challenges Slepwood' I said.

Bob was regarding me. 'You know how dangerous this is Bettony. I would never ask you to do it.'

'You haven't asked. It's my idea.'

Bob's expression was a mixture of happiness and concern. Will was less happy, and insisted that I get not only a full physical check but also a psychological one too. My experiences could have had long-lasting, hidden effects, he worried.

The meeting broke up soon after. Will caught up with me on my way to see Benedict and Potts.

'You don't have to do this, you know,' he said.

I reddened. 'You mean because I'm a woman?'

'No! I don't mean that at all.'

'Have you told Bob he doesn't need to do it as well?'

'No.'

'So why tell me?'

Will replied, hoarsely, 'I... I worry about you not coming back.'

'Oh.'

There was a moment's silence while we both thought about everything that could be behind that sentence. I realised I was not unhappy with it.

'Anyway,' Will said. 'We'll need to run those tests on you before you make a final decision. If you're not fit to go you won't have to decide.'

I already have, I thought. And I was pretty certain the tests would be ok.

CHAPTER TWENTY ONE

I quite enjoyed the tests. I took them a couple of days later, turning up at the sick bay in t-shirt and shorts as instructed. The room was empty now, Dave had been allowed to return to her quarters and Benedict had been given the room next to mine. Will was in professional mode, pleasant but detached, giving his full concentration to his work. I think he barely even noticed me.

I lay on a narrow bed at the end of the room. Running the length of the bed and fastened on to its side was a horizontal plastic lip, about half a metre wide and reaching all around the bed underneath. Behind my head, on the end of the bed, was a monitor and keyboard. Will somehow made small metal beads stick to my forehead, to the back of my neck and to my upper arms. He stood at the keyboard. I heard him tapping. A solid cylinder pushed out from the lip, sliding smoothly over me until it enveloped me from my neck down.

'A count to five,' Will said. He pulled another piece of the cylinder out to cover my face, counted to five, then slid it back. He did this three times, then tapped on his keyboard again and the main cylinder returned to the lip.

'So I'm now looking at the results Bettony and I have to say it's bad news.'

My heart began to sink until I remembered Will's gentle humour. 'It's all ok isn't it?'

'Yes. I'm afraid so. Leave those Renshaw beads on for a moment Bettony. Come and have a game of Tickle the Sparrow.'

'Did I hear you right there Will?'

Tickle the Sparrow was a card game, for which Dave Green joined us. The rules were fairly simple and involved trying to pair up with one of your opponents to beat the third, while at the same time cheating both of them. I thought it sounded unlikely for a game from Abbuth, but it was fast-moving and light-hearted and a lot of fun. We played for half an hour and Will won by a whisker from Dave

Green, with me some way back. Will thanked Green, removed the beads from my forehead and arms and returned to his monitor.

'Yep. Psychological feedback is all very healthy.'

'What an interesting way of assessing someone.'

Will smiled. 'Why shouldn't healthcare be fun?'

** ** **

After all we had been through, it was an incredible relief to be back on the Four, especially now that the narks, as Mrs Ponch called them, had been rooted out. Once a day Bob and Kevin would take Vinny out for a walk, the rest of the time he was confined to quarters. Despite untangling the TV and getting the dark stuff back to the frozen world, Kevin had found a way to get us back there side-on. (That's about as technical as I can get.) In other words, the Four, with the Two (and the lorry) in tow - literally in tow - could sit in this version of Sputteridge with time pretty nearly suspended. Using this reality would make it much easier for us to get the Two to the transition point undetected, Bob explained. It was also a good place for Kevin and Dildow to work on the Two without losing any more time.

It took another week for Benedict to get up and about, and longer for Dave. I got to be pretty good at Tickle the Sparrow, playing against either Benedict or Dave Potts with Will, Dildow or one of the other Daves making up the three.

Benedict said he would be happy to guide us to the site of where the mental health institute would be on Erce, although the idea of actually making the transition back there clearly terrified him. Bob assured him he would be able to wait for us in the frozen world.

Benedict spent some time working with Bob on Slepwood's accent and speech patterns. He explained the subtle differences in pronunciation that Bob would need to master. I offered Bob what help I could, listing words that Slepwood favoured and describing his casual, sadistic brutality. Bob was saddened by this, but on the whole he seemed to relish the idea of impersonating Slepwood. Apparently Bob had been a keen member of an amateur dramatics society back on Abbuth, but had never had the chance to shine in a lead role. In some peculiar way he saw this as his big chance.

The second week I was Benedict's guide around the Four. Suitably blinkered, we were even allowed into the engine room. Kevin refocussed a couple of mirrors and allowed Benedict to look at a bottle of cider, which then did the jumping in the air and disappearing thing, much to Dildow's annoyance and Benedict's astonishment. Like a conjuror, Kevin flicked a switch and a moment later two identical bottles suddenly appeared, sliding towards each other and then merging together into one. Benedict was even more astonished, although I'm not sure Dildow was. As we left the engine room harsh words were being exchanged, or at least being uttered by Dildow, whose cider it was. I took Benedict outside, and tried to explain to my friend the science behind what we had seen, and behind the apparent stopping of time. I don't think he followed much of my explanation. Then again, I'm not sure I did. But he was impressed.

** ** **

The evenings were getting interesting as well. But that's none of your business. That was between me and Will.

** ** **

We transitioned briefly back to Earth, again taking the Two and the lorry with us. This time there was no Sputteridge, just open country. Kevin kept both TVs and the lorry blanketed. I felt sad, thinking of my time in the police house, a building that had been borrowed from another world, in a spectral village that no longer existed. But my car was still there, parked up against what was now just a hedge separating an overgrown lane from bracken-covered heathland. We pulled the "police aware" sticker off it and drove to Truro. It felt odd, being back in my car, in my own world. In fact, I felt like a stranger.

A stranger in my own life. How weird.

We did the thing with the cashpoint. It was fun watching Bob's embarrassment. I bought some new jeans and tops, then we found a

243

high-end gents outfitters. For the benefit of the shop staff Bob adopted the role of my farmer-uncle, who I was advising on what to wear for my forthcoming wedding. In his dark blue suit, white shirt and blue and yellow-spotted tie, Bob looked eerily like Slepwood. When he asked me what I thought he spoke as Benedict had coached him. It was so accurate it made my stomach lurch.

Once we had got Bob kitted out (and also re-stocked on provisions), Kevin moved everything back to the frozen place. It offered safety for us, but had the big drawback that the lorry couldn't be driven faster than ten miles an hour. Anything above that and it threatened to overheat.

Using the map book I had bought in Truro, Benedict had placed the institute near to where Aylesbury would be on Earth, which meant a journey of close on three hundred miles.

'Its official name is Hablock Mental Correction Unit,' he said. He grimaced. 'Destruction would be a better word than correction. It's a fearsome place. Why they insist on preserving a veneer of respectability is beyond me but that's the way the Regency works. Everyone knows what it really is but everyone pretends it's something else.'

He was confused by the road layout, which he said was very different on Erce. Realistically, it was going to take several days to trundle the lorry and the Two over to the transition point, and that was assuming we didn't get seriously lost. We thought there was a strong chance that the road layout in the frozen place would be different again. The frozen gift shop didn't have a map book, we planned to get one on our journey.

We had a couple of trial runs with the lorry. There was a petrol station outside the village, and we discovered that the fuel pumps worked in a similar way to the beer pumps, seeming to borrow from our time-space when we were holding them. The lorry was an old-fashioned design, but that meant it was happier going at low speeds. It was also pretty straightforward to drive - and I have to say, quite a lot of fun. The plan was to take a back-up car as well. If the trip was successful, we would need extra capacity for bringing people back to Sputteridge.

'Why don't we just pick a car up in Aylesbury?' I asked.

Bob looked shocked. 'We try to create as little disturbance as possible,' he said. 'Imagine if you left your car to go shopping and when you went to collect it, it had suddenly disappeared and turned up three hundred miles away. You'd feel pretty confused.'

I wondered how I would feel if I went to collect my car and discovered it had mysteriously put six hundred miles on the clock. Not as confused as if it had disappeared completely, I thought. I never really noticed the milometer much.

Nor the speedometer, to be honest.

The day came for our trip. Kevin and Dildow had entangled the Four's Booze Condensation with some similar alcoholic fumes on the Two. This would make sure that the Two would return to the same frozen point in time, with Benedict and the lorry waiting for it, rather than at some different point the next day. They'd had less success with communications, which Dildow suspected was due to the strange behaviour of time-space. Kevin had walked over to the far side of the bay and spoken into his comms unit, only to hear his own voice saying Dildow was probably right. Dildow, waiting for Kevin's communication, could hear somebody yawning.

They agreed that the problem was fixable, but they didn't have enough time. (From what I could see, time was something they had rather too much of, although it was about as useful as a load of wire coathangers that had been left in the wardrobe for too long.)

But enough of such scientific complexities. Kevin had taken the repaired Two for a couple of test transitions and declared it roadworthy (or universe-jumping-worthy, I suppose). (What Kevin actually said was the Two complied with section twelve subsection one of the health and safety directive on pre-utilised but subsequently damaged interquantal transport, amended for ad-hoc repairs as authorised by the officer in charge... blah blah blahdie blah. I don't know what I ever saw in him apart from six foot three inches of sculptured muscles and a strikingly handsome chiselled face framed by golden flowing hair. Obviously.)

Early one morning (by our time, there being no mornings or afternoons or anything else on the frozen world) we got the Two loaded onto the lorry, and four of us set off. I was driving the lorry, with Benedict navigating. Bob and Will were following us in a large MPV - basically a big hatchback with seating for seven. Mrs Ponch had asked Will to come along. He had brought a worryingly large amount of medical kit with him, stacked in the back of the MPV.

Away from Sputteridge, it was very tiring driving the lorry. I negotiated the narrow lane for the first mile or so without any real problems, but once on the busier main road I had to pick my way around a lot of cars, all frozen in time. The steering wheel was heavy and the manual gearchange needed a lot of strength. Now that it was weighed down with the TV, the lorry was also difficult to control. The fun element of driving it soon disappeared. I pulled in at the first service station after an hour's driving, and liberated a map book. We had travelled six miles.

'Everything's in English, have you noticed?' I said. 'All the road signs. So is this.' I held the map book up.

Bob nodded. 'Think about it Bettony. You met yourself in this place. You were on holiday, just as you were when you found us. This reality must be very close to your own.'

I compared the road map with the one I had bought on Earth, in Truro. There were a few minor differences - Coventry for example had completely ceased to exist - but it was recognisably England. We decided that I would take over navigating, with Bob driving. I felt a lot happier knowing that this was - more or less - a country that I would be familiar with.

We headed towards the main dual carriageway out of Cornwall, taking a route which kept us well away from Truro, trying to avoid as much traffic as we could. After a while Bob asked me to direct him down country lanes, which he thought would have less cars to steer around. This worked well until we came to a van coming the other way. It blocked the lane. There was no way past it and Bob had to reverse for twenty difficult and slightly short-tempered minutes until we found an alternative route.

Eventually we reached the dual carriageway, where we stopped and had lunch by the roadside. It had taken us three and a half hours to drive twenty miles.

Progress was much faster on the dual carriageway. Cars were well-spaced and the extra lane made it much easier to get round them. Often, the biggest problem was to keep our speed to ten miles an hour. Benedict didn't drive, so Bob, Will and I rotated the driving - an hour on the lorry, an hour in the car, an hour's rest. We were aware that there would be no sunset to mark the passage of time and had agreed to stop at six o'clock by Bob's watch for something to eat, then drive until ten and try and get some sleep. We ate just before the dual carriageway merged onto the motorway at Exeter. The M5 was busy and the cars were closer together, but we used the hard shoulder and driving was even easier.

It was ten-fifteen in what should have been the evening when we got to the motorway services near Taunton. We stopped the lorry, had a well-earned bottle of beer, and found some unoccupied rooms in an on-site hotel. We had managed a hundred and ten miles.

I was shattered.

** ** **

We had a breakfast of stolen sandwiches, bottled water and orange juice. We refuelled the lorry and were on the road again by eight am Bob-time. We made good time for the first three hours, until we reached Bristol and the meeting of the M5 and M4. The number of lanes increased around the motorway interchange, but so did the number of cars, vans and lorries. The hard shoulder had disappeared and vehicles were tightly-packed. Bob had taken over driving the lorry again, I was following in the MPV. It took an hour for him to pick his way around all the traffic and get us onto the M4. He led us on for another half an hour, then pulled to a stop and climbed out of the cab.

'Lunch,' he said. 'I'm pooped.'

Will took on the lorry after lunch. We were still making good time on the hard shoulder but traffic on the motorway itself was becoming steadily denser. Several times, Benedict expressed astonishment at the number of people and cars.

It was mid-afternoon when we arrived at the accident.

It was an accident that had not quite yet happened. A car was swerving onto the hard shoulder, which was what made Will stop the lorry. Cars on the inside lane were also braking hard, their weight thrown forwards, bonnets dipping downwards. There were rubber marks behind some tyres, showing that they were in the process of skidding.

The big problem was in the middle of the three lanes. Not far in front, a small car was in the process of slewing from the outside lane into the middle one, directly into the path of a large van. The van must have braked hard. A family car had just hit it in the rear, and it must have been at some speed; the car's bonnet was already in the process of buckling and folding upwards.

A large SUV had in turn made contact with the rear of the family car. It must already have been driving very close. Once again, the family car was taking the force of the collision. The car was unable to take the force of two simultaneous impacts, front and back. It was beginning to fold together. A crack had appeared across its rear window, and the entire back of the car was beginning to crease inwards.

Will had climbed down from the cab and was inspecting the still-frame carnage.

'There must be something we can do,' he said. Then he added, 'Oh no...'

He was looking in the back of the family car. Anguish was written across his face. I hurried over to join him.

A man was in the driver's seat, his face contorted by shock/fear/surprise. There was a woman in the front passenger seat, mouth open, eyes wide, left arm raised in some futile gesture. And in the back was a child seat, occupied by a toddler with a look of complete terror on his little face.

'We've got to do something,' Will repeated. He pulled at the back door and after a moment it responded, clicking and opening, slowly at first then faster as it borrowed from our space/time. I watched a spider-web of cracks slowly spreading across the back windscreen and a memory of the pub's window, shattering as the bullet hit it, flashed across my mind.

'I can't get it undone,' Will shouted. He was pushing at the release buckles that held the childseat in place. 'They won't budge.'

'Maybe they've locked,' I said. 'The car's braking hard, they must have tensed.'

Bob and Benedict were pulling at the front doors, without success. Will ran back to our MPV, then reappeared with a scalpel. He used it to saw at the straps that were holding the child in place. I was watching the rear parcel shelf. Very slowly it was starting to push forward into the back of the child seat. At first Will's knife had no effect, and then with that strange speeding-up effect it sliced through first one and then another strap. Will leaned forward.

'What are you doing?' I cried.

'I've got to get him out before he's crushed to death.'

'Wait!' Bob called. 'Think about the physics Will. He'll be moving at incredible speeds in his own world. The inertial shock on his brain will kill him.'

'I've got to do something,' Will said. 'So I'll do this.'

He pulled the seat restraints aside, then leaned forward further into the car and wrapped himself around the toddler. The whole of the back of the car was beginning to buckle now; even as I watched, the roof was very slowly folding down towards Will.

'Please hurry Will,' I said.

'I can't. I'll know when ... ah, here we go. What a strange sensation.'

The toddler was coming to life. I saw his eyes move first, focussing on Will's face, close to him. Then his arms moved, and within moments Will was gently lifting him out of the seat and out of the car, his hand supporting the back of the little boy's head. The child was clearly terrified but he clung on to Will as he carried the tot across the lanes, across the hard shoulder and onto the grass verge.

'Bettony!' Bob called. 'We need help here!'

Between them, Benedict and Bob had managed to get the front passenger door undone. But the car's slow-motion buckling was making it impossible to pull it open. I climbed in the back, picked up the scalpel that Will had dropped, and reached forward to saw at the seatbelt. A low moaning noise had begun to fill the cabin all around me.

'Bettony you've got to get out of there,' Bob shouted. 'The whole thing's collapsing onto you.'

'We can't just leave them!'

The seatbelt gave way. I climbed on top of the woman and began kicking at the passenger door from the inside. It was maybe six inches open. The space around me was contorting, the front and the roof and the back all beginning to compress.

'Bettony! Get out!'

I gave one last desperate kick and the door buckled outwards, making enough space for me to slide out. Instead, I folded myself around the woman, trying to bring her into our space/time as Will had done with the child. It was very peculiar. She started to turn her head, her eyes seeking me out in wild surprise. The low moaning noise began to lift in pitch, and the whole developing accident around me began to speed up. Then there was a weight on me and my arms were pulled away from the woman. Things slowed down again and a very powerful grip lifted me out of the collapsing car.

We fell backwards, Bob still holding onto me. The gap through which he had pulled me had closed over, the car had already concertinaed to two thirds its original length. I realised that I was screaming and trying to get back to it but Bob was holding me in an iron grip.

She was still in there. They both were. They were both in the process of being crushed to death and somehow I had to get back into the car and get them out. They must live. This child needs them to live!

Eventually I was too tired to struggle any more. Between them, my three friends got me back to the side of the motorway.

'The child was small. Somehow I was able to lend it some of the physics of our time-space,' Will explained. 'Enough to get it out. The woman was too big. Instead of fusing her with our world, she was taking you into hers.'

'We need to move,' Bob added quietly. 'We're not immune. Eventually all this carnage will spread to where the lorry and the car are.'

I was sobbing uncontrollably but managed to blurt out, 'What about the boy?'

'I've put him at the top of the grass verge,' Will said. 'He'll be safe up there. Someone will look after him. Bettony! - No! You must leave him now.'

'We could ta-take him with us,' I sobbed.

'No. He will have people here. Uncles or aunts, grandparents, people who will need him as much as he will need them.'

'You- you don't know that.'

'No. I don't know that. But there's a good chance. With us, he would have no-one.'

'Bu-but you're, ... you're all so good...'

'There are good people here too Bettony. Come on. We need to go.'

'They'll wonder how he got there.'

'Yes they will. Thrown clear in a miracle escape is probably what they'll say. Come on. We have to go.'

** ** **

We were all very quiet for the rest of the day's journey. We made it to some services at a junction between the M4 and the dual carriageway to Oxford, where we planned to get some rest. Nobody wanted to eat much, but we all knew that we had to. Nobody said much. We found rooms and I lay down thinking I would never sleep. Suddenly I was woken by Bob banging on the door. Will was already up, I had slept for seven hours.

'Not far now,' Bob said over breakfast. His cheeriness was. strained, but I appreciated the effort he was making. We had to concentrate on the task ahead, I knew that. Not much more than seventy miles to go. And then we would be in real danger.

It took another ten hours to get to the transition point. The first part of the journey was easy enough, more trundling down the hard shoulder of the M4 in the general direction of London. Then we took a dual carriageway north, which was slow going. Traffic in this part of the country was heavy, and often the gaps between vehicles was too small for the lorry. We used a lot of grass verges. The final part was a busy single-carriageway main road. Once again grass verges (and bicycle lanes) saved us. Then we rumbled over a couple of grassy fields and unloaded the Two.

The idea was to transition to somewhere close to the institute but where the Two could be concealed. Benedict had an idea that there was a lot of woodland at the back of the building and that's what we were aiming for.

'What happens if we try to transition into a tree?' I had asked back on the Four.

'It would show up in the transition co-ordinates,' Dildow had said. 'The Two wouldn't accept them. 'You wouldn't move.'

We resisted the temptation to do a quick transition to see how close we were. Instead it was more sandwiches and bottled water, and then we slept as best we could. The MPV's seats folded down to make a reasonably comfortable bed for me and Will; Benedict stretched across the three front seats of the lorry, and Bob simply lay down on the grass.

When I woke up Bob had already made the first transition. No more than three seconds, it was enough for the Two's cameras to take images of the whole surrounding area. We crowded into the Two and peered at the screens, squeezing into the gap behind Bob's chair. The first few images were of trees, which drew congratulations from Will, Bob and myself and smiles from Benedict. It was the next which showed us how well we had done. Trees again, but behind them, in the distance, some vaguely familiar buildings.

'That's it,' Benedict said. 'My father used to take me with him sometimes when he had someone to interview. I would run and hide in those very woods.'

'That's dreadful,' I said.

'He wanted to introduce me to my future career.'

We filed out of the Two. Bob went to the MPV and got changed into what he called his Slepwood clothes. And then it was time to go. My heart began thumping. Everyone was suddenly very quiet; very serious.

'You won't have long to wait,' Bob said to Benedict and Will. 'The way Kevin's got the Two entangled with the Four, you can expect to see us back here a few seconds after we set off. If not sooner.'

My legs were shaking as I followed Bob back into the Two. He sat at the controls, sealed the door, and tapped at the screen. I felt that slight lurch. Bob turned and looked at me.

'Now then youngster,' he said. 'Let's get you back where you belong.'

CHAPTER TWENTY TWO

Slepwood returns

The shock of hearing that voice, that phrase, turned my legs completely to jelly. Bob smiled, and for a moment I saw the warmth in his eyes.

'How am I doing?' He asked.

'A bit too good.'

'You certainly look like a terrified captive.'

'I'm not surprised. It's how I feel.'

'Right then. Back into character my darling, as my old director would've said.' He flicked a switch to open the door.

We stepped outside, into woodland. The sky still had that trace of orange and a familiar acrid tang hit the back of my throat. Bob gripped my arm and marched me towards the institute. 'I'm not hurting you am I?' He whispered.

'Yes but you have to. Don't relax your grip Bob! Stay in character my darling!'

I didn't have a clue which door to choose at the back of the building, so Bob led me around to the front. I stumbled as we went up the steps and realised how strong Bob was when he effortlessly pulled me upright. No wonder it had taken Slepwood, Kevin and Vinny to subdue him, I thought. Bob burst through the doors and into the clinical reception area. A single uniformed guard was standing at the counter talking to the woman behind it. They both stared at us in astonishment.

'What the hell's up with you two?' Bob snarled. 'Have you forgotten how to salute?'

He aimed his last comment at the guard but they were both so terrified that when the man stood to attention and produced his salute, the woman jumped to her feet and did the same.

'Sir!' The guard said. 'My lord ... what do you want me to do?'

'What the hell do you think!'

'Shall I get Commander Tyne?'

'Of course you shall get him! Now!'

The guard ran from the room. The receptionist was still standing to attention behind her desk. She looked at me and we shared a moment of mutual terror.

'Sit down!' Bob barked at her. She sat down, still saluting. 'Put your hand down you fool and get back to work!'

I had no idea how Bob was going to play this. He had deliberately excluded me from the plans that he had put together with the help of Benedict and Mrs Ponch. They wanted my surprise to be as genuine as possible.

No problem with that one.

'Thought you were clever didn't you? Not so clever now eh?' Bob snarled at me, pulling me about by my arm. 'But you're back where you belong now and the next time you leave this place it's going to be in small pieces.'

The guard returned, followed by a frightened-looking middle-aged man in uniform. He glanced at me and then at Bob.

'My lord,' he said. 'We were told you were dead.' His voice was shaking. His fear seemed only to inspire Bob to new heights of anger. But like Slepwood, the anger became very controlled. Quiet malice burnt from him.

'Who told you that, Tyne?' Bob's voice was barely more than a whisper.

'I - er - I don't remember my lord.'

'I think you do. I think you're going to give me a list of names of people spreading that rumour. If you don't I shall have to assume it was you who made the rumour up.'

This is no exaggeration. I watched a dark wet stain spread across the front of Tyne's pale grey trousers.

'It was Wendle sir. Wendle told me there were stories that you had been killed and that she -' He looked at me - 'had escaped with the other one. I didn't believe him my lord.' His tone became wheedling. 'I've wondered for a long time if Wendle was a recidivist -'

'The other one died, Tyne. Eventually.' Bob dropped his voice even further. 'A full list, Tyne. Handed to me. By you. In person. One hour from now. It'll give you something to do while I finally get something out of this one.' He shook me about again. 'I assume you haven't made any progress with the rest of them?'

'No my lord - yes! Yes we have.'

'Liar!'

'No my lord! One of them has told us how to make one of their nucular bombs. At least he began to before he died and we think -'

'Liar! Bring me the paperwork to show me. You know the penalty for lying to a Regency Lord Lieutenant!'

'No!' Tyne wailed. He took a moment to gather himself, then added, 'I have it on my desk my lord.'

'Here! Now! In fact bring them all here as well. All of them. I'm tired of wasting time. I have discovered one of their little weapons myself. We're going to use it to have a little fun with them.'

'All, my lord? You know that the one called Tellbert is in a coma.'

'Tellbert...' I glanced at Bob. There was a moment when his mask fell, and I saw the shock on his face. It took him a moment to recover himself. Tyne was so terrified I don't think he even noticed. 'So get one of them to carry her,' Bob said. 'But get them all here.'

Tyne hurried away. I watched him punch a number into a keypad next to the inner door, then open it. The guard had returned and was standing stiffly to attention. The receptionist had her head down, pretending to work. After a few minutes, accompanied by more guards, a sorry-looking group of people began to straggle into the reception area. Two of them could not walk unaided, and were being supported by their colleagues. One looked like a duplicate of Vinny, I guessed this was the real Vic Terrugo. They were all bare-foot and wore loose-fitting tops and baggy trousers that stopped halfway down their calves. The clothes may all have been white originally. A smell had followed them in and quickly filled the reception hall.

There were five of them altogether. I found it difficult to look at them. It was an understatement to say they were scared. A couple of them were appallingly thin. They all stood huddled together in the middle of the reception area, looking fearfully at Bob. Whatever Bob was feeling, he was hiding it well now. He looked like evil incarnate.

Tyne returned with a sheaf of papers in his hand. He was followed by another guard carrying a white-clad figure over his shoulder. The guard said 'I'm sorry my lord the inmates were too weak to carry this one.'

Bob grunted. 'What about Bucklan?' He spat.

For the first time Tyne looked puzzled.

'You killed Bucklan yourself, my lord.'

Bob recovered quickly. He grunted again, then said quietly, 'Your treasonable idiocy gets me so angry Tyne that I can hardly think.'

At the word treason the receptionist and all the guards froze. The guards nearest to Tyne edged away from him. Bob watched them, paused a moment, then addressed the guards.

'Bring them all outside. We're going to have a little fun with them. I've got a new toy to play with.' He pulled me about again. Nice timing Bob, I thought, but that's too gentle. I exaggerated my stumble and fell towards the floor. I was slightly too successful. I left it until too late to move my arms, and took much of the force of the fall on my face. I felt my nose crack. When I gathered myself to my feet again, blood was dripping from it. I felt no pain though. Not surprising really, adrenalin must have been coursing through my veins. The prisoners were staring at me, but there was no shock on their faces. I guessed they had been through a lot worse.

Bob sent Tyne away to work on his list and had the guards march everyone else outside. He led the way back towards the Two. I wondered how he was going to distract the guards. There were too many for us to deal with, we could expect no help from the prisoners and in any case the guards were all armed. Three of them carried rifles, the other two had pistols sitting in holsters at their waists.

We struggled through the woods and Bob opened up the Two and disappeared inside. The guards stared at it, then at each other. Bob reappeared carrying a large linen bag. He dumped it on the forest floor and pulled a small metal box from it. This was about four inches by three, and an inch deep.

'Playtime,' he said. 'What we need now is someone to try this thing out on.' He looked at the guard who had witnessed his outburst against Tyne. 'Have you heard any rumours about me?' He demanded. The guard shook his head. He looked petrified.

Bob seemed to consider for a moment. Then he motioned to the guard who still had the unconscious Tellbert draped over his shoulder. 'Put her down here,' he said.

The guard dumped the poor woman on the ground and quickly moved away. She was completely lifeless and he let her drop, but luckily she landed softly on a bed of leaves. Bob placed the metal box on her, stood back and counted 'Five...four...three...two...'

There was a sudden crack from the box. The woman's body arched, as though in pain, and she disappeared.

Even the guards were surprised. The prisoners gasped.

Bob affected to look disappointed. 'Of course we didn't really see how painful that was,' he said. He looked around at the prisoners. 'I hope you get the idea though.' He looked at each one of them, then spoke in Enceldic, I guessed he was repeating himself. He pointed at one of the weaker prisoners.

'Bring him here.'

The guards brought the man closer. Bob smiled, menacingly.

'How about you tell me all about nucular power?' He whispered, repeating himself in Enceldic. The man's eyes widened in fear, but he shook his head and didn't speak.

'Lie down.'

The man lay down. He was panting with fear.

'Last chance,' Bob said. The man was panting faster and was quaking. Briefly, his terrified eyes met Bob's, and he summoned the strength to shout defiantly 'Beth!'

It was easy enough to guess what that meant.

'Shame,' Bob said. He dropped another metal box onto the man's chest, stood back and once more began counting down from five. Once more he only got to two. The man arched his body and screamed in pain as he too disappeared.

One by one the prisoners were brought forward. Trembling with fear, one by one they refused to tell what they knew. One by one they were dispatched, men and women alike, each one screaming in agony. The guards were becoming uneasy. Perhaps even they had some kind of morality. Perhaps a massacre of defenceless people twitched even their consciences. They soon looked as terrified as the remaining prisoners. But none of them did anything to stop Bob. At one point an evil smile lit his face.

'This is fun,' he said. 'I thought it would be.'

Two left now. Eyes wide in terror, the next man was brought forward.

'I'll tell,' he said. His whole body was quaking. 'Everything you want. I'll -'

He was cut short. Bob pushed him roughly to the floor, threw a box at him and watched him go.

'Sir,' one of the guards said. 'My lord. He was going to talk.'

Bob turned on him. 'He's the one idiot who's already told us all he knows!'

Nice improvising Bob, I thought. He picked up another metal box. 'Would you like a go with my new toy?'

'Sir. No my lord,' the terrified man replied.

I could hear shouts in the distance. Very faint. But not good news, I thought. Bob must have heard it too. He pulled the last prisoner forward and threw him to the ground, and dropped the metal box onto him. We watched the man disappear.

'Who's next?' He smiled, looking at the guards. They all backed away. I wondered if they thought they were in danger. After all, as far as they knew, apart from me they were the only witnesses to a massacre.

The shouting was getting louder. One or two of the guards began to turn their heads. But apart from that, they were all transfixed by what they had seen. None of them moved. Bob threw the bag into the Two, then pushed me in after it.

'She's going to give me some fun of a different sort,' he said. They all stared dumbly at him. One of them began to smirk.

Bob was closing the door when the first shot hit it. He slammed it shut and launched himself into the chair. I could hear more bullets bouncing off the Two, then that slight and very welcome judder. Then silence. Bob leaned forward on the desk and put his head in his hands.

'Never again,' he said.

'You were abazing Bob.' I said through my swollen nose.

'I am never doing anything like that ever again.'

I put a hand on his shoulder and realised he was sobbing.

** ** **

I opened the door myself. I stepped out onto the field, surrounded by zombie-like people in dirty white overalls.

I found out afterwards how confusing the time difference had been for Benedict and Will. We had disappeared in the Two, then around twenty seconds later the first of the prisoners materialised. After that they turned up every few seconds.

'Thank goodness, really,' Will said. 'We didn't have time to start worrying about how you were getting on. Just those few seconds, then Merriat Tellbert suddenly appeared, lying unconscious on the ground. We knew what to expect but I hadn't anticipated how bad Merriat would be. We dragged her out of the way and concentrated on moving each person as soon as they appeared. Bob was supposed to position them slightly apart to prevent bounceback and I think they would have been ok but we couldn't risk it. And they were all completely confused. I was giving them a shot of Peridown Two and Benedict was basically just helping them back to the ground. It was frantic but it was all over in less than a minute and then you were back, thank gods.'

Will had barely begun triaging when I wandered out of the Two, blood still dripping from my nose. He took a minute out to fix a soft plastic clamp around my nose. What felt like a hundred small bee-stings came from it, they had a wonderful effect and the bleeding stopped pretty much straight away. Then he and Benedict between them carried Tellbert to the back of the MPV, where he fixed a drip up. I watched them, and suddenly realised I wanted to sit down. In fact my legs gave way.

Gradually, Will worked his way through the Abbuthians. I don't know how much of their stunned reaction was due to the Peridown, and how much to the complete disorientation of thinking they were about to die, suffering agonising pain, then on the moment of death finding they were suddenly in a field, in a very still world, next to a

260

lorry and a big car, with a rather dishy young medic attending to them. Certainly they were all quiet, sitting and staring into space while Will cared for them.

In all this time there was still no sign of Bob. Once the use of my legs returned, I went back to the Two. He was still sitting at the desk, his head in his hands.

'You were trebeddous Bob,' I whispered. 'You did it. You saved theb. All of theb.'

'Thank you my friend.'

Neither of us moved. Bob stayed hunched over the table, I stood behind him and kept my hands on his shoulders. After a long silence, I said, 'You saved their lives.'

'I'm so sorry that I hurt you old friend.'

'Ah! You didn't. That was be. I didn't think you were being rough enough so I threw byself to the floor.'

He didn't seem to hear me.

'It was awful Bettony. I could feel some of his evil, just from acting out the part. And the fear that it generated in those people. Not just in our friends. In those soldiers as well. They thought they were taking part in a massacre and they were too terrified to do anything about it.' He took a deep breath. 'A massacre. We can't judge them Bettony, those soldiers. I could feel their complete terror of me. How many people would have behaved differently?'

'But you did it Bob,' I repeated. 'You saved all of the prisoners. You rescued them. Everything we planned to do, you did it.'

'But I didn't!' Bob almost shouted. For the first time, he lifted his head. 'I didn't get the paperwork on nuclear power!' He turned and looked at me, his face blotched and desperate.

'Think about it. He'd actually brought it from his office. He would have given it to me. He had it in his hand! But I was so focussed on getting our people out that I sent him away again.' Bob groaned, and dropped his head back into his hands.

'Think of the damage they can do with that knowledge!'

CHAPTER TWENTY THREE

A change of plan

Will eventually worked his way through those we had rescued. He had given Bob a shot of Peridown, and my friend was lying among them on the grass, sleeping. The prisoners were also sedated.

'I need to get these people back to Abbuth as soon as possible,' Will whispered. 'Even the facilities on the Four won't be enough for some of them.' He flicked at a blade of grass on his knee. 'The effect of the transition box has pushed Merriat Tellbert right to the limit. I'm not at all sure she's going to survive. She needs some serious intensive care as soon as possible.'

Will, Benedict and I were sitting together, away from the others.

'We can't go yet.' I explained about the paperwork.

Will shook his head. 'We're going to have to leave that Bettony. Hopefully they won't have enough information to be of use to them. You said yourself that they are still using steam engines on their railways.'

'They can be remarkably tenacious where Regency power is involved,' Benedict murmured. 'They will see nucular power - whatever that is - as a way of cementing the Regency's grip on Europa. Sepana will fall into line. The Confederate States of Northern America are rumoured to be ready to join an alliance...'

'I've got a plan,' I said.

They reacted almost as one and I have to say they could have been more encouraging. Benedict said, 'Oh dear,' and Will's version was, 'Oh no.'

It was, I thought, a pretty neat plan. Like all great ideas, it was astonishingly simple. OK, I admit, like all great jewels it needed to be polished. There were a few flaws. But it was a winner. I was surprised that Will and Benedict couldn't see that.

'My first reservation,' Benedict said, 'is that time here is more or less stopped. So waiting here until nightfall could take quite a long time.'

'Bob's in no condition for any more excitement right now,' Will said. 'He's experiencing something akin to post traumatic shock.'

'The alarms would go off. The area behind Reception has movement detectors which are switched on at six o'clock. I know that for a fact Bettony because I set them off once, as a boy. As I said, the Regency can be remarkably tenacious where their power is concerned.'

'Loading and unloading the Two, on and off the lorry, is extremely arduous. Think how many times you would have to do it.'

'Tyne would have locked his office. And even assuming that the paperwork is still in the room, he would not have left it lying around. It would be locked in a cabinet somewhere.'

'These people need proper care, as soon as possible, if they are to survive.'

I was disappointed. But I was determined. We had to do all we possibly could to try and make sure the Regency did not gain access to nuclear power. As someone once said, we talked about it for twenty minutes and then we decided I was right. In truth, as someone very different said, there was no alternative. Our amended plan was basically mine, but with the flaws polished off.

** ** **

Will was with the prisoners, ready to reassure them before joining me, when I started the lorry up. The noise woke Bob, who wanted to know what was happening. A period of negotiation then followed between Bob and Will. You may remember that one of my first descriptions of Bob was of a man who combines authority with reassurance. I discovered now that you can add bloody-minded stubbornness into that mix, a quality which it soon became apparent Will also quietly possessed in large measure. I switched the engine off and watched the entertainment while Bob and Will went head to head. Bob was the senior officer. Will, as medical officer, calmly insisted on his authority in matters of health. Bob wanted in on my plan. Will was adamant that Bob was in no fit state, and that he, Will, was the man for the job. The two of them had what I can only describe as a well-mannered but extremely firm discussion. I was interested to note that, in contrast to many such arguments I had witnessed on earth, each was prepared to listen quietly to the other's point of view before heatedly repeating his own.

A compromise of sorts was eventually reached. Bob would help with the loading and unloading of the Two, and would pilot it, but would take no further part.

Matters were then further complicated by Benedict. Perhaps he had been feeling left out. Certainly he now joined the conversation and insisted on accompanying me. This sparked another round of discussion. I watched the entertainment, from the relative comfort of the lorry's driving seat, and regretted not having any popcorn. Benedict pointed out his familiarity with the building. Bob seemed to take Benedict's intervention as a resetting of the discussion, and rejoined the fray. He felt he would offer a more muscular presence. But Will was completely decided on that one, and held his ground, backed up now by Benedict.

And that was how it remained. For some bizarre reason they all shook hands. Bob hurried over to the lorry. I reached down and shook his hand. I didn't want to feel left out. Bob smiled.

'Come on Bettony let's get this thing done. It's a crazy scheme of yours but we have to try something.'

The animated discussion had completely re-energised Bob. The slumped defeatism of earlier had gone. His eyes sparkled. I remembered Will's previous subtle mindgames - the way he had encouraged us to relish our adventures, the way he had used Tickle the Sparrow, and his comment, Why shouldn't healthcare be fun. I wondered how much of what had passed was his way of pulling Bob out of his trauma.

I tried to catch Will's eye, but he was tending to his patients. His face was studiously blank.

Bob and Benedict hooked the chains around the Two, and we got it loaded onto the lorry. I drove back to the road, then followed Benedict's guidance. We travelled five miles further away, stopping once to pick up two plastic buckets and several large packs of bottled water. At a point where the road dipped into a valley, I pulled onto another field. We got the Two set up and crammed into it. Bob piloted the three of us back to Erce. I could sense Benedict tensing as he realised he was back in his home world. I remembered his terror, back when we were on the Four and he thought he was being asked to do this. I admired his courage.

The valley we transitioned to was wooded and remote. For my plan to work, we needed Erce to be in darkness when we arrived at Hablock, and this seemed the simplest way to do it. We made ourselves comfortable outside the Two, had a sandwich and waited for night to fall. Sitting in the quiet wood with Benedict put me in mind of our escape to Cornwall. I wondered how Mrs Colshaw was getting on. Despite her snobbishness and the distaste she had shown for us at first, she had been very helpful. Helpful to Benedict anyway.

Eventually it got dark. It must have been late summer now, and warmer than when we had last been on Erce. The last of the birdsong died away, replaced by furtive rustlings in the undergrowth. We waited, ready if necessary to jump into the Two and transition away to safety, but there was no sound of a search being made for us. I think I dozed; Bob's voice came as a shock.

'Two am local time. Time we were moving.'

We had got what we wanted. We were locked into 2am in Erce. We transitioned once more to the frozen world, hitched the Two up to the lorry and I drove us back.

Will was waiting for us. 'Are you sure you're up to this?' He asked me. 'You've had a stressful time of it.'

I nodded. It was true, I felt tired, but this had to be done. One way or another. And if the prisoners were to stand their best chance of survival it had to be done quickly.

We drove across the fields, as close as we dared towards where we guessed the institute would be. We unloaded the Two and transitioned. Not bad. We had veered off to the right but not far.

Two more transitions. In the darkness of Erce we were getting closer and closer to the institute. In the strange daylight of the frozen world we got closer and closer to the back of a small housing estate. We could look over garden fences, and we could see a footpath that led into the estate, but there was no access for vehicles from where we were. On Erce we were ten metres away from the back of the building, its dark shape looming in front of us. On the frozen world, we had to give up and start again. We trundled back the way we had come, past Will and his patients, and found a way around the local road system into the housing estate. We had basically driven around most of a large circle. This time when we transitioned we were directly in front of the institute but still a fair way away. We transitioned a couple more times, making our way down a road in the estate, edging closer. At last in the darkness of Erce we were directly in front of the building, a couple of feet from the steps leading up to the doors.

'This is it then,' Bob said. 'The next transition should put us into reception.'

We took some very careful measurements. Back in the frozen world we made the same measurements and scratched some markings into the road. We loaded the Two onto the lorry yet again and trundled it forwards a few more metres, lowering it painstakingly onto the markings.

We filled the two buckets with the water we had collected and placed them outside the Two. One last look around to check that things were in the right place, and we crowded back inside.

I was clutching tightly to the bag Bob had used. It had a few things in it, including two of the remaining metal boxes. Bob had told me they had been put together by Kevin and Dildow. They were single-use, designed specifically to transition one person from Erce to the frozen world. They also delivered a painful but harmless electric shock. The idea had been to make the each prisoner's "death" look as realistic as possible.

I wasn't looking forward to using them.

'Ready?'

Benedict and I both nodded. There was the tiny judder. Bob checked the screens.

'We're in.'

Heart thumping, I led Benedict out of the TV and stepped into Reception. It was dark but we both knew this place well enough to work our way to the inner door. I punched the same code into it that

I had seen Tyne use and it clicked open. Behind us, the Two silently disappeared.

There was a moment of silence after we stepped through the doorway, then alarms began to screech. Even though we had known it would happen, my heart rate doubled.

Benedict hurried down the corridor, in the opposite direction to the room where Slepwood had questioned me, towards a row of office doors. He stopped next to one of them. 'This is where the facility commander's office used to be,' he said, raising his voice over the alarms. 'I hope they haven't moved it.' Like all the doors it had a frosted glass pane set into its top half. Sure enough, the words Commander Tyne were embossed on a metal strip just below the glass. We had a brief try at opening it, punching different numbers into the keypad next to it without success. It was hard to concentrate with the alarms screaming our presence. I dropped my bag to the floor, pulled a hammer from it and swung it hard at the lock. It bounced off. It would take too long to break down the door this way. Instead, I smashed the glass. I tried to knock every bit of glass out but the alarm was screeching, my heart was thumping, I knew there wasn't much time. It was hard to concentrate. When I climbed through I could feel sharp edges ripping into my clothes and my skin.

Benedict passed me the bag then climbed though himself. Neither of us was very big; Bob would never have got through. Then again, Bob would probably have barged the door down. Behind us, the corridor burst into light. Still no sign of people though.

We were in an outer office; it looked like this belonged to Tyne's personal secretary. Benedict ran to an inside door.

'Locked.'

Enough light was coming through the shattered window for me to see a set of keys in a tray on the secretary's desk. I grabbed them. The third key fitted. We were into Tyne's office.

Benedict flicked the light on. No point in hiding now. There were shouts in the corridor, competing with the screech of the alarms. All the noise was muffled as I closed the heavy door and locked it leaving the key in. We only had seconds. Between us we ransacked the room. I thought there might be a chance that Tyne had returned the paperwork to his desk. No such luck. Someone tried the handle. People began hammering on the door. We ignored their efforts to get in and carried on with our wild search. The hammering on the door increased in ferocity. Heavy as it was, the door was not going to last long. We searched on, hands shaking as we pulled papers from drawers and shelves and files, glancing at them then throwing them to the floor. There were too many places to look, and too many of the cabinets were locked. The hammering continued. The doorframe began to splinter.

'Plan B' I shouted. I pulled the two plastic drinks bottles from my bag and threw one to Benedict. We had got rid of the water and they now contained a yellow liquid. We sprayed the room, trying to avoid getting any petrol on ourselves, soaking the papers that were strewn over the floor. The doorframe was giving way as we lit matches and threw them about the office. Flames burst into violent life all around us, we threw the bottles into them and what petrol fumes were left in the bottles exploded with deafening bangs. Benedict had grabbed the two metal boxes from the bag. Surrounded by fire, with guards bursting into the room a few feet away from us, he threw one to me and I watched his body arch in pain as he disappeared. I flicked my own switch and shouted in agony as pain shot through me reaching into every nerve in every part of my body. There was an instant of terrifying empty darkness and then I was in the purplish light of the frozen world, standing on the estate road. I had the sensation that the road was lifting upwards, buckling my legs as it pushed up to flatten me against it. I could smell smoke and had a vague idea that my clothes were on fire but Bob was in front of me and was throwing a bucketful of water over me, drenching me.

I closed my eyes, lay back and groaned softly.

'It was Plan B then,' Bob said. 'Are you two all right?'

'I think I am. Soaking wet, but all right. How about you Benedict?'

'Same.' He blew a deep breath out. 'Mission accomplished, let us hope.'

** ** **

Bloody hell! This stuff really is dynamite!

Crean leaned back and took a drink of coffee.

There had been stories about the fire at Hablock. Rumours that something seriously bad had happened. That precious information had been lost; precious prisoners too, killed in the fire. The official line was carelessness in management, which was the reason given for Tyne's disappearance. He had volunteered to go away for re-education apparently. Crean smiled grimly at that thought.

What about Ben eh? Crean glowed with vicarious pride. And the woman! She was incredible. Crean longed to meet her. He read on.

** ** **

Both Benedict and I were exhausted but we had to help Bob load the Two up one last time. Benedict sat in the cab, working the simple levers which controlled the chains. Bob and I fixed the hooks and stood back.

Everything looked ok at first, the chains tightened and the Two began to lift into the air, moving ponderously upwards as usual and bumping against the back of the lorry as it did so. It cleared the back and the tightening chains began to pull it into position, dragging it onto the flat bed of the lorry. It was a clumsy procedure and it always sounded as though the lorry's winding gear was being tested to its limit, but we had watched it happen many times by now.

Benedict succeeded in getting the heavy Two almost halfway onto the back of the lorry. But then it began to tilt, and very slowly to slide backwards. In our tiredness we hadn't secured one of the chains properly. Instead of being locked into place, one of the hooks began scraping along the side of the TV. It moved slowly at first, still biting into the metal, but suddenly came loose with a tremendous snapping noise. We ducked as chain and hook whiplashed high above us. I have no doubt that had they been lower they would have decapitated us. In ducking, Bob stumbled awkwardly and fell forwards. The Two lurched down, sliding off the end of the lorry and trapping my friend against the ground. For one awful moment I thought it had crushed him beneath it, but I saw it had hit the ground with one corner. The other corner was in the air, still held by its hook, and was the only reason that Bob was pinned and not crushed to death. I was screaming at Benedict to carry on lifting the TV. The winch mechanism was struggling, it could never have been designed for so many lifts of such a heavy load. At first the higher end of the TV also began to drop, then the gears crunched and it raised enough for me to help pull Bob out from beneath it. Immediately after I did so a second hook snapped loose and the whole of the back of the TV crashed to the ground. It rested at a crazy angle, the back digging into the concrete and the front still leaning against the back of the lorry.

I helped Bob to his feet. He started to straighten up, then gasped and bent forwards.

'Bob!'

'It's all right Bettony. I'm just winded. My word!' Bob straightened up more slowly this time, wincing with pain. 'That was extremely close. Thank goodness the second hook held. Ouch.'

We helped Bob into the cab and he operated the controls while Benedict and I re-attached the hooks. We stood well back when the chains tightened and began once more to drag the Two onto the lorry. Benedict and I were both shaking. We were also both bleeding from where the glass had cut into us. Bob insisted on driving back, leaning forwards over the steering wheel and braking every so often. I guessed he was pushing the ten miles an hour limit. I looked out of the window. As far as getting the Abbuthians out and destroying any information they had been forced to give, we had done all we could.

It didn't take long for Bob to get us back. Will cleaned our cuts and put something like sticky tape over them. He poked and prodded at Bob, who winced a few times but pronounced himself ok. Neither Benedict nor I were badly hurt. But now that this most dangerous part of our venture was over, I was - very suddenly - very tired.

I lay back on the grass and immediately I was asleep.

CHAPTER TWENTY FOUR

More Vehicle Theft

'We need to get moving Bettony.'

Bob was shaking me awake. I sat up and looked around. The MPV was gone, although Abbuthians were still sitting or lying around on the grass.

'You've been asleep a couple of hours. Will set off a while ago with Merriat. Benedict's gone with him.'

'How are we going to get these back?'

'We're going to have to borrow another vehicle. Not something I wanted to do but we've no choice. Come and meet Perric Flepstern.'

Bob led me over to the Abbuthians. A couple of them were still asleep. Bob introduced me to one who was sitting up. The man shook my hand. His grip was weak and when he looked at me his eyes were unfocussed. Bob spoke gently in Enceldic and Flepstern seemed to see me for the first time. He half-smiled and answered quietly. Will had started to teach me Enceldic but I hadn't yet progressed much beyond asking where the toilets were, although I recognised the term for Thank You.

'He says, thank you for risking your life to save his,' Bob translated. 'I've told Perric we'll be back soon with a vehicle to take everyone to the Series Four,' he went on. 'Come on Bettony. The sooner we can get this lot back the better.'

Flepstern looked at me and spoke again, and Bob responded. I guessed it was more gratitude. Bob didn't translate though. I asked him what Flepstern had said. Bob looked slightly embarrassed, then muttered, 'He said, your nose looks very painful.'

We trundled the lorry back to the main road and headed towards Aylesbury. We found a garage with another MPV sitting on the forecourt (one previous owner, low mileage, fsh). After a few minutes rummaging through drawers in the office we discovered the keys. Bob was deeply uncomfortable about the whole thing, but we had no choice. We trundled our way back to the field and in less than an hour we were on the road. At Bob's suggestion I led the way in the lorry, and he followed with the Abbuthians.

It was a tiring journey back to Cornwall, especially since there was no-one now to share the driving. We planned to stop every couple of hours, but after not much more than an hour I pulled to a halt. It felt as though my arms were being pulled from their sockets. Bob took over in the lorry.

I wouldn't say it was a strained atmosphere in the MPV, but it was pretty quiet. None of Abbuthians spoke much English, and anyway they weren't in much of a state for conversation. Perric Flepstern was sitting in the passenger seat next to me. He smiled and nodded from time to time, and clearly wanted to talk to me. Sometimes he would speak a few words in his own language, pointing in front or to the side. All I could do was to smile back at him. Before long, like his colleagues in the back, he closed his eyes and his breathing became loud and regular as he drifted into sleep.

Silence made it harder still. A suffocating tiredness was pressing into my skull, becoming heavier and heavier. I had to stop again, before we reached the motorway. I just pushed the chair back, closed my eyes and was gone. What seemed like two minutes later, Bob was shaking my shoulder. His tone was apologetic. 'We have to move, Bettony. It's not that far now to the services. You can have a proper rest then.'

'How long was I asleep?'

'Two hours. You've been through such a lot. You must be exhausted. Can you get to the services?'

I nodded. I got out of the car, threw the contents of a bottle of water over my head and face, and got back in. 'Let's go.'

There was one hairy moment when I realised I had closed my eyes and just managed to pull myself back from sleep in time to steer the MPV around a van. When we reached the services I left the Abbuthians to Bob. I stumbled to a bedroom, flopped onto the bed and was asleep.

The journey seemed to take forever but somehow we got back to Cornwall. The worst part was when we passed the accident.

Without really wanting to, I had been looking out for it. In fact it was hard not to see. Things had developed somewhat. The people carrier was still being crushed from front and back, but had now reached the point where it was looking more like compressed metal and less like a car. And still it was being squeezed together. Other vehicles were beginning to slew this way and that in a freeze-frame dance of death. I glanced over to the grassed bank leading up from the hard shoulder; sitting at the top, frozen in time, was a little boy with a shocked look on his face. I thought about his parents, still in the car, and I was nearly sick. I wiped tears away from my eyes and forced myself to concentrate on the road.

At least I hadn't lost my appetite. A continual diet of service station sandwiches wouldn't have been my choice of meals but I ate hungrily whenever we stopped. Sleep came quickly, too. The hard part was waking up.

I was dreading the last few miles of the journey. My fatigue headache had been getting stronger and stronger over the past couple of days. I knew that despite this I would have to concentrate hard once we left the dual carriageway. The single track roads which we would have to follow from the dual carriageway would still be clogged with cars, all the way back to the lane to Sputteridge. But there was good news when we left the dual carriageway. I never thought I would be pleased to see Pierre DeLondon, but there he was with Dave Green, waving at us by the roadside. Green also seemed to be relieved to see us.

'Will and our new team member arrived back safely with their precious cargo some hours ago,' DeLondon said. 'He shared with us the change of plan and brought us up to speed with what you have been putting yourselves through. Dave and I volunteered to reach out to you and take on the driving for the final stretch of your journey. My goodness, is your nose ok Bettony?'

I stared at DeLondon in reply, and he hurried away to talk to Bob.

'We've been here three hours' Dave Green muttered with some feeling. 'Just the two of us. Dildow dropped us off three hours ago.' His face when he looked at me was the face of a man who had taken a psychological beating. 'Three robust hours ago,' he sighed. 'That man cannot communicate without the use of tired and meaningless clichés.' Then he asked, 'What did you do to your nose?'

'It's fine, Dave. Honestly.'

Green took over driving the lorry, with me as passenger. Bob sat in the MPV with DeLondon. I was worried about my friend. Bob had been moving with more and more difficulty, I was sure that he was in a lot of pain from his injury. When I looked at him now, seated next to the greasily healthy DeLondon, I realised how ashen-pale my friend was.

We set off. I closed my eyes and let fatigue wash over me. Despite the tiredness I couldn't help laughing at Dave Green's description of what it was like to lose three hours of his life, alone with the clichés of the Technical Community Team Interaction Leader. Eventually Green picked his way around all the cars and campervans, all the lorries and the vans. We turned off the main road, onto the lane and trundled back to the Series Four.

Back to Sputteridge.

** ** **

The first person to greet us was Mrs Ponch, waiting outside the doorway. She actually gave me a hug! It felt good to be welcomed back by everyone and to see my friends again - Dave Potts was up and about now - but what I really wanted to do was to sleep. I was dog-tired. As soon as I could I dragged myself off to my room and collapsed onto the bed.

When I woke, my headache had cleared. I stood under the shower for ten minutes before I dug out some clean clothes and made my way to the kitchen in search of food that was as far removed from service station sandwiches as possible.

I was finishing somebody's leftover lasagne when a fully-restored Dave Potts found me.

'We're going home Bettony!' She opened a bottle of beer and poured it into two glasses. 'My hero! Benedict's been telling us what you've been doing but I want to hear it from the donkey's mouth.'

'The horse's mouth.'

'Sorry the horse's mouth. Treat this as a welcome back drink. We can't really celebrate yet. There's still so much to do. Do you know that Gorran Halke was one of the people who you freed? He was the head of the new security department. The head! Can you believe that? They set up a department to deal with spies and it gets headed up by one of the spies! I bet you've never heard that one before!'

We clinked glasses. I took a deep drink of the beer and felt it soak into my body, relaxing and refreshing me.

'What that means, of course, is that the people from Erce - from the Regency - have infiltrated very deeply into your society.'

Dave nodded. 'Mrs P's got some heavy calls to make. Will says he's been telling her to get back asap so... so the people you rescued can be treated properly, but she says she needs to wait and come up with a clear plan. She won't know who to trust when she does get back, and she's only going to get one clear shot at things. And she's got Pierre as well...'

We both thought about that.

'Why does she trust Pierre?'

'Dunno. He's ok though Bettony, I'm pretty sure of that. And he agrees with her. I think he's right, too. We're going to be most effective if we move against the Regency immediately we get back, but we need to be sure of what we're doing.'

'What does this Gorran Halke say?'

'Not a lot yet. He's in a bad way... Anyway. Tell me all about your exploits. What happened to your nose?'

I told Dave what we'd been doing. It was gratifying to see her reactions, especially when I described how Benedict and I had set fire to Tyne's office.

'Benedict didn't tell me about that. All he said was you'd burnt some papers before you left. And he didn't say how close the guards were to catching you.'

'Maybe he didn't want to worry you.'

'Mmm. Maybe.'

A thought occurred to me. I couldn't completely keep the grin from my face. 'And were you worried? About Benedict?'

'Maybe.'

'I like the way you've got your hair now Dave. Letting it grow longer suits you.'

'Thanks.'

'Shoulder length.'

'Yes I know. I can look in mirrors.'

'What does Benedict think?'

'Oi. Enough.'

'Yes Contessa.'

Dave smiled. 'I never thought when I signed up for this that I'd be letting myself in for all this stuff. Eating eggbane, getting shot, on the run across half of some alternative Britannia... kidnapped by a sadistic lookalike of our esteemed COO... a death-defying journey in a small boat...'

'Well neither did I, and I didn't sign up to anything. And I don't think it's all over yet.'

'No.'

I got the feeling that there was something Dave wasn't telling me.

A voice spoke with quiet authority from speakers somewhere in the kitchen ceiling.

'Bettony and Benedict, would you please join us in the Council Room.'

** ** **

Benedict followed me into the Council Room. Mrs Ponch sat with DeLondon. There was no Bob, which surprised me. A very thin man also sat at the table, next to Kevin. His face was unnaturally pale. I recognised him as one of the prisoners who could not walk unaided. He looked desperately ill but managed a weak smile to greet us. Mrs Ponch introduced him as Gorran Halke.

'What you did in Erce so brave,' he managed. 'I thanks you many times.'

I smiled in appreciation but I had to ask Mrs Ponch, 'Where's Bob?'

'Ah.'

'Bob is another one whose bravery we salute,' oiled Pierre. 'Despite his injuries his robust frame -'

'What injuries?'

'Bob was more badly crushed by the Series Two than he fessed up to you,' Mrs Ponch carried on. 'He has some quite severe internal injuries and there has been some internal bleeding -'

I couldn't stop a cry from escaping my lips.

'Is he all right?'

'Will is with him.'

'Is he all right?'

Bettony, please sit down. Bob is all right for the moment but like several of the people you sprung, he needs specialised care back on Abbuth. He's ok for now. Bettony please sit down! You can't see him at the moment. Will is with him and has stabilised him. Everything we can do for him we are doing. Just the same as for our colleagues such as Gorran here.'

I glanced at Halke. His eyes were closed and he looked asleep.

'Let's get back straight away,' I said. Since the news about Bob nothing else seemed to matter. 'Get these people to hospital.'

Mrs Ponch spoke sympathetically. 'Bettony, they'll be all right for a short while. We need to use whatever little advantage we have and this small element of surprise is most of it. I'm going to use the Series Two to make a short trip to Abbuth. You know that the time malarkey in this frozen world means I'll probably be back pretty much instantaneouslously. The Council Senior responsible for science is an old college friend of mine... what would you call her?' She drummed her fingers on the table. 'Secretary of State for Science?'

'I suppose we would if anybody thought science was important enough to have a secretary of state.'

Mrs Ponch raised her eyebrows at that. 'I'm going to go directly to her,' she continued. 'If I can, I shall also involve our top peeler. We have nowhere near as many rozzers as you do in your world, and they are more concerned with the rehabilitation of offenders than anything else. Still, it's all we've got. We can't approach our research facility security colleagues because we know we wouldn't be talking to the real Gorran Halke.

'I want you both to join me. Benedict, I would be relying on you to alert me if you suspect anyone is from Erce. Bettony, I've said this before but please forgive me for saying it again, you've got a keener sense of suspicion than we have. I want you to tell me if someone doesn't seem on the level or even if something just doesn't feel right.'

She looked hard at the two of us. 'You've both been through a shitload of trouble. On top of that Bettony, you must be knackered after all that driving. If either of you don't want to come along, that's fine, I understand. No problemo.'

'I'm with you,' Benedict said quietly.

'Me too.'

Mrs Ponch smiled her gratitude, and DeLondon murmured a few words to Halke. He half-opened his eyes, whispered 'Thanks you pair once more many times,' and closed them again. Mrs Ponch nodded to Kevin, who picked the man up with no apparent effort and gently carried him away.

'Gorran wanted to be here to express his thanks,' DeLondon said. 'Bettony, what you have done has been far beyond anything we could have expected of anyone. You have the deeply heartfelt thanks of us all.'

For once, he sounded genuinely sincere.

✶✶ ✶✶ ✶✶

I was surprised that the Two was fit to transition, but Kevin had given it the all clear. Between them, Kevin and Dildow had also sorted out some of the more bizarre problems with communications. We would be able to use Kevin's handheld comms unit to talk to someone on the Four. There would be a significant time lag though. Getting on for fifteen minutes by the time we got to Devon, Dildow reckoned.

Mrs Ponch explained that her friend Brink Stellish, the Council Senior with responsibility for science, lived near what I would know as Okehampton. We were going to take the Two into Devon and hopefully transition directly into Brink's garden.

'She's a real homebird these days,' the captain added. 'It's what a lot of them do. She's got her office at home and transmits in for council meetings. I'm pretty sure she'll be there. She's got a beautiful home and a lovely family.'

We had a few minutes to get ready, then joined Mrs Ponch in Reception. The lorry was waiting outside, with Kevin sitting at the wheel and the Two loaded onto its back. Mrs Ponch and Benedict joined Kevin in the cab and I climbed into the Two.

Altogether the journey took nine hours. Every couple of hours, Kevin would stop and we would all get out and stretch our legs, then Benedict and I would swop. Each time we did, Mrs Ponch would solicitously ask if I was all right. Each time she did, I would reassure her that I was fine.

This was more or less true. Being bounced around at the Two's desk for the first part of the journey was very unsettling but I managed to find an empty plastic box. It soon contained quite a lot of half-digested lasagne. No way did I want to slow the journey down with extra breaks. The sooner we could get this over and get Bob some proper care, the better. Anyway, once we were on the dual carriageway things improved a lot. I even fell asleep a couple of times.

Eventually we got to Mrs Ponch's first guess for a transition point. She was as calm and authoritative as ever, but I sensed a growing excitement. Not surprising, really, I thought. From what I gathered she had been close friends with Brink Stellish. More importantly, she was finally getting back to Abbuth.

We unloaded the Two and squeezed inside. There was a faint odour of lasagne. Kevin looked nonplussed when I waved goodbye as I was closing the door. I guess it's not standard procedure to wave.

There was the now-familiar slight bump. I pushed the door slowly open and peered outside.

We were definitely in somebody's garden.

I was on Abbuth.

'We're here,' Mrs Ponch exclaimed, pushing the door wider and leading us out. 'I recognise the garden. How about that! Bull's horn!'

We walked into one of those still, summer late afternoons when magic seems to hang in the air. The air itself smelt flower-scented sweet. It was a beautifully-kept garden. A large, well-tended lawn was broken up by areas of shrub and flowers. Here and there, trees cast long, lazy shadows. There was a garden hammock. Despite its size, it was welcoming and homely. I thought for a moment of the manicured hostility of Rob and Carol's garden. Nothing like this.

Mrs Ponch strode towards a tall, wide-shouldered woman crouching over a flower border.

'Brink!'

The woman straightened up. A look of alarm flashed across her face and was instantly replaced with astonished delight.

'Zag!'

The two women hugged. Stellish looked at Benedict and me curiously, and spoke in Enceldic. Thanks to my tuition from Will I was able to make out the word for 'however' and possibly also the word for 'what'. Mrs Ponch then talked rapidly in a low voice for a short while. I noted that she made use of the word 'The' in both singular and plural. Brink Stellish continued to glance at us, each time with her face registering more and more surprise.

Mrs Ponch was now clearly introducing us. Brink smiled and held out her hand. I wasn't sure that Abbuthians shook hands as we did, but I shook it anyway, and it seemed to be ok. I managed 'Hello, my name is Bettony' in Enceldic, which went down well. Benedict stumbled through a much longer sentence, which could possibly have included the Enceldic word for "cheese", and went down even better. Brink responded with a stream of Enceldic, which Mrs Ponch translated as the usual hello and welcome, please call me Brink, and led us indoors. We followed her through french windows, across a large and comfortable living room and into a hallway. Brink pushed a door open and we entered a sizeable study. She sat behind a large leather-topped desk and motioned us to chairs in front of it. Something about the room spoke of power.

Mrs Ponch turned to me and Benedict. 'You must excuse us for a while,' she said. 'I'm going to go through everything we know.'

The two women engaged in a lengthy conversation. Mrs Ponch did most of the talking, every so often she would turn to Benedict or me for clarification of a particular point. Stellish's face became grimmer as the conversation progressed. Several times, I picked out the name Gorran Halke. At one point Brink reached out to a control panel that was set into her desk but Mrs Ponch spoke sharply and Brink pulled her hand away. I was impressed with the authority that Mrs Ponch seemed to command, even with the equivalent of a senior government minister.

After some time there was a knock on the door and a man pushed it open. Once more there was surprise and delight at Mrs Ponch's presence, and curiosity about Benedict and myself. We stood and shook hands with someone who Mrs Ponch introduced as 'Morgan, Brink's lifepartner'. The man retired from the room, and reappeared some minutes later carrying a large tray with a teapot, cups and saucers and plates of cake and biscuits. There followed a very enjoyable pause, when I discovered that tea is apparently pan-universal and biscuits on Abbuth can be every bit as good as the ones that my friend Simon's mum used to make. Then Morgan the lifepartner removed the cups and plates and himself, and things became serious again.

Brink seemed to be struggling to accept what she was being told, every so often she would shake her head or sigh. Terse words were exchanged. Several times she repeated the name Flepstern with some incredulity. Each time, Mrs Ponch was firm in her response. There was more sighing and more shaking of heads. Consciously or not, the two women were now lowering their voices. Translated by Mrs Ponch, Brink began to question Benedict and me in more detail. Benedict was asked a lot about the Regency; my own experiences of Hablock were examined exhaustively. Eventually the lifepartner reappeared, wearing a very fetching flowered apron and smelling of cooking. Dinner, it seemed, was ready.

We ate at a large table in the large kitchen. This was a very large house. A young woman joined us, who Mrs Ponch introduced as

Brink's secretary Angered but who was very pleasant and didn't look cross at all. Angered spoke a good approximation to English.

The conversation over dinner was light. Neither Brink nor Morgan spoke English, but Angered and Mrs Ponch translated the gist of what was said for Benedict and me. The two women were clearly making an effort to appear relaxed, but as soon as dinner was over it was straight back to the study, with me and Benedict in tow. We were consulted less in the post-prandial session, which got rather heated. Eventually things quietened down and there was a lot of nodding as Brink wrote a series of notes using paper and pencil. She used the control panel, apparently with Mrs Ponch's agreement this time as there was no objection. A slim, wide screen slid smoothly out of the desk, and Brink video-called someone, questioning them at length. She seemed to be satisfied by the replies she got. The call was ended and Brink exchanged a nod of heads with Mrs Ponch. Brink made a second call. Mrs Ponch turned to me and Benedict. 'Well that was hard work,' she whispered as Brink spoke again to her screen. 'Brink was rather more difficult to convince than I thought. But we've agreed a course of action. Brink is getting in touch with Mec Reesom and Osian Jelks. Mec is head of the rozzers and Jelks is Gorran Halke's deputy.'

'How do you know they haven't been replaced?' Benedict asked mildly.

'First, neither of them were among the people who Bettony and Bob rescued. Second, Brink has just spent some time talking to Osian's lifepartner who has no doubt at all that she is still hooked up with the real McCoy. I know this isn't conclusive, but it's the best we can do in the circumstances. Mec's lifepartner is on a climbing holiday right now which is a bit of a bugger but we'll have to wing it. From what you've told me the Regency would struggle to replace women because of the bigoted nature of their society so we should be ok.

'Brink is going to ask Osian and Mec to arrest the doubles of all the people you rescued. Even if one or both of them are narks they're going to struggle not to do as Brink asks, because they'd be revealing themselves. If they both refuse we'll have to rethink. Assuming we can get the doubles arrested and detained, we immediately start DNA testing, beginning with Osian and Mec and Head of Council Torrance... Who is not going to be very happy about being kept in the darkroom about all this but we can't help it. We need to keep everything as contained as possible. At the same time we get Bob and the kidnappees back and get them to hospital. It's not the best plan ever but we're thinking on our toes here.'

'On your feet.'

'Yes that too.'

Brink had finished her second call. She looked meaningfully at Mrs Ponch and nodded.

Mrs Ponch stood up. 'Right, Osian's on the game. Brink's going to speak to Mec Reesom next but with Brink and Osian behind it I think our plan is a runner. She'll be on the game. We must get back now. Given the time malarkey, we'll be getting the Four back to Abbuth in what will be a few minutes from now as Brink sees it.'

We left the beautiful garden and immediately were back in the frozen world. In this place, time was important in a different way. We needed to get Bob and the rest treated.

CHAPTER TWENTY FIVE

I discover Benedict's views on beer

If Kevin was startled to see us reappearing so quickly he didn't show it. He didn't ask how things had gone either. Mrs Ponch didn't seem surprised. She told him that things were going to plan and the priority now was to get the invalids to Abbuth.

'How are the comms Kevin?' She asked.

'Approximately as we predicted. The gap between us sending a message and it being received by the comms operator in the Series Four is sixteen minutes and five point seven seconds. This is within -'

'That's great, well done. May I borrow it please.' Mrs Ponch clicked the little handheld comms unit on and said, 'All going according to plan. Get them back please Pierre. Plan A. Please confirm that you have received this.'

'Er... is Pierre controlling the comms unit on the Four?'

Mrs Ponch gave me an icy look. 'Pierre is acting captain in my and Bob's absence. Dildow is on Comms. She will pass the message on.'

We loaded the Two onto the lorry and set off. Some time later the little comms unit crackled into life.

'Hello Captain, confirm message received,' Dildow's voice said. 'We are ready to transition. Dave Green's gone to tell Pierre. See you soon.' Unable to contain her excitement, she added in almost a whisper, 'By the time you get this we'll be on Abbuth. We're going home!'

Mrs Ponch turned to me. 'Pierre will seek out Osian and provide whatever reassurance he can. Osian has said he will use the facility's security people to detain the Regency narks until Mec gets there to carry out a formal arrest. We will need a law passed at Council to compel individuals to undertake the DNA test. Brink was going to push for an emergency motion after she talked to Mec.' Mrs Ponch smiled. 'Hectic days Bettony! My goodness. But so far so good.'

Given the different behaviour of time in the frozen world there was no need for us to rush back now, but there was still a sense of urgency. It could have been difficult keeping to our ten miles an hour limit. Fortunately we had someone who would put emotions to one side and scrupulously follow the plan as previously agreed. Kevin was exactly the right person to have at the wheel. Kevin had already driven for nine-plus hours though, and I was in no condition to help. I was still tired from my efforts in Erce and in driving back, what was effectively one long day ago. Mrs Ponch decided that we should stop to sleep at a services off the dual carriageway.

Eventually, and in reasonable shape, we arrived back at Sputteridge.

It was strange seeing the gap where the toilet block/Series Four had been, especially knowing that it and everyone on it were now in Abbuth. We unloaded the Two next to the pub and Kevin took the controls. He was taking Mrs Ponch first, along with the entangled lorry, then coming back for me and Benedict.

'We'll see you in the blink of an eye!' I said brightly.

'Not this time Bettony,' Mrs Ponch replied. 'Now that the Series Two is going to join the Four on Abbuth there won't be anything in this world to lock time between here and Abbuth. It will probably run concurrently... or something. So don't worry if we're not back for a while.'

The Two and the lorry disappeared. There was a slight gust of wind as air rushed to fill the space they left.

'Or something?' Benedict repeated.

We stood in that weird but now familiar silence, both of us rocking slightly to keep warm. After a minute or two I said, 'Come on Benedict. I'll show you the pub.'

'But how will they know where we are?'

'They'll guess. Trust me.'

At first Benedict was uncomfortable with the few drinkers scattered immovably around the bar. I pointed out the barman, and we agreed how he looked like Rob from the hot world. Feeling a bit like a tour guide, I showed Benedict where the bullets had smashed slowly through the window and where they had gradually buried themselves in the wall. Benedict was suitably impressed by that; in fact, I would say he was shocked. Dave hadn't told him about this part of our adventures. The glass looked as though it had long been replaced, the wall had been filled in and repainted a soothing beige.

Benedict was less impressed with my demonstration of how to pull a pint, which he felt was stealing. He sipped at his beer and grimaced.

'I don't even like beer.'

'Don't you drink much alcohol?'

'I used to enjoy the occasional sherry.'

I wondered how Benedict's embryonic relationship with Dave would withstand their very different approaches to the amber nectar. Not my business, I thought.

Thanks to Slepwood I no longer had a watch, and thanks to his recent lifestyle neither did Benedict, but quite a long time seemed to pass. We wandered out several times, just to make sure that Kevin hadn't returned for us. Benedict protested when I suggested frying up a bacon sandwich, but hunger was making itself felt.

'If we can't pay for this, can we at least do a few chores for them?' He asked.

'How weird would that be for them? Suddenly finding things cleaned or moved? Remember we're living in a few moments of their lives.'

'Hmm.'

The bacon was a little crunchier than I had intended but we both enjoyed it. Benedict ensured that everything we used was scrupulously cleaned and put back in its place. Still there was no sign of Kevin or the Two.

'At least they've restocked on pies since Dave Lanyard was here,' I said.

'Hmm.'

More time passed. I had another pint and Benedict a glass of water. We were getting tired. I liberated a couple of spongy beach mats from the shop and laid them out alongside where the Two had transitioned. It was not in any way comfortable but we slept. Or at least I did. I had no way of knowing for how long.

We spent quite a while in that frozen world. I borrowed a child's watch from a selection in the shop, promising Benedict that I would replace it before we left. (It was in the shape of a troll's face, the hands were fastened to the troll's nose.) It was interesting seeing the watch spring into life as I fastened it to my wrist. It made me think of the motorway accident, when for a few moments Will and I had crossed the time gap between our world and this one. I wondered how the little boy was, and felt a sudden sadness for him.

According to that watch, Benedict and I were in the frozen world for two days. We went for a few walks, but we neither of us wanted to stay for long away from the transition point. I was sitting on a liberated beach chair reading a newspaper when I heard footsteps hurrying down the lane.

'Angered! Slow down!'

Angered put her hands to her face, which had turned red. 'Ouch. Zagretia did warn me about that. Ow! We must hurry though.' She looked at the human statues scattered around the village square. 'This is so strange. And the light... it's all wrong. Where's the other one?'

'Benedict? He's... powdering his nose.'

'What's wrong with his nose? Is it the same thing as yours? Anyway, can you get him please?'

'He'll be out in a moment' I replied irritatedly. I was getting fed up with people commenting on my nose. 'What's wrong Angered?'

She spoke quickly and was clearly on edge. 'Things haven't gone quite to plan. The Series Four transitioned ok and Strikken Flange very quickly got his patients into intensive care so that was good. Brink got hold of Mec Reesom after you left. Mec was sympathetic, but she insisted on involving Head of Council Torrance. I think she talked to HoC Torrance's secretary, actually, Tweek Golgood.' It was clear from the way that she spoke that Angered had little time for Tweek Golgood. 'Of course he was only hearing a brief, second-hand retelling of the whole thing from Mec, who had only had it at second-hand from Brink. A lot must have got missed out. And then

Tweek had to pass it on to HoC Torrance himself. By the time the information got to the Head of Council it must have lost a lot of important detail in the retelling.

'Anyway, whatever the reason HoC Torrance was furious. He refused to sanction Brink's emergency motion for DNA testing and when he heard that Osian was using his people to detain five senior administrative members of the research facility, he went assorted fruit and nuts. By now Zagretia had also transitioned back to the facility with Kevin Thaghrum. Ah.' The pub door swung open and Benedict wandered out. 'Here's Benderdick. How's your nose? It looks ok to me. Better than hers anyway, it's not swollen or anything. I'm sorry but we must go. It's urgent.'

Benedict looked blankly at Angered then at me.

'Things aren't quite going to plan' I growled as we followed Angered up the lane. 'Mec Reesom has involved Head of Council Torrance.'

'Oh. Hmm... What's that about my nose?'

'Nothing.'

'Brink and Zagretia had a storming video conference with HoC Torrance,' Angered cut in. 'I was watching. He's suspended Brink. He has no direct authority over Zagretia but he basically accused her of being one of the Regency people. He's ordered Mec to arrest her.'

'What!'

'I know.'

'What about the five who we know are spies?'

'The last I heard, Osian had ordered his people to keep hold of them. He was taking the late train down to Sputteridge. The man who I think you know as - Peer? - Dun-Dun-Dullundundun? - Has assumed command of security at the science facility.'

'Do you mean Pierre DeLondon?'

'Probably. Can you walk a little faster?'

'No. Not without bursting into flame. Pierre!'

'After Gorran and Osian, he's head of security.'

'Bloody robust hell. I never saw that one.'

'I'm sorry?'

'Carry on. And you're still walking too fast Angered. You absolutely must slow down. I've seen what going too fast here can do.'

Angered reluctantly moderated her pace. 'Mec's on her way there as well, with her own people. There's going to be an almighty confrontation.'

Angered had driven down to the facility on Brink's instructions, to be a link between her boss and Mrs Ponch. The head of the science facility had been easier to persuade than HoC Torrance - hardly surprising really, he had all the evidence in front of him. The absolutely key thing, Brink had told Angered, was not to allow the spies the chance to return to Erce. Once Mec Reesom had seen the five kidnapped Abbuthians - spoken to Gorran Halke, even - she would be able to confirm to Torrance the truth of Mrs Ponch's story. With me and Benedict there to corroborate it, the crisis would be over. It was simply a question of carrying out a holding operation until then.

'I might still get to change my name after all,' Angered said.

'How do you mean?'

Angered relaxed slightly. She half-smiled. 'I'm lifepartnering a week today.'

'Oh congratulations. Does the woman take the man's name then, even here? That's a bit traditional, isn't it?'

Angered laughed. 'Well, not quite. My partner's not actually a man. It's usual in our lifepartnering ceremonies for partners to swap last names. We don't have to, of course. It's just a sentimental way of showing your commitment to your lifepartner. Men and men, men and women, women and women. We usually swap our surnames.'

And then a memory from Hablock hit me so hard that I staggered. Pieces of a jigsaw that I didn't even know I had suddenly fell into place.

'Are you ok Bettony?' Benedict asked.

I couldn't speak. I simply nodded.

'Here we are' Angered said, 'here's the Series Three I used.' We had rounded a corner in the lane and in front of us was an electricity substation. Angered headed for it. 'Come on, no time to lose!'

The Series Three was bigger than the old Two. Angered secured the door behind us, there was the usual little bump, and we pushed the door open again.

And stepped triumphantly into a gap between two lines of men and women awkwardly holding guns and pointing them vaguely at each other. There seemed to be a general air of embarrassment. Everybody was now turning to look at us.

The people to our left looked the most uncomfortable. They were also holding the bigger guns, and there were more of them. Although they were dressed in a variety of casual clothes they all had some sort of identification which was hanging around their necks on straps and catching the sunlight.

The people to our right were similar, except their identifications were clipped to their pockets, there were less of them and only about one in three of them held small pistols.

Mrs Ponch walked out from the people to our right, and came over to us. She looked amazingly calm and authoritative. She even managed a small smile.

'What a shit-awful way for us to welcome you back to our world,' she said mildly. Then she turned to the line to our left, speaking first in English - 'More proof for you, Mec' - and then in Enceldic.

The woman Mrs Ponch had addressed took half a step forward from the people on our left and spoke. I didn't need to understand the words. It was obvious that she wasn't convinced. Or even interested.

Why should she be, if she was following the instructions of her Head of Council?

It was time for my bombshell.

'Tell her this, Mrs Ponch,' I said in a loud voice. Both lines of people turned to stare at me. Mrs Ponch raised her eyebrows. But she nodded, and said 'Go ahead.'

'Tell them that when we were at Hablock -' pause for translation by a puzzled Mrs Ponch - 'Bob Jenkins didn't only free five people.' Pause. Translation. People stirred.

'He also asked for someone else.' Pause. Translation. Everyone staring at me. This felt good. Adrenaline was coursing through my veins; I was the centre of attention. Bettony Gullivant was about to save the world. This one, anyway.

'I have only just remembered this bit.' Pause. Translation. A few raising of eyebrows.

'A lot has happened since that day. I think if I told you everything that had happened you wouldn't be surprised that I forgot! But I have remembered now, mainly because I have just discovered your practice of exchanging names at your lifepartnering event!'

Somebody politely stifled a yawn. A few people sighed. Come on Bettony I thought, you're starting to lose them. Keep it brief and to the point.

'Your Head of Council's name was not Torrance before he lifepartnered, was it! It was Bucklan! And I know this because the Regency people at Hablock told Bob that Bucklan was dead! Mec Reesom, I call on you to challenge the orders that HoC Torrance gave you! That man is a fake!'

Pause. A wide-eyed stare from Mrs Ponch, who nevertheless translated.

Sharp intakes of breath. I had the full attention of everyone now, apart from those who had turned to look at Mec.

'Bettony, you're not quite right' Mrs Ponch said gently. 'Bucklan was not Head of Council Torrance's name. It was -'

A figure broke ranks from the line to my right. DeLondon! I cursed myself for not following my first instincts. Bucklan was DeLondon! But DeLondon was heading with surprising speed straight for the line of people in front of him. What on earth... Someone had broken from that line also, and was running directly at us. Mec Reesom was charging at us, gun in hand.

Two Bucklans? This was getting confusing. DeLondon had altered course now to intercept Reesom. She had paused long enough to steady her pistol and aim at me but as she was squeezing the trigger DeLondon collided heavily with her. There was a muffled explosion as the gun went off, trapped between the two bodies. Both of them fell to the floor. Reesom struggled to roll free from DeLondon's weakening grip, but before she could raise the gun again people from both lines had reached her and were struggling with her.

I watched her shake them off for one moment - long enough to push the gun barrel into her own mouth. There was another loud bang and the back of Mec Reesom's head exploded outwards in a hail of blood and fragments of bone.

I didn't faint. Definitely not. But I sat down very heavily. I was vaguely aware of Mrs Ponch talking to me, and of Benedict being sick.

CHAPTER TWENTY SIX

'You can see him now.'

The nurse pulled the door open for me. I thanked him and entered the bright clean room that contained one bed. Sunlight and birdsong filtered in from a big window that had been part-opened to let in a light, warm September breeze.

Bob turned his head and smiled at me.

'Hello my friend. Do you know I've got another two weeks of this?' he grumbled. 'Hey come on Bettony, you're only meant to cry when I get worse, not when I get better. I'm on solid food and everything.'

'I'm sorry I haven't visited you before now. I did come and see you the day after we got here but you were still unconscious. Then we had to go through everything in a lot of detail with Osian Jelks. After that there were all sorts of medical checks and after all those Bart Torrance wanted to meet us. Then Will said we should go on holiday to get some rest. Oh sod it! Why can't I stop crying? It's relief Bob, knowing you're going to be ok.'

'I know.' My friend smiled and reached out to squeeze my hand.

I wiped my eyes again.

'Bart's a nice man,' I went on, 'but the story he'd been given by Mec Reesom was all lies. She was a Regency replacement. But you knew that.'

'It was a stab in the dark to be honest,' Bob replied. 'When we were at Hablock - When I was Slepwood - I looked at the people they brought into Reception and tried to see a common link. It wasn't that difficult. They were all in key positions of authority, both within the facility and outside. Gorran Halke was a good example. If I was right, Mec Bucklan should have been there as well. I chanced my luck. Sadly, I hit the bull's horn. I hadn't realised that she'd just lifepartnered though. Although she hadn't, of course. Not the real Mec. That had been her replacement's first task.'

'They still haven't found her lifepartner.'

'I know. It's not looking good for him is it?'

We fell silent for a moment or two.

'Did you know about Pierre DeLondon, Bob?'

'Nope. Only the Captain knew. He was a recent appointment to Halke's department, so they thought since no-one knew him he would be a good person to have on board. In a sort of undercover role.'

'He certainly had me fooled.'

'Yep me too. Zagretia was aware that not all her crew were who they were supposed to be. Pierre was there to watch her back. For the months we were stuck on Earth, he studied your world to pick up his character. He thought he couldn't just fade into the background so he decided to stand out as a bumbling fool. He spotted pretty quickly the link between how stupid people are on Earth and how much they use clichés. Particularly the word "robust", for some reason. He actually modelled himself on several human resource managers at a couple of your larger public sector organisations. He was able to follow them through their habit of sending out confidential but unprotected emails. Actually, we never found out what useful purpose human resource managers achieve...'

'Me neither. So all that business about being rubbish with technology...'

'No that was genuine. He was utter shite with anything more complicated than a knife and fork.'

'I'm going to his funeral tomorrow...'

I got control of myself again after a few minutes.

'Sod this' I repeated, wiping my eyes again. I'm supposed to be here to cheer you up.'

'It's fine Bettony. You're cheering me up by being here. And your Enceldic is really coming on.' Bob looked at the bag I was carrying. 'What's in there then?'

I sniffed. 'Well first of all, you need to know that we've got permission from Doctor Penck. And also Mrs Ponch, sort of.'

'Sort of?'

'Yes. She said I could go back to tie up my affairs.'

'You're having affairs?'

'It's just a phrase Bob! It means sort out my house, my savings, all that stuff.'

'Oh.'

'So Kagh and I spent a day pottering around Truro... and we thought you might like this. Fresh from the frying pan.'

I pulled an insulated box out of my bag, set it down on the tray in front of Bob and opened it. Inside, there were plastic boxes. I peeled the lid off one and a wonderful aroma drifted out. Bob's eyes opened wide with delight.

'Bettony! You didn't - it isn't!'

I grinned. 'It is. Chicken curry from the Golden Bridge. Boiled rice. And a side order of crispy pancakes, no egg.'

'Bloody hell! This beats a bunch of grapes!'

** ** **

So that's about the end of my report. Everyone will know all the other stuff. But just in case you've been living in a cave somewhere, here it is...

Bart Torrance resigned, in spite of a lot of efforts to persuade him not to. He said his error of judgement in ordering the arrest of Brink Stellish was unforgiveable. About the last thing he did was to ask me to write this. He said it's important that a full record is kept of everything. Hopefully, with no spies left here and no TV to connect them to us, that's the end of any threat from the Regency and their world.

The same people who failed to get Bart to stay on did manage to persuade Mrs Ponch to stand for Council. The elections are in a couple of months' time. Brink is currently acting Head of Council.

Benedict has moved to a university town which bears an uncanny resemblance to Oxford. He already speaks Enceldic like a native and is studying a foundation course in Poetry and Drama. In September if all goes well he takes the entrance exam for the university. In the meantime he's working as a waiter and occasional pianist in a restaurant called William's, and any time left over from all this and seeing Kagh (and the rest of us occasionally) he spends as a scene-shifter/general odd job man for a local amateur dramatic society. He says it feels as though he's died and gone to heaven.

I did wonder if anyone would protest about me and Benedict being allowed to stay on Abbuth. Who knows, one day we might even help to bring children into this world. Do they really want to risk adding our possibly dodgy genetic code to their own? But apparently, the genetic differences are completely insignificant. As Mrs Ponch had tried to explain to me, you have to dig down a long way to find even the most insignificant difference. They think that all the variations between their world and ours (and every other version of Earth) can be put down to what happens in society. If you're brought up in a society where you are told you're not very bright, then that's how you behave. Or a dim person brought up with the privilege to believe they are clever will act as though they are... even though they keep on making dim mistakes. The Abbuthians think that violence perpetuates itself the same way. They think they're lucky that their society developed in a slightly better way than on other worlds. That early in their social development they became locked into a virtuous circle just as other places can become locked into a vicious one, where ignorance and destitution just repeats itself.

I hope they're right. Their ideas certainly explain some of the people we vote for back on Earth (although maybe not why we vote for them). When I look at this beautiful world though, and how different it is to our own, I sometimes wonder if they are.

** ** **

It was done. Hugo Crean read through the last page of his report and made his final crossings out. He yawned, stretched and checked his watch. Four fifty am. He wandered along to Peckler's office and logged into the sly idiot's machine. Called up the master copy of the Sputteridge file. Made a note of the date and time of its origin. Made all the adjustments as per his own, much-annotated copy. (This took longer than he expected. There was so much to cut out! So much to change! And he had to get this right. There would be no second chance and the consequences of somebody spotting something were too dreadful to contemplate.) Crean was beginning to sweat by the time he finished. It was six thirty by now, and it was not unknown for Peckler on occasion to start work very early. He altered the time and date on Peckler's machine and saved the amended version as the original, with the original's timestamp. Changed the time and date again, to that on his own copy, and sent it to print. Reset the date and time once more, this time to the present, sent his own summary to print and switched the machine off. Destroyed his full hard copy in Peckler's own shredder.

Crean sauntered down deserted corridors to the print room and picked up his summary and the much-amended full report. He returned to his own office and spent ten minutes fraying the new original. He put his slim summary and the bulky (and now dog-eared) new 'original' onto Peckler's desk, then went back again to his office, put his head back and slept.

Crean was still asleep when Peckler passed his open door, half an hour later. Something else to store, Peckler thought. Something to use against Crean when the time was right. But Peckler was surprised to see the two reports on his own desk with a polite handwritten covering note. He made himself a coffee and sat down to read.

And slowly, surprise and pleasure formed and mingled like little fluffy clouds in Peckler's brain. This was a good report. Had he finally started to knock Crean into shape? Peckler was a smooth political operator. Crean came from a powerful family and Peckler knew the kudos he would get from making something of the boy. Of course, he reflected, that could be why they had placed Crean with him. It was well-known that Peckler was a reliable executive who could get the best from his staff.

This was nicely phrased too. Not Crean's usual drivel.

Peckler had an idea. He would let the boy present this to the committee. If it bombed, Peckler would make sure that Crean got the blame. If it flew, Peckler would take the praise. He might even be able to get rid of Crean. Promotion would mean not only the gratitude of Crean but that of his powerful family.

And of course if it bombed he could use that to get rid of Crean too. Peckler read on, interested in the content and impressed by the style.

II

One of the many bonuses of having a Hinton education was that it gave you confidence. Confidence in the sublime superiority of your own abilities. (Often, it gave confidence in the sublime superiority of their own abilities to men who really shouldn't have had it, because they didn't actually have any. But that was never a hindrance, either to their confidence or to the chances and appointments that came their way.)

Hugo Crean adjusted his tie, smiled at himself in the bathroom mirror, and went out into a hushed corridor. He made his way down the corridor to where a uniformed guard stood against another door. A couple of minutes later, and a green light flashed on above the door. The guard opened it and Hugo walked into a large wood-panelled room to face the Committee on the Advancement of the Defence of the Regency.

They were seated the other side of a long, dark-wood desk. Five of them. Peckler sat this side of the desk, to one side. Best suit on. Crean walked over, suitably deferential, and waited to be invited to take the seat in front of the committee. The chairman (it would always be a man) looked up, gave a brief nod. Crean sat.

'Hugo Crean.'

'Sir.'

Silence. The members of the committee returned to their copies of his report. Peckler picked his own up and pretended to re-read it. Crean thought about lunch.

He could really eat a steak. The thing was though, he'd had a steak yesterday.

'What do you make of all this?'

The chairman's question brought Crean gently back to the present. He composed a suitable reply. In other words, the sort of reply that they might expect.

'What one might expect from a woman. Rather lacking in objectivity or detail. Somewhat emotional.'

A grunt from the chairman. A small nod.

299

'We know they can do this...' the chairman searched for the right term. Failed to find it. '...This... jumping about stuff. We got our hands on one of their smaller vehicles a while ago. Well, you know that of course from what you've read. We've used it to great effect. RLL Slepwood used it to place a number of our people in their command structure. Lost the bloody thing now of course. Bloody fool.'

'Sir.'

'The thing is Hugo. The thing is this. They've got technology far in advance of anything here. We get our hands on it, the opportunities are endless.'

Damn right there, Crean thought. He said, 'Sir.'

Hugo, Peckler thought. They only met him a couple of minutes ago and its Hugo already. And I'm still Peckler. The arrogant inbred bastards.

'And some of these other places. Like the one this silly girl came from. They've developed nucular power and made bombs out of it. Massive bombs, one of 'em will wipe out a city. You only need to drop one or two and your enemy waves the white flag.'

Crean nodded. 'Sir.'

The man to the chairman's left looked up from his papers. What's the chances that this will be an intelligent question? Crean thought.

'Crean you say?'

None. 'Sir.'

'You a Hinton man?'

'Yes sir.'

'Not the Crean who captained the rugger team about six years ago? When we whipped the arses of the Yarrow boys?'

Crean smiled. 'It was nine years ago actually sir.'

'Was it? Was it by Jeremy?'

'I remember that game,' the chairman said. His face cracked into a smile. 'Biggest victory by either side for thirty years. I was sitting next to Tolly Bargton. He's a Yarrow man. Should've seen his face.'

The two men chuckled.

'As I recall,' the man on the left said to Crean, 'you broke the leg of the Yarrow Lock.'

'It was a complete accident sir.' And it was. When he saw the bone sticking through the flesh, Crean had nearly been sick. Now, he forced the briefest of smiles. Enough to imply, *we both know it wasn't.*

The man on the left chuckled again. Said, 'Good show.' He turned to the chairman, as though seeking confirmation. 'Eh?'

The chairman nodded. He allowed another brief smile. 'Bloody good show. Tankshift, his name was. I saw him not long ago. Still walks with a limp.'

All the members were smiling. One of them shook his head at the impetuousness of youth.

'Is he - one of us? This Tankshift fellow?'

'God no. Something in the theatre I think. Father owns a company selling dishcloths or something.'

'Bloody deserved it then.'

More chuckling.

The members returned to peering at Crean's report.

'The thing is. The thing is this. We need that bloody big machine of theirs. And we need more of their scientist-types. We never got anything out of the buggers Slepwood brought us.'

'Sir.' The poor bastards... Never? So the Sputteridge report was correct? She got all the survivors out?

'We've got a few of our people over there. Got a bloody good man in a key position. What's his name Peckler?'

Peckler stirred.

'We call him Wellbeck sir. Codename Wellbeck.' There was a hidden subtext to Peckler's words. *Don't tell him the name.*

'Hmm.' The chairman frowned. Several of the other members were looking at him. He clearly wanted to tell Crean. Eventually caution got the better of him. Even so, he couldn't resist saying,

'You'd recognise him anyway Hugo. He went to the, er, ... *right school.*'

There was some coughing. The chairman looked around at his colleagues, as though asking a silent question. There were slight nods in reply and pointed looks at Peckler, who also gave the smallest of nods.

'Would you excuse us for a few moments Hugo?'

'Sir.'

Crean left the room. Steak again, he thought. After this I deserve a treat. He took up position in the corridor at a respectful distance from the door to the committee room.

But maybe today plain fried. Just a touch of garlic.

His mouth began to water.

The door opened. Whatever conversation had taken place had been brief. Peckler came out of the room. No-one could have guessed at the jealousy seething beneath his amiable exterior. Crean knew it was there though. The thought made him strangely happy.

'Hugo,' Peckler said. 'Can you rejoin us please?'

'Of course.' *Hugo.* Doesn't take you long Pecky does it?

He returned to the chair and once again waited for permission to sit. The nod of assent this time was much friendlier. The chairman picked his report up and waved it about in front of him.

'Hugo, you can see from all this that Slepwood has managed to let these fools get one over on us. As I've told you, er - Wellbeck - is a good man but we need someone else there. Someone who will send us something that's more bloody use than this.' He waved Crean's edited version of Gullivant's report around. 'Someone keen of wit and strong in frame.' The chairman's face cracked into a full hideous grin. 'Someone not afraid to break a leg or two.'

A stirring of amused assent from the other members.

'Dangerous business of course, but nothing you can't handle. I'm sure of that.'

Are they really doing this?

'What do you say?'

'I say thank you sir. It's a wonderful opportunity.' *It certainly is. Not in the way these idiots are thinking though.*

Nods of approval from the committee. A smile from Peckler. Crean glanced at his boss and for the benefit of the members watching, politely mouthed 'Thank you sir.' Thought to himself, I know what you're thinking Pecky. Free of the young twerp at last!

Peckler nodded a benign acknowledgement. This was also, without any doubt at all, for the benefit of the members watching.

'Good show,' the chairman said. 'Just what I expected from a Hinton man. Good show.'

'Bloody good show,' the left hand man said. 'Well done Peckler. You've unearthed a good one here.'

A couple of nods at Peckler, who smiled his thanks. They all stood and there were handshakes all round. Peckler led Crean away.

'Congratulations Hugo.' Still the benign superior.

'Thank you sir.'

'You'll need to go back to combat school to sharpen up.'

'Sir.'

'You may as well take some leave until then. Is there anything outstanding?'

'Thank you sir. No, nothing outstanding unless you would like me to do some more analysis of the Sputteridge file...?'

They both knew what the answer to that would be.

'I think you've done a thorough job on Sputteridge.'

You have no idea. 'Thank you sir.'

Peckler held out his hand. 'I'm off to lunch now. Why don't you clear your desk and head off?'

'Thank you sir.' There were going to be two lunchtime celebrations, Crean suspected. 'One question sir?'

'Yes?' A touch of irritation. Peckler was impatient to be away.

'If they've taken the vehicle back how shall I get there?'

'Oh there's no need to worry about that. We'll recover it. No problem there.'

Crean nodded. Wellbeck, no doubt. 'Thank you again sir for everything you've done for me.'

'It's been a pleasure Hugo.'

On that note of mutual insincerity the two men parted. ACLL Peckler looked forward to a life without that supercilious slacker Crean to babysit. He would do his utmost to make sure his next trainee assistant was more... malleable.

Hugo Crean thought about how he would soon be escaping to a freedom that he had never imagined could be his. And hopefully, to a chance to meet that amazing woman.

** ** **

THE END?

POISONOUS REPTILES

The Second Sputteridge Chronicle
Rose Mandelson

Hugo Crean has made a mind-boggling leap across realities. Using a stolen Transition Vehicle he has jumped from a dysfunctional society ruled by a corrupt elite called the Regency, to Abbuth, a world whose fair-minded if rather naïve and party-loving occupants have made remarkable scientific progress. Hugo's mission was to consolidate the Regency's grip on Abbuth and to help pervert their science to advance the Regency's military power. Hugo has no such plans. He intends to warn the Abbuthians of their peril, and also to meet Bettony Gullivant, the feisty hero whose journal forms the major part of book one of this series - Dangerous Physics: Adventures in Sputteridge.

Unknown to anyone, Hugo's contact on Abbuth – TMB – is a psychotic killer who is pursuing a private vendetta against Bettony. TMB hunts Bettony across realities but completely underestimates her. Pretty soon, the hunter becomes the hunted.

The fast-paced story moves across different variations of Earth including one populated by a lethal cross between a turtle and a snake, and a world which seems to be centred around celebrity game shows and nostalgia tourism. Along the way, Bettony meets up with old friends and discovers how Bob has had his own mission sidetracked by the opportunity to appear in a holiday theatre production.

ISBN 978-1-7397814-6-0

CONCORD: SABOTAGE

Allen M. Trager

When Humans nearly destroyed themselves with catastrophic climate change and the resulting wars, they were contacted by the seven-billion-year-old galactic federation known as Concord. The aliens granted Humans probationary membership in Concord and helped us begin to reverse the damage done by centuries of neglect. Select individuals were allowed to serve as crew on Concord spaceships. Five hundred years later, Emma Fuji is the sole Human among a million aliens aboard a spaceship the size of Pluto called Violet Enforcer.

An unknown group begins sabotaging surveillance drones in several systems, and Violet itself is nearly destroyed. Initial suspicion that Humans are responsible is dismissed out of hand. But a Human-crewed ship is vaporized by the same tech, and a group of fanatics on Earth who have renounced any dealings with Concord claims responsibility. Humans are once again under suspicion.

The goal of the Renouncers is to convince humanity to withdraw from Concord, and if they are truly responsible they'll get their wish. Unfortunately, history shows that Tribes that resign or are banished from Concord don't last long. If Humans are responsible for the tens of thousands dead so far, it will mean the end of the Human race.

As the number of sabotaged systems continues to climb, Emma and her closest alien friends race to prove that Humans are blameless. Ranging across an entire quadrant of the Milky Way, Emma and her team search for clues to the true identity of the saboteurs.

In the end Emma's strength, intelligence, and compassion are nearly enough to solve the problem. But the final evidence is revealed by the charm and instincts of the galaxy's most famous canine, Moondog.

ISBN 978-1-7397814-2-2

SATAN'S OLDER BROTHER

A C Arnold

Constable Lloyd Pratt, not quite the pride of Girlston Police Force, suspects organised crime lurking in the shadows, everywhere he goes. He sees it where others see dogs fouling the streets. But when Lloyd's blundering attempts at crimefighting bring him into contact with a pair of desperate bullion robbers, his inability to grasp reality gives him the chance him to succeed where Special Branch fail. Although he never quite understands at what.

And when Lloyd enlists his friend Steve into the fight against wrongdoing, a misunderstanding over his favourite phrase The Ungodly ushers his friend into a nightmare world of supernatural terror.

Lloyd's brother Terry, who no-one would call a thief, not to his face anyway, and his sister, who is definitely not a psycopath, also have their parts to play, as does a local butcher of repute who never sells stolen meat. As Christmas 1988 approaches and big-time crime comes to Girlston the tension builds. Only one man, languid and nonchalant, stands between the forces of darkness and true British justice.

Only Lloyd, anyway.

Available on from www.186publishing.co.uk
Amazon.co.uk
Amazon.com